RAPUNZEL'S
DAUGHTERS

RAPUNZEL'S DAUGHTERS
AND OTHER TALES

EDITED BY
JOSIE BROWN, ROSE MAMBERT
& BILL RACICOT

PINK NARCISSUS PRESS

This is a work of fiction. All the characters and events portrayed in this book are fictitious or are used fictitiously.

RAPUNZEL'S DAUGHTERS and Other Tales.
© 2011 Pink Narcissus Press

Individual stories © their respective authors.

Scene headings in "The Death of Urashima Taro" are taken from the speech "I've Been to the Mountaintop" by Dr. Martin Luther King, Jr.

Cover illustration by Ciaran Gaffney
Cover design by Duncan Eagleson

Published by Pink Narcissus Press
P.O. Box 303
Auburn, MA 01501
www.pinknarc.com

Library of Congress Control Number: 2011921409
ISBN: 978-0-9829913-1-2

First trade paperback edition: July 2011.
Printed in the United States of America

Contents

Introduction

Fairy tales occupy a unique place in our literary lives. They are formative influences, showing us how to live, warning us from danger, and providing some parental control where necessary. They feature enduring characters whose stories remain deeply embedded in our consciousness, no matter how old or serious we become. Still, we must leave them after a point; when we close the covers of our books or the movie comes to an end, these influential characters are frozen at the moment of Happily Ever After. Though we remember their stories, we can't take them with us.

We challenged these authors to take classic fairy tale characters beyond the covers of their books, and to see whether or not things were actually so happy in their ever afters. Our authors answered the call by presenting us with deeply human characters, with further adventures, and with challenges to our own sensibilities. The outpouring of submissions for this anthology speaks volumes about our enduring connection to fairy tale characters, and about our continuing desire to explore the worlds they inhabit.

This collection features a broad range of authors and styles, and we are proud to offer up such variety not only in the stories themselves but in the people who wrote them. These different authors were drawn in by a myriad of tales from all over the world, some well-known and some more obscure. The one connective thread between all of these stories is a deep desire to continue our acquaintance with the fairy tales from our childhoods, and to bring them with us into adulthood.

We hope not only that you will enjoy this anthology, which is home to some exceptional writing and storytelling, but that it will encourage you to think about the fairy tales of your childhood, and wonder where your favorite characters are today. Maybe you can see some of the Beast in the mailroom clerk, or Cinderella in the woman who lives down the hall. Perhaps that lady in the subway station looks more like an old crone or the boy walking to class more like Prince Charming. Our hope is that whatever – or whoever – you see, it is a little more magical than it was before.

Josie Brown
Editor

Cinderella

"Cinderella never did bag that prince."

James S. Dorr is a prolific short story writer and poet working largely in dark fantasy and horror with occasional forays into science fiction and mystery. In the past he's been a technical writer, city editor on a regional magazine, full time non-fiction freelancer, and semi-professional musician. Among his influences he includes Edgar Allan Poe, Ray Bradbury, Allen Ginsberg, and Bertolt Brecht.

James has published two collections, Strange Mistresses: Tales of Wonder and Romance *and* Darker Loves: Tales of Mystery and Regret, *along with three to four hundred appearances (fiction and poetry) in magazines and anthologies from Aboriginal Science Fiction and Alfred Hitchcock's Mystery Magazine to Xenophilia and The Yellow Bat Review. He is an active member of Science Fiction and Fantasy Writers of America and the Horror Writer's Association, an Anthony (mystery) and Darrell (fiction set in the US Mid-South) finalist, a Pushcart Prize nominee, and a multi-time Honorable Mention in* The Year's Best Fantasy and Horror.

Latest news can be found at jamesdorrwriter. wordpress.com.

"Cinderella is such an iconic story it's almost the American dream in some ways, hard work and un-complaining virtue at last rewarded. In fact, I've written at least two other Cinderella variants in the past. 'The Glass Shoe,' however, is a sort of deconstructive version – or, perhaps better stated, de-mythologized. 'It ain't necessarily so.' I wrote it last August as the mid-term election season was building up steam which added a dollop of cynicism: What would one make of Cinderella in an age where 'spin' often seems to count more than truth? This is one answer – but mainly I wrote it because it was fun."

The Glass Shoe
James S. Dorr

Cinderella never did bag that prince. It's only a myth, a story she told later. It was actually her second stepsister, the one the legend says chopped off her toes to fit in the slipper, who ended triumphant. She was also the one who drank too much, so when the time came that the prince and his lackeys showed up with the glass shoes, she wasn't feeling any pain to speak of.

There are some who said she took some funny pills as well. That may be true. In any event, unlike Cindy's older step-sister – the one who had her heels shaved to the bone – this second stepsister just slipped her foot in as smooth as silk, not bitching or moaning like her elder sibling, but smiling all the way.

"What's all that red stuff though?" the prince asked, noticing that both the transparent shoes were filled with blood by now.

"Scarlet stockings," the second stepsister said, being quick of wit. "They were a gift from my poor deceased Daddy." But the thing was she was genuinely pretty, and big busted too, and was wearing one of those off-the-shoulder bustier things, with the laces in front like all the girls wore in those days, scoop-necked, you know the kind I mean. Suffice to say, the prince was easily enough distracted.

So they were married. Cinderella, whose feet were

12

naturally small – but her breasts were too, and her nose was large – never even had a chance to enter the contest. In a sort of hissy-fit she refused to go to the wedding, but second sister did give her the shoes afterward, as a kind of present. "Think of it as a *booby* prize," is what the second stepsister actually said, gratuitously curtsying as she did so, so Cindy could get an eyeful of what she meant. "Not even princes care that much about feet."

But Cinderella used those shoes. For the rest, she got implants and a nose job, also an ear tuck and hair extensions, and her acne cleared up of its own accord. Fairy godmothers had a lot of talent in those days, but not even they could control what would stare back the morning after from the bathroom magic mirror. However, "Cin," as she called herself now, was if not truly beautiful at least presentable, so she went out on the county fair circuit, modeling the glass shoes. She made sure everyone saw that her feet fit them. In this way she started the myth that it was actually she who had copped the crown.

It scarcely mattered, nobody cared about princes and princesses. Hell, most people didn't even bother to vote. It only got worse as time went on, too – Cin had some "tell-all" books ghostwritten for her to help boost her speaking fees. Some people even believe them to this day. She eventually got herself elected Governor of Montana some years after, but the job didn't suit her.

It didn't have to. Everything by then was PR. One of the slippers finally broke, being glass after all, but she still has the other. She also hunts and fishes, and she keeps the shoe on her mantelpiece between an elk head and a stuffed muskellunge.

Fairy Tale/Nursery Rhyme

"Why, Mister Swinedown," I said. "It is your heart I desire."

In addition to writing fiction, Rev DiCerto is a working musician and a medical editor. Apart from "The Spyder," he has two CDs nobody has ever heard, one of which was produced by a former Allman Brothers Band member and recorded in Nashville, and a short story called "The Saga of Anund the Berserk" in Pink Narcissus's Elf Love anthology.

"The theme for 'The Spyder' came about as a whim. I was working at home and e-mailing back and forth with an old friend and mentioned the theme of the anthology. We started throwing out the most ridiculous fairytale postscripts we could think of. If memory serves, there was originally supposed to be a lot of ninja training in this story.

"I'm currently drafting out the third book in a series of fantasy novels based entirely on Viking mythology, culture, magic, and literature. The second is due for editing and pruning; the first is too long to be accepted as a first novel. Write your congressmen and demand more novels that represent Vikings as three-dimensional humans."

Although there are no vikings or ninjas in "The Spyder," it is still a clever story and a vastly entertaining read.

The Spyder
Rev DiCerto

As I stepped across the threshold into the Mother Goose Public House, I could feel all eyes upon me. The main salon was smoky, ill-lit, and filled with a most offensive odor of stale beer, tobacco smoke, and rank sausages. A hush descended over the room, but a cacophony of diverse conversation soon resumed as the manifold beady eyes returned to cup, companion, or cards. A brief scan of the room revealed my quarry: a hulking gentleman with furry sideburns in a shoddy topper and a hairy greatcoat. I adjusted my dress and took a seat at his table. I had arrived promptly at four in the afternoon, as I had promised. Tardiness would not serve me in the least in this endeavor. There was a propriety which I felt it imperative that I observe.

"Evening, Miss..." said Mister Wolfe.

"Good evening, sir," said I.

"'Fraid I didn't quite get your name." My companion's voice was a deep-throated growl, aggravated, no doubt, by years of smoking and gin. His massive hands, with their hairy knuckles, were wrapped around a tankard of ale. This was not at all the sort of a gentleman with whom a young lady ought to be seen in public, but he was the only one to whom I could turn in this time of need.

"My name is unimportant, Mister Wolfe," I said. "Besides: I hardly think it to be the part of a man such as yourself to feel fear of such a one as me."

A smile passed across the face of Mister Wolfe that could only be described as – and I beg your pardon for the use of the term – wolfish. "True enough," he said, and, upon my word, he licked his lips. "You are a little one."

I could scarcely resist the urge to retreat into the umbrage of my bonnet, and yet I managed to maintain my composure. The weeks of visiting with witches – the city of London was simply swimming with them in 1898, and they were for the most part humbled by want of food, let alone currency – had taught me a courage that had been hitherto alien to my admittedly somewhat meek character. I persevered.

"Have you contacted the gentleman in question, Mister Wolfe?" I inquired.

Mister Wolfe's smile vanished, a fact that brought me no end of glee. "Oh, I have. Right tricky work it was, too." He began to scratch his left palm with the claw-like nails of his right hand.

I held firm in my resolve. "You have been paid quite handsomely already," I said, setting my chin in an attitude of determination. "And you shall be paid the remainder upon completion of your duty."

Mister Wolfe let out a sigh that sounded even more like a growl than did his speaking voice. "Right," he said, in a tone of resigned impatience. "Well, the gentleman you wish to see happens to be visiting in town this very week. He says to call at his rented flat tomorrow evening at eleven."

The hour seemed natural enough to me, considering

the nature of my business with the gentleman. However, it left me precious little time for the completion of my lone remaining errand, which was imperative if I was to be successful in my endeavor. "Thank you, Mister Wolfe," I said. The leering smile returned to his face, but I chose at this time to simply ignore it. "Where shall I meet you, then?"

"Ten-thirty, outside Victoria Station."

I did not allow him to see the shock I felt at the mention of such a respectable neighborhood as the location for an occult ritual. Instead, I rose, as primly as ever a proper girl did.

"Oh, and Miss," said Wolfe. I turned back to him. The leering grin was wickeder than ever. "Be sure to wear something nice."

Indeed!

I had changed into a more modest dress for tonight's errand, one of deep royal blue, with long gloves and a veiled bonnet that suggested not just propriety but also a certain conservatism – which, I must say, stood out in contradiction to my youth. Nevertheless, I felt that such attire, with a less pronounced bustle and less lace about the neck, would set the gentleman upon whom I would be calling at his ease. He was not a man renowned for an overabundance of sense, but he did have his worth. At any rate, an outfit that would capture the depraved attention of Mister Wolfe was quite another matter from one that would reassure the reputedly timid Mister Swinedown.

In my younger days, I would have found Jermyn Street after dark a most frightening place. However, since my great fright two years earlier and the time I had spent chasing witches, it now elicited no greater reaction from me than any other section of the city. In fact, I found myself rather enjoying the raucous activity of the place.

When I found the house I sought, I was taken somewhat aback. Certainly here was a house that could withstand even the mightiest of gales. I had expected it to be constructed of brick, and in this I had made no mistake. But I had also expected it to be rather small and poorly constructed, with few windows; the structure was in this regard the utter opposite of what I had envisioned, being rather a tall and imposing block of a building, with gargoyles and sculpted ledges, and twin gas lamps with crystal covers on either side of a shiny red door with an ostentatious brass knob. Perhaps, then, Mister Swinedown did not regard his home to be the impregnable and irreplaceable sanctuary that he was said to. It was all the same to me; unflustered, I ascended the stairs and knocked with the great, polished knocker, which was duly inscribed with the monogram "S."

When he opened the door and regarded me with a piggy little eye through the crack afforded by the still-set chain, Mister Swindown proved to be a tiny, pink-skinned man with flabby jowls and a round face. His suit was of the finest cut, however.

"Hello?" he said, in a frightened little voice.

"Good evening, Mister Swinedown," said I.

"I don't know you, Miss," said he, and would have shut the door in my face then and there, had I not set one dainty little foot in the opening in the nick of time.

"I am so terribly sorry to trouble you, sir," I said. "But I would require only a moment of your time. May I come in, please?"

He looked most uncomfortable at the prospect of opening the door. "I am afraid, Miss, that I can not open the door. You see, I am a rather wanted man."

I gave him the sweetest of my girlish smiles. "Your troubles are well known to me, sir," I said. "Indeed, it is about Mister Wolfe that I have come to speak with you. I assure you, I shall be brief."

"Then Wolfe is after you, too?" he asked. I could tell that his resolve was beginning to break.

"Mister Swinedown," said I, "I cannot begin to describe to you the sense of utter dread which that gentleman's leering smiles instill in me. And if I am to discuss him with you, is it not safest for both of us if it were to occur within your sturdy brick house, rather than upon the front stoop?"

Mister Swinedown nodded and opened the door. He led me through the front hallway and into a small parlor. There he sat upon a velvet couch. I took a seat nearby on the ottoman in front of a chair by the fire. Mister Swinedown reached for the bottle of sherry that stood on the table, surrounded by crystal glasses, but I shook my head.

"I will not be here long enough for that to be necessary, Mister Swinedown," said I.

My host nodded. "What, then, brings you here, Miss – I am sorry, but I am quite certain that you have not yet told me your name."

"I have not," I said. "And I should feel much safer if I did not."

Mister Swinedown nodded. His expression showed that he understood quite well how any person – and in particular a pretty young woman – who had caught the attention of Mister Wolfe would be inclined to remain anonymous. "Then what is it that I can do for you, Miss?"

"There is something that I need from you," I said.

An expression of discomfort crossed my host's face. "Miss, I have no money to lend, if that is what you are after," said he. "Nor will I permit you to share my sanctuary with me. Between myself and my brothers, I assure you that these premises are quite fully inhabited."

"That is not what I need from you, though, Mister Swinedown. I have not come to you for money or for sanctuary."

The pink little man looked relieved at this, and his posture returned to one of relaxation. "Very well, then, Miss. What is it that you desire of me?"

I stretched out my right leg, and his gaze strayed to the silver buttons on my shoe. In some discomfort, he looked up to my face, flushing, for I had hiked my skirts up enough for him to see my silk stocking from my ankle nearly to my knee. I gave him a smile and a longing look. "Why, Mister Swinedown," I said. "It is your heart I desire."

The man looked utterly shocked. His pink face turned red, then purple, as I leaned toward him. I hiked up the skirt a bit more, and reached for my garter.

"But Miss—" he said.

I drew the silver revolver from my garter and shot him between the eyes. He let out a squeal as he toppled over backward. I returned the pistol to its holster and leapt to my feet, then dragged my host to the center of the floor. He was stone dead.

I drew the silver-bladed knife from the sheath on my left ankle and drove it into his chest. The still-warm blood coursing over my hands sickened me, but I persevered. I had learned a lot from the witches. The silly little creature. I had said I wanted his heart. Had he not believed me?

And had he truly believed that it was his house, and not his heart, that kept Mister Wolfe at bay?

I emerged from Victoria Station at ten twenty-five to find Mister Wolfe awaiting me under a gaslight. Neither his coat nor his hat had grown any less tatty in the past day's time, and he smelled like a great wet dog. There was an eager look in his eyes from the moment they lit upon me. I had dressed in a far more girlish and fetching fashion, with a pronounced bustle, a tight corset that accentuated my curves, and a flowered bonnet. I had heard that Mister Wolfe had an eye for young girls. Certainly I had heard rumor of one or two who had fared most horribly at his hands, and another few who had only barely escaped his machinations. He licked his lips.

"Well," said he, "don't you look nice!"

"Good enough to eat?" I asked, and affected a giggle. I was going to be sure the nature of our association was no mystery to him, once the inevitable had occurred.

"You do, at that."

"Well," I said, "shall we be off, Mister Wolfe?"

He looked hungrily at me, then nodded, barely able to conceal his shortness of breath, and led me up the street. We walked for some minutes, and I must confess that I was most uncomfortable as we went, never feeling certain when Mister Wolfe would set upon me. At length, as we reached a dimly lit corner, my companion pointed right, down a dim alley. "It's down there," he said.

I nodded and allowed him to lead me down the alley. The light from the street quickly faded. I heard the scurrying of rats. A baby cried out in one of the buildings above, and I heard a drunk muttering to himself. There was dread, but no true surprise, when we fetched up against a high wooden fence. I turned and saw the huge silhouette of Mister Wolfe towering over me.

"Is this the place?" I asked.

"Oh, aye," said Wolfe. "Now, Missy. Let's have a look at your knickers."

"No," said I.

Wolfe chuckled, like the barking of a St. Bernard dog. He seized me by the neck with one vast claw of a hand, and slammed my back against the fence. Had I not the heart of Mister Swinedown among the various affects in the carpetbag that I carried, I feel certain I should have been injured; but as it was, I merely laughed. Wolfe stopped.

"Why are you laughing?" asked he.

"Because, Mister Wolfe, you cannot harm me."

"That's what you think, Missy."

"Then try."

I felt his hand squeeze at my neck, but though I felt some small pressure, it quickly ceased to build, as though he were attempting to squeeze the bole of an oak tree. His arm began to tremble. I giggled, and he laid his other hand to my neck to aid its fellow. He squeezed for all that he was worth, until his frame shuddered with the effort and I heard his breath come gasping. I giggled again.

23

"Have you had enough yet?" I asked.

He released me with a burst of foul-smelling breath. "Curse you!" said Wolfe. "How've you done it?"

"Though I am certain that you shall know all in due time, Mister Wolfe, I will not reveal my secret to you now. However, there is the matter of my knickers. Do you still wish for a glimpse of what is beneath my skirts?"

His shadow stood quite still, and I was certain that he was in a state of great doubt. Finally he said, with a shuddering breath, "Yes. If you're keen to show me." I could hear his wolfish grin.

I reached down and began to slowly hike up my skirts. I could hear him sniffing in the darkness. "I'll show you," I said. "So long as I will still get what we arranged, and be brought to the gentleman."

"We'll see about that," he said.

I pressed the silver revolver to his nose. "No," said I, "you will take me to him. Now. As big a fool as you are, Mister Wolfe, surely you now realize that you cannot harm me, but I can harm you. Or has your famed nose gone stupid as well? Can you smell what is in the chamber of this pistol?"

He growled. I declare it, the man truly growled at me. "Silver," he said. "Bugger."

"Now take me to see the gentleman, and aid me in my endeavor this evening, or you will die," I said. "Then we need never see one another again." Finally I could be certain that Mister Wolfe would deliver on his end of our bargain, being exhausted of other options.

The man who opened the door to the fourth-story flat

was much younger than I had expected, only a year or two older than myself. He was handsome, and well dressed. He did not appear in the least bit surprised to see Mister Wolfe, but he did start somewhat at me.

"Mister Crowley," said Mister Wolfe. "This is the young lady I told you about." Mister Wolfe was positively sheepish before me.

"Do come in," said Mister Crowley. He stepped back from the door and admitted us to the flat. The parlor was well appointed but not opulent. A fire burned upon the hearth, and there were candles lit. A circle had already been drawn on the floor. "And you are?"

"You shall know in good time, Mister Crowley," said I. "Can you do, then, a summoning, as Mister Wolfe has told me?"

Crowley, dressed in a silk jacket with an ascot, smiled faintly and nodded. "I have done several such ceremonies," he said. "I have been involved in the occult arts now for some two years. I might go so far as to say that I need the practice."

"Very good, sir," I said. "Then let us begin. It is a demon which I wish to summon."

"Have you brought the blood of a black goat? Did Wolfe here tell you about that part?"

"Indeed, I have everything that is required of me," I said.

"Then the last thing that I must ask of you is the name of the demon."

"If he has another name, then I am unaware of it. The name I have learned is Spyder."

Mister Crowley nodded. "That should be sufficient," he

said. I handed him the bottle of goat's blood, and he began the ceremony.

For a girl as proper as I am, a ceremony involving the blood of a goat, the drawing of pentacles, and the intonation of ancient chants is no pleasant prospect, and it was with no small degree of trepidation that I withstood this one. Again I was glad of my time with the witches, for their smaller rites had gone a long way toward preparing me for what I experienced in that tiny London flat that night. At one point, I came near to swooning, but Mister Crowley came to my aid, and then went on with his chanting. He smeared the goat's blood over the circle drawn on the carpet, then dabbed it in each of the corners of the pentacle. What was left he splashed into the center of the design as he began to intone the demon's name, in a voice that grew ever in its volume and its intensity: "Spyder! Spyder! Spyder!" He opened one eye and gestured for me and Wolfe to join in, and we did. "Spyder! Spyder! Spyder!"

A strange smell began to fill the room, at once sulfurous and sweet, as though a flame had been set burning in a sugar mill. It stung the nose. I opened my eyes and saw a vast, dark shape taking form in the midst of the pentacle. As we chanted, it grew ever more solid, until a glistening, black spider, flecked with red patches, stood corporeal within the circle. Its legs swatted at the borders of its earthly prison, but it could not break free. Mister Crowley dropped his arms and ceased to chant, and Wolfe and I followed suit. Crowley stepped toward the circle until he stood at its very edge.

"You are the demon called Spyder?" he asked in authoritative tones.

"I am," the creature chattered.

"This woman has asked that I summon you. Do you know her?"

"I do not."

Mister Crowley turned toward me. "Do what you will," he said.

Swallowing my overwhelming terror, I stepped up to the edge of the circle, and picked up the carpetbag that I had set down there and opened it. "Do you remember me, Mister Spyder?" I asked.

"No."

I pulled out the silver bowl, and pulled off the waxed paper that I had used to cover it. A milky, cheesy odor mingled with the smell of sugar and brimstone in the air. "Do you recognize this?" I asked. "Is it familiar?"

"No."

I leaned forward, then remembered myself and looked to Mister Crowley. With a bemused expression on his face, he shrugged and nodded. I bent down and placed the bowl of curds on the floor, just within the circle, before Spyder's mandibles. The demon's legs bent and it brought its face nearer to the bowl.

"You?" it asked. "That was you?"

"It was I," said I.

"This is a gift?"

"It is."

The spider's mandibles dipped into the wide bowl of curds and whey. I could hear its mouth working as it ate. I reached under my skirt with both hands.

"Mister Crowley," I said, "please, in the future, inform any demons with whom you have converse that it would be most unwise to ever again interrupt Miss Muffet's breakfast."

The silver revolver in my right hand blasted away, six shots, emptying even as I brought its twin to bear. The pistol in my left hand drew perfect aim on Wolfe even as the spider collapsed to the floor, its eyes forever dimmed, ichor oozing over the carpet, its eight legs shuddering in its death throes.

"Gentlemen," said I, "it simply isn't proper to frighten a lady while she is eating."

East of the Sun and West of the Moon

"At once she felt as if she'd crossed a boundary, a border into a new land, and there was no turning back."

Suzanne Lilly is a writer and an elementary school teacher. Her work has appeared in numerous places online and in print, and she has placed and received honorable mentions in online writing contests. Suzanne Lilly writes light romance, young adult, and middle grade novels. She is also the feature writer for the Fiction Writing section at Suite101. com. She blogs at TeacherWriter.net and can be found twittering as @suzannelilly. She has a Master's Degree in Teaching and is a graduate of the Long Ridge Writer's Group, a member of the Romance Writers of America, as well as its Young Adult chapter. When not writing, she is knitting, cooking, reading, or swimming.

Suzanne's writing has appeared online in Common Ties, Chick Lit Review, Mysterical-E, WOW! Women on Writing, Fandangle, The Deepening, and other websites and blogs. Some of her nonfiction work has been published in paper and ink in Cat Fancy, Advanced Healing, Pearson Education, and The Dixon Tribune.

"I always loved the dreaminess of the original fairy tale, 'East of the Sun and West of the Moon.' There's something magical about the title, a sense of being everywhere and yet nowhere at the same time."

East of the Sun and West of the Moon Redux
Suzanne Lilly

Every day for the past thirty years had proceeded in the same stultifying routine. Madeleine would rise from her king-sized bed in their cold penthouse suite and put on her riding boots. As she rode the horses she held tight onto their manes while they galloped across the fields. It gave her the sense of freedom and adventure she'd felt all those many years ago, riding to her beloved on the North Wind.

Charles, on the other hand, preferred fishing in Central Park. This was a natural inclination, considering the time he'd spent as an enchanted Polar bear. Each day he would return with a fish to fry for their noon meal.

She would come home from riding flushed with wind-burn on her cheeks. She would cook his fish in Tuscan extra virgin olive oil and fresh basil from the hothouse. He, in return, would comb out her long wind-tangled hair with her golden brush and tie it back with a single golden ribbon.

Every afternoon, Madeleine idly stared out the tall west facing windows of the penthouse, reminiscing about more exciting times. Charles sat watching the stock market reports on CNN, cheering whenever his fortune grew.

One day, as she sat by the window in the golden rays of the setting sun, she looked down on the street below and saw a

young woman, not much more than a girl, talking and gesturing to the doorman. From her vantage point high above the
street, it looked as if the girl was quite agitated.

"Who could that young girl be?" she wondered out loud.

"Probably some panhandler," her husband commented.
He didn't bother to look away from the television to see whom
she was talking about.

Thirty years of solid comfort had fattened his soul and
left hers hungry. She went downstairs to the doorman.

"Edmund, who was that girl standing here talking to
you just a moment ago?"

"No one to worry about, ma'am. Just a tourist."

"What did she want?" Madeleine draped her long hair
in front of her right shoulder and smoothed it with her hands.
A light wind from the North pulled a few strands loose.

"She wanted to go upstairs to your penthouse, but I
turned her away."

At that moment, the girl came running toward them
from around the corner of the building. A gust of cold air
pushed her closer to them and she stumbled.

"Please ma'am," she said breathlessly, "I've traveled so
far to meet you and your husband."

"Really?" Madeleine smoothed her hair again, pushing
the strands back into place.

"Yes, I've read the story of your love for one another,
and I had to come find out if it could possibly be true."

"Of course it's true, child. We've been together for thirty
years. Nothing could separate us."

Even as the words left her lips, she gazed at Edmund's
warm golden brown eyes and thick dark hair. She thought of

how they contrasted with her husband's polar ice blue eyes and thinning white hair.

"The city is extremely cold today, and it looks as if a storm is blowing in," Madeleine said. "Why don't you come inside with me? I have hot tea and cookies." Charles would never notice, so immersed was he in the stock report.

Edmund gave her a look of consternation and stepped protectively between Madeleine and the girl. "Ma'am, are you sure this is wise?"

"I'm certain, Edmund. We'll be fine." She looked at his full lips and licked her own.

The young girl followed her up to the penthouse kitchen. She clasped her cold fingers around the warm teacup and nibbled on stale cookies. She admired the fine marble counter tops, the Italian tiled floors, the mahogany cupboards.

"My husband has been very kind and generous to me," Madeleine explained.

"And you've been so kind to me," the girl replied. "Here, let me give you this as a token of my appreciation. It was a gift to me on my eighteenth birthday." She handed Madeleine a small golden pendant in the shape of an apple.

Something stirred inside Madeleine's heart, a deep and distant memory, but she couldn't put her finger on it. She did, however, put her finger on the golden apple pendant, and slipped it around her neck. At once she felt as if she'd crossed a boundary, a border into a new land, and there was no turning back.

"I have a spare bed in the den, if you'd like to sleep here tonight. You're welcome take a shower in the maid's quarters."

The girl accepted her hospitality and stayed the night.

In the morning, when Madeleine rose for her usual ride, the young girl was gone.

The morning was windier than usual. Her husband complained of the waves on the water in Central Park and said it made it harder to catch a fish. He did bring home a small one, which his wife dutifully cooked for him in the Tuscan extra virgin olive oil with a bay leaf from the hothouse. After his lunch, Charles used the golden brush to untangle his wife's hair.

He lifted her hair and gently kissed each bone along the nape of her neck. His lips caressed her shoulder and swept over her neck and up to her ear. "You were wonderful last night," he whispered. Madeleine wondered what he meant, since the night had been no different from any other.

That afternoon, the girl again appeared at the main doorway to the building. Madeleine watched as Edmund waved her away and the girl refused to go. She went downstairs and placed her hand on the doorman's arm. "Thank you Edmund, but the young woman is welcome to come upstairs with me."

Madeleine fed her pasta for dinner and offered her the spare bed again. The grateful young girl took a golden hair clip out of her locks and gave it to Madeleine to express her thanks. Again, a shadow of a memory stirred deep within her. She realized how much the girl reminded her of her own younger self. She knew she shouldn't accept the gift, but the beautiful clip had such a warm golden color, and it would help keep the wind from tangling her long locks. She brushed away her doubts and placed the clip in her own hair. The next morning, the young girl was gone again.

That day proceeded as every other day. She rode, he

34

fished, she cooked, he ate, then he brushed her hair. It was exceptionally knotty, for the cold North Wind was howling around the corners of the building and through the city streets. It took him longer than usual to brush it out, and when he was done, he wrapped his arms around her and whispered how much he enjoyed their lovemaking the night before.

Madeleine had spent the night curled up in her own warm bed alone.

At sunset, the girl arrived again. This time Madeleine was downstairs waiting for her.

"I appreciate your kindness these past two days," the girl told her, "but tonight I don't have anything to give you but this gold spinning wheel charm. My father bought it for me when he gave me a book of fairy tales."

At the mention of fairy tales, Madeleine turned to her. "Give me the charm," she said and turned it over several times in her hand. The shadows of memories clarified, and Madeleine understood the turning of the magic. The girl waited patiently as Edmund pulled Madeleine to the side.

"Are you sure you want to do this?" he asked her.

"I want nothing more," she said.

"The third time is a charm. After this, there's no turning back."

Madeleine fingered the golden apple pendant around her throat, adjusted the gold clip in her hair, and hooked the gold spinning wheel charm onto her own bracelet. She gave the girl the key to the penthouse. The girl quickly went upstairs before Madeleine could change her mind.

Madeleine smiled into Edmund's warm eyes. "I went to the bank this morning," she told him. "I transferred all of

Charles' money. If we're quick, we can catch a plane to Italy tonight and be basking in the balmy Mediterranean sun tomorrow."

Edmund threw his cap into the bushes and hailed a cab.

Snow White and Rose Red

"She was the light and the blossoming of spring, and I the dark twilight of autumn. Together we were whole."

Juniper Talbot grew up in the woods creating and living Faerie Tales with her sister. In her experience, the beast is always more desirable than the charming prince he turns out to be, and the Prince never has an equally charming brother waiting in the wings for the rejected sister to marry.

Juniper's story "Color of the Sky" appears in the Elf Love *anthology.*

Not to be confused with the more famous fairy tale, "Snow White and Rose Red" is a Grimms' tale about two sisters who encounter a bear.

The Bear
Juniper Talbot

They say I married his brother and moved to a neighboring kingdom. In this way, the story can have a happy ending. They say I married his brother because it's what they want to believe. Perhaps in a way, I did marry his brother, since in the end, we truly became one.

It happened like this.

I loved her more than anyone, and she loved me. My sister. She completed me, and I completed her. She was the light and the blossoming of spring, and I the dark twilight of autumn. Together we were whole.

I barely remembered our father, and she never knew him, still a babe in our mother's womb when he died. Our mother's love for her dead husband seemed to pass over us then, becoming grafted instead onto two rose bushes, which grew in front of our cottage on either side of the door. One bloomed with blood red roses, the other with roses white as snow. Mother tended these roses with the loving care she had once granted to us, but gradually Mother began to think of her two daughters only in terms of her darling rose bushes, til we lost our names and identities entirely. I, the elder darker one, became known only as Rose Red, while my sister, the younger and fairer, became Snow White.

The love my sister and I had for each other was fierce; a barrier against our mother's overwhelming grief and gradual abandonment. We knew no fear, no loneliness as long as we had each other. The forest, the dark, the chill of winter, the anguish of our mother could hold no sway over us. We were complete in each other; the light and the dark half combined in perfection. We believed it would be this way with us forever: Snow White and Rose Red. But forever is too long a time and Fate has a way of intervening when least expected.

All that we had known changed the night *he* came to our door, seeking haven from the snows. When we heard the rap on the door that first wintry evening, I saw fear flicker across my sister's face for the first time. In the simplicity of our young lives and the bond we had with each other, Snow White and I had had no occasion to know fear. I should have known then, with that brief flicker in her blue eyes, that something was about to work its way between us – that Change in its unpredictable and nuanced way was about to enter our lives. I should have run to the door, and bolted it hard against the ensuing blast. Instead, we hesitated, my sister and I, staring into each other's eyes, trying to savor the last moment before the world we knew began to slip away forever.

"Answer the door, Rose Red!" my mother called from her bench by the fire.

Struggling to my feet, I went to the door. As I lifted the latch and pulled it open, I saw at first nothing but blackness. A strange, musky, earthy scent assaulted my nose, however, and skittered through me like so many fiery pinpricks. A sensation I had never felt before blossomed in my belly, and I stood frozen on the threshold, my dark eyes staring into darkness.

"Rose Red! Who's there?!" my mother called.

At that moment, I realized that the blackness I saw was a living, breathing mass of fur. As I stepped back, the stranger stepped forward. Through the crack of door I had pulled open, his huge hulking form was revealed.

He was a bear. Not any bear. Snow White and I had encountered many during our rambles in the woods, but never had we seen such as this. He was massive, and stood firmly on his back legs as would a man. He towered over us by more than a head, all but cracking his skull on our ceiling beams. It was the scent that emanated from his wiry black fur, however, that overcame me the most. I was used to the musky dank smells of the earth and found them comforting and familiar, having made my bed on the forest floor so many times before, my sister curled tight against me. He smelled of earth, yes, and familiar damp must of humus, but there was more. Whatever strange odor poured from him captivated and intoxicated me like nothing I had ever experienced or imagined. I wanted only to bury my face in his black fur and drink in his aroma, running my fingers through the coarse hair, and pulling my body ever closer to his beating heart. I stood still, however, dumb and staring.

Snow White regained her composure quickly, and politely invited the bear to take a place by the fire. Mother slid back her bench, and dropping to all fours, the bear lumbered to the hearth. He sank, exhausted, next to the flames.

"Child, will you sweep the snow from my coat?" the bear asked my sister, his voice rumbling from a deep place.

"Certainly, sir," Snow White replied, jumping up to fetch the broom.

As I watched my sister sweep the snow from the black

hide, a pang of jealousy shot through me.

"What is this?" I asked myself, shocked. How could I ever feel jealous of my sister – she was my soul, my heart, myself! I looked away, unwilling to take in more of the homey scene, and busied myself with re-fitting the latch in the door, and wiping snow from the stoop.

When I turned back, Snow White had returned to her seat, and the bear had fallen into a deep slumber. I stood – reeling and uncertain, a strange fire smoldering in my belly.

That's how it began. The bear left in the pre-dawn light before Snow White, my mother or I awakened. Although each day after that seemed to carry forward with a sense of normalcy, something in me churned. Nothing was normal for me. Each evening the bear would return, rap on the door and wait to be let in. Each evening, I breathed in his scent as Snow White swept the snow from his hide. I envied her this task, but couldn't bring myself to say so. I wanted everything to be the same, but I knew that it never would be again. Something had come between Snow White and me, and I knew we were caught in its grip, unable to flee. Although I tried to find joy in the simple things Snow White and I had once shared, I hungered more with each passing day for the evening and the inevitable rap at the door that was reshaping me in ways I could not under-stand and could not resist.

Sometimes in the dead of night, I would pull away from my sister's gentle arms and sneak to the hearth where the bear slept. I would wrap myself as close to him as I dared, and breathe in the smell and warmth and dark danger of him til I felt him stir with the first light. I would then scurry guiltily back to the sleeping arms of my sister and dream of black fur til full dawn reached the window.

The winter passed in this way, and we watched the snows slowly vanish. Little did I know what suffering this change of seasons would bring.

One evening, when the smell of spring was high in the air, and the song of the tree toads could be heard from the window, no rap came on the door and no bear lumbered to his accustomed place by the fire. Though I waited long hours into the deep of night, well past the time when my mother and sister took to their beds, he still did not come. The bear had intimated that when spring came, he would need to return to his cavern home to guard what was his to guard, but somehow, I never believed the day would come. Now it had, and I was lost.

Throughout the ensuing spring, I was plagued to distraction. Sometimes Snow White would cry, wondering why I seemed so far away. But the sweet blue eyes of my sister had been replaced in my heart by the bottomless brown pools of the bear's, for which I longed without solace. Her light could no longer hold a candle to his dazzling darkness, so like my own.

At night I would dream that he had come back to me, that I lay down beside him on the hearth and buried my face once again in his deep scent and wiry black fur. I would press so close to him that my heart would beat with his, and my body would meld with his, and my dark hair would tangle in his dense coat, until there was no Rose Red any more – only Bear. Until one day.

Besides my distracted obsession with our winter guest, the spring and summer had been far from normal. Snow White and I had encountered a very grumpy dwarf on two occasions, who despite our efforts to rescue him from difficult situations, left only in anger, cursing at us without a morsel of gratitude. We thought very little of it, knowing that the forest folk have their own ways and it is best to have as little to do with them as possible.

On this particular day, however, we spotted our grumpy fellow just as he was being lifted away in the hungry clutches of a large eagle. Snow White and I both grabbed the dwarf and pulled him to safety, ripping his coat in the effort. Just as he had done in the past, the dwarf stamped and shouted at our clumsiness in ripping his coat, with no thanks for saving his sorry skin. Snow White began to laugh at the silly creature, and I felt the first glimmer of a giggle about to erupt from my throat – the first my poor sweet sister had heard from me in a long time.

Just then I heard a branch crack, and a dark, earthy musk-like scent filled my senses, wrapping me in my long awaited dream. All thoughts of Snow White and the crazy dwarf left me as I turned to face *him*. I knew him instantly. He stood as tall and large as ever I remembered him, and though he caught my eyes with his fathomless pools of brown for only an instant, all the pent-up desire flooded through me, my belly kindling with flame. The dwarf, on the other hand, had frozen at the sight of the bear, looking frightened and guilty. With one definitive swat of his giant paw, the bear knocked the dwarf to the ground, and the nasty little man never moved again.

Snow White ran to the bear and hugged him, but I,

jealous once more of my beloved little sister, stood rooted to the ground. Even as I watched the two beings I loved most in the world hold each other in friendly embrace, I knew that now at last, I could be fully complete. My dark could be joined with his dark and finally made whole. What I had shared with my sister all those years, I knew now was just a small taste of the satiating feast that lay ahead when I would at last be united with my bear.

The bear stood back from Snow White, and turned toward me, the fervor in his eyes seeming to match my own. I took one step toward him, eyes locked, knowing with every part of my being that my endless dreams would at last be fulfilled.

Then without warning, the air cracked. The earth shuddered. Something crucial and irrevocable snapped, as blinding light split the sky in two. I was shaken to the core and stunned, deaf and blind.

When my senses returned, I saw with growing horror what lay at my feet. A lifeless mass of wiry fur coiled oddly on the ground, only vaguely resembling the tall, imposing bear I had loved and known. I must have stared stunned for a long time, but at last, I looked up. Where my beloved bear had been only moments ago, a fair young man with vacuous pale eyes now stood, staring at me, confused and unrecognizing. He turned toward my sister, and I saw their gaze lock in recognition and delight. They fell into each other's arms, light embracing light. The dark lay dead and discarded at their feet.

What came next is a blur. I remember something about the rude dwarf and an evil spell placed on a young prince, causing him to go about in the shape of a bear. I remember hearing of a plot for the dwarf to steal the wealth of this prince-bear. And then hearing of how the spell was broken, and the treasure retrieved when the dwarf at last lay motionless in a heap, the claw marks of a bear scarring his cheek.

All this I remember only dimly, like a dream that flees into mist with the morning light. What I remember clearly is falling to the ground and burying myself in the still warm skin of my black bear. Drinking in the fading aroma that so intoxicated me. I hear my sister call to me dimly. I feel hands try to drag me away. I hear my own throaty growl of protest, as I bare my teeth and claw at whatever comes close.

I must have lain prone on the ground wrapped in my bear's skin for a very long time, but I don't know. I remember dark and light and dark again many times over. At last I crawled my way to the opening of a nearby cave whose familiar scent of bear hide called to me. I believe this must have been his lair in those lonely months when he no longer warmed himself at our fire. His scent was stronger there, and I could dream of him as I lay wrapped in his skin.

When at last the snow started to fall, I began to remember other things – other eyes. I remembered blue eyes. Although the face they belonged to was blurred, I felt an old yearning I could not name. I scraped my way out of the cave draped in dark hide, and lumbered aimlessly through the woods. As the sky began to darken, I caught the twinkling of many lights not far ahead. Impelled forward by the haunting memory of those blue eyes, I made my way, until at last I found myself at the gate of an opulent dwelling. Light and warmth blazed from every window, and something old and melancholy stirred in me. I hunkered my way under the weight of the skin to the closest window, and peered inside. By the fire sat a man and a woman and an old woman. Mother. Sister. The words felt strange in my mouth, yet somehow warm. I scratched lightly on the pane, and two blue eyes turned to mine. I don't know if she saw me, but a shock of recognition stole through my body. It was more than I could bear. I turned then and lumbered back to the safety of my cave.

As the long winter days passed, I felt myself becoming more and more at one with the skin of my bear love. My own course dark hair began to entwine in the fur of his coat. My fingernails grew long and yellowed, curving almost like claws, and the fierce dark hunger in my eyes burned like his own once had. My skin, crusted with dirt, began to stick inside the hide til the skin became my own, never leaving my body. The heft of the hide bore me down, and I walked now with a heavy lumbering gate. I was becoming complete.

Occasionally, I would still hunger after a sight of those blue eyes, and would find myself staring into the window where the strangers sat in warmth and companionship. I could no longer understand their speech, and my own came only in low grunts and growls. I could however feel those blue eyes on mine, dimly calling to some place buried deep in dark fur and heavy hide.

Whether she ever knew me or recognized me, I'll never know. All I know is that, as dark became one with dark, and light became one with light, there stood little but emptiness between us.

On the last night I visited the lighted window, I saw something I didn't understand. A small mewling package of pink and blue lay on the lap of the one I had known. A strange light seemed to shine around it, and my dark eyes, no longer used to light, found it hard to bear. The blue-eyed one held it close, and it cuddled and slept. Some long forgotten desire awoke within me then, and I clambered and grunted at the window. Blue eyes stared back at me in abject terror, and raced from the room with the small pink thing clutched to her breast. I slumped to the ground and lay there in confusion, until at last sleep overtook me.

I awoke suddenly in the pre-dawn light to a loud wailing sound. Instinctively, I ran toward the woods, now hearing the baying of hounds and trample of hooves close on my trail. I ran for my life, knowing full well that I was the hunted. Although I was fast, my heavy skin bore me down, and I soon found I was no match for the swift hunters and their hounds. As I neared my cave, the hounds fell upon me, gnashing at my skin and face. I felt my blood spill from me, but fought on with my claws and fangs.

The twang of a loosed arrow warned me only seconds before it split my heart that death was on its way. Trailing blood, I limped the last paces to my cave and crawled deep down inside. The hounds continued to bay at the opening, but soon I no longer heard them. I felt my blood pour into the skin of my beloved, wetting the dark fur with crimson the color of red roses. I thought only briefly of white snow and blue eyes, wondering if my death had come from them. I knew now, without the slightest doubt, that my dreams were all coming true. I would at last be truly united with my beloved, that dark would know only dark. Finally, I would be complete.

Little Red Riding Hood

"Reliable evil sources include the wicked witch, wicked step-mother and the huffing puffing wolf."

David Sellars is a fiction writer and copywriter currently working in Tourism Marketing on the beautiful island of Jersey. Outside of work and study, he is a romantically hopeful fisherman, a keen kayaker (as long as there are rods involved) and avid player (but mainly watcher) of most sports. Traveling is a serious passion, and if he doesn't venture off island often, the walls close in.

David blogs, writes short stories and is currently working on an MA in Professional Writing as well as his first novel The Silence for which he will also write the screenplay. His preferred genres include dark romance, horror, thrillers, crime, travel, fairy tales and comedy. He can be found at www.davidsellars.blogspot.com and www.davidsellars.com.

"I have always been interested in fairy tales, and as part of the Professional Writing Course we were encouraged to write in a genre we liked, but approach it from an entirely new angle. The style I've written this in also reminds me of cartoon shorts which used to appear pre the main feature in cinemas."

The title of his story – "A Wolf's Guide to the Fairytale" – says it all.

A Wolf's Guide to the Fairytale
David Sellars

We've all heard the stories from times past, when girls in pretty scarlet capes wandered alone in the woods on their way to delivering wine and cake to their ailing grandmothers; of how wolves have tried over and over again to devour both of these feeble souls but have nonetheless wound up dead themselves. Well here it is, a 10-point "idiot's guide," incorporating centuries of knowledge on the legend and how to successfully hunt and consume your own Little Red Riding Hood (LRRH) and her Grandmother.

1. First you have to find yourself a LRRH. This part is easy – go to any enchanted, forbidden or fairytale forest and ask around. Reliable evil sources include the wicked witch, wicked stepmother and the huffing puffing wolf. Make it clear that you do not wish to trade fairy tales with these inept characters.

2. Once located, observe LRRH from afar, making sure you aren't seen.

3. LRRH will have a mother and a father, who may or may not be a woodcutter. LRRH will eventually be given rations to take to her sick Grandmother – these are usually wine and cake. She will leave mid-afternoon and be told not to deviate from the path so that she reaches Grandmother's cottage as quickly

as possible. Follow her and make sure you keep out of sight.[1]

4. Once on the path and away from view of her parental home you should seek to interact with LRRH. She is gullible and innocent; she will not fear you. The trick here is not to eat LRRH (as luscious as this may seem) but to find out the exact location of her Grandmother's house. It is located deep in the woods so make sure LRRH is precise and you memorize this. I cannot emphasize this enough – see point 6 below.

5. Suggest that there are some wonderful flowers in the forest for LRRH to pick for her Grandmother; be sincere but firm. Whilst LRRH is searching for flowers, this will enable you to get to the cottage before LRRH.[2]

6. Locate the cottage.
WARNING! There are many other cottages located in these forests so you need to make sure you find the right one. Avoid any house made of straw or sticks, and despite the glorious aromas, under no circumstance enter one that is built entirely of gingerbread!

7. Knock on the door, and pretend to be LRRH. The Grand-mother is old and probably senile so this shouldn't take much convincing, she'll encourage you in.

8. Make no small talk; time is of the essence, so gobble up

---

[1]   *Werewolves, do not fear as LRRH always ventures to Grand-mother's house on a full moon.*

[2]   *Werewolves, ensure that LRRH does not pick wolfsbane or this will give her the upper hand later in the fairytale.*

Grandmother as quickly as possible, borrow some of her night clothes, especially the nightcap and glasses, as these have been especially good camouflage garments throughout the centuries, and jump into bed as LRRH will be arriving shortly. Do not fall asleep.

9. When LRRH arrives, invite her in. You will be desperate to devour her to take the taste of Granny out of your mouth but there is a procedure that needs to be adhered to. LRRH will comment on how big various parts of your body are. Depending on which fairytale you are in this will differ but reply to comments with, "All the better for seeing, smelling, touching you, etc.," until she replies with the fateful, "Oh Grandmother, what big teeth you have," and then you can say, "All the better for eating you with, my dear," and this is your cue to eat that gloriously irresistible plump young flesh.[3]

10. LRRH's father or a random woodcutter will come into the house after hearing you snore loudly – understandable after a big meal. Now, depending on the fairytale you are in, you will either be hacked open or silently opened by shears to allow LRRH and her Grandmother to escape. You might even be filled with rocks by LRRH so that you are too heavy to move. Regardless of how you are supposed to die, the obvious course of action is not to fall asleep in the first place (caffeine can help – The Mad Hatter provides a great brew on a regular basis) and merely run off into the woods to survive the fairytale (howling with delight should you wish).

---

[3]   *Despite the temptation, chew up LRRH as you eat her, believe me, you'll thank me for this should things go wrong here on in.*

The Tinderbox

"And what had *Karl done to her, while she slept on the back of his dog?"*

Richard Jay Goldstein lives in Santa Fe, where it's nice and quiet, thanks. He's a retired ER doc, has been writing for about 20 years, and has published 40-some stories, essays and poems in literary and sci-fi/fantasy/horror presses, including a few anthologies such as Virtually Now *(Persea Press), in which he shared space with Octavia Butler, Ursula K. LeGuinn, Stephen Dixon, Margaret Atwood, and others. He has also been twice nominated for the Pushcart Prize.*

"I was inspired by this very call for stories. The story of the magic tinderbox has always fascinated me. When I was a kid I had an illustrated copy. The dogs with big eyes drew and repelled me. And like many fairy tales, it is really quite horrible, and the protagonist extremely unlikeable. I welcomed the chance to get things straightened out."

No doubt Hans Christian Andersen would approve of this enchanting and sophisticated sequel to his original tale.

The Fourth Door
Richard Jay Goldstein

There are many strange stories of the old days told in the northlands, where the summer sun shines at midnight and the winter nights seem to last forever. Wild lights like curtains unwind across the dark sky during those nights, shedding strange powers on the frozen land below. It is said the brittle northern lights were much stronger and brighter long ago than they are now, and brought with them powerful magic that lured strange creatures out of the silent ancient forests.

We have largely forgotten those old days, and so we think many stories are fanciful and untrue, but which in reality were as true as what we now call history.

The Magic Tinderbox is one such story, but the story everybody knows is only the beginning...

...for the story goes on to tell of the grand festivities celebrating the wedding of Annemette — meaning *bitter pearl* — the princess of Denmark, and how these festivities were full of ambiguity and confusion for her.

On the one hand, the story explains, Annemette was marrying Karl, a handsome and resourceful soldier, as had been foretold when she was a child by a witch woman. On the second hand, Annemette's parents, the king and queen, had just been mauled and killed by Karl's magical dogs with huge eyes, a horrible event. On the third hand — for three-handed trolls were common in the forests of Denmark in those days — the king and queen had imprisoned Annemette in the Copper Palace for many years and allowed her to see no one, and no one to see her. They were fearful of the witch woman's prediction, of course, but still it was a cruel thing to do.

During the feast Karl became drunk, as soldiers will. Although he had put on the airs of a gentleman when he was living in the town and spending gold like a sailor — or rather, a soldier — he was really a very coarse person.

Drunk, his face red, mead dripping from his moustache, standing unsteadily on his chair, he related the tale of how he had acquired his wealth and his fabulous and dangerous dogs. He told how he had met a horrible witch on the road, and how she had shown him the eerie hollow tree, and how to enter the underworld beneath it. He described the enchanted caverns, with a hundred lamps burning, and the three doors hiding treasures of copper, silver, and gold. He terrified the crowd when he told of the three great dogs — one with eyes as big as saucers, one with eyes as big as mill wheels, and one with eyes as big as a tower is round. But he had bravely tamed all three with the witch's protective apron, and taken away as much gold as he could carry, as well as the tinderbox which the witch had asked for.

"But when I came out of the tree," shouted Karl triumphantly, spraying the front row of listeners with saliva, "and asked the old witch what the tinderbox was for, she refused to tell me. *It's for lighting fires,* she said, and would say no more. So I cut off her head. A service to the kingdom, if you ask me. One less ugly witch."

And now Karl squinted at the crowd, and suddenly did not seem quite so drunk. "As you know," he growled, "the tinderbox summons my dogs. They bring me whatever I want, and kill whoever I say." He let that sink in, then told a lie. "And the tinderbox works for me alone, since I freed it from the cavern. If anyone else tries to use it, the dogs will come and kill them and return the tinderbox to me."

Karl resumed his drunken jollity. "The dogs brought me Annemette when I first came to town, at night, while she slept." He winked lewdly. "I stole a kiss, and perhaps more. And now she is my wife and queen!" Karl waved at the band to start playing, which they did, a bright polka. He jumped down from the chair, grabbed Annemette, and whirled her onto the dance floor.

The crowd cheered, yelling, "Long live King Karl! Long live the Queen!"

As she was swept around by Karl, Annemette began to have second and third thoughts about the whole business. Her memories of being carried on the back of the terrible dog were dreamlike and vague. What had Karl done to her while she was in that enchanted sleep?

Back at her place at the grand table, Annemette called for more mead for her new husband. She raised her glass too, but only sipped at it. Finally Karl was utterly awash, drooling, barely able to stand. Annemette had two serving men help her steer Karl out of the ballroom. As they left the crowd cheered and elbowed each other.

The servants closed the heavy door of Annemette's private apartment. Karl grabbed at her, but she eluded him. "Come on," he protested, his voice wet and slurred, "you're my wife now. Come here."

"Not when you're drunk," she said, and the next thing she knew Karl had fallen across her bed, snoring.

Time passed, as it often does, while wild lights swirled across cold skies.

Annemette and Karl lived together in the Copper Palace, as king and queen, but hardly as man and wife. Annemette became cold and unforgiving. She thought more and more about the wanton killing of her parents, even though she knew she herself had chafed under their imprisonment. And what *had* Karl done to her, while she slept on the back of his dog?

At first Karl visited Annemette's bed often. She submitted to this silently. But his visits became less and less frequent, and finally stopped altogether. He took his pleasure with courtesans, who at least pretended passion.

Money was never a problem in the Copper Palace. In fact, shortly after becoming king, Karl issued a decree that there would be no more taxes. He had no need for taxes, when he could summon a magic dog at any time. This made him very popular with the people.

Whenever the coffers ran low, Karl would take his tinderbox from the pouch around his neck, where he always wore it, and strike it three times. In a few moments the door would crash open and the great horrible dog with eyes as big as a tower is round would burst in.

"Gold," the King would cry.

The dog would disappear, then reappear moments later with a big sack of gold held in his dripping jaws. There seemed to be no limit to the gold.

Otherwise, Karl rarely reached for his tinderbox. What did he need the big clumsy dogs for when he had servants standing ready in every room?

Annemette was walking alone in her private garden, wrapped in furs. As she passed a locked gate a young girl suddenly appeared, holding the bars of the gate with both her small hands.

"Please, your majesty," said the girl, "may I speak with you?" She wore a ragged dress with a strange blue check pattern that was oddly difficult to look at. She was very thin, and pretty. Her blue dress was also thin, but she did not seem cold.

Annemette thought about calling her guards, but instead unlocked the gate and let the girl into the garden. "What is it?" she asked.

The girl curtsied. "I am Gudrun, your majesty. I would like to serve you. I'm young but I'm strong. I would do any sort of work — sweeping, sewing, cooking, anything."

"And why should I hire you, Gudrun?" said the queen. "I already have maids and cooks and seamstresses and servants of all kinds."

"Because my mother Saffa lived and worked in the Copper Palace long ago, when you were a baby," answered Gudrun. "Your Majesty." And she curtsied again.

"Saffa..." said Annemette. "The name is familiar. Yet...."

"My mother was the witch woman who foretold that you would marry a soldier," said Gudrun. "Which seems to have come true," she added, daringly.

59

"I was a little girl then," said Annemette in wonder. "But I remember that the witch…"

"Her name was Saffa," interrupted Gudrun, not adding *Your Majesty*.

"Yes, *Saffa*," continued Annemette. "I remember she was made to leave the palace, and the kingdom. That was when my mother and father locked me up, they were so fearful the prophecy would come true."

"Yes, Your Majesty," said Gudrun. "She left the palace. But now I am here, and I will stand by you."

Annemette stared at Gudrun, suddenly chilled.

Hendrik, the old King of Sweden, sailed across the Kattegat from Sweden with a large retinue of courtiers, mapmakers, and ambassadors, leaving his son Alberik to rule in his absence. The King of Sweden wished to discuss with the King of Denmark the disposition of the island of Hlesey which lay in the middle of the Kattegat. Half the residents of the island called themselves Swedes, and half Danes. In some cases these halves were married to each other, and there was no peace in the land. The perplexed people had called upon the kings to decide once and for all to which nation the island belonged.

The passage across the Kattegat was not an easy one, since the clear cold waters were deep, with dangerous rocky reefs all around, the weather whimsical, and shifting lights in the sky above. It was therefore a great honor to Denmark and its king for Hendrik to be the one to visit. Hendrik was old and beloved and had been king for many decades, whereas Karl was a brand-new king, and his accession was somewhat questionable.

Karl met Hendrik's ships personally, along with troops and bands and acrobats and dancing girls, showing proper deference and bad taste. The Queen stayed home. At the palace King Karl treated the Swedes to a big feast and of course drank too much. He sang a number of lewd ballads while standing on the table and accompanying himself with knife-on-goblet percussion. Queen Annemette quietly left the room early.

King Hendrik listened politely to a few of these ballads, then excused himself and retired, pleading age and exhaustion.

The next day the two kings met in the Hall of Meeting, where the wan winter sun shone briefly through the tall windows. Karl was hung-over and out of sorts. Really, when it came down to it, Karl was generally in short supply of sorts. As he slouched in his Chair of State, he appeared to be fiddling with something under his shirt.

"So, then," said King Hendrik, "even though Hlesey is not particularly valuable, its inhabitants deserve a just settlement of this jurisdictional matter."

King Karl of course knew nothing about Hlesey. "Well, if it's not valuable," he said irritably, "why don't you just sign it over to me?"

"I feel," said King Hendrik, "that I must consider the feelings of those inhabitants of Hlesey who consider themselves Swedish."

"Oh, to hell with all of them," swore King Karl. "If they mattered they wouldn't live on godforsaken Hlesey. Tell you what. I'll smoke on it."

King Hendrik blinked in astonishment, but the Danish scribes and courtiers in the room turned pale.

King Karl pulled up a silver chain which hung around

his neck and pulled out the tinderbox. He opened it and struck a spark, one time, two times, three times. All the Danes hurried out of the hall when Karl struck the first spark, but the Swedes just stared dumbly. In a moment the great door flew open and there were the three horrible dogs, their enormous eyes shining, their huge jaws dripping.

King Karl waved his hands and the dogs fell howling upon King Hendrik and his retinue. The dogs seized the Swedes one after another, shook them until their necks cracked and the blood flew, then tossed them high in the air, letting them fall broken onto the stone floor.

The dogs did not catch every Swede. A few slipped out the door and ran for their lives.

Finally the slaughter was over. King Karl waved again and the dogs padded out the door and vanished. Mangled bodies lay all over the Hall of Meeting. The Danish courtiers crept back in timidly.

"Clean up this mess," ordered King Karl. He wrinkled his nose at the stench and rose to leave.

"Your majesty?" said the chamberlain, bowing.

"Well, what is it?" grumbled Karl, holding a perfumed handkerchief in front of his nose.

"Sire, some of the Swedes managed to... ah... escape. If they get back to Sweden, and... ah... report, Prince Alberik — who is.... ah... now *King* Alberik, I... ah... imagine — might take it... ah... poorly."

"For God's sake, man," thundered King Karl, "do I need to think of everything? Send men after them, and stop them. And if Alberik tries something stupid anyway, I've always got this." And Karl held up the tinderbox.

Pursuit was undertaken, but the Swedes had a head start and a good reason to hurry, and made it to their boats without being caught.

"Gudrun," sobbed Annemette, "what can we do?" She threw herself across her bed.

Gudrun sat beside the queen and stroked her hair. "Do not cry, your majesty. There is always an answer."

Queen Annemette continued to sob. "But Gudrun, he is so *wrong,* about *everything.* Now he has likely brought war with Sweden down upon us. The people should never have acclaimed him king when he killed my parents. He should not have killed my parents in the first place. I should never have had to marry him. He is *evil.*" Annemette sat up, tears streaking her face. "I mean, what kind of qualification for being king is murder? He is a common soldier. He knows nothing of governing."

Gudrun looked thoughtful. "As to that, my queen," she said, "many kings began their rule with murder, and some of them might have been decent kings in the end. But here, dry your eyes. I will tell you what to do."

Queen Annemette dried her eyes, and blew her nose. "I am ready," she said bravely. "Tell me what I must do."

"You must go to King Karl," said Gudrun, "You must go to him, and tell him you had a dream, and in the dream the Swedes came with a great army to attack the Copper Palace. He will scoff at your dream, because he has the mistaken belief that he is a hard-headed practical man who is never superstitious. But you must then say that you are fearful, and beg him to fortify the palace more strongly."

"He will never agree to that," interrupted Annemette. "He thinks the Swedes are cowards."

"That is right," agreed Gudrun. "But he will say that fortifications would cost too much. That even his magical dog could not haul that much gold. And then you must tell him your dream also showed you how he could obtain riches beyond what even he has imagined, with his mere three dogs."

"I see," said Annemette, beginning to smile. "So even if he has no intention of fortifying the palace, he will want to know how he can get these greater riches."

"Exactly. Then we have him."

"Just for argument's sake," said Karl. "Let's say I wanted more wealth than I already have. Which I don't. What would I have to do? According to your silly dream."

Annemette leaned back on the couch on which she sat, and tried to look dreamy and mysterious. "In the magical underworld beneath the tree," she breathed, "where you so bravely found your magic tinderbox, there is a *fourth* door. Or so my dream said. And behind this door is another dog. But this dog does not guard a chest of copper or silver or gold. It guards a chest brimming with diamonds."

"A fourth door," mused Karl.

"But of course," said Annemette, "it was just a silly woman's dream."

Annemette watched secretly through a keyhole as Karl, in his own room, dressed himself in commoner's clothing and a traveler's cloak, the hood of which he pulled low over his face. She watched as he drew back a tapestry, revealing a hidden shelf. From the shelf he took a box, and from the box an old apron with a strange blue check pattern which was oddly difficult to look at. He put the apron in his pocket, took his tinderbox, and left through a window.

"I must explain something to you, Your Majesty," said Gudrun to Annemette. From a cloth bag she pulled out a dress and showed it to Annemette. "This is the dress I wore the day I first spoke to you."

"Yes, I remember it," exclaimed Annemette, "and it's the same strange blue check pattern as Karl's apron."

"That is true," said Gudrun. "I told you my mother Saffa was the witch woman who predicted you would marry a soldier. But what I didn't tell you is that she was also the witch woman Karl murdered. She wanted the tinderbox not to use, but to hide under a spell, so it would not fall into the hands of some greedy adventurer like Karl. She kept her end of the bargain. She pulled Karl out of the underworld, and let him keep whatever gold or silver he could carry. But he killed her anyway."

And here the story tells how Karl went back to the forest and to the dead tree where he had first met Saffa. Nothing had changed except there were red wildflowers now growing where he had cut off Saffa's head. Karl climbed the tree and descended into the underworld, as he had before. He did not worry that there was no one to pull him out, for now he knew he could summon a dog to carry him.

In the enchanted hallway below, the hundred lamps still burned. There were the three doors he had seen before, behind which were the dog with eyes as big as saucers, the dog with eyes as big as mill wheels, and the dog with eyes as big as a tower is round.

But, sure enough, in the shadows at the end of the hall was a fourth door he had not seen before. He took out the witch's apron and opened the door.

Behind the fourth door was a room filled with light, a hard crystalline light reflected from a million diamonds which spilled from a huge chest. In front of the chest sat an enormous dog. As Karl stepped into the room the dog began to growl with a sound like distant drums. Saliva dripped from its jaws like tiny diamonds falling.

This dog had no eyes at all.

Karl spread his witch's apron before the dog, as he had before. In this way he had tamed the other dogs, and they had laid themselves quietly down on the blue-checked cloth. But this dog had no eyes. It did not see the apron and did not lie down. Instead it leaped forward and seized Karl with its huge teeth. It shook Karl until he was broken and empty, then threw his body out into the hall. The fourth door slammed shut. Karl's body sprawled crumpled on the floor. The tinderbox rolled from his pocket and lay in the shadows.

Finally, the story tells how Alberik, the new king of Sweden, crossed the Kattegat with an immense army, to avenge the death of his father Hendrik. Annemette met him at the shore, alone, with only her maid Gudrun beside her. She begged his forgiveness for the death of his father. She also agreed to cede to Sweden the island of Hlesey. Alberik was struck by Annemette's grace, intelligence, courage, and beauty.

66

It also helped when she told him Karl was gone for good.

Alberik suggested that he and Annemette rule Hlesey jointly. He forgave her for the death of his father, which had not been her doing, and who had been, after all, a very old man.

A year later Annemette and Alberik were married, uniting their lands. This fulfilled Saffa's prophesy a second time, since Alberik had come to her as a soldier at the head of a great army.

But Gudrun went alone one night to the forest, and to the dead tree. She set fire to the tree. When the flames subsided there was no trace of the entrance to the underworld hall.

The tinderbox has not, so far, been seen again.

Tam Lin

"Only she had run into the North Forest and brought back a prince of the First People, all copper skin and strangely long fingers."

Elizabeth Zuckerman spent her early authorial years redeeming villains until she realized that they were more interesting left evil. She has since devoted most of her waking hours to the attempt to make heroes more interesting. She lives in Philadelphia, and plans one day to own a sword so that she can test its strength against her pen.

Other short stories by Elizabeth can be found in Whortleberry Press's collection *Free Range Fairy Tales* and in Drollerie Press's forthcoming anthology of urban-fantasy Greek myths.

"'Tam Lin' is one of the classic 'Beauty and the Beast' stories, complete with the classic characters: the brave heroine, the otherworldly lover, the powerful female antagonist. Those stories were always my favorites – among all the passive princesses, Beauty and Janet and Psyche stand head and shoulders above the crowd. 'Tam Lin' poses a particularly unique dilemma, with the hero entering the heroine's world at the end instead of shepherding her into his. Nothing comes easily in the ballad – there was no reason to assume that this biggest change of all would be any different!"

Unearthly
Elizabeth Zuckerman

Whenever she had doubts, which was oftener than she liked, Jennis told herself that, in essence, her situation was quite ordinary. Who really knew the person you married, anyway? There were depths in her own father that her mother chose to ignore, and weaknesses in her mother of which her father was blissfully unaware. One way or another, everyone married a stranger.

And the things that set her engagement apart were, she told herself, things to be proud of. Everyone else she knew had settled down with someone plain and boring. Only she had run into the North Forest and brought back a prince of the First People, all copper skin and strangely long fingers. She had led him away, bold as you please, from under the nose of his Artist mother, and he had used his own Artistry to hold back her enchantments. He loved her and the baby swelling under her loose cotton dress. He had run away from his own people to join hers. That was the important thing.

Sometimes he caught her telling herself that. "Where are you?" he asked her one night, as they made ready for bed. There was no point in not sharing a room, not with his child straining the seams of her clothes. She started at the sound of his voice; he spoke the language of the Continent with a soft halting accent that drew out the vowels. In the light of the last lit candle, he glowed like polished metal.

"I'm here," she said, embarrassed.

"Yes, and no." He blew out the candle and sat beside her on the mattress. The straw crackled under the weight of their bodies. "Your mind hides, sometimes. I never know where you go."

Jennis pushed her doubts away. There was no reason to doubt. He was here, in all the beauty that had made her reckless that first time. Their thighs pressed together; his hands were warm on her face. She made herself ignore how it frightened her that his fingers could reach the top of her head while his palms cupped her cheeks. "Nowhere important," she said, wrapping her hands around his and pulling them to her waist. "Nowhere as nice as this."

"I love you," he said before he kissed her.

She woke first, as always. He had never needed to start an early-morning fire for breakfast; he could have rolled out of bed and used his Artistry to create fire out of nothing. But he was a light sleeper, so she took care to keep quiet as she laid the tent of kindling and lit it with a few well-struck sparks. A cold breeze slid through the open window and made her shiver. She crouched in front of the infant fire, shielding it until the flames caught.

When she got up, her father stood behind her. His face was damp and flushed; she guessed he'd thrown a handful of cold water on it to wake himself up. "Jennis," he said. "We need to talk."

"About Temmolin," she said, using the name she'd given him. None of her people could pronounce his real name; it rippled off his tongue in a string of liquid vowels, but she stumbled hopelessly over it. At first that hadn't been a problem; they had never spent much time talking, after all. But when she became pregnant and needed a name to call him in front of her parents, she chose the name they'd given to her baby brother, born eighteen years ago and dead within a month. She'd hoped it would soften her parents, and it had. But here was her father, awake half an hour before sunrise, his eyes alert above the dark circles that ringed them. So not as softened as she'd hoped.

Her father sighed. He sat down on a stool by her fire, staring into it as she scooped a handful of flour into a clay bowl. "I'm glad he's marrying you," he said. "I'm glad you chose a man who's decent. I'm even glad he never leaves you alone – I wouldn't want you to marry someone who didn't want you."

He still hadn't turned to face her. "But..." she prompted, wiping flour off her hands.

He raised his head, and she wished he hadn't. She knew that look in his steady eyes, that set of his mouth. He was going to be stubborn and right, and there was no way for her to talk him around.

"But he's First, Jennis," her father said. "He scares me. And the thought of you being in his power scares me."

"He wouldn't do anything–"

"I know that," he interrupted. "I know he wouldn't hurt you on purpose. But he doesn't think like us."

Jennis' eyes narrowed. "He's not an animal, Da. He's not like the people we know, but he's a person."

"I *know* that. Will you please let me talk?"

The note of agony in his voice shocked her into silence. Her father closed his eyes and took a breath, letting it

72

all out before he looked back at her. "I want to be sure that you know what you're getting. Because for all that he is, your Temmolin, he's not one of us. And he's not going to become one of us once you two are handfast. You're sixteen; you're a woman grown; you make your own choices. But if you marry him, you need to marry him knowing that."

There were tears in her eyes, but she couldn't tell whether they meant that she loved her father, or whether she was angrier at him than she'd ever been in her life. "All right," she said. "I know it." She turned away, back to the handful of flour waiting to become bread. She dipped some water from the nearest bucket, mixing it in with her hands.

She didn't take her hands from the dough until she heard her father leave. Then she sagged, her elbows on the table, bracing herself on them as she sobbed as quietly as she could. It wasn't fair that anyone else should have doubts. She was the only one supposed to worry. She could deal with herself. She couldn't think away other people's worries.

They were married six days later, at Temmolin's insistence. "As soon as possible," he'd said over dinner.

"Can you provide for Jennis?" her father had asked, staring evenly at Temmolin across the rough wooden table.

"Of course," Temmolin had said, sounding surprised. "I'll make a house tomorrow."

And he had. He'd woken up early, for him, and gone outside to pick a spot. At the northern edge of the village, he'd stood still for a moment as if gathering his thoughts, then put out both hands palm down toward the earth.

It had split open.

Jennis, who'd followed him on his search for the perfect site, had seen her neighbors shriek and stumble backward, clutching at each other, staring in terror at Temmolin. She herself had stood paralyzed next to him, a mouse drowning in the sorcerous gaze of a snake.

She had seen him work Artistry before. He had shown off at their first meeting, calling sparks of golden fire from the air and making them dance, while she rested her head on his naked shoulder and laughed in wonder. Of the battle with his mother, she had seen very little, but the sounds behind them – trees groaning as they split in two, fire thundering over the broken trunks, a screaming tunnel of wind that made her narrow her eyes almost to blindness – had been more than enough.

But those had not been her places. It was different in the village, being watched, seeing her betrothed as everyone else did.

The house built itself out of thin air. Foundations, walls, windows, an impossible second story resting on top of the first. The roof was grace itself, two golden walls of thatch gliding like birds to a perfect point at the top. Temmolin let his hands drop to his sides and smiled.

Within her, the baby moved.

She gasped, one hand flying to her belly. "What is it?" Temmolin asked, but Jennis shook her head. Her hand pressed hard against the spot where her child had turned over. She had sung it lullabies, stroked the place where it lay, whispered to it late at night when her voice was the only thing to break the silence. Not once had it moved, until now.

Stay asleep, she thought. *Don't wake up to this.*

After that, her father asked no more questions about Temmolin's ability to provide for her. No one wanted any more demonstrations of Artistry. Their wedding was an event, for all that it was thrown together in four days and Jennis had no time to make a new dress. Everyone cheered when her father knotted a linen rope around their joined hands. Everyone also got very drunk on wedding ale.

By the time they retired to their new house, it was dark. The moon was almost full, and so bright it hurt Jennis' eyes to look at it, but Temmolin carried a torch nonetheless. The door didn't even creak as he pushed it open.

She paused on the threshold. "What's wrong?" he asked. He tilted the torch so the light fell on her face.

Jennis looked away. "Nothing," she said. "Well, something. I'm a little afraid."

"Of me?" He stepped closer.

She held herself still so she wouldn't flinch away. "No," she said. "Of the house." She'd had too much ale as well, she realized. If she hadn't, she would never have said any of this. But it was coming out now, and she couldn't think fast enough to stop herself. "This is the biggest house in the village, and you just pulled it out of the ground. Like it was nothing. You said you were going to make it, not build it, only I didn't understand what you meant."

He had beautiful long features, narrow and elegant. Now they tightened into a mask. "This is who I am, Jennis," he said.

It seemed to her that she'd had this conversation before. "I know!" she said. "But – I didn't know, *really*. And it scares me. Not you. Just – seeing it. What you are with it."

Temmolin drew in a harsh breath. Her vision was blurry; she couldn't make out his expression. "But you like the house," he said. "You like having it. You like not being in your parents' house. You like that it's the biggest house in your village."

Jennis blinked. "Well," she said, thinking about it. "Yes."

"So it's all right with you that I'm an Artist, as long as you don't see me doing Artistry."

This was all wrong. This wasn't how she'd imagined her wedding night. She didn't know why they were having this conversation, or how it had become a fight. They had never fought before. The desire to finish this was an ache in her, as persistent as hunger or lust. "Yes," she said. "That's fine. That's wonderful." She reached out before she could talk herself out of it, catching his hand, drawing it to her lips.

Temmolin doused the torch. She was too dizzy to wonder how. He pulled her into the house's darkness; she locked her arms around his rigid shoulders. "I'm sorry," she whispered.

He relaxed, a little. "I love you," he said, and led her into the bedroom.

Jennis had dowry rights to five of her father's acres, since her husband had no land of his own. The morning after their wedding, Temmolin ate the sausages and biscuits she made and went out to the fields to work their land. She had offered to come and help, since he'd never farmed before, but he shook his head. "I'll be back soon, anyway," he said. "No point in you making the trip."

She put this ridiculous boast down to a desire to please her, and washed the dishes with a smile.

He walked back in barely a minute after she was done. Only then did she notice that he had no hoe or spade with him, no bag of seeds. Jennis felt her stomach clench. "What are you doing?" she said.

Temmolin shrugged. "I plowed," he said. "It was easier than I thought."

His tunic and trousers were immaculate, except for the dust of the village streets. He hadn't even broken a sweat in the late spring heat. There was only one possible conclusion. "How?" she asked anyway.

He looked back at her, his eyes suddenly cold. "You said you didn't want to see it," he said. "And you didn't."

Jennis knew instantly how it had been. He would have stood on the edge of the soil, as he'd stood on the edge of the boundary of their new house. He would have looked like a prince, standing tall and golden over the bent backs of her father and brothers and friends, his black hair rippling loose like water. He would have closed his eyes, held out his hands, and the land would have obeyed him just like she did: opening, surrendering, giving in. In a few moments, he would have accomplished what it took an ordinary person days to do.

She had to make him understand. He was her husband, and she loved him; she had to be his guide.

"Temmolin, you can't do that," she said. "Not in front of everyone." Jennis heard her own voice indistinctly, as if she were shouting across a field in a strong wind. She made herself focus. "You can't set yourself apart like that. It'll make them angry."

"And scared?" he asked. "Like you? Are you angry?"

She was, but she couldn't tell him that. She said, "We live here. I grew up here. I know how this works. If we make them angry, they'll punish us. Valca won't trade for her milk or her beef; Jerin won't sell us any lambs come next spring. They've got to see you working as hard as them, or they'll turn on you."

"And you feel the same, I suppose."

Why did he keep bringing it back to her? How much more clearly could she say it? Jennis took a slow breath to calm herself. "What I feel is that this is important for us," she said. "I want us to live here. I want you to belong here, with me."

Temmolin laughed. She had never heard him sound bitter before. He said, "So I'm meant to pretend I'm one of you, then? When everything about me screams that I'm different, you want me to ignore what I am, and ignore that they know what I am, and pretend I'm like them in the hope that they'll decide to play along?"

Her patience was running out. "You came here," Jennis said. "You left your world and came to mine. If it were the other way around, I would listen to what you told me."

His mouth tightened, and for one shocked moment she thought he might strike her. But he stepped back across the threshold instead. Two strides took him back into the street.

Jennis ran to the door. "Where are you going?" she called.

"To borrow your father's plow," he said over his shoulder, without looking at her.

Before midday, her enormous house had been visited by nearly every woman in town. *That husband of yours. It*

78

gave me shivers, seeing what he did out there. Can't you make him stop? She'd talked to them all, smiling and polite, the good girl they'd known for sixteen years. She'd brought out some honey cake she'd thrown together as soon as Temmolin had left in anticipation of such visits. To every one of them, she'd given the same answer.

I've talked to him. This is all new to him, you know. He's very sorry about it. He won't do it again.

Temmolin came home exhausted and sweaty, with his beautiful hair tied up in a rough workman's knot. Dirt clung to his elegant fingers and stained his linen trousers. He ate her mutton pie without comment, staring dull-eyed into the distance. Jennis put her arms around him when he was done and kissed his neck, feeling the bulge of her stomach nudge his stiff back. "I'm so proud of you," she whispered. "Thank you."

He put up a hand and touched her arm. "I love you," he said, expressionless.

Jennis gave birth in midwinter. Temmolin waded through knee-deep snow to fetch Garna, who'd presided over Jennis' own birth. Garna took one look at her patient, who had retired to her bed when the pains got bad, and nodded as if pleased. "You'll have an easy time," she said. "You're built to bear."

"This is easy?" Jennis demanded. "It hurts!"

"Always does," said Garna. "You!" she added, turning to face Temmolin. "Hot water, fast as it'll boil. Bring a kettle up here, and don't come back until it's done."

This was Garna's usual method, Jennis knew: give the husband one task so he can feel that he helped before getting him out of the way. She stared at Temmolin's face, hoping to gauge his thoughts, and felt gratified by the flash of fear in his dark eyes.

Besides, she told herself firmly, if he was afraid, there was no point in her worrying too. She didn't have any energy to waste on being afraid. She had a baby to push out.

Afterwards, Garna called it one of the easiest births she'd ever seen. Jennis remembered it differently. There were long stretches where nothing happened, nothing at all, until she thought in a panic that the baby simply wouldn't be born, and when the swift sudden contractions finally came, they tore screams from her that were part relief. She rode out the contractions as if she clung to a spar in a storm, desperate and panicky and determined not to let go. She used her screams as defiance, throwing them like stones at her own fear and pain. *Listen to that!* Jennis told herself. *I'm not ready to give up. You can't make me. I am going to win this, and my baby will be the most perfect child ever born on this island.*

And he was. He came at last in a gush of liquid, sliding like a fish from between her thighs. Garna wiped his face clean with linen soaked in warm water, and he let out a high ferocious cry that brought tears to Jennis' eyes. "Let me," she croaked, her throat hoarse with screaming.

He nestled in her arms, still wailing. Jennis stared at his tiny toes and flushed skin. His face was wrinkled like an old man's; his eyes squeezed shut as he cried. Instinctively, she put him to her breast. She felt the tug on her nipple quiver in the pit of her stomach. Her heart pounded against his fragile skin. It was all she could do not to crush him to her as love swept her helplessly away.

At her request, Garna fetched Temmolin from the tavern. She heard his footsteps thud heavily against the stairs. He threw the door open, and their son began to cry again, but Jennis cradled him close until he hushed.

They had agreed on names beforehand, names acceptable to her people but easy enough for him to pronounce. "Look, Merin," Jennis whispered, lifting her son from her breast. "This is your father."

Temmolin dropped to his knees by the bed. He looked from Jennis to the child and back, as if he couldn't trust what he saw. Little Merin reached out a tiny curled fist – he would have very long fingers – and touched his father's face with his knuckles.

Temmolin began to cry.

Garna suggested she stay in bed for the rest of the day, and perhaps the next if she felt weak. Temmolin did not let her lift a finger for six days; he rubbed her aching back, cared for Merin when she slept, even cooked surprisingly well. They were six glorious days of leisure; she couldn't remember ever being so well looked after. But at last she was ready to get up, and she tiptoed downstairs to surprise him.

In the kitchen, Temmolin sat a safe distance from the fire, cradling Merin on his lap. Both their eyes were shut. Their hands were pressed lightly together, palm to palm; it was the first time she'd seen Merin's hand open. It struck her how much he looked like his father, and that it made her uneasy. *If I can see it, everyone else surely will,* she thought. *They'll wonder how much he's like his father.* She could imagine their fear, even understand it, and that thought worried her even more.

The timing, in retrospect, struck her as obscene. Before her eyes, before she'd quite framed her thoughts, the two of them rose off the floor and hovered weightless in midair. Merin's eyes flew open, and he laughed his sweet baby gurgle.

Her gasp broke sharp and ragged from her throat, but Temmolin heard it. Still suspended in the air, he opened his eyes. His face was a mask; hers, she knew, was all too easy to read. This was different from dancing lights in a sunlit clearing; it was worse than an impossible house born from the earth and air. Her husband was dancing her son down a solitary path. They were already isolated enough by their neighbors' fear; if anyone knew about this, it would destroy what goodwill remained. She knew it with the absolute certainty of panic, and knew that somehow she had to make him understand it at last.

But he still floated over the floor, and his eyes were hard as rock as he looked at her.

"Stop it," Jennis said. "Please."

They came down, as gracefully as they'd risen. Only when she saw her husband touch the floor did Jennis step into the room. She lifted Merin out of Temmolin's arms. "Please don't do that again," she said. "It frightens me. And if anyone else saw..." She trailed off, feeling the hopeless inadequacy of words. "It's the same as with plowing, and the house. You can't make us even more different." He was stone-faced still, and she cried with sudden fury, "Are you even listening to me?"

Temmolin was looking, not at her, but at Merin in her arms, still giggling with the memory of flight. "He likes it," he said. "It doesn't scare him." Temmolin's mask slipped, and she saw the longing in his eyes. To be a father, to raise his son as he had been raised, to show him all of the world – it was no different than what she wanted with Merin, was it? Jennis had a momentary vision of Merin making sparks dance for some unknown girl, and knew how fear would taint the wonder of any girl who saw it; knew, because she felt it in herself, here, now, her feet on the cold floor and cold leaking into her love.

She made herself be harsh, as harsh as Temmolin. "You can't teach him any Artistry. It won't be good for him." She hugged Merin close, ignoring how his giggles had turned angry.

"It's in him," said Temmolin. "He'll be an Artist, like me. You have to let me–"

"I don't!" she cried. "I don't have to let you do anything! Merin's my son, and he lives in my town, and I won't let him suffer because you can't accept what he is!"

"But I do." Temmolin never got loud, as she did. His anger was soft and cold as snow. "I accept everything he is. I love him for it. I want you to do the same." He took a step toward her. He had dropped his mask completely, and the pain on his face was clear. "Jennis. He's my son too."

"Then do him a favor," she said, her patience gone, "and don't turn him into you."

But it wasn't that easy. She could forbid her husband from doing Artistry, even when she wasn't there. She could smile at her neighbors as if nothing was wrong. But she had brought Artistry into her home, and only now did she understand the price.

Valca's wary glances slid off her like water when she traded wool for milk. When Jennis patched up the seam of a jacket that her neighbor Corvan had split while cutting fire-

83

wood, he barely met her eyes, although she had brought the jacket to his door to return it. An invisible barrier surrounded her whenever she appeared with Merin on her hip; people stepped away, looked down, avoided contact with her and especially with him. Even in her parents' house, where she went often these days to escape the oppressive silence of her own, Jennis could feel the same undercurrent of fear, circling her like a vulture, endlessly patient, waiting for the moment when she'd stop fighting.

It only made her fight harder. She held Temmolin's hand whenever they went outside the house, partly for the simple comfort of touch and partly as defiance in the face of fear. She told stories of Temmolin and Merin, ordinary stories, utterly lacking in anything stranger than the astonished love of a father for his son. She paid extravagant false compliments on his behalf, praising Valca's cheese and Olach's ale with words that she placed in Temmolin's mouth. It helped, a little. As yet no one had turned from her. They accepted her husband for her sake. It was good – at least, it wasn't bad – but it made Jennis angry to get so little in return for so much work.

And it was impossible to convince herself that it was worth it when she was the only one trying. Jennis had been glad at first that Temmolin had begun to feel their neighbors' wariness. She had thought it would rouse him to action at last. But instead he drew in on himself as the winter inched forward, his aloof silence giving the lie to Jennis' frantic inventions. He saved all his affection for Merin, and it was sweet to watch them playing, but it drove Jennis wild that he couldn't connect his beloved son's future to the villagers' dislike. At night, the only time they were alone, she raged at him, demanding to know why he was so determined to have them hated by everyone. "I don't care about everyone," he would say. "I care about you and Merin."

"Then do something!" she would tell him. "For our sakes. So that we can be proud of you. If things were different, if I had come to you—"

"I wouldn't care what you did, or what my people said," he interrupted harshly. "It doesn't change who you are."

It does, she thought. *I was never this angry before. You were never this cold. We're not who we fell in love with anymore.*

But that, more than anything else, she could not say. It was too dangerous to tell him, almost too dangerous to tell herself.

"It's not the trappings I want," he said, stroking her hair. "It's you. I love you."

The first time he said it, she let herself find in his words the comfort she desperately wanted. But he said it often after that, as if he had noticed with relief that it worked to silence her, and soon it sounded so rote on his lips that she wondered if he even meant it anymore.

Merin caught a cold late winter. Jennis squeezed drops of lemon juice into a small spoonful of honey and let him suck the mixture off her finger, but he could barely get a good grip on her before he had to let go and draw a sniffling breath. Temmolin seemed frightened, which in turn frightened Jennis; what if the First were too weak to survive even little ailments? What if Merin couldn't fight it off?

"I can burn it out of him," Temmolin said, after four

hours had rendered them weary and ready to snap.

What scared Jennis most about that suggestion was how reasonable it seemed. "I'll take him to see Garna," she said, not looking at Temmolin. "If she can't do anything..."

There was no need to finish the thought.

The cold midday sun threw thin shadows onto the earth, dark under a light dusting of snow. Jennis wrapped Merin up so closely that only his nose and mouth stood free of blankets. Garna's house was not far, but she refused to take any chances. At the last minute, Temmolin threw on the coat she had made for him and accompanied her. She was glad of his presence, warm and solid and as frightened, for once, as she was.

Garna lived in the center of the village, easily accessible to anyone. She opened her door to Temmolin's remorseless pounding. "Merin's sick," Jennis said at once. "We can't – we hoped you might–"

It sounded ridiculous; it gave no sense of the frantic rocking and doses of honey that were only a few minutes old. But Garna let them in, unwrapping Merin by the fire to take a closer look at his chapped lips and to feel his heat-flushed neck and face. "He'll be all right," she promised after a quick glance, taking the baby into her arms. "I'll make a posset for him. You sit down and get warm."

Jennis obeyed, weak with the absence of failure. Temmolin put his arm around her. She leaned gratefully into his body, hoping that the contact would communicate the second most important message, after the safety of their son: *My people can heal him, too, and more safely. We are worth your effort.*

She was so glad to have Merin restored, and so cheered by Temmolin's hoarse thanks to Garna, that she had half crossed the central square before she noticed the stares. But when she felt them – hot on her back, sharp as knives – she turned. People were looking out from their houses, leaving their doors open to the cold; some had even stepped outside for a better view. The snow fell more thickly as Jennis looked back to see why.

The path they had walked from Garna's house was clear. Not a single snowflake had fallen on it. Everywhere else, the snow was clinging fast and white, but in the narrow channel where she and her family had walked, the ground was brown and soft.

Merin giggled in her arms and pointed down. Bright shoots of grass sprouted under his command, spreading all the way back along the path.

Jennis couldn't think. Her mind was frozen with cold and fear. Everyone had seen; her son was an Artist, and they knew it, and there was no point in pretending they didn't.

She would never remember the look she threw her husband: wide-eyed, beseeching, hopeless. All she would ever remember was that suddenly Temmolin was there, his hand held out over Merin's forehead in a pose of deliberate theatricality. Jennis felt heat move from Temmolin's palm into Merin, heard her son give a thin cry, saw Merin reach out again toward the ground.

Nothing sprouted. In fact, as she watched, the grass that Merin had grown began to wither, bending in the wind.

Temmolin faced the villagers. Jennis wondered wildly if he meant to attack them. But instead he bowed low, a suppliant before his masters. Words died in her throat, shriveled like Merin's grass. This had not been what she had wanted. She had wanted him to woo her people, not kneel before them and sue for their pardon. Tears stung her eyes, but she blinked them away and stood in the cold beside her husband until the villagers granted him absolution, slipping silently back into their houses.

Temmolin straightened as the last of them retreated. Humiliation had carved lines into his face that had not been there a few moments ago. "I'm so sorry," she whispered.

"Why?" he asked. "I've cured him. He's safe. He's one of yours now."

Disbelieving, she looked from Merin to Temmolin.

"Just now," he said. "It's all gone. I've burned out his birthright. He's as safe as you could ever want him to be."

She put a hand on his arm. He flinched away, and she saw that humiliation was not the only emotion that had marked him. "I don't know what to say," she whispered. "I've never seen anything so brave."

His laugh hurt her ears. "I'm not brave, Jennis. Don't start thinking I'm a hero. I abandoned my people, and all I want now is not to be abandoned in my turn. And it seems now that I'll pay any price to be safe. Even if it's not mine to pay." He looked down at Merin, snug in her arms; she wondered if he would ever look happy again.

Jennis reached out again and took his hand, gripping too tightly for him to pull away. "It's cold," she said gently. "Come home." When he still did not move, she stepped close to him and laced her fingers between his. She said, "I love you."

Two tear tracks lined his cheeks as he raised his head.

He looked as though he had never properly heard the words before. "What is it?" she asked.

"After all this," he said, "that still means something."

His hand tightened on hers. Snow crunched softly under their feet as they walked home.

The Three Feathers

"To be murdered in your bed would be a blessing."

Dy Loveday has degrees in anthropology, sociology, social work and social policy. She has published several non-fiction publications through the Government of South Australia (policy, strategic plans, operational frameworks and the like) as well as a few non-fiction articles about Aboriginal well-being published by Flinders University.

Dy is married to a wonderful man who makes great cups of tea and doesn't complain (much) when she gets caught up in her writing and forgets to eat dinner. They have two crazy dogs, a smart cat, an Alexandrine parrot and an eighty-year-old that inhales chocolate and fantasy and looks like Twiggy. She will also read anything, even the tiny writing on the back of shampoo bottles when she's in the shower.

"As soon as I read Grimms' 'Three Feathers,' I knew that I wanted to write the sequel. The hero was a 'simpleton' - chosen by the king to inherit the kingdom. His two brothers were urbane, clever and collected, but missed out on winning the title through their own arrogance. I wondered how these two would feel about their 'simple' brother being chosen, and figured they'd make perfect villains. Then I thought about all the times that I've been polite, fantasized about getting rid of rude dinner guests, wanted to zap obnoxious colleagues, and the outline for 'Three Brothers' was born."

The Three Brothers
By Loveday

Simon swallowed the full-bodied Cabernet past the lump in his throat. His brothers' jibes continued to wreak havoc on his appetite. But finding the right words had never been easy, so he just glared at them, hoping they'd stop their petty insults and allow them all to eat in peace. Just. This. Once.

The oak tree outside the dining room rustled in the darkness, scraping against the mullioned windows. A faint breeze crept through a cracked pane, rippling across the white linen tablecloth like a ghostly hand reaching for his wife, Kikki. In the middle of the table, three large white feathers stood upright in a silver urn, a reminder of the quest the brothers had been sent on before their father's death.

From his vantage point at the head of the oak table, he could see the pleasant smile fixed on his wife's small, pale features. Most women would have divorced him by now, but Kikki never complained.

Half their problems would be solved if only his brothers would leave them alone in the crumbling castle. It was barely habitable, so one would think they'd take their puny inheritance and find heiresses to put up with their sly ways. They were both golden-haired and handsome enough. But since their father's death six months ago, they'd settled into the fortress as if it belonged to them. And their behavior worsened, day by miserable day. Perhaps they found more joy in watching Simon's marriage drain away like his waterlogged crops near the swollen river.

"The carpet is stained," said his brother Jon, in a loud brash voice. Eric, the middle brother, failed to hide a snigger in his napkin. "We will have to throw it out."

Kikki's navy blue eyes glanced up, before moving back to the food on her plate. She continued to coax the oyster out of its lair, prying it from its shell with a tiny fork.

Fury washed up Simon's spine like a tidal wave. "Ugh… that … ugh …well … umm." Unbearable silence. A tide of heat rose up his cheeks as his brothers looked at him expectantly. His wife kept her head down. Clever woman.

"Did you have something to say, Simon? Can I get you a pencil? Perhaps that would make it easier." Jon's voice was tender, all the more deadly for it. They all knew Simon couldn't write. When he tried to concentrate, the pen fell from his limp hand as if he tried to grasp a formless cloud. His writing looked like a monkey had scribbled it on a cave wall. He'd inherited the kingdom despite his inability to scribe, ride a horse or speak clearly.

"Brother, let Simon be. You know he is incapable of defending himself. Let him scrabble back to his rooms to finish his meal. Kikki can stay and keep us company." Eric gazed at Kikki. With a wicked smile, he reached across and grasped her small hand in his. To her credit, she didn't cringe, merely picked up her goblet and took a small sip, her hand a limp victim in Eric's giant paw.

Simon's chair screeched on the parquetry. It toppled over, catching the tablecloth on its way down, dragging his meal to the floor. The cloth caught on his leg, entangling him in its folds. He stumbled on his short leg, grasping the table to stop his fall. Food and wine covered his trousers but he ignored it.

"Mis... mis... mistake." Simon raised his knife and tossed it on the table, where it vibrated, embedded to the hilt in the wood.

"What, brother? Are you upset? I agree it is unfortunate that your wife spilled her waters on the carpet. All for the sake of birthing a stillborn child. And lost her betrothal ring. Your most precious gifts to father before his death are gone. The means by which you won the kingdom." Jon gave him a bright, dazzling smile, his eyes dark and malevolent. "You're useless, brother. Without them you are nothing. Once the people know you'll be deposed. To be murdered in your bed would be a blessing."

"It shall be mine," said Eric, with a far-away look in his eyes.

Jon regarded him with an evil glare. "Hardly. I am the eldest and handsomest."

"Rubbish. People take offence to everything you say. You'll get your throat slit."

"Well, let's agree. It shouldn't be *him*." The brothers nodded, turning to Simon.

"Save us the trouble and do yourself in," sneered Jon.

Fury wound its way up Simon's spine. He raised his fist and thumped the table. What he needed was a sword to run his bloody brothers through. The carpet could be cleaned and the ring found, but mentioning the loss of his child was unforgivable. They stared at him as if he were a violent predator. His wife paled and shuddered, face drawn, and something inside him cowered in shame. But the other part of him, the tired, lonely part of his soul, reared up and took over.

His hand flexed and opened, fingers widespread. Anger sparked in his chest, running down his arm in a hot pulse of fire. Energy swirled, iridescent blue and red flares glowed on his fingertips. The smell of sulfur flooded the air. He pointed and bolts of electrical current flew across the table. Jon opened his mouth in a rictus of terror, not realizing until it was too late. Eric ducked, trying to dodge the dazzling light but it veered around a candlestick and followed him, zapping his skin and turning it red, then carbon black. The brothers' blackened bodies cracked, then crumbled within the lace and silk clothing, leaving two scorched feathers drifting above the table, in the faint breeze.

Simon trembled from head to toe, panicking. He couldn't speak, couldn't move. The anger was so strong, so deep inside. He raised his hands, looked at the broad palms. What had he done? Kikki's face swung into view. She caught his stare, her gaze moving from his hot face, the spilled food and the two empty seats. She picked the napkin off her lap, folded it slowly, and put it on the stark white table. Pulling back the tablecloth, she revealed two large toads, sitting amongst all the finery on damask covered chairs.

Kikki straightened and stood, pushing back her chair. She snatched a lonely white feather from mid-air and poked it into her dark, upswept hair.

"You took your time. Let's go to bed," she said.

And so they did.

Cinderella

"Well... I no longer need to rely on mice and rats to keep me fashionable. Who needs a Fairy Godmother when you have a Prince with a fathomless wallet?"

Melanie Rees works as an ecologist and spends much of her time playing in wetlands, which are currently not all that wet. She has also held jobs playing in dirt, playing with fish and playing in treetops. When she is not up a tree or stuck in the mud, she writes speculative fiction. Her stories have been published in various venues, including Antipodean SF, The Future Fire *magazine and* Infinitas Newsletter, *and the* Shades of Sentience *anthology. She lives online at flexirees.wordpress.com and in the real world lives in South Australia in a house made of straw.*

"So they live 'happily ever after'... In many fairytales the endings are so neatly wrapped up that I felt it would be interesting to unravel the stability fairytale protagonists reach and present that in a modern day scenario, such as seeing a shrink. Whilst trying to think of different disorders that characters would need to see a therapist for, a fashion segment was airing on a television program I was watching. This made me think of vanity and Cinderella seemed like the perfect character to explore that ailment, especially considering the contrast with the underlying message of the original Cinderella stories."

Dr. Zum:
Psychotherapist to the Surreal
Melanie Rees

Floral perfume wafted into Dr. Zum's consultancy room as he opened the door. The woman before him lifted up her oversized glasses and perched them on top of her honeyed hair, which was meticulously curled into a tight bun.

"Welcome, Miss..." Dr. Zum prompted, holding out his hand.

"It's Mrs, but I'd rather keep my name secret." She glided into the room, her brilliant blue dress a stark contrast to the motley brown carpet and furniture. "I don't need the castle's paparazzi snooping around for gossip about me."

"I assure you that all therapists keep their clients' names confidential."

"Still..." She placed her gold-coloured handbag on Dr. Zum's desk, and with a silk handkerchief she dusted the tweed sofa and sat down cross-legged.

Dr. Zum moved the surprisingly heavy handbag to an adjacent coffee table and sat down on the chair behind his desk.

"Be careful with that! It's a limited edition. Made by the Fairy Godmother herself."

Dr. Zum looked at the handbag; it looked more like a

suitcase. You could fit a pumpkin in there. He turned back to the woman who was brushing down her dress with her handkerchief as if his sofa had contaminated it with dust. This was going to be a long session. He stared at the clock on the wall and the drawn out ticking of the second hand.

"So…" Dr. Zum took a deep breath hoping the answer would be simple. "What brings you here today?"

The woman sniffed and dabbed at her eyes with her handkerchief. Dr. Zum doubted that eyes that rigid could shed tears.

"I'm aging fast. Varicose veins, puffy ankles, a saggy bosom." She tried to heave her chest out, but her tightly strung corset kept everything firmly in place. "The Fairy Godmother has only been moderately successful in dealing with my crow's feet and plumping up my cleavage."

Dr. Zum stared at the clock again as it approached midday. He felt the seconds aging him. With notebook and pen in one hand, he dragged his chair from the desk towards the sofa and sat in front of the woman.

"Aging happens to us all." Dr. Zum scratched his receding hairline with the back of the pen.

"Yes, but my Prince wishes to find company elsewhere… with younger princesses," she sniffed. "He's been visiting balls in other parts of the realm. Official duty, he tells me. But I know better."

Can't imagine why, Dr. Zum thought as he twiddled the pen between his fingers. "Perhaps you need to remind your husband of what attracted him to you in the first place."

"It was the dress I wore to the ball. He adored me. My stepsisters and all the lords and ladies at the ball cooed over my glamorous robes. But I have bought every dress imaginable. I don't know what else I can do."

"Don't you believe he saw more in you than your attire?"

"Oh, he tells me that it was my graciousness, my sweet nature, how I shared my oranges and lemons with others at the ball. But he also told me that the lone brown clog I found under our bed was one of mine. Trust me that shoe was such a fashion *faux pas*, I wouldn't be caught dead in something so drab. How can I believe anything he says?"

"Have you considered trying to reconnect with that person inside, the person who he fell in love with? The person in here." Dr. Zum patted his heart. "Throw away all the dresses. They aren't who you are."

"Am I not entitled to a little luxury after slaving away most of my childhood... thanks to my stepmother? I've never had nice things before."

"That's not what I'm saying." Dr. Zum leant forward. "Do you think that maybe the glitz and glamour of palace life has changed you at all?"

She rubbed her chin, deep in thought. "Well... I no longer need to rely on mice and rats to keep me fashionable. Who needs a Fairy Godmother when you have a Prince with a fathomless wallet?"

"That wasn't what I meant either. Who were *you* before you met the Prince?"

"No-one. I was nothing but a cinderwench."

"Based on what you've said, it seems your prince thought you were gracious and kind and your inner beauty was—"

"So what you are saying is that I need to find whatever it is he saw in me that first night." The intensity in her voice ratcheted up a notch and she perched forward on the sofa. "But the prince ogled over my dress when we danced..." She stood and waltzed on the spot; swaying back and forth she seemed to drift off to another place. "I was young and beautiful back then."

"Okay, that wasn't quite the direction I was hoping the conversation would go. Think deeper."

She shrugged. "It *was* a beautiful dress. It glistened in the light and swayed as I danced."

Feeling a headache coming on, Dr. Zum clasped his forehead. "When you took off the dress, was he still interested in you?"

"Why yes." She sat down and seemed to contemplate this for a second. "Yes, he was. I was in my rags cleaning. They came to try on..."

"He saw you in plain clothes and still fell in love with you," Dr. Zum prompted.

"So you are saying I need to rekindle the beauty he saw during that first night at the ball, but not just focus on the dress."

Dr. Zum nodded and turned his palms upwards in his 'tell me what *you* think' gesture.

"You're right! When we met he wasn't just focused on my glamorous dress." She leapt out of her chair. "Oh, you are good, doc."

Dr. Zum sank back in his chair. He still had the touch.

"He came and tried on my lost... Oh, how could I not have seen it before? It wasn't the dress he fell in love with at all."

"Of course it wasn't." Dr. Zum sighed in relief. "Your prince saw there was more inside than–"

"It was the slippers!"

"Huh?" Dr. Zum's mouth fell open. "That wasn't–"

"You're good, doc. He was obsessed with my petite feet in those beautiful glass shoes. Not these puffy balls dangling at the end of my ankles."

Dr. Zum shifted in his chair and held up his hand, motioning her to sit down. "Wait a minute, you're misinterpreting–"

"Thank you, doc. You said I need to rekindle the person he fell in love with so I just need my Fairy Godmother to do some reconstructive work on my ankles and feet."

"Wait a second. I think we need to discuss –"

"Who would have thought the answer would be so simple?" The clock on the wall chimed as the hour hand struck twelve.

"That's my cue." She picked up her handbag, which suddenly turned into a turnip. She looked at the vegetable dangling from her hand and then turned to the doctor. "I don't suppose you know any good Fairy Godmothers whose work lasts, by any chance?"

Chicken Little

"Why don't you go find out what Mr. Loxy wants, then come straight back and tell us all about it?"

Marlena Frank spends her days as a computer programmer, but has recently discovered the joys of writing. Her two cats are her muses, and fantasy is her realm of choice. She finds it hard to contain all the stories demanding attention, but she's working on releasing them one word at a time.

"I have books of fairy tales lying about that I've accumulated since childhood, and thought that maybe I'd get a neat idea by flipping through a few of them. When I came across the very short Chicken Little tale, I recalled how bad I felt for her. Chicken Little is a character who is rather naïve and riles all of her friends into a panic that ultimately leads to their demise. I wondered – what would happen if the sky was truly falling? Not necessarily in the fantasy sense: images of a steampunk London being bombed amid a bleak backdrop came to mind, and I knew I had what I wanted."

Marlena has been published online at Short-Story.Me! and was also chosen for their anthology that was published in December. She is currently working on a horror/supernatural/southern gothic tale that refuses to be locked into a category.

More details can be found on her writing website at: http://lenafrank.wordpress.com.

The Sky is Falling
Marlena Frank

Carefully, cautiously, the five ladies followed the swish of Mr. Loxy's reddish cloak to the dark warehouse. This part of town was bad enough by itself, but the building looked like it had barely survived the last bomb raid. The shutters were singed in places and several of the windows had been boarded up. The doorway had partially collapsed, leaving only a small opening where they could enter.

"And you're certain that it did fall from the sky, yes?" He was tightening his fingerless gloves as he spoke, and the five shorter women had to move quickly to keep up with him.

"Yes, yes," Ms. Little whispered. "Out of the sky like a fiery bolt from the heavens! You don't think it's really..."

"I don't know, but I can check a few things to see if this truly is an invasion. We must be certain before we take such claims to the High Minister. Follow me." Loxy dropped his top hat into the crook of his arm and crouched down low as he made his way into the building, leaving Ms. Little and the rest alone on the dark street.

"Do you think we can trust him?" Penny whispered at her side, her eyes wide as she stared at the building as though it spewed hellfire.

"I don't think we have a choice!" As sketchy as the place looked, Little thought it'd likely be safer to be indoors than out. She looked to the others, all four of them cowering and glancing upwards in apprehension, not quite sure if they should trust the mysterious man's claims, or take their chances out in the open. Little gazed up into the pouring rain, clutching the black umbrella in her hands; she could see the dark shapes moving behind the clouds above like giant whales swimming through the skies. If only she could she could see their markings! She could only hope they weren't the enemy's airships.

"Do you ladies truly think it's better to face bombs than an old building?"

"Well, he doesn't exactly look trustworthy," Loo whispered, her purple feathered hat looking like a drowned pigeon in the pouring rain. She exchanged concerned glances with the other ladies.

"I can't believe this! You think me a liar, do you?"

"Oh that's just not true, dear!" Lucky insisted, patting her reassuringly on the arm. "We just... we'd just rather not. Why don't you go find out what Mr. Loxy wants, then come straight back and tell us all about it?"

"Oh yes, that's an excellent idea!" Penny leapt up. "Go find out if he's a true gentleman, and let us know!"

Little sighed, wondering not for the first time why she'd decided to get this gaggle of gossips involved in the first place. "Very well then, ladies. But you'd best not run off as soon as I turn my back."

"Oh no."

"We'd never think of it!"

"Perish the thought!"

Taking a moment to muster her courage, Little gathered her golden skirts and petticoats, then crouched down to climb in through the doorway behind Mr. Loxy. The hallway was dark but thankfully very dry. She shook shut the umbrella as she stood. There was a slight smell of mold, and now that she was indoors she could hear the heavy, grinding sound of machinery in the distance.

Mr. Loxy was at the end of the hallway, top hat now replaced on his head. He seemed even taller in the tiny corridor as he waited patiently with his hands clasped behind him. "Oh, excellent! I was wondering for a moment if you were really interested, or simply pulling my leg with this tall tale."

"I'm... quite sorry, Mr. Loxy. My friends – they aren't quite as trusting as I am, though I am loathe to admit it."

Mr. Loxy frowned, looking as though he was not particularly surprised by the news. "But you, Ms. Little? You are not so easily frightened, I hope?"

"I don't believe so."

"Excellent. Well then, let me show you my instruments, and if we've any luck I should be able to prove your claims." And with a great flourish of his cape, he turned to the door behind him where he began turning wheels and pulling levers, seemingly in random directions.

"What are you...?"

"It'll take just a moment!" With a final thrust, the door gave a resounding churn as a hiss of air shot out and the door lifted smoothly up above his head.

"Don't be frightened, please. This way."

He led the way through, and despite her fluttering heartbeat, Ms. Little followed. Down the long hallway they crept, Mr. Loxy maintaining a rapid pace the entire way. His long legs made short work of the winding path, but Ms. Little had to trot to keep up. The mechanical grinding noise was growing louder.

"What is that?" Her voice sounded very small.

"Oh, that's the Calcinator."

Ms. Little blinked in confusion, and started to speak as they took a sharp turn. But as the hallway suddenly opened up into the massive room, she was at a loss for words.

The room was a giant glass dome tiled up every wall with hexagonal glass inserts. The rain fell down the sides of the room in tiny rivers, making crisscrossed patterns across each of the glass pieces. But the most incredible oddity was a giant metallic pipe that ran up the center of the room and into the heavens. It emitted a steady flow of steam above their heads, and all along it churned and swiveled gears large and small, some with squared teeth, some with pointed ones, and some without teeth at all. The number of moving parts that played across the surface was dizzying, and the grinding noise of the equipment only intensified the vertigo.

Then she realized that the room was open to the outside. In fact, at the very top of the room was a cutaway almost as if someone had cracked the end off an egg. The pipe was actually pumping the steam outdoors. And above the pipe, floating as if on a cushion of air, was the remainder of the ceiling, shielding the entire room from being flooded by the pouring rain above.

"How on earth!" she breathed.

Mr. Loxy smiled, gesturing wildly up to the edifice. "Welcome to the Calcinator, my dear. Isn't it beautiful?"

The room was incredibly warm, and quite humid with the addition of the moisture outside. She dabbed at her fore-head with a handkerchief. "Forgive me, it is quite lovely. But honestly, how is this supposed to help us?"

"Ah yes, here, put these on." He retrieved the strangest goggles she had ever seen. They looked normal at first glance, but had sliders on the sides very much like a microscope. She slid them over her head with a bit of reluctance. They smelled strongly of sulfur.

"What are these –"

"The Calcinator puts off quite a bit of heat when it's actually on. It can be quite... dangerous."

Ms. Little pointed at it in shock. "It's not even on?"

"No, not at the moment." Loxy took off his top hat and dropped it onto a side table. Little hadn't realized it before, but his short-cropped hair was a vibrant red. Just like the machine, this man seemed a being from another world.

"Now, Ms. Little, do you have the bauble that fell earlier?"

She reached into her velvet purse, placing her fingers around the cold metal within. She pulled it out, still marveling at the cold copper that gleamed when brought under the ruddy light.

Loxy leaned forward, flipping his goggles to different colors as he examined it within her hand. "Hmm, yes. This does indeed look like one of their carpet bombs. A dud perhaps, but it does resemble it."

She could feel the blood drain from her face, "A... a dud? You mean to tell me I've been travelling across London with a bomb in my satchel?" Her breathing was becoming ragged as the pitch of her voice increased.

Loxy grimaced as he glanced up at her, an eye behind the green lens studying her closely. "Really, it could be far worse, my dear. Take a seat."

She sat down at the only available seat beside the Calcinator. But the heat it was pumping off was unbearable. She was feeling light-headed, and barely noticed as Loxy took the failed bomb from her hands.

"You'll want to strap yourself in."

"Excuse me?"

Loxy motioned down to the straps at her side, and Ms. Little blinked a moment before snapping the strange buckle across her waist. Then he started pulling more levers and turning rotating pulleys as the Calcinator began to spin – slowly at first, then picking up speed. The breeze was cool though, and refreshing after the still heat from earlier. It was only when she felt her body being pulled against the belt that she realized that they were ones spinning, and not the Calcinator.

"My God," she gasped, but her voice was lost in the whirr of the spinning room. Loxy waved at her, trying to get her attention, his vibrant hair spilling out behind him as he pointed up above them. As she raised her eyes once again she realized that the entire ceiling was spinning with them, staying at a constant pace, only this time she didn't see the sky above or the pouring rain. There was blackness behind the glass and tiny dots of red light that she soon realized made out a map of the entire British Isles, from Ireland to England. Then one of the panes of glass went clear again just over London's East End.

"Mr. Loxy, I think it's broken!" She had to raise her voice to be heard over the device. She glanced over and saw him standing perfectly still, looking upwards for a moment before continuing his notes. His hair was a crazed animal in the wind, but he barely seemed to notice. She watched as another window pane went clear and another, until London was nearly boxed in from the empty glass panes. "What does it mean, sir?"

But Loxy kept silent, and continued his scribbles for several minutes before finally pulling down a large lever at his side. He dragged his long, thin fingers through his hair in a vain attempt to tame the impossible mess. The Calcinator started to spin less quickly, and the breeze ceased to whip across her face. When the device finally stopped, she could still feel the vibrations moving through her hands and legs as though she were still in motion. The world still felt as though it spun, though Mr. Loxy seemed unhindered by it.

"Ms. Little, I appreciate your bringing this to my attention. I'm sorry to admit that I am restricted from using the Calcinator without the strictest of evidence, which you so willingly provided me."

She was finding it hard to find her voice, but at least the world had finally stopped spinning. She unbuckled the belt around her waist with shaking fingers as Mr. Loxy continued.

"I realize this might be difficult for you to understand, but your actions may save numerous lives today." He was at his desk scratching out a quick letter across some thick linen parchment. "Once I send this off to the High Minister, I'll be able to speak more. I must request that you do not leave this room until I return. I'll be just a moment." And with a quick nod, he moved into the next room. She could hear a door open and some discussion, but she was still trying to find her legs. She was fairly certain she couldn't flee from the odd room if she wanted to. Standing up only made the dizzying sensation worse, so falling back into the chair seemed the only safe option. It would certainly not be ladylike to make a giant mess of Mr. Loxy's clean floor.

In a couple of minutes he returned, though in much less of a rush than before. "Come, Ms. Little, we need to get you up and to a safe location." The tips of his fingers were icy cold as he helped her to her feet.

"I'm quite sorry, Mr. Loxy. Your device, it –"

"The Calcinator?"

"Yes, I'm afraid it rattled me quite fiercely."

"I apologize, it does tend to have that affect when you first experience it, though with a bit of rest you should be right as rain." They were moving through a tunnel, another dingy one like before, but in a different direction. Little could only hope they wouldn't be utilizing another dizzying device. She wasn't sure her nerves were up to the task.

They came to another door, much larger than the last and with many more gears and pulleys. When he finally pried it open, there was a loud bang as the giant latch pulled back. The inside was quite bigger than she'd imagined, and quite a bit busier than any other location in Mr. Loxy's laboratory. Men and women alike, dressed in simple white garb, were moving to and fro about the room. And huddled in every corner were groups of people, many people – perhaps hundreds.

"What on earth?"

"I'm afraid this is where I must take my leave, my dear lady. And may I thank you again for your incredible discovery."

"Please, Mr. Loxy – you must explain what in the world

is going on? Who are all these people, and what are they doing here?"

Loxy stood straighter, clasping his hands behind his back as though he were giving a lecture. "I'll put this simply, Ms. Little: the city of London is likely to be bombed. Horrifically – very likely today. We've had intelligence point to several possible routes, but no one knew where or when the attacks would begin. There have been rumors for the past year, but nothing complete. The dud you gave me earlier was all the proof I needed to run the Calcinator, which locates and displays precisely where any airships are hiding nearby. As you saw with your own eyes, and if those readings are correct, then our fair city is quite surrounded."

Ms. Little couldn't believe her ears. Was she really the first person to realize they were under attack? "I – I don't understand. Why don't you have that Calcinator running all the time? Why shouldn't we always have that spinning device monitoring the skies for such a deadly strike?"

Just as the question escaped her lips, the hundreds of candles throughout the room flickered and then went out, submerging all of the people within the giant room in complete blackness. A few children started crying and several of the white-clad men swore, struggling to relight whatever candles they had on hand. Mr. Loxy just laughed, "Well, precisely this."

"What happened? There was no breeze, or anything!"

"The Calcinator thrives off heat, my dear Ms. Little. And as such is sucks it out of anything it can find. It took me years to perfect it, so now you simply have candles that are put out, ovens that flicker and die, and embers that become immediately cooled. Although its use is restricted, at least now

I'm not completely banned." Candles throughout the room were slowly being relit, casting an eerie glow on the tall man.

"And before? What did it use before, Mr. Loxy?"

He paused for a moment, searching her face for something, perhaps understanding. "Like I said, anything it can find. Needless to say, I was lucky to survive. Some of my associates were... not so fortunate." He sighed heavily, collecting himself before extending his hand.

"But truly, Ms. Little, congratulations are in order. You have served your country well this day, I just hope we were quick enough."

He took her hand in his, and grazed his chilled lips upon her skin. "Good luck, Ms. Little. May we see each other again soon."

"Yes, and good luck to you, Mr. Loxy. And thank you... for believing me."

He smiled before bowing deeply. "You are more than welcome, my dear lady."

He turned to head out the door as more people poured in from the streets. Ms. Little was thrilled when she spied Penny, Loo, and Lucky all huddled around one of the benches; she'd have quite a tale to tell them. When the first of the bombs finally fell, more than half the city was prepared and confined to the safety of the shelters and all because a single woman found the courage to report a trinket that had fallen from the heavens.

The Handless Maiden

"Father wept and said it's because you're tainted with your grandmother's curse, your mother's blight."

Alison Balaskovits was born in the Chicago land area. She received her B.A. in Creative Writing and Literature at Loras College in Iowa and is currently working on her MFA in Fiction at Bowling Green State University in Ohio. After, she plans on escaping to a nice little flat in England with an earless cat named Oppenheimer.

Her work has previously been seen in The Allegheny Review, Pindeldyboz, *and* Children, Churches and Daddies. *She has an upcoming re-telling of Hansel and Gretel in* Mad Hatters Review. *Her biggest influence is Angela Carter's disturbingly beautiful collection,* The Bloody Chamber, *and each time she sets out to write a retold fairy tale, it is with that high standard in mind.*

"A Girl Without Arms" was inspired by Grimm's "The Handless Maiden" which, after Red Riding Hood, is the author's favorite fairy tale.

Dark, complex, rich with symbolism and layers of meaning, "A Girl Without Arms" is not an easy story to interpret, and arguably the most challenging piece of the collection.

A Girl Without Arms
Alison Balaskovits

When she asked, her father lowered his voice and told her that her grandmother was a witch, made of woman's cruel magic: poisons and childbirth. The villagers spat on her doorstop for luck and overcharged her for breads and meat. What else but a witch's heavy laughter made the udders on the herd overflow and run like piss? The villagers shivered at the noise and put their fingers deep in their children's ears and bottled the milk. It tasted sweeter than honey. Unnatural. They ran grandmother out of town by slapping her breasts until they bruised and bled. They cast her tender daughter to the ground and marveled at the stones embedded in her face.

And Father said her mother flogged herself with a whip of braided horsehair and dull nails. She put her jagged back on display in the square each morning, and the villagers wept at the sight. They made garlands of magnolia and lily of the valley for her hair. They commissioned a stronger whip of leather and glass. Madonna, they called her. Notre Dame. They bowed their heads and asked her blessings. They rolled loaded dice to take her to their rooms each night and watch the vicious act with their belts undone. When she put on child they gripped their hair and wailed and wondered how it could be. When her child was born her back convalesced to pink baby skin. The villagers could not look upon her without violent retching, and

116

so she put on a shift of pale tulle and went into the woods.

And Father said he took her into the swell of his own home because he was a kind man of means and because he did not like his own children, nor his wife's slew eyes. He bounced her on his knees and lanced the round blisters on her hands from churning the daily butter. She grew quiet and beautiful and obedient, and he loved her.

When she asked, her father said it was the black-eyed devil come round to ask for her hand. Of course her father did not give his favorite away. He gave his other daughters, the one with horse teeth, the one with the red birthmark, the one with a single eye, and tossed out his wife as well. Then he placed a heavy crucifix around her neck and on every wall so everywhere she looked there was suffering.

Father wept and said it's because you're tainted with your grandmother's curse, your mother's blight. It is on your hands and arms. Everyone who looks at you can see where you've come from. The devil has come to collect his own. She cupped her hands to catch her father's tears, and he used fresh soap and sandpaper to scrub her fingers and elbows raw. She raised the salt water over her head and poured it over her body to burn away the rest.

Father said he shut her away in his bedroom to safeguard her from the villagers, who would see her lineage in her arms. Roused by the devil, they will tear her apart. She is safest under covers. She is safest without candlelight. She is safest against the swell of father's fat belly, big enough to hold her still and keep her warm.

When she asked, he told her not to ask anymore.

When she acted, she took the dull butter knife she hid

117

in her skirts and put it to the place of elbow and bone. Slow she brought it down, slow she carved, low she moaned when it ripped muscles and fractured bone. Then the locked door shook and whined on its metal hinges and burst open. Behind it was the man her father called devil, all long hair and pale eyes. With her permission, he took the sharp axe on his belt and swiftly removed her other arm. He watched her arrange her arms with her toes on the pillows. One vertical. One horizontal. Meeting in the middle. She laughed when he took her in his arms and carried her down the stairs, out of the house, through the village, and into the dark woods.

Peter Pan

"It was about the time he started calling me Tinker that he showed up in Never with that little tease Wendy."

At the University of South Carolina, Southern writer J. Michael Shell studied under the great American poet and novelist James Dickey. Internationally published, Shell's fiction has appeared in the Shirley Jackson Award nominated Bound For Evil anthology, the Panverse Two All Novella Anthology, Hadley/Rille Books' Footprints anthology, Space and Time magazine, Spectrum Fantastic Arts Award winning Polluto magazine, Tropic: The Sunday Magazine of the Miami Herald, and The Benefactor, to name just a few. He has also had a novella podcast on Nil Desperandum, and Sniplits – Audio Shorts To Go has produced one of his stories for MP3 download. Though he has been characterized by the anachronistic title "Old Hippie," Shell insists the correct appellation is "Last Hippie."

"'Confection and Confession: An Overdue Account' is one of my favorites. As a child, Peter Pan was my hero, and as I grew older I couldn't help imagining a relationship between Pan and Tink. He was just too magical for Wendy, who I thought was an inhibiting factor and not at all suited to life in Never."

His novel The Apprentice Journals is scheduled for release by Dog Horn Publishing in 2012.

Confection and Confession:
An Overdue Account
J. Michael Shell

My name (my *real* name) is Tinklette Marabelle bon Fiereste. It was that idiot Peter who saddled me with my better-known, though thoroughly unflattering, "nickname." I didn't mind so much when he occasionally called me "Tink," but one day, out of the blue, he started calling me "Tinker."

"Tinklette!" I informed him. "A tinker is someone who fixes pots!"

"How about 'Tinker *Bell?*'" he insisted. "It fits you perfectly!"

"How vulgar!" I insisted right back. "I am *bon Fiereste*, a true-born Fire Sprite, not some common fairy you can call by pet names!"

"Oh, don't be so stuck up," he told me. "Sprites and fairies look pretty much the same to me."

That made me angry. So angry, in fact, that I shed two tears, which nearly burned his house down, tree and all. "Now see what you've made me do," I said, when he finally got the fire out.

"I thought all Fiereste take an oath not to magic humans!" he accused, as if I'd burned his house on purpose.

I didn't speak to him for a week after that, and should have stayed away for good. But he was cute and brave, and a little bit bad — qualities that stirred up quite nicely in that mostly human boy. And, yes, I had a terrible crush on him, and eventually assented to his calling me Tinker Bell. I even turned a deaf ear when he told people I was his fairy. It's not something I'm proud of, and I should have made him stop. Fairies, after all, are nothing but tarts and trollops.

There are three kinds of glamorous creatures in the world, in case you didn't know, and fairies are pretty much the bottom feeders. They have no code of conduct whatsoever, and will use their glamour on any human male who wanders into their realm. They are also the least proficient in the magical arts. I have more magic vested in my little finger than half a dozen fairies could produce on their very best day. That's why they have to gang up, as they do, to glamour a single frail human. Didn't know that about them, did you? Well, it's true. And once they've got a boy good and glamour-ed, they're loathe to give him up. They may keep him for days on end in that state. You might think it's all harmless fun, but it isn't. There's many a fey-shy boy in the world who was made that way by a fairy dalliance. Even pixies (who aren't much better than fairies) have enough common courtesy to let their victims go before trauma to the mind is done.

Pixies and fairies are the *other* two kinds of glamorous creatures, but *we*, the Fiereste, are the first. In the ugly language that English has become, we are known as "Fire Sprites." And though Peter insisted that we all look alike, we are, in fact, quite different. At least we Fiereste are. Pixies and fairies, I must admit, are hard to tell apart.

Anyway, that is how I came to be known as you-know-who, a horrible pejoration of my beautiful name. And the worst part is, it was done merely for effect — so it would *sound* better when Peter called my name in the heat of battle. That's something you have to understand about Peter — image, to him, was everything. In fact, he'd often call to me, while sword-fighting pirates or wrestling Indians, saying, "Mirror me, Tink!" That meant he wanted me to glamour the air in front of him to reflect. Then he'd actually strike poses as he was fighting. It's a wonder he never had his head cut off while he was doing that!

All ego, that was Peter. It was why he wanted not to grow old. It had nothing to do with any grand notions of childhood as an ideal condition. It was vanity, plain and simple. I was many times tempted, in spite of my oath, to plant a gray beard on his smooth, supple chin.

It was about the time he started calling me Tinker that he showed up in Never with that little tease Wendy. I could take or leave her brother, John, but Michael was an absolute charmer. I was sorely tempted to keep him when Peter finally got tired of the Darlings and kicked them out. I'm sure you've heard the story that it was Wendy who dumped Peter, but just because that Scotsman said it, doesn't make it so. He was, after all, human, which is why, I think, he took her part. He knew the *true* story, or at least most of it. I can be absolutely sure of that, because it was *I* who told it to him. I don't like to go into the details, which are rather embarrassing, but he tricked me one night with an old Celtic spell that contracted me to him for a hundred years, or until I delighted him with a tale. For the most part, the story I told was accurate. There was one minor detail that I fudged, but it wasn't the part about Peter giving Wendy the boot. It had, rather, to do with a certain green cake, which I'll get to the heart of in due course. Now — let me start

123

at the beginning, that I may correct the inaccuracies and out-right lies that have all these years been circulating in the form of Mr. Barrie's notorious tale.

Peter, as was his habit, had been slumming around in the Mortal Lands – in particular, a place called London. (Peter should have been called "Tom" for all his peeping into windows.) During one such excursion, he heard the barking of a dog as we floated above a large and moonlit abode. "Hear that, Tink? That shaggy beast senses us and wants to scare us away from what it protects."

"What is there worth protecting in this place?" I asked him. "Everything in this realm marches toward death. It's a portrait of inevitable decay. Let's go home to Never. I'll dust you down when we get back, and feed you frosted moonbeams."

"Not now, Tink," he said, ignoring my enticements. I can't tell you how that boy frustrated me. He was looking through a dormer window high up on that home, when I heard him coo, "I've never seen such a beauty in the land of the dying. See how peacefully she sleeps."

"So *let* her sleep," I told him — perturbed now, and wanting to go home. "If you don't come with me this instant, I'll leave you here, and you're not likely to find your way back to Never without me."

That got his attention, and he said, "Would you really leave me, Tinklette?"

"Why I haven't left you before this amazes even me, Master Pan. Now come along. Perhaps if you pay attention this time you'll finally understand the directions and can come here by yourself — instead of dragging me along to keep you from getting lost."

"I know the way, Tink — second star to the right and straight on till morning," he smiled.

"Don't be an idiot," I told him. "Either follow me or stay here and gawk at that tart in the window. I'm leaving."

Needless to say, Peter joined me. He wouldn't have lasted long in old London-Town. But apparently he paid strict attention to our route that night, because not a week later he showed up in Never with those Darlings tagging along. Contrary to the Scotsman's lies, I had *nothing* to do with their escape from the Dying Realm. Peter must have pinched a bit of my dust one night as I slept, in order to fly them out. While I shan't go into the particulars of our relationship, suffice it to say that staying perpetually young does not preclude one experiencing the passage of time — not even in Never. Peter *was* a boy, but a very *old* boy, and was not immune to the callings of desire. In fact, perpetual adolescence can be a particularly anxious state. So, as I've said, he may have purloined a little of my dust one night while I was in his very near proximity, and spun-up to his size (something we Fire Sprites can do, while pixies and fairies, of course, cannot).

As I've said, that Scotsman was a liar. Not only was I not aware that Peter had finally gotten the directions straight and gone to London without me, but I had no idea that he'd returned with those Darlings in tow until I saw them silhouetted against a lovely evening sky. As for Tootles shooting Wendy down with an arrow, I had naught to do with it. Those lost boys were miscreants! In fact, when I say "lost" you may read "abandoned." They were a foul lot more in need of a warden than a mother. Was I there when Tootles loosed that bolt? Could I have stopped him? Yes and yes. But just because I chose not to get involved in protecting what was obviously trouble on the wing, should I be labeled conspirator, and even *instigator?* Those beastly boys blamed the whole thing on me, and Peter, egomaniac that he was, believed that faddle about my jealousy. Can you imagine — a Fire Sprite jealous of a human girl? Why, *had* I been jealous, all I'd have had to do was wait a little bit till age consumed the trifling amount of beauty she possessed. And as for Mr. Barrie's assertion that Peter regularly "cuffed" fairies, that may or may not be true. But if he'd ever raised a hand to a Fire Sprite (and this one in particular) he'd have joined James Hook in shopping for prostheses.

Peter was, indeed, piqued at the boys for shooting his little prize out of the sweet Never air. He had quite a temper, actually, and a bit of a mean streak. As punishment for their archery, he kept the lost boys up all night building a shack around his London tart. He was refusing to speak to me (and I enjoyed the respite), but it didn't last long. Peter *was* the Captain and Hero of Never, but without me, as will become apparent, he was just another lost boy. Anyway, he kept the gang, including John and Michael, up all night constructing that hovel. Once it was built, Wendy insisted that it be called "The Darling Household," and that she be referred to as "Mother Darling." When they started that game, I took my leave as it was giving me bouts of nausea.

What they were up to in the "Darling House" or the

"Wendy House" I will not speculate upon. But just the fact that she was one young girl living in the company of ten dirty boys (two of whom were her brothers!) did not bode well for our lady's reputation. Even pixies and fairies, who are both (as even Mr. Barrie has mentioned) fond of orgies, had nothing kind to say about young Wendy. In fact, her reputation grew so ill that the pirates were simply *infatuated* with the idea of capturing her. And the Mermaids, who were much too fond of Peter, tried on more than one occasion to drown her lovely bones in their lagoon.

One such occasion was the night the pirates captured the Indian Princess Tiger Lily. Though I realize Mr. Barrie was reconstructing the tale I told him for the entertainment of children, I, for one, see it as a distinct disservice to the young to sugar-coat the nature of a world (and if you think Never is bad, take a good look at your own).

Pirates are pirates — they pillage and plunder and rape when they are able. And while those pirates who'd captured Tiger Lily may very well have left her to die on Marooner's rock, that was not their main intention when they brought her there in that dinghy. Fortunately, I'd gotten word of Lily's capture and was following right behind — floating on a kite young Michael had abandoned to the wind a day earlier. Had I flown, they might have seen my light, but down on the water, and behind them, I was well concealed. I also knew that the boys were out there somewhere with Peter and Wendy. I was hoping Wendy would feel like swimming, as that lagoon was practically infested with Mermaids. Had they gotten hold of our girl, naught would have remained. Mermaids are lovely creatures, but their fish half is barracuda, and their appetites are sharp as their teeth.

Anyway, I was just about to sneak onto the pirate's dinghy and loose lovely Lily from her bonds when Peter began imitating Hook's fell voice. He was really quite good at it, and bade the pirates let Tiger Lily go. Amazingly, they did. Then Hook swam out to join the party, and Peter couldn't help but brag. The jig was up.

Well, and of course, there ensued a brouhaha in the waters all around as the pirates leapt in after the boys, and the boys swam into the fray. As this juvenile aquatic carnage commenced, I dusted Michael's old kite, took Tiger Lily by the hand, and we floated up above the fracas. "Put me down, I want to fight!" Lily said.

"Wouldn't you rather stay up here with me?" I asked. "I could shrink you down a bit, and we could lounge upon this kite." Lily was such a *lovely* girl, but she was also a tiger. She escaped my grasp, then did a wonderful swan-dive into the lagoon. I missed her immediately.

Eventually, I saw the boys, along with precious Lily, commandeer the pirates' dinghy and head back for the mainland. The pirates, who'd actually given Peter quite a thrashing, were headed — swimming like Olympians — for their ship. Why didn't they finish Peter off? Why were they swimming as if for their lives? I'll tell you, and it will expose another of Jamie Barrie's gross inaccuracies.

First of all, there was no crocodile, much less a crocodile who'd swallowed a clock, much *much* less a crocodile to whom Peter had fed the evil Captain's hand. That was merely a clever rumor inspired by me and spread by Peter to frighten and infuriate Hook. In fact, Peter still has the Captain's hand stored away in a little cask of salt. A bright ruby ring adorns its anorexic forefinger.

Once the rumor took, I fetched for Peter a gross of little wind-up toy duckies that clicked just like a clock as they swam. Peter always carried one of those with him in case of a pirate encounter. That night in the lagoon, the one he was carrying probably saved his life. You can imagine how hilarious it was to me, sitting high up on my kite, to see the pirates swimming hysterically away from that little, clacking toy ducky!

Before long, the pirates were out of sight, and I noticed that Peter was stranded on Marooner's rock. Wendy was there also, laid out dead-tired from her extended swim, and I could see several mermaids pawing at her feet. Had they gotten hold of her — well, I shan't reiterate. But Peter managed to pull her up a bit, and the mer-gals lost interest for the nonce. The tide, however, was taking an inexorable interest in their little island, and would soon be over their heads. With the ruckus of the fight over, there would only have been poor, exhausted Peter to fend off the mermaids, and I do not think he was up to it. Wendy would have been fish-kibble.

Now here is a part of the story that truly angers me as Mr. Barrie related it. According to him, that kite simply floated down of its own accord and carried Wendy off to safety. Balderdash! Though I will not deny her relative beauty, Wendy possessed her fair share of, shall we say, baby-fat. Not only did I have to dust that kite again to hoist her chunky bottom back to dry land, but I twice had to physically push it back up, as even my enchantments groaned under her weight. And that was just the *first* time I saved her wretched life — but we shall get to that cake, as I've said, in due course.

Once I had put Wendy safely down at the doorstep of her house, I chased a Never-Bird out of its nest and flew the little structure out to Peter. Never-Birds are very like enormous pigeons, except much tidier. The nest was cozy, and Peter and I enjoyed a leisurely and comfy sail, snuggled down into it, back to the mainland. When we arrived at the Wendy House, I asked her, quite politely, if she wouldn't mind making us up an omelet of the two lovely Never-Eggs I retrieved from the nest. "Do I look like the cook?" she asked, indignantly (and, remember, I'd just saved her meaty buttocks from being gnawed by toothy mermaidens).

"No!" I told her. "You look like the mother!"

The following day, Tiger Lily showed up with her braves to negotiate an alliance with Peter and the boys. It seems she was grateful for their assistance in coming to her rescue. "What about me?" I asked her.

With a bashful little smile, Lily said, "Yes, thank you, Tinklette Marabelle, for also thinking of me in my time of need."

"I love to hear you say my name," I told her, and I *did*. "Now, I require a *kiss* for my brave endeavors."

"Oh no, you naughty Sprite," Lily blushed. Then she whispered to me, "I like braves."

"I like them, too," I whispered back. "I like everybody."

As part of the treaty agreement, Lily and her warriors agreed to stand guard while Peter and the boys (and you-know-who) took refuge in the underground lairs to recover from their battle. Being somewhat overextended myself, I joined them and put out my light for to sleep. Now you must understand that when a Fire Sprite sleeps, extinguishing her light, she is literally dead to the world. It is a compromising condition to be in, I admit, but when we awaken we are always refreshed and at the peak of our power. The *problem* is, the only thing that can wake us is ourselves in a dream, and we simply won't do it until we're thoroughly rested. Which is why and how I slept through the pirate attack that overwhelmed the Indians. Fortunately for Wendy, I also slept through her scheming attempt to take Peter from Never for ever and ever.

You may wonder how I came to know the intimate details of Wendy's game while I was thoroughly extinguished in sleep. It's simple — I watched the whole encounter from my dream. I'm surprised, actually, that I didn't wake myself to take her to task. Her plan was (all along, I believe) to attach herself like mistletoe or some other poisonous, parasitic plant to Peter and the boys, then feign homesickness and a longing for her family. When she told the boys that she simply *must* return home, all but Peter asked the pitiful question that her plan had precipitated, "Then who shall be our mother?"

That is when she sprang her trap. She would, she told them, take them all home to her very own mother and father, who would adopt them. Ha! Confronted with that motley bunch, Wendy's mother would have fainted. None the less, that is what she told them — fully expecting Peter to not want to be separated from his crew. But Peter, though he'd played Wendy's "Mothering" game, was not one to be coerced. He was a rebel for true, and contrary by nature. "Go then," he told them all. "Tiger Lily's braves are standing guard above. I'm sure they'll cover your retreat out of Never."

Unfortunately, Lily's braves were actually bound and gagged and headed off to Hook's vile ship, the Jolly Roger. In another attempt to sentimentalize Peter, Wendy shed a tear (as cold and calculated a tear as I've ever seen) and bade him take his medicine (another of her games) on a regular basis. Then she and the boys shimmied up the hollow trees that served as egress to and from the underground lair.

While all this was going on, Hook and his pirates were waiting above. With his ear to one of the hollow trees, the Captain heard every word of Wendy's little show. As she and the boys emerged, they were, one by one, bound and gagged for transport to the Roger. Now Hook had *everyone* captive, save Peter.

You may be saying, "But Tinklette, Hook also did not have *you* as captive," and that would reveal that you know *nothing* about Fire Sprites. Had Hook, or any other corporeal creature, ever attempted to keep me captive, it would have been on their dying day.

Now you must understand that, normally, Hook and his full-grown pirates could never gain entrance to the underground lairs, as the hollow tree entrances were carved only big enough for the passage of boys. And though the Scotsman blamed the widening of one of those passages on one of the lost boys (I believe he mentioned Slightly) it had actually been widened to accommodate Wendy's Rubenesque arse. And this, of course, allowed Hook to drop down into the lairs, where he found Peter — unsuspecting and fallen asleep. Peter could nod off at the drop of a hat, and Wendy's little show had apparently bored him to slumber.

When Hook entered the lair, he immediately saw Peter stretched out on a bed in divine repose. When asleep, Peter appeared almost cherubic. Now here is one thing Mr. Barrie got entirely right — every great pirate, though he be fierce and manly, exhibits also a feminine nature. When Hook saw Peter's angelically sleeping countenance, something stirred in him and he could not strike. "Dagnabbit all!" I heard him swear. "I cannot muss him with dagger and sword. He's far too cute!"

Then Hook saw the medicine he'd heard Wendy speak of, sitting on a table. Being vile to the core, Hook always carried a bit of poison on his person, and this he poured into the medicine bottle. Then he climbed back up through the wider tree and commenced to use Peter's very own trick upon him.

Making his voice sound exactly like Wendy's, Hook called down through the hollow tree, which gave his words an echoing, dreamy quality, "Peter, my love, *please* take your medicine! It's all I ask and my final request."

Now, though I was witnessing this from my dream, I was very much asleep, and nowhere near rested enough to wake myself. But when I saw Peter rise and head sleepily for that bottle of poisoned medicine, I quickly ran to the mirror in my dream and said to myself, "Wake up, you fool!"

"Who are you calling a fool?" my reflection replied. "It isn't time."

"But Peter's in danger!" I cried.

"Oh, just let me sleep for five more minutes."

In an act of desperation, I hurled my very best dream necklace at the mirror and broke it to a thousand shards. It was perhaps one of the greatest sacrifices I made for Peter. If you've ever wondered how Fire Sprites can arise from sleep with their hair perfectly coiffed, it is because we fix it in our dream mirrors before we wake up. To this very day, I awake a tousled sight because I broke my mirror to save that boy.

When I opened my eyes, I saw that Peter had poured out the medicine into a great, huge spoon. Quick as a flash, I flew to him, just as he opened wide. He was about to place that poison on his tongue, when I dove into the spoon and splashed it dry. That's right, I did not drink it as Mr. Barrie implied, but drenching myself in it was almost as bad.

Poisons work differently on Fire Sprites that they do on pirates and boys. This particular poison, rather that sickening or killing me, caused me to spin-up to human size, and I could not spin back down. Big is not something we Sprites do well, and the only other occasions on which I did it was in order to hold and be held by Peter. So when he saw me like that, being a boy, he thought that's what I had in mind. "Don't touch me!" I cried to him. "I'm poison!"

Peter smiled and said, "You're surly, for certain, but I wouldn't call you poison."

"Hook poisoned the medicine, you jerk," I told him, not a little miffed. Not only was my dream mirror broken, but now I was spun-up and big for who knew how long. In fact, I was so big I wouldn't be able to go up even the widened-out tree.

"The poison really made you big!" Peter laughed, coming fully awake now. "In fact, you're bigger than Wendy."

And *that* was the only time (almost) I ever hit him.

Captivity, as I may have implied, is something a Fire Sprite cannot abide. But captive I was, as my poisonous size prevented my exiting the underground lair. "Don't worry," Peter told me, holding his aching jaw as I paced around. "I'll think of something to get you out."

"Well, be quick about it," I yelled at him, coming just a bit unglued, "before I cuff your other cheek!"

"Okay, Okay! I've got it! I'll just go up to the lagoon and fetch a bucket of water to wash the poison off you."

"And leave me *alone* down here? It will drive me mad!"

"It will be a short trip," he said to himself. But I heard, and cuffed him again.

Now I will admit that being in the same room with a hysterical Fire Sprite is an untenable position to be in, but he might have tried to calm me first before he made that mad dash and shimmied up a tree and out. "You come back here!" I cried, holding back my tears with all my might, lest I ignite my prison and perish in the blaze. Fire can't harm a Sprite when she's normal size, but spun-up like that we're as vulnerable as humans.

It seemed forever, but finally I heard Peter calling down the tree. "I'm back, Tink!"

"Hurry, then!" I screamed. "I can't take it anymore."

"I'll lower the bucket down on a rope," he called back. "You can pour it over yourself."

"Can't you just bring it to me?" I cried back.

"You're too big," he answered. "I'm punch-drunk already!"

It was then that I whimpered, and he must have heard it. Whether or not he risked coming down because he loved me, or because he was afraid I'd cry and burn down the lair, I cannot say. But he wasted no time dousing me with that water, and very slowly I began to shrink back to normal size.

As I was diminishing, Peter asked, "You don't, by any chance, know where Tiger Lily and her braves have gotten off to, do you?"

"The pirates have them," I said, smiling as I watched my fingers go dainty and small.

"And Wendy and the boys?"

"Pirates," I said again.

"We'll have to save them, you know," he told me.

"I suppose," I told him back.

"Have you any more of those wind-up duckies?" he asked.

"Will a duck's foot fit in a puddle?" I answered.

Together, we smiled.

For some reason, fights and thrashings and war are of the greatest interest and entertainment value to human kind. So I should probably go on to tell you all about the great skirmish that ensued, and how Peter saved everyone and ended the villainous life of Captain James Hook. It is, after all, what J. M. Barrie would do, is it not? Well, I am *not* that vain Scotsman, and I'll tell you no glorious lies. The fact is, Pan would *never* have killed Hook, even if the opportunity presented itself. He *needed* Hook. In a way, he *was* Hook. What, after all, is a yin without its yang? No, those two were inexorably bound up, and Peter would have withered away in no time without his arch-nemesis to keep him on his toes. So even though there was some fighting, in the end it was just another wind-up ducky toy that scared the pirates away. When it was done, Wendy threw her arms around Peter's neck and cried,

"Oh! You're my Hero and Savior! I must take you home to Father and Mum!"

"Forget it," he told her as I fluttered down and landed on his shoulder. "I'll take Sprites over mothers any day. And this Sprite here," he told her, "is going to fly you home right now. I strongly suggest you don't give her any bother along the way, as she's had a very trying morning."

"*Well!*" Wendy harrumphed.

"A deep subject," I advised her, as I dusted her and her brothers. "Now get a move on before your parents replace you with a cat, or a canary, or perhaps a little green turtle."

Once I'd herded the Darlings through their dormer window, I closed the bars and welded them shut with a few precisely-shed tears. I could hear a commotion inside, and a dog barking, and can only remember thinking, "I hope it eats them."

Now you have heard the *true* tale of Peter and Wendy and the lost boys (who are still, of course, lost. Those Darlings never would adopt them). "But what about that *cake*?" you are probably asking. Well, don't worry — I've simply saved my confession for last.

As it happened, Wendy was, as usual, making a nuisance of herself and mothering every boy in Never. It was, of course, disgusting. But it was the day I heard Peter himself call her "mother" for the very first time that I ordered the poison cake. Yes, it was I, not Hook. Hook couldn't blow his nose without my knowing about it, much less plant a bright green, poisoned cake on the Wendy-House doorstep. And, *no*, I didn't break my oath. There was no magic involved at all. I simply paid Hook's baker to make the thing, then gave him a little extra to deliver. So when I told the Scotsman a pirate brought it, I was actually telling the truth.

Wendy was such a little pig! By the time she keeled over from the poison, she had green frosting all over her mouth. I can't *believe* I let Peter talk me into reviving her. I'd actually have done her a better service if I'd let her die. At least she'd have had a pretty corpse. As it turned out, even that poison cake didn't dull her penchant for pastries. She was huge by the time she turned thirty, and when she finally did succumb to her human mortality, a special "full-figured" coffin had to be constructed to contain her girth. Though I'm sure you're thinking otherwise, I took no satisfaction from her obesity, or her demise. I simply wanted her out of Never, and once she was gone I could not have cared less if she rose to become Queen of Jolly Old.

What I wanted was Peter, and I got him — though nothing lasts forever. It seems his eternal youth wasn't so eternal after all. It was a spell, you see, that was secretly placed upon him when he was given the name "Pan." But a spell like that is hard to maintain, and one day he simply grew old all at once.

Now my light is going out — it's the price we pay for breaking our oaths. I say "we" because most of the true-born are fading just as I am. Human or fairy, pixie or Sprite, love takes its toll on us all. I suppose, at least in that respect, we do look pretty much alike.

The Frog Prince

"If you kiss me, I will turn into a handsome prince and ask for your hand in marriage."

Anne Waldron Neumann has published a half dozen literary folktales in, among other journals, The Harvard Review, and American Letters & Commentary, *which nominated one of her stories for a Pushcart Prize. She holds a Ph.D. in English literature from Johns Hopkins University, has taught at universities in America and Australia, currently teaches creative writing in Princeton, New Jersey, and is the author of* Should You Read Shakespeare? Literature, Popular Culture and Morality.

Anne is currently seeking a publisher for a collection of her fables, *Bedtime Stories for Mothers, in which "The Froggy Prince" and her other contribution to this anthology "The Seven Swan Brothers" (page 285) both appear.*

You can visit her site at: www.annewaldronneumann. weebly.com

The story of Princess Camilla's aunts having tea in a restaurant is based on a family incident Anne heard from her mother. Anne has also met many froggy princes in real life.

The Froggy Prince
Anne Waldron Neumann

As usual, Princess Camilla was drinking afternoon tea in the castle's morning room with her three maiden aunts. The aunts nibbled cucumber sandwiches and shortbread fingers and discussed something rather daring.

"Cousin Kitty tried it first with Miss Mabel Ingalls," Aunt Arizelia confided.

"Miss Mabel Ingalls is very advanced," breathed Aunt Bethesda.

"Miss Mabel Ingalls is very advanced in her *ideas*," Aunt Celestine corrected firmly.

"So Cousin Kitty suggested she and I try it together," continued Aunt Arizelia.

Aunt Bethesda was thrilled. "And did you?" she asked.

"Yes, did you?" Aunt Celestine echoed.

"We *did*. But we didn't know where the nearest one was. So Cousin Kitty found the head office in the telephone book. She spoke to a nice young man on the telephone. She told him she was Mrs. Winthrop Dunham, and that she and her cousin Lady Arizelia Stillwater wished to visit a Cobb's Corner Tea House for afternoon tea, but where was the nearest one? And he said, 'How very fortunate, my dear Mrs. Dunham. We have one quite near the palace, at the corner of Central Square and King Alfred Boulevard. And there is another on Ascension Allee, across from the main entrance to the zoo.' So we left Roberts and the carriage and walked across the park to the one at the zoo. We had tea and buttered toast. And – do you know? – it was really *very* nice."

"How does one pay afterwards?" asked Aunt Bethesda uncertainly.

"Yes, how does one?" asked Aunt Celestine.

"One pays the waitress. Cousin Kitty asked me if I knew which one *was* our waitress, and I said I *thought* she was wearing a black dress with a frilled white apron. A gentleman at the table across from us laughed so pleasantly – admiring my memory, I suppose. Really, we had a most delightful time."

After tea, Princess Camilla escaped the aunts for a walk in the palace garden despite the drizzle. There, she was accosted by a loathsome toad – or was it a frog? "If you kiss me, I will turn into a handsome prince and ask for your hand in marriage," the frog promised.

Through the window of the morning room, Princess Camilla could see the aunts still nodding agreement around the tea table. She picked the frog up and kissed him. And thought suddenly, as she did so, "I should have asked whether he will turn into a *kindly* prince, or a *well-read* prince, or..." But it was too late. A handsome prince stood before her holding out his hand. She took it. It was cool, limp, and slightly damp.

"How do you do?" the prince said formally, without quite meeting her eyes. He clicked his heels and bowed stiffly. "Prince Wilfried of Hoch-Nieder-Oberthal eternally at your service, dear lady. With the permission of your father, your mother, or any of your nearest relatives, I hope you will grant me the honor of your hand in marriage." The prince's voice was somewhat too loud and rather monotone.

The aunts had clustered at the morning room window and were watching with undisguised curiosity. "I accept your offer with gratitude and pleasure, my lord," Princess Camilla said hurriedly, before she had time to change her mind. "And how soon after the wedding may we return to your kingdom of – where is it? – Hoch-Ober-Niederthal?"

"Oh, we must remain in *your* kingdom, dear lady," said Prince Wilfried. "I wish to continue my study of the fascinating water spiders with which your ponds and streams abound. Besides, my wicked older sister, who turned me into a frog with her witch's spells, already rules Hoch-Nieder-Oberthal quite resolutely in my stead, and I am reluctant to challenge her. Though I feel sure that, in exchange for my continued silence about her spells, she can be persuaded to send me an allowance to maintain me in modest comfort in *your* delightful castle, which I see behind me, and with whose water gardens and their diverse aquatic fauna I am already most happily familiar."

The aunts were smiling and tapping on the glass of the morning-room window. Princess Camilla felt her lower lip beginning to tremble. But Prince Wilfried had already waved a limp hand at the aunts and was walking without a backward glance toward the French door that led to the morning room. Princess Camilla hurried after him.

At the wedding breakfast, Prince Wilfried told his new bride's maiden aunts all about the curious habits of water spiders, both male *and* female. His voice was as usual somewhat loud and monotone. But, as the aunts were all a little deaf, they were rather pleased than not. Indeed, they were fascinated by the prince's description of his researches. "Our dear niece must be very admiring of your thoroughness and knowledgability," said Lady Arizelia.

"I think it is charming for a young man to have a scientific hobby," breathed Lady Bethesda.

"I am sure we are *all* delighted to have a new interest to discuss at mealtimes," added Lady Celestine firmly.

"Ladies, you are too kind." Prince Wilfried fixed his eyes on a corner of the mantel and bowed stiffly from his chair. "I look forward to meeting you and my dear wife every day at breakfast, lunch, tea, and dinner to report regularly on my researches. I shall hold myself always ready to accompany my dear wife on any afternoon calls or receptions of state her royal duties require. My mornings and evenings, I must, of course, save for scientific study." And he bowed again, this time more or less in the direction of the silver tea urn and Princess Camilla, who felt a sudden urge to blow her nose.

Aunt Arizelia smiled understandingly. "From what you have told us of water spiders and their interesting though bizarre habits, I can see how important evenings are for your collecting expeditions."

"And the clear morning light is essential for arranging and examining my specimens in their glass cases," Prince Wilfried continued. "Perhaps, ladies," he offered modestly, "you would not object if I brought part of my collection to the table from time to time to show you its progress?"

"Not at all," said Lady Arizelia.

"We should be delighted," said Lady Bethesda.

"My dear boy, need you ask?" cried Lady Celestine.

"And perhaps you will allow us in turn sometimes to invite our cousin Mrs. Winthrop Dunham and her dear friend Miss Mabel Ingalls to hear your reports. Miss Mabel Ingalls, I feel sure you will find, possesses the true scientific temperament." Aunt Arizelia and Aunt Bethesda nodded agreement. Prince Wilfried bowed once more and smiled vaguely at the door-knob.

A year and a day after her wedding, Princess Camilla was drinking afternoon tea with Prince Wilfried and the maiden aunts in the castle's morning room. Her face looked thin and pale, but the aunts knew she did not like her state of health inquired into. So Prince Wilfried and the aunts, having already discussed the curious habits of water spiders, were now talking about something else rather daring.

"Cousin Kitty tried it first with Miss Mabel Ingalls," said Aunt Arizelia. Aunt Bethesda and Aunt Celestine thrilled with anticipation.

"Miss Mabel Ingalls is so very advanced," murmured Prince Wilfried admiringly.

Princess Camilla looked out the window. It was drizzling. She felt tired and somewhat chilled but thought she might nevertheless walk in the garden after tea.

Hansel and Gretel

"Hansel and Gretel, what have you done?"

Jonathan McKinney lives in Winchester, Kentucky with his wife Charla and their three children. He enjoys PC gaming, particularly Team Fortress 2, playing Texas Hold 'em with friends, and lazy Sundays.

Jonathan's story "Shiny Eyes" has appeared in Close Encounters of the Urban Kind and Dead Worlds Vol. 6. As a special submission project he also has a two part story titled "Love's Enduring Embrace" on the websites wilywriters.com and edgeofpropinquity.net.

"I thought first of Hansel and Gretel, thinking what a traumatic experience they went through. Some residue of that probably would have lingered in their young minds, not to mention the fact that their parents came up with a horrid plan to get rid of them anyway. So I found myself asking myself what if Gretel liked the idea of burning more people, and the story boiled onto the page."

Aroma
Jonathan McKinney

The old hag's skin grew blisters everywhere the fire licked. Sister watched through the rusted iron bars of the oven as she held the old hag at bay with the locking mechanism, a large iron bar that fit into a slot on the right side of the oven. Sister's eyes watered from the heat and finally she closed them. The sounds and smells were enough, however – the shrieking, and the burning flesh.

Sister opened her eyes, at home now, done reminiscing on the old hag's death. Their father had lied to them. Their mother, alive and well – not their stepmother as the village believed – had greeted them upon their return home with the blood-crusted cane.

Brother's plumpness had helped him endure the beating, but Sister hadn't partaken in the witch's treacherous hospitality. A week home, Brother's hefty body had diminished, now nearly bones again beside her in bed.

"Gretel," her mother called. "Food, now!"

Sister gritted her teeth. She flipped the covers off, and nudged Brother who stirred beside her on the bed. She put on the apron that hung beside the door, and ducked through the opening from under the stairs that led to their tiny room. "Hello, Mother," she greeted, needing both eyes to see the massive thing called Mother.

Fat fell in layers from all sides, spilling over the seat of the kitchen chair. Mother's mouth, a tiny dot in an endless supply of chins, pursed. "My first meal hasn't been prepared and it's three crows into the day. Have we lost our manners?"

"No, Mother," Sister replied.

Sister opened the pantry cautiously to avoid acquiring new bruises from falling food, and collected what she needed for breakfast. After three trips to and from the pantry, the pleasant smells filled the cottage. Brother shuffled in with a sponge and a small basin. He lifted the folds of mother's flesh and washed away dirt and grime. Sister set the first of three dishes in front of Mother.

Greedily the large woman dived into the dish. Others watching may have believed this her first meal in ages, but just yesterday she had partaken of her regular seven meals a day. When the food was devoured, mother wiped her chins and smiled. "You ungrateful children may have the rest."

Sister let Brother eat most of the crumbs. Father came in carrying a small squirrel already skinned and dressed. Sister smiled at her father, who now just looked at her grimly. "Father, dear," Mother said.

Father threw the squirrel atop the cutting board and grimaced. "Yes, Mother?"

"Suppose you take these two out into the woods today for a third time. Maybe this time will be the last?"

Sister's face grew red. She knew her father would. Her rage was hidden but unabated since she'd realized her father had lied when he told her at the old hag's house that Mother was dead. The gold coins she and Brother had found were mere fakes, obviously another lure the hag used for travelers. In response to Mother's question, Father simply nodded.

Sister studied mother, calculating the size and girth of her, and purposefully let a small piece of bread spill from her pocket. "Oh dear," Sister exclaimed.

Mother stood up quickly. Her stomach pushed the table forward, and knocked Brother to the floor, who, after the few crumbs, had returned to cleansing Mother. "What's that?" Her grating voice amplified in the tiny kitchen.

"Gingabbre," Sister mumbled.

"Speak up to your mother, Gretel," Father ordered.

"Gingerbread," Sister replied, eyeing the floor intently, and shuffling her feet.

"And just where did that come from?"

Brother jumped in front of his sister. "The witch, mother, she..."

Sister punched Brother lightly on the back. "That's our secret, Brother, she need not know."

"Need not know, do I?" Mother yelled, grabbing the cane painted red by Brother and Sister's infractions. She pointed it at Brother. "Tell me, or Gretel gets what you deserve."

Mother always tried to play them against each other. Whipping one for what the other did. Brother cleared his throat. "In the forest when Gretel and I became lost, we came upon a house made from Gingerbread."

Mother's eyes grew wide. "Liar," she called, lashing Sister across the forehead. "Liar, liar, liar," and with each "liar," Sister received the cane across her brow.

"I'm not lying, Mother we'll show you. Your cart will pass comfortably between the trees where she lived."

Mother nodded. "Yes, you will."

Gretel grabbed Mother's traveling bag, a large sack of imperishable food, slinging it upon her shoulders and grunting with each step. Outside her mother climbed into the cart with its steel-reinforced wheels. Father hooked both mules up. Mother leaned over to Father and whispered, "We finish it today."

Sister and Brother led the way into the woods hand in hand as the cart led by their father followed. Mother ate from her bag, spilling crumbs along the path for the woodland creatures, the very same that had eaten the children's trail just a week ago. "Are we there yet?"

Sister turned to look at Mother. "Around the next bend, Mother."

The gingerbread house came into view, and Mother began to drool. She licked her lips, and rocked forward, the cart creaking under her weight. The mules groaned at being stopped so quickly when her feet hit the ground. Blubber bouncing, she hurried to the house and threw two handfuls of gingerbread down her throat. Sister opened the door to prepare the oven while Brother collected some wood.

Soon the fire raged inside the oven, and Mother stepped in through the hole she'd eaten in the wall of the house. "What's that delightful smell?"

Sister smiled. "We found some food already in the oven and ready to warm up. Come over and have a whiff." The squirrel, which no one had seen Sister lift from the cutting board at home, now cooked inside the oven. Sister doubted her measurements as Mother waddled over to the oven. Mother peered inside and sniffed heavily. Sister used the large iron door, throwing her shoulder against it with all her might and glory, to shove Mother's girth inside the large oven. Brother ran over to help her and they managed to close it as Father, drawn from tending to the near-dead mules, peered in the door.

"What's going on in here?"

Neither Brother nor Sister gave an answer.

Father, seeing Mother's fat squeezing through the rusty iron bars of the oven, cried out. "Hansel and Gretel, what have you done?"

Mother screamed as the smell of the squirrel mingled with her own. Sister sniffed heavily much like Mother had, and moved back from the oven as Father approached. He heaved the door open and tried to remove Mother. Father's vain attempt gave no ground. Sister imagined it would take the help of the mules and half the village to budge Mother now.

Sister once again closed the door, but now upon her father too. Brother asked, "Gretel what are you doing?"

"He left us in the woods. He's responsible as well."

Sister frowned. She could no longer see Mother, burning behind Father's back, but as with the witch there were still the smells and sounds. Their deaths mimicked their lives: Father wore silence in death as Mother screamed and cursed. The smell just before the flesh burned, when the meat was cooked, Sister adored.

The door closed completely as Mother's fat body cooked from the heat, and Father joined her in their final resting place. Brother and Sister collapsed just outside the door, their backs to the oven. Sister cried.

Brother grasped her hand. "It's over."

Sister wept. "I know, awful isn't it? There's no one left."

Brother looked into her eyes. "You have me."

Sister shook her head. "That's not what I mean."

Brother nodded then smiled. "There are some kids in the village that were making fun of me. Well, us."

"Really?" Sister brightened up. "You're not just saying that?"

Brother moved Sister's hair behind her ear. Gently he traced a finger across the sores Mother's cane had raised upon her brow. "Really."

Sister's eyes twinkled and a smile stretched across her face. "We'll need to get us a bigger oven."

Beauty and the Beast

"Maybe it's because I get tired of ravishing Lady Gaga, I snapped – those overly done hats, those huge shoes, the whole shtick."

The stories, poetry and humor of Larry Lefkowitz have been widely published in the U.S., Britain and Israel.

Larry is currently seeking a publisher for his literary novel about a literary critic, his assistant and the wife of the former – she wishes to have the assistant finish an unfinished novel left by her late husband. Several chapters have been published in print and online.

"I saw a serious Beauty story and my humorous approach came to the fore."

Humorous indeed, "Getting Along With Mr. Wrong" proves that not even legends are free from the problems of married life.

Getting Along With Mr. Wrong

Larry Lefkowitz

*One day Beauty got bored with the Prince,
who was boring indeed, unlike the Beast,
who had character. Beauty told the Prince
so after an especially boring day with him.
Shocked, he immediately returned to his
beastly state.*

Beauty, I queried her over our cups of tea (mine
cinnamon, hers strawberry-lemon), what are we to do today?
It's overcast, best we stay indoors – you know what rain does
to my fur.

Beauty didn't answer, caught by a magazine article
about Lady Gaga.

Beau-ty, I repeated. Beauty liked my spaced-name
pronunciation, preferably with a Noel Coward accent.

She looked up. Did you say something, Beast?

I did. I enquired as to what we should do today.

Beauty sighed in that dramatic way of hers, stolen from
a BBC reenactment of one of Jane Austin's novels.

I suppose, she said, turning the pages of the magazine
absently, you will ravish me.

Yes, it cannot be ruled out, though it gets increasingly
fatiguing. And you comply so nonchalantly lately. Not like in
the old days when you would beat on my chest and–

154

Yes, I know, Beast. Something's changed. She said this without looking up from her magazine.

Maybe we should vary the routine. I could dress up as – what's his name? The actor you like. The Caribbean buccaneer. Or go back to some of my past routines. You remember? The bagpipes? *Roamin' in the Gloamin'*?

How could I forget? It was like being ravished by an octopus. And that skirt!

Kilt. I was deep into the role. An adherent of the Stanislavsky method of acting. And you made a fine Lolita in our little Nabokov tribute.

She looked up from her magazine. They were ok in their day. You were naughty to try to vary The Legend.

A case of the flesh being willing and the spirit weak. I had pangs of conscience every time I did it.

Still, it was preferable to the boring old ravishing according to The Legend.

Beauty, I won't stand for disparagement of The Legend. Admittedly, repetition breeds boredom, but ravishing is what the Legend of Beauty and the Beast demands. One or two ravishings a day.

More like one a day lately, she corrected.

I'm getting older Beauty. Beasts age, too, you know – not just rock stars.

I know. Your ravishings lately – how can I put it? – have not only become less frequent, but somewhat... Beauty hesitated, and then circled her hand vaguely in the air.

Tepid, I ventured.

Pre-cise-ly, she said, imitating my enunciation of one of my favorite words, which she claimed I borrowed from

155

Margaret Thatcher.

Maybe it's because I get tired of ravishing Lady Gaga, I snapped – those overly done hats, those huge shoes, the whole shtick.

I adore Lady Gaga, Beauty replied.

Next thing, you will want a tattooed rose on your delicious shoulder.

A chastity belt, she shot back.

Her new cheekiness probably came from Lady Gaga. Or Britney Spears. What a contrast to the passivity of her Gothic novels stage. I would read them out loud to her, and then we would ravish. Gothically. But nothing remains as it was, even in legends. Fault our revisionist age. Postmodernism and such. Anybody can read legends as they wish, and not as they were told and passed down from generation to generation.

My reflective silence apparently oppressed Beauty, for she threw down her magazine – with Lady Gaga on the cover! She could not remain peeved for long – The Legend wouldn't permit it. Putting both hands under her chin and leaning on them in her Little Miss Muffet pose, she said, to mollify me, How about a game of Scrabble?

I always beat you in word games, I replied tartly, still miffed.

I'm not as intellectual as you.

If you read the *T.L.S.* as I urged you these last decades, you would be.

Lady Gaga doesn't read the *T.L.S.*

Maybe I should ravish Lady Gaga.

At this Beauty let out a long laugh. I could hardly picture the two of you. You'd have to do it wearing elevator shoes.

An unkind cut. She knew I was sensitive about my height.

Ah for the days when I would sing *Hey nonny no, today we'll go a'ravishing* as I jumped into the air and clicked my hobnailed boots.

Yeah, in your furry, furry voice.

What do you expect – I *am* the Beast.

That's fine for you. What am I? The Ravished, that's who.

We each have our roles according to the parameters of The Legend. Besides, you are Beauty, the epitome of – I stopped, offended, because Beauty had covered her ears, shouting, I heard it all before.

You *shouted*, I pouted. Beauty had never shouted at me before.

She ran to me and gave me a hug. I know, Beastie, I'm out of sorts lately.

Mollified by her hug, I pawed at the zipper of her dress. A flouncy thing with large pasted-on flowers. Lady Gaga's influence at work. How about a little ravishing, Baby, I purred in my Humphrey Bogart voice.

Not today, if you please, Bogie. I have a headache.

What! A headache. A common housewife's excuse. Any housewife worth her apron would give her eye teeth to be ravished by me.

You use a mixed metaphor? She laughed, You're hopelessly behind the times. Housewives would prefer to see others ravished on TV. Like in *Sex and the City*.

I got carried away, hence the mixed metaphor, ergo, the

solecism, I explained to her. The truth is, what with TV and the internet the legends are losing their force. Vintage is out, the ephemeral is in.

She sighed. Maybe we should bow out gracefully. Close the shop. I'll take up aerobic dancing for exercise.

I ignored her wit, but replied to her proposal. After Walt Disney got hold of the Legend, we became but pale imitations of ourselves. I agree to bow out as gracefully as a Beast can, I said to her, but how about one last ravish?

Oh all right, she consented. Then she stopped. Maybe we could make it a game of Scrabble instead – go out intellectually. You might be remembered as a savant and not as a beast.

Why not both? Scrabble followed by ravishing. Feast for the mind, feast for the body.

Ok, I'll get the Scrabble game.

And I'll get my fur-gel.

Rapunzel

"For years she, and every woman in her family, had been searching for a way to rid herself of the monstrous hair.*"*

Amy E. Yergen is a new science fiction and fantasy writer. In August of 2010, she completed her MFA in Creative Writing and Writing for the Performing Arts at the University of California, Riverside. She has lived all over North America including Alaska, Maryland, Alberta, Canada, and Hawaii. She currently resides in California with her family and cat Frank. Find her at amyeyergen.com.

"Rapunzel's Daughters was inspired by my favorite professor. In college I met Wendy, this vivacious, brilliant, and over all a wonderful literature teacher and person. I was amazed by her, she lit up rooms wherever she went, and I wanted to be just like her. She was an independent woman, close to being tenured, and a great mom to her little daughter Nora. This story is an homage to her."

A modern take on the old tale, "Rapunzel's Daughters" is Amy's first publication.

Rapunzel's Daughters
Amy E. Yergen

"Wow, your hair's really long. Have you ever thought about cutting it?" The cashier looked to be about nineteen. *Her dark hair was spiked with gel and highlighted in sections: lavender, white, teal. She didn't wear much make-up except for black eyeliner. Her nose ring was new or infected, because the skin was tinged very red and looked painful. Her name tag proclaimed her "Jordan!"*

Marianne didn't respond at first, even as the girl tossed her perfectly red, ripe tomatoes into a plastic sack with the cans.

"No, you're the very first person that's ever mentioned that," Marianne said flatly.

"Haven't you ever thought about cutting it?" The cruel, piercingly blue eyes of Gabrielle 'Gabby' Miller were frozen on her in disapproval. "Well, haven't you?" Marianne didn't answer. "You look awful. Look in the mirror." She pronounced her words in sharp staccato. Marianne turned around in the Millers' enormous bathroom, not meeting the eyes of Cathy and Cindy. The popular girls.

"Don't you know that everyone says you're a freak?" Cathy asked. Cindy touched Marianne's shoulder, seemingly in sympathy, then turned her forcefully toward the mirror.

Marianne looked into the reflection and saw three

very nearly identical girls. They each wore their hair just past chin length; in ringlets they rolled in sponge rollers every night. The only difference between them was hair color. Gabby's was dark brown, almost black, Cathy's hair was golden brown, and Cindy's was the color of dirty dishwater — but highlighted nicely in the summer which kept it from being mousy. Or so she said.

"Are you paying attention?" Gabby shouted and yanked at Marianne's hair from behind so her neck snapped back like a whip. Marianne didn't answer, she'd wanted so desperately to be Mary and now she just wanted to go home.

The girls in the mirror, girls she should have been taller than, seemed to grow. They leered over her in heels that belonged to Mrs. Miller. Heels Marianne was fairly certain they weren't allowed to wear. Heels much too small for her enormous, overgrown, size ten feet.

There was a rolling sound of a drawer opening and Gabby's small pale hand, with bubblegum pink nails, reached into the drawer that was filled with all kinds of odds and ends: a hair brush, an epilator, baby powder, and a long vicious looking set of scissors. They weren't like some, with the friendly plastic handles in orange or red. The metal was as reflective as the mirror and the blades curved in a sharp point ready to stab something.

"Y– you should be careful, those—"

"Shut up, she knows what she's doing."

"I don't need your help, Cathy. What're you laughing at, Cindy?" Marianne watched in the mirror as Gabby, without even looking at her two conspirators, grabbed a section of hair and tried to slice into it. It didn't work and the scissors made a sound like teeth clunking together.

"I told you, it's not going to work," Marianne said softly. Gabby yanked the section of hair she held again, and Marianne winced. She sawed the scissors against Marianne's hair over and over until they could all smell warm metal.

"What the hell is wrong with you?" Gabby pushed Marianne aside, examining the now dulled scissors. "These were brand new, my mother's going to be so pissed!"

"She's like Cousin It," Cindy snickered. Cathy's eyes lit up and she burst out laughing.

"Cousin It, that's great. That'll be your nickname from now on," Gabby leaned on the bathroom counter trying to contain herself as Cathy sank to the floor unable to breathe through her giggling hiccoughs. Cindy looked superior, then snorted.

"I am? Seriously?" the cashier asked.

"Absolutely," Marianne replied, and lifted her tomatoes out of their bag before the girl did any more damage. She swiped her card and signed her receipt, then turned the cart to make her way out of the store. She shook her head, rolling her eyes. Then cracked her neck. Her head and shoulders ached; as they always did by this time each day. *Cut it off.* She laughed to herself, *If only it were that simple.*

For years she, and every woman in her family, had been searching for a way to rid herself of *the monstrous hair*. It couldn't be cut. It was far too coarse — like strands of iron growing straight out of her skull. She'd dulled and broken countless pairs of scissors trying, but to no avail.

Each girl child born to her family had been delivered with a full head of towheaded curls about half an inch long.

163

And though their hair took a while longer than most children's to begin growing, once it did, it was a nightmare. At the age of ten Marianne's hair was down to her waist. By twelve, her knees. It had finally stopped growing after puberty and settled just past her ankles, trailing no more than two inches on the ground — for which she was actually thankful. Her mother's trailed more than a foot unbraided. Everyone hated it. Everyone except for their great grandmother Edith, who always said *"you should all be thankful to God you are not bald"* in a heavy Polish accent.

Georgia, Marianne's little sister, *was* bald. She'd begun using Nair on her head in Jr. High school and by college she'd saved the money for electrolysis. This was before laser hair removal — although according to Georgia you can't laser off blonde hair anyway. Something about refraction. Or reflection. Or whatever. Georgia liked to consider herself a rebel. And, while Marianne would dearly love to at least try her hair in a bob at her ears, she wasn't sure permanent baldness was the answer.

Marianne fumbled with the grocery bags, which were heavy when transferred all to one hand, and reached into the pocket of her white shorts for car keys. She unlocked the trunk and dumped her groceries all in at once — realizing for the moment that she was almost as bad as the cashier — and slammed it closed. Then walked to the driver's side and let herself in.

The car had warmed from the sun, even though the air outside still held the chill of early spring. She let the door hang open and sat for a moment without buckling her seatbelt. She leaned back — feeling the opposing temperatures of warm car and cool breeze vying for dominance. It made her drowsy and she closed her eyes.

"You have the most beautiful hair." Roger's voice was low, his lips close to her ear. His fingers nimbly found each bobby pin she'd placed with purpose that morning, slowly unwinding the braid that circled her head in one thick, shining, plait. Then the braid itself fell apart, the long waves crimping softly after being released from their tight enclosure.

He sat her down in the chair by the window so the sun shone against her white dress and hair. His easel was already set up with a new canvas, his tackle box filled with pencils and paints open, but as he pushed her down into the chair he followed her, kneeling, pushing hair back from her face, kissing her with his rough, unshaven mouth.

Marianne was not what you might call beautiful. Though she would certainly not call herself ugly, she was rather more on the side of plain than pretty. She had a high forehead, a thin face accentuated by a long, thin, somewhat pointed nose, and what Georgia always said was a Julia Roberts-esque mouth but was really just large and almost horsey. Her skin was the beige-y pale of so many white people, typically Midwestern, and a little freckled over her face, chest, and shoulders from too much sun. She hadn't quite the leathery look of a sun worshiper, but she supposed she was on her way. In the next ten years or so, when she turned forty-five most probably. Well, she liked to garden.

She was tall, nearly six feet, and that was something. She was thin, you'd never know she'd popped out three kids in succession, but that was about the closest she came to the feminine ideal. She had very small breasts, not even a B cup, and wide bony hips leading to scrawny legs and large, flat feet. It was her hair, though, that gave the illusion of attractiveness. The sun-kissed halo brought her the warmth of a pre-Raphaelite painting. Something Roger had told her again and again — and had tried to capture in his hundreds of paintings. It wasn't that Roger didn't have talent, but to Marianne, even in art, she always just looked like herself not some Waterhouse nymph.

And so, because of this, Marianne was afraid that if she ever did find a way to remove her long rope of hair, part of her softness would go with it. Part of whatever had brought Roger to her. It was Roger that had made her love her hair in the first place.

A bird, landing on her windshield startled her out of her daydream and she honked the car horn to get rid of it. Moments later she was buckled in, meandering down the road, not as far into her own lane as she could be – although there was no one else on the road. It was a quiet and lazy day on Primrose Street. It wouldn't last long. It was nearly two-thirty and soon everyone's kids would start popping up in yards and on street corners – home from school. Alice and Adele would be fighting over who could tie up the phone first and for the longest. Abbie would help her make dinner.

She was smiling at the thought of her girls when she pulled into the drive. She stopped smiling as soon as she saw Abbie sitting on the stoop. She stopped the car barely off the street, and sprang out the door, not bothering to turn the engine off. Hardly bothering to pull the emergency brake.

"What's the matter, what's happened?" She was

shocked by her daughter's appearance. The hair she'd carefully washed the night before and braided in a long French braid was covered in dirt, ripped apart so it barely held even the remote idea of a braid — her face was red and tear-streaked and she appeared to have had a bloody nose. On top of that, her shoes were missing.

"The kids at school hate me, I don't want to go back there again, momma. Please don't make m– me," Abbie's face welled up with tears and she began sobbing into her mother's lap. Marianne pulled her daughter into her arms as she began to fill with a dark boiling rage.

When Marianne had her first two girls she'd felt a huge relief. Their hair was fine, wispy, and dark like Roger's. The summer's humidity curled the short tendrils around their faces and shadowed the little dark eyes that matched her own.

When Abbie was born Marianne was torn between joy and concern for the only daughter with the yellow curls that so many generations of Ripunnselles had had. She loved Alice and Adele more than words could express, but she felt separated from them in a way that she didn't feel with her youngest. They were a strange combobulation of Roger and their own unique-ness. And they favored him, she knew, as daddy's girls, much as she had done when her father was still alive.

But Abbie was like Marianne, and the monstrous hair made it more obvious day by day. And now she was repeating the history of torture Marianne herself had experienced.

This last summer Abbie'd turned eleven, and had begun the subtle start of puberty. She'd shot up, tall and skinny and tan. And her hair had grown six inches in three months. She'd spent her days playing kickball with the neighbor kids, and then come home to lie on her bed because her hair was becoming so heavy and hot.

It reached her waist now, and was just long enough that she accidentally tucked it into her pants when she used the bathroom. Something Marianne had often done as a girl. Something that could be painfully embarrassing in Junior High.

This was the third time already, just this week, that she'd come home crying, although it was the first time Marianne had ever seen her in such a state. She'd sat down with Abbie's teacher only two weeks ago. She thought they had this under control.

It was suddenly quiet again and Marianne realized that Abbie had stopped crying and was looking up at her.

"What happened, baby?"

"Everyone always teases me for how long my hair is, but they were never really serious. Usually the girls just said I was too brainy and wouldn't let me play with them. But today our new P.E. Coach said he'd never seen such long hair on anyone and got out a yard stick to measure it. He said I must be a Fundy and, oh ha ha, I must be a Mormon. And I said, no I wasn't, I just happen to have long hair. And he said if I wasn't a Mormon my hair was against dress code and I needed to have you cut it. And I said that I couldn't, we'd tried, but I inherited really weird hair and it just doesn't cut. And he called me a liar in front of the whole class!" Her words poured out in a wave and Marianne struggled not to get up and phone this coach immediately and give him a piece of her mind.

"And then at lunch Jason yanked my hair and called me Fundy Abbie and everyone laughed. And I thought they'd forget about it, but they keep whispering it whenever the teacher calls on me or when I raise my hand or even when I get up to sharpen my pencil! And then at last recess I was walking up the steps to go outside and Kyle yanked my hair so I fell backward into the mud by the drain that never gets cleaned out because we're in a basement classroom."

"And the bloody nose? Did someone hit you?"

"I dunno, it started a bit after I fell."

"Rapunzel! Rapunzel! You're so weird! That's why the witch locked her up, you know. You should be locked up too!" He pushed Marianne down hard and she fell to the ground, with the wind knocked out of her for half a second. Just long enough for him to turn on his heel.

"Why don't you help me bring the groceries inside and then we'll get you cleaned up, huh?" Abbie nodded. She seemed to have recovered after her cry. She'd laid her burden at her mother's feet and probably wouldn't worry about it again, until the next bad thing happened. Abbie sniffed, and walked over to the car. She popped her head in the door, removing the keys from the ignition before Marianne had even made it to her feet. She slammed the door, too hard, and pressed down on the keychain, locking the doors with a loud, automatic, click. Then she stretched out her arm towards Marianne, presenting the ring of keys like a miniature butler. Marianne smiled and patted her daughter on the head. She unlocked the trunk, leaving Abbie only the bread and cereal boxes to carry so she would have a light load.

They stumbled into the house, Abbie hunched down, squatting in front of the open fridge to put the apples and oranges in one crisper and the onions and zucchini in the other. Her hair fell across her shoulder and Marianne saw the dirt and grime caked into the strands.

Long hair was trod on, caught itself up in things, became knotted, and most often, would simply be stared at. This mess, however, was almost obscene. She remembered how lonely she had been her whole life – sticking out like a sore thumb. Until she'd met Roger. She would talk to him again about putting Abbie in a different school.

She finished what she was doing. The cans and crackers and cereal were stored in the cupboard. The milk and ice cream had been saved.

"Okay." She motioned to Abbie, literally caught with her hand in the cookie jar. Marianne giggled as Abbie stuffed the whole thing into her mouth, and then jumped down from the kitchen counter to follow her mother into the bathroom.

She watched Abbie strip out of all her clothes and throw them down the laundry shoot into the basement — which was something Abbie loved to do. Then, Marianne had her sit down in the tub, facing the wall, so she could use the hand-held showerhead.

"It's cold! It's cold! It's cold!" Abbie scrunched up her shoulders and squealed.

"Sorry, sorry," Marianne laughed softly, spraying away from her daughter until the water adjusted. She began at the top, parting the hair with her nails and rinsing from the root down. Abbie grabbed the shampoo and poured buckets into her palms, soaping herself until her hair, and the entire bath, was nothing but bubbles.

"I think that's enough," Marianne said, prying the shampoo from Abbie's hand. It made an audible pop as it slipped from her fingers and she whined, but let it go.

She heard the front door open and close, the voices of her other two daughters arguing. She smiled at the sound of their feet clamoring up the stairs to their bedrooms. Then frowned as she wrapped Abbie in her own fluffy pink towel.

"Why can't you just try something sharper?!"

"What do you want me to try, Marianne, a chainsaw? Stop being hysterical."

"You don't make Georgia keep hers!"

"No one could make Georgia do anything she didn't want to do. Anyway it's bad enough with one hooligan in the house. You shouldn't be trying to follow her example; straighten up and act like a lady. Your father and I are in agreement, so don't bother running to him. I'm not ruining any more scissors on your hair. And that's final."

"You know, sweetheart, I told you I didn't think we could cut your hair, that I've never been able to get a pair of scissors through mine. But I don't think we really tried on yours."

"But you, and grandma, and Auntie Georgia—" Abbie began.

"I know, honey—"

"But, don't you want me to be like you?" Marianne felt filled with shame.

"Oh sweetie. I want you to be like *you*. I think we should try."

"Yes, please," she said, her voice muffled against the bath towel she was wrapped in.

Marianne got out her sewing shears, so like the ones that Gabby had tried to use on her years ago. She tested their sharpness on a piece of paper, then knelt down so that she was the same height as her small daughter. Her wet hair was the color of dark clover honey, if you could comb honey out over a smooth, flat plane. Marianne took the scissors, holding her breath, and closed them over her daughter's hair.

Sniiiiiiiip, the hair buckled with a sound almost like crunching snow. The effort required was intense and she could see a red ring forming across her hand where she held the scissors. She nearly considered wire cutters from the garage. Still, the strands fell to the ground, releasing Abbie from their burden with every slice.

Abbie's hair now extended just below her shoulders, much the same length as her two older sisters'.

"Oh, honey, I'm so sorry. I never thought–" But Abbie didn't seem to hear her. She twirled sideways, trying to spy her hair from the back and did a little dance that left her towel sliding to the ground. She didn't seem to notice.

"Oh awesome! Yes!" she clapped her hands and gave a little jump into the air. "Thanks, mom!" she cried, before disappearing out the bathroom door, a few hairs still sticking to her towel and shoulders.

Marianne, knowing she'd done the right thing, began retrieving the long mess of hair from the floor. As she was dumping it into the waste basket she stopped. She reached back into the trash and picked out a strand of Abbie's damp, rejected hair. After a brief moment she stuffed it into her pocket. Then she switched off the bathroom light and closed the door.

Urashima Taro

"Sometimes I catch myself looking out at the sea and wondering: if I scratched open my gills, if I braved the journey again, would the Dragon Palace still be there, would Otohime still live?"

"M" is, among other things, the Roman numeral for 1,000, the name of Fritz Lang's first talkie, a mediocre perfume, and an X-Men character. "Shaw" may be a name of Britannic origin meaning "dweller in the wood" or a Gaelic name meaning "wolf," but it may also be an Anglicized spelling of certain common Chinese or Jewish surnames.

Fangoria has said that M's writing "should not have been as compelling a read as it was." Readers who enjoy "The Death of Urashima Taro" might also like "And Points Beyond" in the 2010 Semaphore Anthology, "Feral" in 69 Flavors of Paranoia, or "The Further Adventures of Vance Headstrong and His Time Traveling Bicycle" in Schlock magazine.

A full list of publications can be found on M's blog at mshaw.wordpress.com.

"'Urashima Taro' is the kind of open-ended story that begs to be added on and reinterpreted. This particular take on it was born from the fact that some (but not all) versions of the tale end with Urashima turning into a crane, which in Japanese folklore is a divine animal that lives for 1,000 years. Where would Urashima be, and what would he have lived through, by the end of this life?"

"The Death of Urashima Taro" holds the distinction of being the only story in this anthology with Japanese origins.

The Death of Urashima Taro
M. Shaw

We've got some difficult days ahead.

It is not so very bad to be old, on the earth, when one has known the sea. True, I am weak and often tired, and the West Coast winds lash my face when I walk to the tea garden in Golden Gate Park; but the sun is to be seen on most days, and to be old is to be near immortality.

The sea does not suffer the weak to live. It is a garden where small, pointy teeth are grown with greater urgency than oranges, grapes, peaches, strawberries in California. If you were to, say, rescue a small turtle on a beach out of sentimentality, and if that turtle's father were a god of the sea, and the god asked you to make an audience at his undersea palace, that you might be thanked as was your due – a god told you this – and you were to accept, you would soon discover how poorly you fit there. You would have to swim very cautiously (quickly would not be an option, everything would be quicker than you) to reach the palace, even with gills.

My gills have closed up, healed over like an old piercing.

Here is what 999 years old looks like: my legs remain mostly vertical, though they are stick-thin and have the tendency to fold up in a way that you might find disturbing. My back is curved almost at a right angle, so that my shoulders run parallel to the ground. I used to have jowls but now these have worn away, so that my neck appears long and stringy, my head a half-deflated helium balloon tethered to my little shoulders, now merely sustaining itself against the ground rather than striving toward the sky. My nose has become very long. The nose keeps growing, you know, throughout life, and now mine appears practically a beak. I am bald, of course, my cap waxed and buffed by the elements until it shines red.

If you are having trouble with the image, let me tell you that if you were to examine the cargo manifest of a certain Dutch vessel leaving Dejima in the early 1600s you would see where someone had written "an extremely old Oriental man," crossed it out, and written underneath, "a crane native to this country," intended as a gift to the King of England for his menagerie.

The ship, incidentally, fell to pirates on the way back to Europe. I remember these things with more vividness than you would credit. They are to me as something that happened ten or twenty years ago would be to you. Remember the Korean War? Sometimes I picture the merchant's face, trying to sell a slave at the market in Sierra Leone, when the Frenchman spat at him and called him mad for trying to sell a bird as a man-servant. I laugh, though it sounds more like a croak. If I laugh in public, sometimes passers-by ask if I am all right.

I came to California to build a railroad, stayed to wash clothing, found fortune elsewhere. I am quite a good fisherman.

But it doesn't matter with me now.

Several years ago I saw an article in the *Chronicle* about the Emperor coming to the premier of a Charlton Heston movie. He was, I think, in his fifties at the time and not yet what you would call an old man, though perhaps not a young one. There was a picture that I looked at, trying to find Otohime's face in his. After all, the Emperor traces his lineage to her son, though that son was alive centuries even before I was born, if the story is true. Why would I think that I could find her in any human face? She was like no one else.

The Dragon Palace was not made of coral or crystal, but we did not have the words to describe it back then. It was so clean, and we lived so near the elements. You cannot escape them in Nippon, even in Edo – no, it's called Tokyo now. Even in the Tokyo of today they live in wind and storms at the pleasure of the gods. If you saw it at the end of your perilous swim, you would have had to say it was made of crystal because that was the only thing you could think of that was so clear and so solid at once. You would never have seen *Star Trek*.

What? Being old does not make things that are new invisible to me.

And Otohime. Understand, she was not beautiful like a person. She was from a world of little light, or at least where the light was not so harsh as our sun. Her skin was not thin, in the manner of certain fish, but pale, so pale that from beneath the neck of her kimono I could see the faint, pulsing light of her heart. I wanted to hold that heart between my two hands, simply to keep it from getting too cold (but it was warm in the Dragon Palace, which you cannot appreciate as I could). Her face was like one you would see in a drawing, with eyes wide open and expression unmoving; but that is not the way people look at one another really, and when someone does look at you that way it is unnerving.

I was not unnerved. When I saw that face, I knew it as that of the little turtle I had cradled in my arms and placed gently in the shallows, away from the cruel boys who prodded her shell with fishing spears. Even if she had not showed me how her people change their forms, I would have believed.

At the Dragon Palace I had the marvels of science laid out before me, in an age of the world when most mortals had never heard this word "science." After all I saw there it would have been easy to decide that there are no such things as gods. That there is no such thing as magic. That all our myths and legends were born of our inability to understand what is occasionally placed before us. But then there was that tamate-bako. I was not kept young by the unimaginably advanced technology of the Celestials; it was a box made of paper, a half-millimeter-thick veneer that separated me from time.

Because I've been to the mountain top.

If you were going to write a newspaper article about me and you addressed me as Urashima Taro, I would tell you that name is part of an old story. A true story, but nobody has called me Urashima Taro for hundreds of years. They say "Urashima-jiji," or "Old Man," or "Pops" like the youngsters in Golden Gate Park. This is my identity, to you. I am old.

When I opened the tamatebako given me by Otohime as I left the Dragon Palace, I thought that what I became was old. 300 years, give or take a score. Every time I have thought myself old, it has been an illusion produced by lack of fore-knowledge. I never comprehended how old I was yet to become. When I went to the Dragon Palace I thought myself, if not old then at least mature; much the way I am sure the hipsters on Haight think themselves, if not mature then by some measure wise. All I can say of age is that the young lack a sense of time. They are unable to conceptualize how very long life is, or how short.

Perhaps you have heard of this thing called "relativity." I will not blame you if you have not, for I myself have only known of it for less time than you have been alive. It says that what we call "space" and what we call "time" are one and the same, and consequently that one's movement through time depends on the speed at which one moves through space. You may understand my experience at the Dragon Palace better if you understand that the vessel in which Otohime came to this world was capable of moving through space at incredible speed. Not only this, but that as it now sits at the bottom of the sea where it is so very like a palace, it is still moving at a velocity greater than anything our science has made, but in a way that cannot be perceived with the eye, just as the movement of light cannot. Thus it is true that I dwelt in the Dragon Palace for three days, and it is also true that when I returned to the surface 300 years had passed. There is no contradiction.

Sometimes I catch myself looking out at the sea and wondering: if I scratched open my gills, if I braved the journey again, would the Dragon Palace still be there, would Otohime still live? And then I remember that all the years I have seen have passed in perhaps a week by her measure. Unless she has since returned to the surface, her world would look similar

179

indeed to that of my memory. Only I would be different.

But if I were to say that I am old, I would not be wrong. Cranes live for 1,000 years and I am the eldest of my kind. Any older than me would be dead.

By the way, did you know it is said that someday soon we may send a man in a little metal capsule to the moon? The moon! 1,000 years and such a slow, clumsy step we have taken toward the splendor of Otohime's world. That is how short life is.

And I don't mind.

At the tea garden I often request fortune cookies. I enjoy these little novelties because when you live for 999 years, every message they bear is true. Almost none of them are true of my future at the time I read them, but now these ones are true of my past; they have merely reached me late. For example, not a few paper fortunes predict romance and I have known romance.

I was married in Nippon, yes. To whom did you think I swam from the Dragon Palace? Why would I choose to leave a dominion of the Celestial Plane only to swim with a million slippery creatures that would tear me apart almost as soon as they would forget they had ever seen me? Would you leave Heaven to see your mother again?

In the Dragon Palace you never grow old. Your old age is kept in a box made of paper. You are loved by everyone; and because everyone loves you, they give you the paper box containing your old age when you go. They tell you that leaving will do you no good, that you will never see your loved one again, that while you are consumed by a grief that each of them wholly feels herself (because they love you) you must understand that there is nothing you can do. Loving you, they will at last allow you to leave if it is truly what you want.

I did leave, because I had to see for myself. Or maybe because I foolishly preserved some hope that if I swam fast enough I could reach the land in time to see my wife again. And when I did get there, and saw that Otohime had spoken truly, I opened the tamatebako which I knew to contain my old age because, delusional from the swim and the grief, I kept a similar hope that it might contain my past along with it.

Remember, I did not understand relativity back then. The past is not a country that you can visit. It is a temporary physical state, and once it is gone there is no way to force it back into place. I cannot put my old age back inside that paper box. Otohime's people cannot undo entropy. In place of visiting the past, we must visit memory.

And this is why the fortune cookies are important to me. One forgets much in 1,000 years. Even important memories become buried in the mind's obscure recesses and will only come out when their names are properly called. I do not remember my wife so much. We were married for the blink of an eye, in another age of the world, and when I open a fortune cookie and read "One whom you have long admired will turn your way. Lucky numbers 4, 11, 13, 23, 31, 35" I sometimes catch sight of a strand of hair come untied over the back of a neck, the suggestion of an endearing look cast upon me, two hands tying a net with practice. I never see a face, however. When I try, it is Otohime's face that I see. That one I will never forget.

Like anybody, I would like to live a long life.

Perhaps I have been dishonest, if dishonesty means telling only half of the truth. I left the Dragon Palace not only to return, but to escape. I was afraid of the Celestials, the combination of love and power that they command. All I had done was rescue a goddess who had taken the shape of a turtle, I who took lives from the sea every day. I was not worthy to live among them, and I feared that one day they would realize this and the penalty would be severe.

The irony in this is that I did face a penalty, in the form of having my age returned to me, for betraying their benevolence with doubt. Ah, but even then I was allowed to keep some small bit of their gift. If it were not for that, I would have turned to dust when I opened the tamatebako. No mere human lives 300 years, after all.

Certain of my kind (and there are others, make no mistake) prefer the sky, as I did once. I first came to America – no, it was called the New World then, on the sky. I could return on the sky to Nippon if I so desired, though the journey would be hard, to live out my final days in the land of my birth. I know, however, that when I arrived at Honshu it would not truly be the land of my birth.

When one is young, say 400 years, the sky holds no small appeal. With your whole life ahead, sailing on the wind when you have mastered the art creates the illusion that immortality is already yours, that you truly command all beneath you. In my age I have come to dread the sky. In my final days – and yes, I believe it is down to days now – I know that I will soon ascend into the sky never to return. I worry that if I catch the wind under my bony forelimbs and take off, I might look down and see my body beneath me. I know that to fly is not to command. 1,000 years teaches one just how little of the world is to be commanded by anyone at all.

When I die I will fly up to the Celestial Plane, possibly bearing some worthy soul up with me if the tales are to be believed. To fear this would be pointless, yet I do not know what will happen when I arrive. Will I be taken to task for betraying Otohime? Will I be sent back for another millennium until I become worthy? Though it seems so short a time in perspective, I am not sure I could bear it.

Longevity has its place.

The torture of California is that it fancies itself Heaven. In truth it is little more than a pleasant country, warm, fertile, brilliant in its small way, and eternally governed by youth cast in bronze masquerading as godliness, just naïve enough to convince themselves that they are. I among them know better, but my voice has grown too heavy to tell them how small they are.

In the Dragon Palace you never grow old; you are loved by all; are purified by everything you touch; dwell in beauty and radiance for all your days; want for no joy, know no vice; may have all this forever, if only you are willing to discard your mortality that is so very useless.

Tomorrow I will return to the Dragon Palace. I will brave the sea again, one more time, for my Otohime.

I am ashamed and cannot bear to return. I could not bear their eyes, wondering if they wonder if I will betray them again.

I will decide tomorrow. I will walk out on a pier by the ocean and see where my spirit is moved. California, small comfort and small beauty and transience, or–

Tomorrow. Tomorrow.

But I'm not concerned about that now.

Today a man (me) died in California and another man (39 years old – a child!) died in Tennessee, across the desert and the plains and the mountains and just across the river, another country. I came to see him. Came to see this man who, in his 39 small years had earned what I dwelt humbly under Heaven for 1,000 years hoping to deserve. He carried himself as though nothing worried him, nothing at all, but when he saw me, at first he looked at me as if I were not what he had been expecting. I could read the salci of his brain where he wrote "an extremely old man," crossed it out; wrote "a very large bird," crossed it out; wrote "an angel" and drew his quill across the page with a flourish. I believe my old, dry tear ducts kicked a bit. At that moment I knew that this man, whom I had never met, loved me as no one had since I last emerged from the sea.

He sat upon my shoulders. He weighed nothing at all.

And I bore him up. Into the sky, toward immortality. We did not speak to each other, he and I, but I believe that some sentiment passed between us, some commonality, and I believe we understood each other, though our experiences up to that point cannot have been materially similar.

It is not so very bad to live for 1,000 years merely in

order to become an instrument of mortal redemption. I have been to the Dragon Palace, and I know the meaning of those 1,000 years: ten days with the Celestials will balance them. The great joke, I suppose, of all that time on the earth was that I never required redemption. To swim in the sea but once would have been enough.

Diamonds and Toads

"She also learned that talking in her sleep could lead to her bed becoming a real bed of roses and diamonds and other precious stones, none of which were pleasant to sleep on."

E. Craig McKay is a retired college professor. For years he's written non-fiction: wine, food and travel articles for Canadian magazines, and movie critiques for Canadian newspapers. He has written also under the names James W. Marsh and Craig Gambarotto-McKay. Craig is a member of the Writers' Alliance of Newfoundland and Labrador. He lives in Newfoundland and Labrador, Canada during the summer and Almunecar, Spain in winter. Find him online at ecraigmckay.com.

Craig's previous publications include: "The Pledge" in Renaissance Magazine, and "Life in a Box" for Hall Bros Entertainment. He was selected as second runner up for flash fiction by the CBC Literary Competition.

"In addition to wondering what 'happily ever after' would really mean, I was intrigued by the positive potential of spewing forth toads and snakes as well as the unexpected drawbacks of producing jewels and flowers. How would such apparent curses and blessings affect the respective recipients? The results were as much a surprise to me as I hope they will be for my readers."

Away With Words
E. Craig McKay

In days of old, in a land of lakes and forests green, there lived two sisters. Linda, true to her nature, was kind to a woodland elf disguised as an old woman, and the elf caused diamonds and flowers to fall thereafter from her lips at every word. Her nasty sister, Fanny, was rude to the same elf and was saddled with the unhappy situation of producing toads and serpents from her mouth.

This changed the life of both sisters. As one might well imagine, Fanny was not the first choice at dinner parties, whereas Linda became much in demand.

Unhappy Fanny went off to live in isolation in a forested area. The population of vipers and toads in the region rose to the point that most people began to avoid it completely. The snakes preferred to eat birds' eggs to the numerous toads, so while toads and snakes were everywhere underfoot, song birds disappeared completely from the nearby countryside. Fanny acquired a serious dislike for snakes. However, even though she had taken a vow of silence, the resident population was already enormous. Finally she moved to Ireland.

For Linda the future looked bright. The wealth, which spontaneous production of jewels brought, allowed her to live well and to travel in better circles.

A local dandy, Prince Beaumont, learned of her strange

power to produce jewels in this novel manner. The prince decided that she would make an interesting acquisition. He charmed her and carried her off to the castle where he married her and they settled down to live happily ever after.

Or so the story ends, but life goes on.

Fanny did well in Ireland. Since she was not as stupid as she was disagreeable, she acquired skill as a mime and earned a decent living performing at town fairs. Since people often assume that quiet individuals are great thinkers, and mimes are popular at charades, Fanny was well thought of and admired. Ironically, this new-found approval transformed Fanny into a better person. Contrary to expectations she lived happily and quietly in a cottage by the sea.

As for Linda, well, forever is a long, long time.

Within a few weeks Linda discovered that life as a princess was not the proverbial bed of roses. She also learned that talking in her sleep could lead to her bed becoming a real bed of roses and diamonds and other precious stones, none of which were pleasant to sleep on.

Not that her bed was crowded. It was immense. Her suite was immense. Everything at the castle was on a large scale. It was also very lonely.

She had maids, to whom she dared not speak for fear of breaking her word to the prince and his father, the king, not to let anyone outside the royal family know of her secret skill. She had ladies-in-waiting and attendants before whom she must likewise remain speechless. It was the same at all public functions.

Linda lacked the social skills which she would have grown up with at court. She knew not even simple country dancing, let alone the highly stylized and intricate dances popular at court. Even had she spoken any foreign languages they would have been worthless since she was condemned to remain mum.

The negative side of her ability to spew out flowers and jewels had been made obvious on the way back to the castle after meeting the prince in her clearing. At first he was amused, even pleased by stopping and dismounting to gather up the jewels she produced. But, as they neared populated areas, he cautioned her to guard her tongue, or in effect, to keep her mouth shut.

The king, Beaumont II, although clearly as eager as the prince to benefit from the riches of her speech, seemed more than a bit disappointed by her low birth and lack of political connections. She had even heard Queen Gloria complain that the jewels were not of the most fashionable cut.

Soon Linda began to feel more like a golden egg-laying goose than a treasured wife and soul mate. The king had even scheduled a daily recitation period for her during which she was taken to a very private chamber where she was encouraged to talk continuously for one hour. The subject mattered not, as long as she produced a reasonable pile of rare stones. The castle had no shortage of flowers in the meeting chambers and banquet halls.

The queen's verdict was, "She is a peasant; her parents were peasants; do what you like, my son, we do not wish to associate with her."

The prince was not very supportive. He was usually off hunting, riding, shooting, tramping about in the forests with his men-at-arms and young aristocrats, or doing any number of things to which she was not invited.

On one of the rare occasions when she was alone with the prince, Linda tried to explain her feelings. "I wish we could do some things together, Beau. I get so lonely sometimes," she told him while being careful to keep the resultant flood of jewels from spilling to the floor and clattering on the marble.

"Your role is here at court; I must maintain my position among the warriors and nobles of our land. If you are required to do anything, you will be informed. Meanwhile, you had best speak only in the treasury room where we have a carpet to prevent the jewels being marred by contact with hard stone floors." He turned and left the room. Linda carefully dumped the diamonds, emerald, and rubies into a small purse which she would take with her to the treasury room at her appointed time.

Even courtiers, eager to improve their position at court, ultimately gave up trying to ingratiate themselves with her. There is only so much you can say to someone who never responds.

It might have been easier for Linda if she could at least write notes to exchange thoughts. Unfortunately, a young girl who lives in a remote cabin in the woods, where she is forced to do menial work for her mother and sister, is not given a thorough education. Linda could neither read nor write, was unable to do simple arithmetic, and had only the foggiest notion of history, science, or geography.

Linda was pretty and cooperative, but her good nature was concealed by her enforced silence.

It was not surprising that she soon became morose and yearned for a simple life where she could hope to have a friend.

Even her former existence started to seem preferable to the gentle trap she was now in.

She appealed to the king to allow her to move to one of their hunting lodges where she could at least commune with nature. After taking proper precautions that her production of treasure for the royal coffers would continue unabated, the king agreed.

The lodge chosen was not far from where Linda had been born and had lived the first seventeen years of her life. The lodge was well-guarded, so no stranger ever ventured near. The prince came a few times, but clearly had other activities which interested him more. The king was content that his quota of treasure continued to be produced and was periodically transferred to his vaults at the castle. The queen was relieved to be rid of such a hopeless social misfit. Linda was lonely, but learned to enjoy her quiet country life.

Linda was provided with tutors at her country retreat so that she might learn the social graces required of a member of the royal family. One of her tutors was a monk who taught her to read and to do arithmetic. The young monk, Alfred, was a patient and skilled teacher. Linda made good progress and was soon able to read simple books and to perform mathematical calculations. It opened her eyes to possibilities she had never dreamed of.

One day Alfred discovered that Linda had prepared a series of cards with words on them. By using the cards, and writing out the occasional word on blank cards, Linda was able to hold a conversation with the monk without speaking.

Linda had arranged her first message to Alfred on the table where they sat together for her lessons. The cards presented a simple message: "Reading is good. Now, I would like to learn some practical skills."

Alfred read the message and then made one correction. He replaced the card "I" with a card which read "We." "Your Highness is a princess of the royal family. The use of the royal 'we' is your right."

Linda smiled charmingly at his little joke, while being careful to keep her mouth firmly closed, and returned the "I" card.

It was Alfred's turn to laugh, which he did with good spirit. "I understand, Your Highness. I will obtain books on whatever subject you wish and will attempt to be of service."

The first thing Linda asked for was books and manuals which would teach her about jewelry and working in gold and silver. The monk brought such books and found that she was an eager student. Over the next few years she became both knowledgeable and skillful in the fabrication of earrings, broaches, necklaces, and rings. When the king died and Linda was called upon to appear with the prince at his coronation as King Beaumont III, she wore jewelry of her own fabrication. She carried it off well.

She had learned enough in a few years that she could function at court. As time passed, people became so used to the fact that she never spoke that it now failed to provoke comment.

The kingdom was wealthy and was thus strongly defended. Peace was upon the land and famine was no longer a threat to the people. Queen Linda took a keen interest in the education of the children of their realm. She and the king had no offspring of their own and when King Beaumont was fatally injured in a hunting accident, the crown passed to his cousin, Carlos, who ruled an adjoining kingdom.

The secret of her ability to produce jewels and flowers by simply speaking had only ever been known by a few people. It happened that when her husband died, no one else living knew of it.

The new king, King Carlos, provided Linda with a small castle and the surrounding lands which contained several lakes and a tract of forest. She retreated from the world and spent the rest of her life within the borders of her lands. As her personal coat of arms she took the image of a mute swan on a placid pool of water. In a small town which sprang up she established a school directed by the monk Alfred for the education of the children. She was content there and was respected by all.

When in old age she contemplated her life, she decided that though her gift had not led to a perfect life, it was much better than what she would have experienced without it. Though she had not always been happy while she lived, she died without regrets.

An obelisk was raised to recognize her contributions. After consultation with the monk Alfred, King Carlos decreed that her simple monument be decorated with a swan wearing a crown and bearing the inscription: *Love and Truth need not speak loudly to be heard.*

Snow White

"Snovhit – Snow White, Halfdan thought – she lives up to her name. Never had Halfdan seen skin so pale, or hair so black. It couldn't be natural."

Duncan Eagleson is an author, painter, animator, leather sculptor, and award winning maskmaker. He contributed art to Neil Gaiman's Sandman, *adapted and illustrated Anne Rices'* The Witching Hour *and made masks for Wes Craven's* Cursed, *the Big Apple Circus, and mask magician Jeff McBride. He is the writer and illustrator of the online series "Railwalker: Tales of the Urban Shaman." He has written and illustrated a number of other comics and graphic novels including the online series "ArcMage," and the short story "Harkinton" for the anthology* 2012: Final Prayer. *You can see his work online at duncaneagleson.com, eaglesondesign.com and maskmaker.com.*

"I wanted to find an unexpected consequence that arose from some central incident or important piece of magic in the tale. Thinking over several tales, it occurred to me that Snow White rises from the dead, and I wondered, could she actually have been something like a zombie or a vampire? Snow White is a tale from northern Europe, and, like many Norse tales, prominently features dwarfs. So I looked for some undead creature in Norse lore, and discovered the aptrganger, or draug.

"What would the Prince do, if his new bride turned out to be a flesh-eating undead thing? Well, he'd go back to the dwarfs for help, of course."

195

Snøvhit

Duncan Eagleson

Rothgar clamped his teeth together and swallowed hard. The corpse of the child in Helga's arms made his stomach lurch. He wasn't sure why. Though barely twenty summers, he had seen men slaughtered in battle, had even given captive warriors the red wings himself, cutting open their backs to drag their lungs out behind them. Granted, he had found that a hard task the first time or two, but even then, neither his stomach nor his nerve had betrayed him, not as they threatened to do now.

Somehow this was different. Perhaps because it was a child. Perhaps because the body was not cut with blades, but torn with teeth, muscles ripped from the bones, the bones themselves gnawed upon, as wolves might do. Perhaps it was because he saw the marks and knew them, not for the marks of the teeth of wolves, but those of a human. Rothgar glanced at his father. King Halfdan was pale and angry, hands fisted at his sides.

"Wolves," the king said quietly. He glanced about at the gathered jarls, huscarls and villagers, as if daring them to disagree. "My heart bleeds for you, Helga. I will send men to hunt these wolves."

Rothgar was sure his father did not believe this the work of wolves. He knew the old man had seen too many wolf kills in his time not to know the difference. He had to recognize the marks as human teeth. But unlike his son, he would have no way of knowing what human teeth had made them.

Helga was drawn away by her husband, and the villagers turned to follow them, to prepare the body for burning. The jarls and huscarls began speaking quietly among themselves, planning for the hunt as they headed back toward the mead-hall. Rothgar sighed and turned away. He would not be joining the hunt tomorrow. He would visit the smithy tonight, and tomorrow he would start for the mountains.

Rothgar shivered in the biting mountain wind and wrapped his cloak more tightly about himself. The cloak was heavy reindeer leather, trimmed with wolf fur and lined with wool, and had been perfectly efficient at keeping him warm on hunting expeditions. The one time he had been in the mountains before, it had been summer, and although he had encountered the dverger, it had been in the lower reaches, nowhere near the towering peaks that hid the legendary gates of Svartalfheim itself. Rothgar was a viking warrior, no pampered southron princeling, yet the bitter cold of the high mountains in winter was something far beyond what he had ever experienced before. He now regretted not having followed his first impulse, which had been to purchase garments from the nomadic tribes that ranged the northern areas of his father's realm. The tribesmen faced the harshest of weather as a matter of course, and they would, Rothgar thought, know the best ways of staving off the cold. Yet when he'd made his decision to come here, he had felt a certain urgency about the errand, and the nomadic herdsmen would not be seen in his country for several months yet. So he had chosen to rely upon the embroidered woolen garments and leather tunic, along with the cloak, which had kept him warm and comfortable on the coldest of hunting forays.

He regretted now having presumptuously taken the smith's hammer by force, though he still saw no other choice. Sven the Smith had glowered ominously and predicted dire consequences of what he called Rothgar's "theft." He was probably right; smiths usually were about that sort of thing. But Rothgar would accept whatever punishment the gods might mete out, if he could only rid his land of this curse. Sven had refused to accompany Rothgar, to guide him and open the gates of Svartalfheim for him. He could have forced the issue, but he had considered that confiscating the smith's second-best hammer was a lesser evil than forcing the man to come with him. He would return the hammer if he was able when all this was done. All his sources had agreed that gaining entrance to the citadel of the dverger required knocking on their gates with the hammer of a smith, and to complete his mission, access he must gain.

Rothgar was seriously considering that he might have to turn back if he did not want to die on these barren crags when he saw the dark shape on the icy cliff that loomed above him. The cliff rose hundreds of feet, sheer gray granite, dusted with snow and rimed with ice, but in the center of the cliff face, a dark shape like the shadow of a pointed arch was free of both. It was tall, a hundred feet at least, and half that across. At first it seemed a strange incursion of some dark rock, black basalt growing in the granite face, but as he approached, Rothgar could see that its edges were far too smooth and regular for it to be a natural formation. Staring through frozen eyelashes, he thought he could make out runes inscribed upon it, but each time he tried to read them, they would change or vanish, only to reappear a second later. There could be no question, he thought: this had to be the entrance to Svartalfheim.

The wind was picking up again, blowing biting snow into his face, and he had to lean forward, head down, to stagger toward the cliff face, plodding ahead, placing one numbed foot before the other. Blinded by the snow, he nearly stumbled into the rock before he realized he had actually reached it. He leaned against the black stone, fumbling at his belt for the hammer. Raising it with the last of his strength, he struck three blows upon the rock, then three more, and finally, nearly collapsing, the final three. His last blows barely had any power to them, and were driven more by the weight of the hammer than by his weakened arm.

Rothgar sank to his knees. They didn't hear me, he thought. I made it all the way here, and they won't open the gates because I can't strike them loudly enough to be heard. Then he sank into unconsciousness.

Rothgar awoke to stinging pain in his hands and feet. He was lying on a pallet, covered by furs, in a dimly lit room that smelled of smoke and iron.

"Hands and feet hurting?" asked a deep, gravelly voice. "Count yourself lucky they can still feel aught at all."

Rothgar knew at once where he must be. "You heard me," he said. His voice was a hoarse croak. "My knocking, I mean."

"Aye, we heard ye. Think ye a pebble falls against our gates that we hear not?"

Rothgar turned his head to see the speaker. The man was short and wide, with a beard that reached his belt. Though his graying hair and beard still showed that they had once been red, his skin was near as dark as that of a Saracen. This was no surprise – Rothgar had met this dwarf before.

"Durin, is it not?" he asked, propping himself up on one elbow.

"Aye, Durin it is, Rothgar Halfdansson." The dverg stepped to the side of Rothgar's pallet, holding out a drinking horn. "Drink this, it will help warm you, and tell Durin why the son of King Halfdan has near killed himself to reach our halls in the midst of winter."

The mead was sweet and warm, and spread a welcome glow through Rothgar's torso.

"It's about my wife," he said. The dwarf chuckled, but there was little humor in it.

"Aye," he said, "Durin judged it would be. Can never say we dinna warn you."

The council chamber of Motsognir was high-ceilinged, cut from the raw stone of the mountain. In the center was a large fire pit, a pile of logs flaming and sending smoke up into the darkened heights above. Ranged about it were finely carved benches, seating enough for a hundred, though only eight now sat upon them – seven dwarfs and one man, with Motsognir himself installed above them in the high seat. They were, Rothgar gathered, all that was left of the once proud dverger race.

The old dwarf king's beard was white as snow, but he carried himself as straight as a young soldier. His raiment was finely wrought with gold and jewels and elaborate embroidery, upon his head he wore the iron crown of the dverger, and at his side rested an extraordinary sword that could only have been the brand of Volund. Their court had seen better days, yet the dverger king had welcomed Rothgar as befitted a visiting prince. His chief councilor, Durin, continued to treat Rothgar with more familiarity and less formality, which Rothgar found he preferred. He had enough of courtly formality at home. Nevertheless, he was a petitioner here, and it would behoove him to follow the old dwarf king's lead. Motsognir would hear nothing of Rothgar's errand until they had feasted on courses of roast pork, venison stew, carrots and cabbage, a roast goose, and finally barley bread with butter and honey. After the meal was cleared away by Vindalf, the youngest of the dwarfs, they performed the rite of sumbel, horns of mead raised to their ancestors and to the mighty heroes of ancient times, Motsognir graciously naming several of Rothgar's forebears, with whom he seemed to have been personally acquainted. Finally, the formalities of hospitality and diplomacy done at last, the dwarf king got round to enquiring as to Rothgar's mission.

"There is a curse upon my land," said Rothgar. "The curse of the draug."

"Aptrgangr." Durin nodded.

"Ye wot," said Motsognir, "that to express surprise at this would be less than honest."

"Aye," said Rothgar. "Durin has already reminded me of your warning, which I heard, but got not at the time. Ye ne'er spoke the word 'draug.'"

"It was not given to us to know such detail. We knew only enough to warn you of an ill fate."

"Before this I had heard only that the draugar were hideous monsters." Rothgar shook his head. "And so they are, but none e'er told me they could come in the shape of beauty and love."

"What form does this draug take?"

"What form? As best I wot, whatever form she chooses. Wolf or cat, beast or bird, she can change her shape at will, or so it seems."

"The king meant to ask," said Durin, "what manner of draug? The drinker of blood? Eater of flesh? Consumer of the spirit?"

Rothgar gave a bitter laugh. "Consumer of the spirit, certes, though I wist that is but the effect, and not the primary source of the creature's nourishment, which I wot you ask after. Children have vanished, their gnawed bones discovered later discarded in the forests. She is an eater of the flesh, so I adduce."

"That is bad," said Durin. "For the drinkers of blood, there are easier remedies. They may be pierced with a stake of ash, exposed to the sun, burned, or buried in salt..."

"Please, friend Durin," said Rothgar, holding up a hand, "speak not to me of remedies that will avail me naught against this creature that lives in my very home. I beg you, rather, speak to me of those deeds that will end this curse upon my people."

Motsognir uttered a somber grunt. "For the eaters of the flesh," he said, "Ye must wrestle them unarmed, naked, hand to hand, and having bested, hold them still to take their head. Moreover, the only blade that will cut the flesh of the draug is that of the draug's own brand."

There was a long silence in the hall, as man and dwarf considered the implications of this.

Finally, Rothgar sighed. "So much have I heard from the hedge-witches and seidhir," he said. "But I see not how that can be done, for she is as powerful in her limbs as any five warriors together, nor does she herself possess a sword, or even a scramasax. I come to you because I ween that this draug would ne'er have walked the earth without the wyrd-craft of the dverger, and hoped ye could grant some rede of more practical aid."

Motsognir looked at the floor, and the others of his court stirred uncomfortably. Durin studiously took out his long-stemmed pipe and began filling it with dwarfish pipeweed. No one spoke. When Durin had his pipe smoking well, he finally broke the silence. "Durin wots as Rothgar the son of Halfdan speaks soothly," he said. "Yet she that became your wife bargained for and earned the magic of the dverger. Seven years Snovhit labored here, our very thrall maiden. When her allotted time was served, we bestowed upon her the magic she had requested. 'Twas only fair and right, and the dverger keep their bargains."

"And to become a draug was her request?"

"Nay," said Skafith. Older even than the king, his face lined and wrinkled, his hair pure white, Skafith's white beard near reached his ankles, and was braided with bones and charms. "Not to become draug, but to have whate'er she wished for. When she came to face the poisoned death her foul mother wreaked upon her, belike she wished for more of life. Yet the Norns do not lengthen a strand again once it be severed."

"And so..." said Rothgar, "this?"

"A spell is spun," said Durin. "It is but a device, a tool. A sword wots not who or what it kills, nor does a spell have the discernment of a human mind. The spell assured her whate'er she wished for, and since she could not be made truly alive again, it made her aptrgangr – a draug."

"So dverger wyrdcraft is responsible for her state, and yet you contend that the dverger themselves bear no blame in this?"

"As ye say. Such result was never our intent."

"And is there no help you can give me? Or my people?"

Motsognir looked grim, Durin shook his head sadly, but Skafith looked into the shadows of the ceiling and cleared his throat. "Methinks there may be a way," he said. He looked to each of the dwarfs there assembled. "Is Snovhit not inheritor of the Jotunbrand, which lies within our own halls? And have not all draugar barrows?"

Rothgar looked from one dwarf to another, watching as their looks lightened, and several nodded to themselves. That they held in their keeping a sword which must belong to his wife he understood, but the significance of Skafith's reference to a barrow escaped him.

Surprised as he was, Edgtheow the Geat managed not to show any sign when he felt something touch his leg. He glanced at Halfdan, but the king was deep in his cups, and seemed not to have noticed. Toes stroked Edgtheow's inner thigh, and Snovhit smiled at him across the table. She'd been flirting with him all evening, and he was aroused, but uneasy, pondering what to do. He was, after all, a guest here, a petitioner at Halfdan's hall, and though he had not seen Rothgar for many years, the man was his foster-brother, and this woman was Rothgar's wife.

"Kina!" Snovhit called to the young thrall. "The king is weary. See him to his chamber." As the thrall scurried to the king's side, Halfdan stirred. "Weary? No..." he said, and then peered about the hall with bleary eyes. Most of his jarls were asleep or retired. "Well, perhaps..." he muttered.

"Come, sire," said Kina, taking his arm, and the king stirred himself and allowed her to lead him away.

Snovhit fixed her luminous black eyes again on Edgtheow. "Perhaps thou art weary also," she said, smiling again, "and I should see thee to thy chamber."

There it was again. She had a peculiarly old-fashioned way of speaking, even when flirting. Edgtheow wasn't sure what to make of this woman. Even in Geatland, he had heard of his foster brother's marriage, though he had never met the woman before, nor even heard of her, which was odd, the son of Halfdan marrying a woman of whom so little was known. Gossip said she was beautiful, and here gossip spoke true. Though she had less meat on her bones than Edgtheow normally liked, she was fair of face, with the palest skin and the blackest hair he had ever seen. And she had a way about her. When she fixed those huge dark eyes upon him, it was nigh impossible to look away.

Gossip also said that Rothgar had saved her from a witch's curse, that she had lain asleep for a hundred years, that she had been a captive of the dwarfs, or a dragon, or a sorcerer. There were a dozen variations Edgtheow had heard, and though he did not doubt his foster brother's bravery or resourcefulness, he had credited none of those tales, at least until now. With her old-fashioned speech and peculiar looks, he could well imagine she might be an ancient princess, transported or preserved through many years until Rothgar had found her and brought her to Halfdan's court. Yet he would believe none of it until he had spoken to Rothgar. It had not seemed polite to enquire of Snovhit herself, nor of the king.

The questing toes had reached his groin, and Snovhit's eyebrows rose, amused, at the hardness she felt there. "Not so far in your cups that you cannot stand, noble Edgtheow?" she said. The velvet voice caressed his soul as the toes continued to caress his hardness beneath his breeks, and Edgtheow knew he was lost.

The pale blue of false dawn on the horizon and the sparkling of the stars promised a clear, cold day ahead. Edgtheow leaned against the wall of the mead-hall, watching the mist rise in the hollows between the hills. Snovhit had been insatiable, and Edgtheow was exhausted but unable to sleep. She had left him in the small hours, and he had finally risen from his pallet, wrapped himself in his cloak, and walked out to see the sunrise.

From the mist a figure appeared, plodding slowly across the silent village. The man was wrapped in a fur-trimmed cloak and carried a long package, wrapped in cloth, the length of a spear, though wider at one end. He stopped abruptly when he noticed Edgtheow.

The Geat walked forward to meet him. "Good morrow," he said. The figure looked around, as if seeking some escape. Closer, Edgtheow recognized him. "Rothgar?"

Rothgar looked back at him, astonished. "Edgtheow?" His face lightened. "When did you arrive here?"

"This – that is, yesterday – morn. But come, my foster brother. What ill betides? You do not embrace me, but stand here hiding your booty, sneaking into your own home like a thief with his swag."

Rothgar glanced guiltily at the package he now held half-hidden behind himself, and Edgtheow thought they both had guilty secrets now. "Ill betides indeed," said Rothgar. "Have ye heard from my father of our woes?"

Edgtheow shook his head. "Naught of any ill did the king speak."

"Yet had he done, he could not have told the half." Rothgar sighed, glancing back toward the mountains.

"Hath been so many years," Edgtheow asked, "that ye would no longer trust your Edgtheow, share with him your darkest woe?"

Rothgar looked the man up and down. The Danish king's son was a big man, but even so, the Geat towered over him. In their youth, Rothgar and his brother Heogar had called their foster-brother "the Jotun," as he had seemed such a giant.

"Aye," Rothgar said at last, "perhaps 'the Jotun' could help me after all." He smiled, and brought the unwieldy package out before him. "Mayhap you are the only man I know could raise this brand. Come, let us seek a fire and some mead, and I will tell you all." Rothgar sighed, and then clapped a hand to his side. "But first," he added, "I have a hammer to return."

* * * * *

Late the following night – or early in the morn two days after, if one reckoned more closely – the Danish king Halfdan stared blearily down the length of the mead-hall, listening to the snoring of his jarls and huscarls. Rothgar and Edgtheow had departed on a hunt early the previous morn. Damn the boy, he thought (though the gods knew Rothgar was no longer a boy), always dashing off somewhere or other. He couldn't stay at home even in the dead of winter. With a groan, he levered himself up from the high seat and turned to leave the hall.

Halfdan Frothisson was not a happy king. His bones ached even in the warm weather. Piles aggrieved his backside with the teeth of vermin and his manhood stood to service only reluctantly now, despite the beauty and attentiveness of his favorite thrall, Kina. And he hadn't the head for mead that he once had.

Halfdan made his way slowly from the hall toward his chamber. Usually, if he drank enough, his knees stopped aching, or at least he ceased to notice them, but tonight pain flared in them like hot coals. He was halfway to the door of his quarters when his daughter-in-law appeared at his side.

"Let me help you to your chamber, my lord," said Snovhit.

Snovhit – Snow White, Halfdan thought – she lives up to her name. Never had Halfdan seen skin so pale, or hair so black. It couldn't be natural.

The woman would be queen soon. His son had certainly married a beautiful one. Normally Halfdan preferred a woman more substantial, but tonight, despite Snovhit's gaunt form, he found her bewitching. She put her arm around him to support him, and he fancied he could feel the softness of her skin through his woolen robes. The old warhorse in his breeks snorted and twitched its interest, surprising Halfdan and embarrassing him briefly. She's my gods-rotted daughter-in-law, my son's wife, I shouldn't be thinking of her like a thrall to be tumbled, he thought, but there it was. They were at his chamber door now, and she was helping him inside, and he was hoping she wouldn't leave too quickly. The pain in his knees was either gone, or just forgotten.

The two young men lay in the gorse at the edge of the garth, watching the hall.

"She has not left the mead-hall," Edgtheow whispered. "Mayhap she will not feed tonight." Edgtheow had not confessed to Rothgar about coupling with Snovhit, but the experience had made it easy for him to believe that his foster brother's spouse was a draugr.

"She is wont always to feed on the dark moon," Rothgar hissed back. "Something is wrong."

"Surely she would not feast upon your father's jarls. She would betray herself."

Rothgar thought about this. It did not seem likely his wife would endanger her position by killing one of his father's men in his own mead-hall. And yet the dverger had warned him that the draugr might sometimes live on the life-force itself, sucking out the pith from a person's soul without drawing blood. This she could do without fearing discovery. "We should go in," he whispered. His foster-brother looked at him dubiously, then shrugged and followed.

The snores of the jarls threatened to bring down the

very rafters of the high hall. Rothgar and Edgtheow crept silently through the hall, the Danish king's son carrying the long package. The high seat was empty. They passed beyond it, and drew into the corridor behind. Rothgar looked up and down the hallway. The door to his own chamber, which he shared with Snovhit, was dark, but flickering light showed beneath his father's door. Feeble moans issued from within. The two moved swiftly down the hall. Rothgar reached for the door, then stopped and glanced at Edgtheow.

"If he's with Kina..." Rothgar whispered.

"We'll back out and he'll never notice," said Edgtheow. Rothgar nodded. Shifting the wrapped weapon to his left hand, he turned to the door again, but Edgtheow whispered, "Wait..." Rothgar watched as his foster brother dropped his cloak, and then quickly shrugged out of his clothes. "Just in case..." the huge Geat said.

Rothgar nodded agreement. The dverger had been specific about this. The warrior who wrestled with the draugar must be naked to prevail.

When Edgtheow signaled he was ready, Rothgar un-wrapped the hilt of the great sword he carried, lifted the latch as quietly as he could, and gently swung the door open. The moaning had become louder, but now stopped. Rothgar thought at first they had been discovered, but they were not. No one bellowed at them, nor did either of the chamber's occupants so much as glance toward the door.

On the pallet, Snovhit lay atop the body of the king. Both were fully dressed. Her head was bent to his throat, his head turned aside, his face white as hers now, clearly dead or dying. Rothgar gave an involuntary cry of pain and grief. He cut his cry short, realizing too late that he had betrayed them, but Edgtheow had already launched himself across the room.

Snovhit reared back and turned as Edgtheow leapt, trying to meet his attack, but the giant Geat was too quick for her and landed on her back, the force of his leap tumbling them both to the other side of the pallet. Rothgar dashed forward, stooped to his father, but for all there was no blood, it was clear that the old man was already dead.

On the floor beyond, the draug and the Geat wrestled. The creature's skin, always pale, had become grey-white and waxy, her form more wiry and muscled, her hands clawed. Grappling her from behind, Edgtheow had wrapped his legs around Snovhit's, and got his left arm beneath hers, his left hand behind her neck, and held her right wrist fast in his right hand. He was taller by far, and easily twice the weight of the woman, who was gaunt as any corpse, yet he held her only with the greatest of difficulty.

"Quick, Rothgar!" Edgtheow called. "The blade!"

Even freed of its wrappings the sword was heavy, an enormous blade nearly as long as Rothgar himself, the massive hilt of weighty gold, engraved with all manner of design. With an effort, Rothgar raised the weapon above his head, and then hesitated. He did not see how he could sever the draug's head without also killing his foster-brother.

Edgtheow seemed to understand Rothgar's predicament and he rolled, using Snovhit's own struggles to turn them over, the draug now below him. He reared back, holding the monster's head down, giving Rothgar a clear shot, the only danger now that Rothgar would strike the Geat's hand as well as the draug's neck. Rothgar brought the sword down with all his strength.

The point of the sword struck the stone flags with a mighty clang, the vibration of the impact ringing through Rothgar's bones. He had overshot – the sword was so long, it struck the floor without striking the draug. Rothgar tugged at it, but the point was buried deep in the flagstone it had split. With a hiss, Snovhit broke free from Edgtheow's grip. Her arm swept up, and the giant blade was ripped from Rothgar's hands. Like a seal diving into water, Snovhit dove into the stone flags and vanished, taking the great blade with her.

Rothgar and Edgtheow stared stupidly at the spot where she had disappeared. The giant Geat looked up at his foster brother.

Rothgar shrugged. "They can travel through stone and earth," he said. "Or so the dverger tell me."

"Then we have lost," said Edgtheow.

"Not necessarily."

As her kind might do, Snovhit the draug moved through earth and rock like a fish through water. She smiled as she swam toward her barrow, reflecting that her foolish husband, in attempting to kill her, had instead ensured her immortality. Thanks to Rothgar, she now bore the Jotunbrand, the giant's sword forged by the smith Volund, the only weapon in the world that could do her harm.

Yet she was troubled. That her husband had wielded the Jotunbrand, however ineffectually, meant that he had visited Svartalfheim, and that the dwarfs had betrayed her, giving the sword into his keeping. She would be avenged on the dverger for that betrayal, but it was meet she gang warily, for though were but seven of them left, the dwarfs were crafty and powerful, and would be dangerous foes.

She emerged into her barrow with relief, and then cried out in anger and surprise. Where before her lair had been a comforting womb of dark stone and earth, now the sharp angles of crystal threw back reflections on every hand, and points of quartz bit at her feet and knees as she staggered and fell. She smelled dwarf, and heard a loud hissing, boiling sound. She turned to flee back into the earth, but found the way blocked, another great crystal grown up to fill the gap through which she had just entered. Snovhit dropped the great sword and gave vent to a scream of rage and hatred that was echoed back at her in vibrations of the crystalline walls of what was now her prison.

When Edgtheow and Rothgar reached the barrow that overlooked the lake, they found seven dwarfs standing before it. Three of them stepped forward to greet the two young men. Motsognir, the last king of the dverger, was flanked by the dwarfish seidhir, Skafith, and his councilor, Durin.

"She is trapped within," said Motsognir.

Edgtheow looked from Rothgar to the dverger.

"We lined her barrow with crystal," said Durin, "and sealed it once she entered."

"And this will hold her?" Edgtheow asked.

"The draugar can travel through earth and solid stone," said Skafith, the bones and charms woven in his beard clicking and clattering. "But they cannot travel through crystal. She is well and truly prisoned."

"And so," asked Rothgar, "she will trouble the Danes no

more?"

"At least until the last of the dverger has passed forever from Svartalfheim," the old seidhir said.

"Now for the final surance," said Skafith. The dwarfs turned, facing the mound in a semi-circle. Skafith began to chant in a language neither the young Dane nor his companion recognized. The other six joined their voices to that of their seidhir, and all raised their hands, each holding a hammer toward the sky. Their chant became louder, and Rothgar felt the earth beneath him begin to quiver and shake. There was a sound like mountains grinding together, and the low mound of the barrow began slowly to slide toward the mere. It vanished beneath the water, as the waves rushed in to fill the hole where the barrow had once stood. Within moments the rumbling ceased, and the waters calmed, and there was nothing to show that there had ever been any mound beside the mere. The dverger ceased their chanting and returned their hammers to their belts. They turned again toward the two men, and the dwarfish king stepped forward.

"Hail, Rothgar, King of the Danes," he said. "For I wot that king now ye are."

"Little enough pleasure does that give me," said Rothgar. "To become king at the slaughter of my sire. And there has yet to be a Thing to select a new king. I may not be the Danes' choice."

The old seidhir of the dwarfs stepped forward, and laid a hand on Rothgar's arm. "One day," he said, "poets will sing of Rothgar, king of the Danes." He turned to regard Edgtheow. "And also of his friend the Geat, and eke of noble Edgtheow's son, a great hero whose name will ever be linked with that of

215

Rothgar."

Rothgar looked at his friend and smiled ruefully. "That my name should be linked with that of progeny of yours pleases me well," he said.

Edgtheow laughed. "My foster-brother speaks like a king already," he said. "An ye speak so on my behalf to Helmut, and persuade him to accept my were-gild, a debt will lie between you and I such as can never be repaid."

"Say not never," said Rothgar, shaking his head, "for such words taunt the gods."

Within the mere, deep in the crystal-lined barrow, Snovhit the draug snarled at the world outside her prison, and then looked down at her own belly. "We need but wait, my little Grinder," she said, and her clawed hands rubbed at the white skin of her midsection, caressing as she imagined the swelling that would soon grow there. "The dwarfs' power wanes daily, and they are not long upon Midgard. Soon they will be gone, and we freed, and then you shall feast upon the flesh of the men who follow my dear husband." She lay back upon the painful points of her crystal prison, and regarded the great sword. "We shall have our vengeance on my Rothgar, and perhaps your father Edgtheow, as well." And though it was far, far too soon for such, she imagined she felt a movement within her belly, as if the monster growing there had heard and responded.

Cinderella

"The eyes of a squirrel magnet glittered back at me darkly, and it mocked me with its spatula."

Nicci Mechler is an artist and writer living in Cincinnati, pursing a Masters in English from Northern Kentucky University, which happens to be over the river and through the woods. She favors red shoes, and always keeps an eye out for wolves.

Her work has previously appeared in The Licking River Review, NKU Expressed, The Lost Cause Review, and various zines. For more about information about Nicci, go to www.evematrix.com.

"Happily ever after never satisfied me. As a child, I always wanted to know what happened after the HEA ending. Who wrote the story but the woman who won the prince and the kingdom? What if Cinderella had secrets? What if the step sisters weren't so wicked? What if the prince wasn't so charming? Wicked women have always fascinated me. Who is the most wicked of them all? I'd keep my eye on the princess."

"Cinderella's Niece" is a perfect story for those who like their humor served with a liberal helping of snark.

Cinderella's Niece
Nicci Mechler

"Happily ever after," she snorted derisively, shaking her head. "It's the publicists that come up with that crap. Believe you me, it doesn't reflect reality in the slightest." A bleached-out blonde curl tumbled free of her shower cap, and a half-inch-long ash from her lipstick-stained cigarette fell right into the bowl in front of her. She didn't seem to notice.

I watched the grey and black speckles disappear into the phlegmy yellow batter, and wondered if I shouldn't just fake a little illness to get me out of the house. But no, I promised Mom I'd do this. She felt a little guilty about how she'd treated Auntie C back when they were teens, and now I was paying for it. I chewed on my pen cap, and stared down at a crack in the lemon-yellow vinyl faux-tiles.

It'd been a few years since Aunt Cindi had walked down the aisle with her Prince Charming. To me, he'd always been the beer gut in the recliner. Time hasn't been what you might call kind to either one of 'em. One hundred and fifteen plus years, two packs a day, and serious gambling problems have made them what they are today. And... I'm still not sure what that is.

The cigarette continued to bob between her lips as she spoke and stirred. Spoke and stirred. Coughed, spoke and stirred. "I was a looker in my day, I tell you. And your Uncle,

219

well. Every girl in these parts was after him, yes they were. His family was rich, powerful..." She started to sigh, but finished in a hacking cough. "He seemed like such a gem when we were first married, but he changed. They all do, I'll tell you that right now." Auntie C's seriousness dissolved as she moved on to her favorite topic – herself. "Did I tell you about the shoes I was wearing when we met? Oh, gorgeous, gorgeous." She continued to prattle on about her conjured footwear, inadvertently sprinkling more ashes into the mixing bowl.

I pushed the black frames of my glasses up my nose, slid off the stool by the counter, and went over to the fridge. Mother'd been in therapy for years after the wedding, always going on about how evil Auntie C was, and how she stole everyone's hopes and dreams away, marrying the only bachelor worth having.

Mom got over it eventually – and started dating married men.

Though, for years, she'd persisted in saying her stepsister was Evil incarnate. Looking around the trailer, I had trouble believing it. Unless you could trap human souls in cheesy plastic knick-knacks, I didn't see any evidence of evil (covert or otherwise) going on around here. Still, mom had asked me to come and look around. She had a feeling something strange was *going on*. She said it just like that too, with *emphasis*. It was my duty, she'd said, to check it out for her, and it kept me from having to suffer through another of my mother's experimental family 'recipes.'

The sound of sugar scraping on plastic continued from behind me, as Auntie C doctored the pre-mixed batter with a little more oomph. I thought Mom had once told me my Uncle was a raging diabetic, but...

I hadn't seen Uncle P.C. all day. He wasn't in his favorite chair when I came in. I'd never seen him leave it on my previous visits to the 'Palace on Wheels' (double wide). It'd been a while since I'd visited them. Since college, my infrequent visits became almost non-existent. Mother's reason for asking me to come here seemed a little silly. I was only slightly uneasy that I hadn't seen my Uncle all day.

I wrapped my hand around the handle, wrinkling my nose in distaste at the pea green fridge door. The eyes of a squirrel magnet glittered back at me darkly, and it mocked me with its spatula. 'Kiss the Cook' it proclaimed, in blood red lettering. I stuck out my tongue at it, a ritual I'd repeated since I was six, opened the fridge, and peered inside. I blinked, surveying the contents of the humming cooling unit. She could have single-handedly kept the Tupperware business going – the fridge was packed. And nothing was labeled. Something moved. I was, for a moment, afraid.

"Uh. Auntie C?" I said, interrupting her nostalgic monologue, "I'm going to get a drink." I leaned against the door, shutting it quickly before anything tried to make an escape.

"Yes, all right, dear," she said, waving me toward the back door with a goopy spoon. The batter was looking a little grey. "Hurry back, I haven't told you about my wedding dress yet."

I cringed inwardly, and stepped out the back door, breathing in a few lungfuls of fresh air. I would have lingered longer, but the yard gnomes were staring at me. I thought I saw one gnash its little gnome teeth. "Smoke must be getting to me," I said aloud, walking down the path toward the garage. It'd been a while since I'd been back here, and the path was partially overgrown.

For as long as I could remember, Auntie C kept the soft drinks for the kids in the garage. She stored them alongside the freezer full of TV dinners and cuts of meat. She had a stockpile worthy of a true paranoid delusional – the only thing missing was a stack of gas masks and some four-foot thick bunker doors. Mom said it had something to do with the Depression. I didn't really try to figure it out, it was safer in fairy-tale families if you just accepted some things, and left the rest alone.

I pulled my cell phone out of my jacket pocket, and dialed up my mother. She answered on the second ring. "Mother. She's telling me again. If I have to listen to the fairy godmother intervention story one more time..."

"Relax, Neva. Just remember what we talked about," she tried for soothing, and missed.

"Relax? I'm wandering around Auntie Cindi's house looking for evidence. I don't see why it has to be me. I was starting to feel like a normal person – no pixie dust or goblins at a party in years."

I stepped into the garage, and kicked something on the floor, sending it skittering across the concrete. It ricocheted off a twelve pack of beer. I bent, and picked up Uncle P.C.'s signet ring.

"That's odd," I muttered to myself, but also to my mother, who was still on the phone with me. I reached up and pulled the cord on the bare lightbulb fixture in the garage.

"What's that, sweetie?" She seemed very interested all

222

of a sudden.

"Why are you suddenly concerned with Uncle P.C.'s fidelity? You don't really think he's, how did you put it?, 'making time' with the witch next door, do you?" I waited – she didn't answer me.

Something caught my eye over by the freezer. Uncle P.C.'s engraved, gold-plated Zippo. That shouldn't have been in here. Suddenly, I had to look, had to know. I moved across the garage, and unlocked the freezer. The lid seemed to be stuck, probably frozen, but I struggled with it, ignoring my mother's soft questions.

I pried open the freezer, and was confronted with something that looked a lot like an Elvis ice cube. Somehow I doubted my Uncle had fallen on there all on his own. (Let alone knocked himself out with a petrified, now dented, T-bone, partially covered himself up with chicken TV dinners, and locked the door.)

"Well, that's just great," I muttered into the phone.

"What?" my mother asked.

"He's in the freezer," I informed her softly, letting the lid drop closed with a hollow thud.

"Damn," she said.

"Damn? That's all you have to say?" I had a bad feeling about this.

"Yes, damn... that half-pint Rumple-whatever won again."

It occurred to me that she'd probably been drinking.

"He won what?" I was beginning to wish that I was adopted.

"The pool, he won the pool. We've been doing it for

years now. The last time I won was back when Snow White got the ice pick," she paused to revel briefly in her former glory, "but that little rhyming bastard's been hot for the last few years. He predicted modus operandi for the last three celebrity fairy tale murders."

"Mom?" I asked.

"Yes, dear?" She sounded a little huffy still, but she managed to sound a bit concerned too.

"Please don't call me. Ever. Again." I picked up a soda, locked the freezer, and turned out the light. She knew I meant it – she'd call back in the morning. Her clock was set different than mine. Ever after doesn't exist, not really.

"Don't be silly, dear."

"Goodbye, Mother." I terminated the call with a little press of a button, and turned back toward Auntie's house. If lady luck was with me today, I'd find my car keys quick. I'd be outta there before anybody could say 'Once Upon a Time.'

Beauty and the Beast

"'Getting old,' Belle sighed. 'It's a bitch.'"

Kate Larkindale is currently a Wellington-based writer, cinema manager, film reviewer and mother to two boys. She is constantly amazed that she has any time for writing, but doesn't sleep much. She can be found online at katelarkindale.blogspot.com.

Kate's stories have appeared in many places of late, including literary magazines such as Residential Aliens, A Fly in Amber, Halfway Down The Stairs, The Barrier Island Review, *and the anthologies* Drastic Measures *and* Daily Flash, *to name a few.*

"Surprise, Surprise" takes place in a modern setting, fifty years after the "Happily Ever After" of the "Beauty" and her "Beast."

Surprise, Surprise
Kate Larkindale

The train rattled to a stop, brakes squealing in protest. Belle was thrown forward, jolted awake by the sudden arrival at the station. She squinted out the window at the platform, searching for the station's name.

"Help!" she cried, leaping to her feet as she saw the sign and realized she was home. Still half-asleep, she gathered her many bags and hurried down the aisle to the door, making it through just as the warning bell began its manic chiming.

She waited until the train had eased its way out of the station before wearily dragging the bags inside. It was early evening and the large sunglasses perched on her nose made everything dim and shadowy. She stumbled once as she made her way inside the station proper, but managed to keep upright by grabbing hold of a handily placed railing. Peering around, she searched the waiting room for her husband.

"Damn!" Belle almost stamped her foot in exasperation. It was not the first time Samuel had forgotten to pick her up.

A line of taxis waited outside the station, drivers lounging against their cars as they chatted and smoked their foul smelling cigarettes. Belle held onto her bags tightly as she walked the line, searching out the most salubrious looking cab before sliding in.

"Thirty-eight Tiergarten Way," she commanded, slamming the door behind her. She sank back in the seat, exhausted again already.

"Don't ever get old," she snarled to the driver.

"Excuse me?" The man spoke with a thick accent. He was dark skinned, but not African, Belle was sure of that.

"Getting old," Belle sighed. "It's a bitch."

"You madam?" The driver peeked in his rearview mirror. "You are not old."

Belle laughed to herself, wishing it were true. She stopped quickly, a pain in her cheek making her wince.

"It's my fiftieth wedding anniversary," she said, leaning forward to talk more intimately with the driver. "And would you believe it? My husband forgot to pick me up from the station. Again." The cabbie looked surprised, looking back at her over his shoulder briefly before turning back to the road.

"How could any man forget you?" The driver smiled, white teeth flashing in the glow of oncoming headlights. Belle ducked back in her seat.

"He's senile," she said, her voice dull. "He forgets most everything. Most of the time he's living in the past. So far he hasn't forgotten me, but it's just a matter of time." The driver grunted and focused on the road ahead. Belle sank back in the seat, thinking back on the fifty years she'd spent with Samuel.

When they'd married, it seemed like a fairytale. Her love for him had been boundless. Her love for him had changed him, made him human. He was not a man who had ever felt that kind of all-encompassing love before and he drank it up, blossoming before her eyes the way plants do after a drought.

227

"You saved me, Belle," he said at least once a day. "Nobody ever saw anything good in me before you."

"It was true," Belle said aloud, startling the cabbie so he jumped. "When I met him, he was in prison for assault. And it wasn't the first time he'd been in either. My Samuel was a bad man back then, a beast. In high school he got in with a bad crowd and after he left it got worse. Sammy never had a good home. His father walked out when he was just a boy, and his mother was too busy to spend much time with him." Belle stared out the window, picturing the well-muscled man she'd first seen in the counseling room of the medium security prison.

"You sure are pretty," Samuel crooned from behind the table. "I like blondes. But are you a real blonde?" He licked his lips and dropped a lascivious glance to her crotch. Belle dropped her hands, allowing her briefcase to cover her lower half as she made her way to the uncomfortable seat across the table from him.

"I'm Belle," she said, hating how shrill her voice sounded in the windowless room. "I'm here for you to talk to. Nothing you say to me in these sessions will be used against you. They are for you, and you alone."

"Maybe I got nothing to say." Samuel leaned back in his chair and she could see he was manacled. She breathed a sigh of relief. She had counseled bigger men before, but none of the others had intimidated her as much as this one.

"He was so full of hate," Belle sighed, looking back at

the cabbie. "There was a man here in town. Gerald Banks. He was a white supremacist. A real bigot if ever I saw one. He took Sammy under his wing, way back when Samuel was just a boy. Sammy never had a father, and Gerald was there. Oh, the poison that man spewed! He's dead now, thank the Lord." The cabbie glanced back over his shoulder but Belle did not notice. Behind her sunglasses, her eyes looked beyond the polished interior of the cab.

"Gerald was like a father to me," Samuel said, eyes clinging to the tabletop before him. "Nobody ever paid me attention. He cared about me. He asked me about school and girls and really wanted to know what I thought about all kinds of stuff. Nobody ever asked me before."

"But he told you things too, didn't he?" Belle tried to break in as little as possible, wanting Samuel to allow his thoughts and feelings to flow freely.

"Sure. He told me a lot of things. He told me the way the world was, the way it worked."

"Do you still believe that's the way the world works?" Belle asked this casually, watching as another prisoner worked his way toward them, pushing a mop up the drab concrete passageway.

Samuel bit his lip and followed her eyes. The prisoner with the mop was tall and thin. The harsh fluorescent lights glinted off the shiny black skin on his bald head.

"You're doing a great job, Henry," Samuel called as the man passed, his face contorting as if he'd tasted something bitter.

The prisoner answered with a grunt and a flick of his

hand, mopping his way past Samuel's cell and on down the row.

Belle smiled to herself and turned back to Samuel. "There," she said. "Was that so bad?"

Samuel remained silent for a moment then shook his bowed head. "I just did what Gerald taught me to..."

"The things that man taught!" Belle shook her head. "It took me almost three years to rehabilitate Samuel. But he worked hard at it. He wasn't stupid, just ignorant and completely in thrall to that bigot. In time his hair grew back and I could see he was not the hideous creature I'd met that first day. No, he was a handsome fellow and by the time he was released, well, I had to admit I was in love with him. Anyone who works that hard to better himself, to free himself from the past is someone to be admired in my books. We were married three weeks after he got out of prison. May fifteenth, 1960. Fifty years today."

Belle's voice trailed off as the cab turned onto the narrow, winding lane that led to her house.

"Number thirty-eight," the cabbie said, pulling the car up to the curb. "That'll be twenty-two ninety."

Belle fumbled with her purse, pulling out a few crumpled notes. "Keep the change," she muttered as she gathered her bags once more.

"Thank you, ma'am. And happy anniversary."

Belle made her way up the driveway with difficulty. The paving was uneven and she could not see much with the glasses covering her face. The car was parked in front of the garage and lights burned in the house.

230

"I hope the damn fool is home," Belle muttered as she staggered up the three steps to the front door.

"Samuel?" Belle called, dropping her bags in the dimly lit foyer. "Sammy? It's me. Are you home?" She shuffled her way into the living room, expecting him to be in his armchair, the television blaring some inanity. But the living room was empty, the TV silent for once.

"Samuel?" she called again, moving through to the dining room.

Candles flickered on the table and a vase of crimson roses sat in the center. Without thinking, Belle raised her glasses to look. A bottle of her favorite Pinot Noir breathed on the sideboard; her best china and silverware were on the table, two places set side by side.

"Oh, Samuel," Belle breathed, suddenly aware of the aromas that permeated the house. "Oh, darling, you sweet, sweet man."

Following the delicious scent, she made her way to the kitchen. Samuel, a floral apron tied around his waist, stood at the stove stirring something. Belle paused in the doorway, not wanting to call attention to herself yet. No, she wanted to surprise him. She'd spent every penny she had left of her inheritance on the surgery, timing it perfectly so she could surprise him on their Golden Anniversary.

Tearing off the scarf that covered it, she ran her fingers through her hair, dyed just yesterday to the honey blond shade of her youth. The sunglasses she'd worn to hide her face fell to the carpet without a sound. Belle ran her fingers across the taut planes of her face, feeling the slightly raised scars at her hairline and wincing. It would be a few more weeks before they stopped tingling.

"Samuel?" Belle stepped toward her husband, her voice low. "Happy anniversary, my love."

Samuel turned, dropping the spoon he'd been stirring with to the floor with a clatter. His face was open, a smile brightening his wrinkled face. As she watched, the smile fell away, his eyes grew frightened.

"Who are you?" he shrieked, grabbing for the knife on the bench. "Get out of my house, you hideous beast!"

Little Red Riding Hood

> *"I pulled my cloak tighter around my body against a sudden chill. The stars were tarnished nails, holding up the sky. I forced a grin. 'Don't worry about it, Kara. Wolves don't wear leather fringe. They wear* fur.'"

Michael Takeda may have worked in a club at some point, but he was never a bartender.

"In writing a sequel to Little Red Riding Hood, I wanted to maintain what I considered to be the key elements of the original tale: the driving force of the wolf (hunger) and the cautionary nature of the tale (don't trust strangers). Fairy tale worlds are alternate worlds, and to stay faithful to that tradition, I set the story in an alternate reality, though one not so very different than our own. The anonymous city in "Wolf" served as a backdrop upon which other issues could come into play, such as conformity and consumerism in particular. Living in America, I often find it alarming how much we consume: not only food, but goods, natural resources, and, in some sense, other people.

"Anyone who's read my story 'Xenium' in the Elf Love anthology probably noticed my obsessions with robots and gender roles – obsessions which have spilled over into 'Wolf.' Writing in Celeste's voice – the 'I' in the story – was some-what of a challenge. I found it hard to relate to her. If it's true that writers insert themselves into their characters, I'm concerned I might be Jules."

"The Wolf in Standard Ration Clothing" is easily the most dystopian story in the collection.

The Wolf in Standard Ration Clothing

Michael Takeda

I trudged downstairs from the kitchen into the workroom, where Mother was working on an antique foot-operated Singer, tailoring a hem, while my sister was savagely stuffing the body of a ragdoll. My mother has always been eccentric. My sister insisted that using technology would save our mother from straining her eyes and back from leaning over the old-fangled machines all day, but Mother wouldn't listen. She said that society's reliance on technology had made the world the conformist wasteland it was today, and that our business was originality, not mass production.

"There's an order on the net for some baklava," I told her.

She peered up from her sewing and propped her glasses in her hair. "I can make some of that," she said. Setting aside the swatch of fabric she'd piled in her lap, she then sashayed past me to the stairs that led to the storage comb. "I'll check the books. Russian, isn't it?"

"Greek," I said. It was my job to know everything.

"There are some things over there that need to be painted," she said, pointing at the shelf. "I've already marked all the colors."

I nodded as Mother disappeared down the dark stair-

235

well.

My sister swung her curly, purple-streaked bob in my direction. "I'm so sick of this. I'll paint if you stuff."

I shrugged. "What's wrong with stuffing?"

"I don't know why Mom gives you all the okay jobs and I get all the crappy ones," she mumbled. "Plus you get paid more."

"Because I'm older, twerp." I was nineteen, Violet three years younger. "You can paint if you want. Just paint within the lines."

"A fucking monkey could do that." She slid off her stool and headed for the shelf of unfinished projects. "Long as I don't end up a freak like you, staying up half the night doing research on pie crusts."

"I don't just read about pie crusts, snotface. Besides, it's important to Mom."

She snorted softly. "What do you read that could possibly keep you up all night?"

"Police reports, mostly," I said, mostly to shut her up.

Violet's hand hovered briefly in the air. She didn't meet my eyes. Then she exhaled softly, and picked out a paintbrush, giving it more attention than it deserved. Finally she muttered under her breath, "Is that why you never go out anymore? Because of what happened to *her*?"

It wasn't a question I liked. I pretended I hadn't heard, instead staring at a piece of Mother's art which had hung on the far wall for as long as I could remember. It had a car bumper in it, wrapped in strips of potato sack and canvas, so tactile that it made your fingers ache to touch it. Across the bumper, under the spotlights, glistened three symbolic stripes of paint: one red, one blue, one violet.

Back on her stool, Violet spoke again, this time with her usual annoying level of shrill. "So, are you, like, going to marry Richard, or what?"

Richard Woodsman: polite, clean-cut, handsome, and he had a shiny badge. He'd been the first on the scene, and the one to break the news about Scarlet's death. That I was dating him was fucked up on many levels, but at least with him I felt safe. "I don't know. I never see him. His department always has him out on assignment."

"At least he makes a lot of money."

"I know, but, what's the point of having money if you don't have time to enjoy it?"

"Men all suck," she decided.

"Are you speaking from experience?"

She gave me a saccharine smile. "Aren't you supposed to be working, Celeste? Stuff!"

I worked in the Honeycombs, a cluster of Bauhaus-style buildings in the downtown zone, where several retailers rented space. Ours had three living combs and a storage comb below, each tiny room stacked on top of one another like a child's toy blocks. Across the hall from us a modeling agency had recently opened. They closed down at five o'clock every day like we did, but it was after closing that they saw the most activity. From my perch in the netbook nook in the top comb, I could look down through the slim window into the corridor, and since I'd been staying home at night I'd seen a lot of people come and go from that office. It did not take me long to solve the mystery.

When I told my best friend Kara about it, she laughed

so hard that her laughter infected me, too. "The office across the hall is an escort service?" she asked. "I can't believe it. And they have men, too?'"

"Oh, sure. Men, women... circus performers. You know, the usual."

Violet's question about why I never went out anymore had struck a nerve. It was true that I'd been cooped up too long. But I hadn't wanted to return to the underground alone, so I'd invited Kara. Now we prowled the dark streets while powdered and perfumed creatures in dark clothes danced by our brightly-clad forms. Kara wore a long, form-fitting dress of sea-green satin that my mother had designed specifically for her. I wore my usual cloak, the one of velvet and as blue as a summer sky in the country. As far as I knew, there were only three such cloaks in the entire world, each made by my mother's hands: red for Scarlet, purple for Violet, the blue one for me.

"That is really freaky," Kara said. The gold glitter on her honey-colored skin sparkled as we passed under a rare working street lamp. "So now that you've figured it out, what are you going to do about it?"

I grinned wickedly. "Maybe I'll go there tonight."

She laughed nervously. "And do what? Pay for sex?"

"Maybe I'm curious."

"But what about Richard?"

"It has nothing to do with him," I said. "And I didn't say I was going to actually have sex with anyone."

Kara gave me a skeptical look, then shook her head with a sigh. "So... where are we going?"

"I'll take you to my favorite club," I said.

238

"I don't know about that. I've heard some weird stories about that place."

She acquiesced nevertheless so I led her into the dark depths of the Korova Milk Bar. She had never been there before, but she immediately lost herself on the spacious dance floor of the Trip Room. I didn't feel like following. Too many people were watching the dancers in true vulture fashion.

The club had the atmosphere of – and was dedicated to – both the book by Burgess and the film by Kubrick. The bar even boasted replications of woman-shaped milk dispensers like in the film, only the milk wasn't full of drugs. Drugs circulated openly through the club by human hands. I recognized most of the hands, but was not looking tonight. Sober, the Korova was an entirely different experience. Everyone here was so self-fascinated, and this interested me. I watched them all as the lights swirled and the music pulsated against my flesh. Some of them watched me back. No words were exchanged. I wanted it that way.

Eventually I wandered to the bar in the back of the Departure Room. I was greeted by the familiar, bitter tang of amyl nitrite in the air. Jules was still working here. He had silver and some other color artistically smeared across his face, but it was hard to discern the design in the dark. I knew him vaguely, had heard he was gay. Like everyone else at the Korova, he was probably involved with the drug trade, though he'd never admitted – to me at least – that he knew the score. Before I'd even sat down, he was ready to take my order. I asked for a beer. He slid the ice-frosted bottle before me without asking for ID. Why ID for a drink when there was a ready supply of drugs in the club that could put you in a mental

239

heaven or hell for three days?

"How are things, Jules?"

"Really busy. You haven't been around lately."

"Been saving my money," I said. "Lots of work."

"Don't work too hard," he said, and gave me a conspiratorial wink before slinking off to tend to another customer.

At the bottom of the bottle is when I found Kara. She was ready to leave, so we headed back towards the Honeycombs. I was buzzed from the dark beer, and my mouth tasted less than pleasant, but I felt like a cloud – soft, all mist. Above us curled a rodent moon, half-gnawed. I'd forgotten how good it could feel to drift through the night, when the heat-haze of the smog was blown away from the wind off the river, when the buildings were quiet and dark.

"I love your mother's pies," Kara said, clearly a bit buzzed herself. "When is she going to make me one of her pecan specials?"

"Whenever you ask."

"This dress she made me is so comfortable." It looked right on her long, lank figure. "I could have danced all night if these standard ration shoes weren't killing my feet."

"That's what you get for buying GX-DR-Cs," I chided. "Faulty insteps."

"Yeah," she said, amazed. "How the fuck do you do that? Is there any item of clothing you can't name?"

"It comes with the trade." All standard ration clothing and accessories were cataloged by a series of letters, followed by a number that represented color. One was white, two black, followed by the primaries. Then came the secondary colors, then varying shades of those colors. Beyond the secondary colors, I couldn't name them all, but colors like chartreuse and ocher were available for any product you purchased. Most manufacturing was done by highly-specialized bots. Type the numbers into the netform, and the machines would spit out your order, no human hands involved. Mother hated it. She believed that modern manufacturing had made life impersonal, that people weren't allowed to truly be individuals anymore, that there was no love in consuming goods made by robots. Hence, her business, Craft Works, had been born. And my sisters and I had been dragged along into it.

"I like that bar," she decided. "I even met a guy tonight with spiky blond hair and a black leather jacket with fringe. Do you know him? I didn't want to give my contact number to a mass murderer..."

Kara trailed off suddenly, crestfallen. "Shit, Celeste! I didn't mean it like that... I wasn't thinking."

I pulled my cloak tighter around my body against a sudden chill. The stars were tarnished nails, holding up the sky. I forced a grin. "Don't worry about it, Kara. Wolves don't wear leather fringe. They wear *fur*."

It was cooler in the building when I got back. Although I had my money chip in my pocket and I had brushed my teeth to remove the lingering bad taste from my mouth, I was hesitating outside the agency door. When a couple finally stepped out, I darted in through the diminishing crack. Standing behind a narrow counter inside the lobby was a tall, thin droid in dark round glasses and a champagne pink zoot suit – a JYS-EF-W-33, if I wasn't mistaken. His modulated voice vibrated through the air. "May I help you?"

An eerie glow from the neon lamps emanated from his silver casing. "I'm looking for some company for the evening," I said, wishing that the beer buzz hadn't dissipated so soon.

"Male or female?"

"Male."

Metal joints whirred and clicked. "Please – this way."

He took my chip, popping it briefly into a slot in his neck. "Do not let the fee influence your selection. All our male escorts are equally priced," he said. Which meant that the women were not equal. I wondered what factor determined a woman's price. Age? Beauty? Body shape? Vaginal size? But I didn't ask, as we had arrived at a room.

I followed the droid inside. A dozen men lounged about, practically motionless, as though they were only manikins on display. I wondered if they were models making money on the sly. I glanced over them quickly, feeling un-comfortable, then surprised as I recognized the man closest to me as Jules, the bartender from the Korova Milkbar, sitting – appropriately – on a barstool.

I looked at the men again, this time with more scrutiny. I passed from face to face. There was something generic about their beauty, all chiseled features and sculpted bodies. Too perfect, and not my type. But I was determined to select one, too committed to retreat. In fact, within me, the anticipation was building as the idea was becoming tangible. A part of me wanted to go through with it, to choose a man I would pay to fuck tonight, and nothing more than that, no strings attached. I realized that there was music playing in the background. I recognized it as classical, which my Mother often played, but you didn't hear it anywhere else – popfuck-rap abounded. The strains of the piano and strings were oddly comforting. I suddenly liked the atmosphere in that room of the agency – I felt powerful.

In no hurry, I studied the merchandise again, and my eye fell on Jules, perched on his chair, seeming extremely bored. Strange how he had looked at me without a spark, a smile, or even a wink of recognition. No, more than strange it was absurd. Absurd and annoying. And yet my gaze lingered on Jules; in the harsh light I could see how pretty his face was, with sloping cheekbones and a square jaw, his eyes heavy-lidded from a trace of exotic Asian blood. The make-up was missing. I was so annoyed by the fact that Jules – the same man who had served me a drink a scant two hours ago – was pretending that he didn't even know me, that it hadn't immediately occurred to me that I could pick *him*.

"I'll take Jules," I said.

Still showing no sign of recognition, Jules rose, smiled at the droid – my host, or guide, or whatever it was – and whisked me from the room, through the building, and out into the night.

"Is it all right if we pick up a few things at the market, Celeste?" he asked, taking my hand. I assumed it an obligatory gesture, but I found it as comforting as the sound of my name on his lips.

"I'm not familiar with the usual procedure, so anything is fine."

He didn't seem bored anymore, no longer a manikin but a sleeping beauty brought back to life. Neon signs threw patches of color as we flew past them, whizzing through his spill of black hair. His smile was as dark and light as a black-bird's wing. "Don't worry. It's included."

In the shadowed labyrinth of the underground market, I watched his deft hands pick out the ripest fruits and plop them into plastic bags. He took my hand again and we returned to the building, only through a different door. After a few twists, we entered a small, warm, dimly-lit basement comb. Behind a counter stood a girl. Behind her, a fully-armed droid.

"Would you like something?" Jules asked. "Something to slow you down, or pick you up?"

"Such as?"

"Anything you want. Benders, tweakers, poppers, heaven, coke, blacks, blues, junk, crank, sleeping beauties, snow whites...?"

"No, I don't think so."

"Perhaps just some Ecstasy, then?" he asked lightly.

I was intrigued by all this black market dealing, but I wasn't in the mood to alter my reality. "No thanks."

"Just one," he told the girl, and she disappeared into a back nook. "Are you sure?" he asked. "It really enhances the experience."

I refused a third time, then the girl returned and handed him a small box, gorgeously adorned with a painted bird, which he secreted away in a pocket.

We continued up a rickety back stairwell, Jules still holding my hand. We wound up in the comb directly over my mother's kitchen. I had always wondered what was up here, but I never would have guessed that it was a room – albeit a very comfortable room – where money and flesh were traded.

"Are drugs always part of the deal?" I asked.

"Mmm-hmm." He withdrew the box and then pressed a spot on the bird's head. There was a tiny click as the box popped open, revealing a secret compartment in which a small blue pill nestled. "To tell you the truth, I got into this business for the X. The agency produces most of the hard stuff on its own. It's pure."

"Ah," I said.

He smiled softly. "I'm going to change into something I think you might like."

He slipped into a nook that I assumed was a changing room, pulling a curtain across the rod. But I was not watching him. The room had captured my attention.

It was almost modest, except for its decor. Sexual paraphernalia was tucked subtly away: oils, feathers, books, bits of leather, chains. Antique night tables, book-shelves, and elegant decorations filled the space, with carpet underfoot, all luxuries in this age. The bed was a marvel of wrought iron and brass fittings. As I was considering going over to the bed for a closer look, Jules emerged from the changing room. His flesh was exposed through a slip of black silk that I recognized as a garter, hooked to opaque stockings. All this hardly concealed by a drape of some gauzy material wrapped around his slim hips. I knew that garters used to be worn by women, but I found the effect on Jules intriguing.

I was still discovering hidden treasures in the room as Jules carried a glass of water over to the bed. "I can still give you half."

"No, forget it," I said. Then, "How many people are there at the agency?"

"About sixty or so. Though only about twenty are men."

"That explains the selection."

"I know what you mean." He trailed a lazy hand through his dark hair. "I don't like most of them."

Because money was involved, I could be blunt. "Really? I thought you were gay."

"Does it matter?"

I watched him silently from my brightly-lit side of the room.

He tilted his head coyly. "Actually, I don't consider myself much of anything. I spend all my time sleeping or working. I don't have time for romance." He fingered the crystal water goblet. "Help yourself to something."

I reached into the bag and pulled out a peach. "Do you want one?"

"Maybe later."

I bit into the fruit. Real peach juice, sticky, sweet, dripped down my chin.

Jules watched me, then stretched his legs, displaying the smooth skin of his thigh between the straps. "Is this what you were saving your money for?"

I half-smiled, amused. "Actually... no. I just came here because I was curious."

"You'd be surprised how many people say that."

"Did my sister say it?"

"Violet?"

"Scarlet," I said. He cocked his head at me, so I added, "Three years older than me. Dark hair. Wore a red cloak with a riding hood."

I watched Jules' fingers as they trailed a slow path

along the goblet's rim, and as he watched me. "I knew her. She used to come into the Korova every now and then." He studied me intently. "I heard what happened. Do you want to talk about it, Celeste?"

It had been a year since that night. Because of Richard, I knew what the Feds knew. Grandmother had been ill, so Mother had sent Scarlet to her house with a basket of baked goodies. To get to Grandmother's house, it was probable that Scarlet had passed through the Woods – the bad part of town. Maybe she'd stopped to talk to a stranger – that part was unclear. All we knew for certain was that some maniac the press had nicknamed the Wolf had gotten to Grandma's house first. He'd eaten half of Grandma after he'd had his way with her. Parts of Scarlet, too. They'd found my sister's heart on a plate on the second shelf of the fridge, between a jar of orange marmalade and a bottle of ketchup. As for the Wolf, he was still at large.

More juice dripped down my chin as my teeth tore into the firm flesh. "I'm not paying you to play psychologist."

"Sure." He studied me for another moment, then smiled sultrily as if he'd just remembered what I *was* paying him for. "So, Celeste... do you like to come?"

"It's not the most important thing there is."

"What's important to you, then?"

"How it feels to have a cock inside me," I told him. His interest didn't seemed feigned. "In that moment, all my troubles just seem to disappear."

He stretched his lean body across the mattress. "I don't think you'll have any *trouble* feeling me inside you."

"I never doubted it."

247

He smiled. "And I thought men were overly concerned with the penis." Then he laughed, and I grinned. "Do you have a lover?"

"No," I said, sucking on the pit. "Although I do have a boyfriend."

"What kind of boyfriend is he if he doesn't satisfy you?"

I dropped the pit, wiping the juice from my chin with the back of my hand. "He's what my mother calls a 'nice boy'."

His hand dropped to his crotch, stroking silk. His voice was a seductive murmur. "I could be your bad boy."

I realized that we were talking too much for the business we were conducting, but the conversation felt good and easy. I reached for the clasp of my cloak, letting it fall to a heap on the floor. "I think that's what I expected."

His smile grew, and his cock did, too. It had been a long time since I'd felt the hardness of a man's body. I really wanted to fuck him now.

"Are you ready?"

I admitted, "I really want to walk barefoot on this carpet first."

His smile was a sly promise. "You can do *whatever* you want."

I kicked off my shoes, socks, and walked towards the bed. Thick pile rose between my toes like sand. I looked down at Jules, spread across a silken, feather quilt. "This bed is lovely."

He glanced across it. "It's too small," he sighed. Then he sat up and looked at me, eyes cutting like surgical steel. "Celeste. Get comfortable."

I padded over to him, removing my shirt, and stood

before him. He set down his glass. Then he reached over to the wall switch and dimmed the lights, striking a mood like a match. He leaned forward to touch my bare arms; I touched his. All of a sudden words seemed pointless. In his eyes, there was a new intensity. I trailed my fingers over his beautiful face. He was very attractive, with a slender, silk body, strings of muscle taut under the golden brown skin. As I leaned down, his gaze grew lazy, wanting, and we kissed. His mouth was full and warm and seeking. My breath got caught in my throat.

The sex got caught in my throat, too.

Morning light tinged the clouds tangerine and turned skyscraper glass into silvery fish scales as I picked my way through the streets, super coffee steaming in my hand. Rusty garbage bots motored down the sidewalk, steel lids clattering against cans. The whistle of the approaching tram warned me off the tracks. The tram screeched by my face in a gust of hot metal and grease, her belly full of men in dark suits and ties, netbooks in one hand, cups of super coffee in the other. They were carbon copies, in the same suits with the same manners and the same ambitions: to be an executive VP and own a car so they wouldn't have to ride the tram.

I hurried on, sipping my super coffee, feeling the synthetic caffeine as it coursed down to my toes. I knew which streets to avoid – those closest to the Woods. One had to or risk being mugged, murdered or raped, even at this hour. I spied some people from the Korova Milkbar slipping down a side street, and I waved. They waved back with cheerful, Heaven-induced grins.

Back home, I found Richard in the kitchen, manilla

folder in hand, conversing politely with my mother. The smell of the baking bread filled me with hunger. Richard rose and kissed me on the cheek.

"There you are," he said.

"Here I am," I agreed.

My mother sent me to fetch Violet, so I set down my coffee and headed downstairs. Violet was curled into the couch, tapping on her texter. "Mom wants you."

"Richard's here."

"So I noticed."

"Is he taking you out on a date?"

"I have no idea."

"You should make him take you to dinner. You never go out anymore. Loser."

"I was out last night with Kara," I said, but I was thinking about what had happened after the Milkbar. I remembered how Jules felt – or, rather, I hadn't been able to think about anything else.

Violet was eyeing me with what appeared to be actual concern. "Are you okay? Your hands are shaking."

I stared down at my hands, then shoved them guiltily into my pockets. "Must be the coffee," I told her. "Now, move it, pipsqueak."

Back upstairs, Violet greeted Richard and then promptly asked him if he were here to invite me on a date. He told her that he was on a case.

I sipped my coffee at the kitchen table. "If you're on a case, then why are you here and not working?"

He flashed perfect white teeth. "But I am working. I'm investigating the modeling agency across the hall from you."

"Really?" my mother asked. "What have they done?"

He opened the file and shook out several sheets of photographs. "We believe that this agency is just a front for a large prostitution ring. We have pictures of some of the suspects. I need to know if you recognize any of them."

"How horrible," she said, snatching the pictures from his hand to get a look. She plopped her glasses on the end of her nose and shuffled through the stack. "And such nice-looking young people, too. They seem so normal."

My sister had jumped up, too, but I just sat there, feeling like a character out of a rural play. *Y'all come down to the whorehouse, y'hear?*

"I'll need you to look over these, too, Celeste."

"Sure."

Mother shook her head. "I don't recognize anyone."

She passed me the pictures and I flipped through them. To be honest, the men I had seen there had all looked alike, with nothing in particular to differentiate them. But for some reason, I felt a strange quiver run up my spine when I came across the picture of Jules. Jules: draped in a long coat with a metallic sheen, standing on a street corner, slim and silvery and sharp like a knife blade.

"Someone you know?" Richard asked hopefully.

An echo from last night tingled my ear, filling it with a hot flush of blood, and making my body vibrate like a cello string: *I could be your bad boy.*

"No," I lied.

At first I was delighted about the late date that Richard had scheduled in his overflowing agenda. I couldn't remember the last time we had gone out. Yet, as the day wore on, the novelty wore off. Underground dealings, though more common than the normal, legitimate kind, intrigued me more. Maybe it was the deception I enjoyed. Maybe that's why I'd lied to Richard.

It was close to the hour when my date would arrive and I was sitting at the worktable alone. Restless, I reached into a pocket and withdrew the little pillbox. It had been too beautiful to just throw away and I had always possessed a weakness for mementos. After some prodding, the secret compartment popped open and I discovered a surprise.

The pill was still safely nestled in the box, unconsumed. My mind wandered back to last night: how Jules had trembled at my touch, how many times his pleasure had been spent as he writhed beneath me, how it had felt... and none of it synthetic.

I shoved the box into the back corner of the drawer and ran to the Korova Milkbar.

He smiled in the darkness when he saw me. Not the usual smile, but with a trace of something more. I told him that I needed to talk to him. Smiling, he agreed, and I waited for him to get off from work.

An hour later, as the music and the amyl nitrite was grinding around in my head, his slender body appeared out of the darkness into my darkness. I set down my milk as he reached for my hand, drawing me out of the club into the burnt-plastic, hot-metal, chemical smell of the streets.

Before I could speak, Jules pushed me against the wall of the club, colors from the neon lights swirling about him as his mouth found mine. He tasted of apples and smoke.

Hot breath corroded my thoughts as it roiled in my ear. "I have to contact the agency. I won't have to go in if I tell them I'm already with a client."

We walked to a nearby netbooth. I leaned against the glass, huddling in my cloak, as he tapped in his code. I didn't know how to explain, or even what I was doing here, so I waited, silent. With a puzzled look, Jules disconnected and met my eyes. "A strange voice answered," he revealed. "Human. Something's up."

"A bust?"

"Maybe." His eyes were cutting, twin blue lasers dissecting me. "We could walk by and see if anything's happening."

I drew the cloak around my cold bones. The weather in the city was a funny thing, prone to change in a heartbeat. I shrugged and followed.

We hastened through the tide of screams and laughter shattering the night, echoing off the concrete, until we reached the Honeycombs. Blue and red lights pirouetted across the windows of my building. The place was crawling with cops.

"Fuck." He looked at me. "If we left anything incriminating in the room..."

Near dawn, I had watched Jules gather everything up and strip the bed, sending our fluid-soaked sheets down a half-concealed chute. We had cleared everything out, except... "The peach pit."

Jules looked at me. That he was debating was clear. It was my DNA in question, not his. But then his expression shifted. "We have to get to the room somehow."

"The Feds know what you look like," I warned him.

"How do you know?"

"You remember that boyfriend I told you about...?"

"You sly bitch." He laughed weakly. "Great. Now what?"

I thought. "I can get in through the front door. If you can get around to the back, I can let you into our storage comb."

The plan proceeded without a hitch. I felt clever. The combs were quiet, my family asleep upstairs. Leaving the lights off, I crept my way down to the storage comb, and turned off the alarm. A moment later Jules was inside, a presence in the dark. Fear of being caught had sent my pulse racing, and, in truth, turned me on.

Jules' voice was all breath. "And now?"

"The vent in the kitchen. We could try to crawl up it. It might lead up to the room."

"You're crazy."

"You don't have to come with me."

His hand around my wrist kept me from turning away. "Celeste. It's too risky."

"And when they find it?"

"It doesn't prove anything."

"It proves that I was in the room."

His grip tightened as I tried to pull away. "You didn't do anything wrong."

"Except pay you to fuck me."

"You didn't pay," he said.

"What?"

"I reversed the charges."

"Why?"

He smiled. In the shadows there was only the barest

glint off his make-up from the Milkbar. "Stupid girl. Why do you think?"

He moved to kiss me. As I leaned into him, there was a snap in the dark, and the comb filled with light. Across the room, with one hand still on the switch, Richard stood. In his other hand, a gun, fixed on Jules.

I blinked. "Richard?"

Richard didn't spare me a glance, focused on Jules. "Step away from the girl, now," he growled. "You are under arrest, *Wolf*."

The trial caused a sensation, with great fanfare in the press, and no one in my family could walk the streets without being mobbed by reporters. I stayed in, suffering nightmares until the doctor prescribed a sedative.

I talked to no one outside the family except for Richard. It was rare that I didn't come downstairs to find him chatting with my mother at the kitchen table, hands wrapped around a cup of oily coffee, a plate of cookies fresh from the oven between them.

It was only on the last day of the trial, as the secluded jury debated, that I finally linked with Kara.

"It was awful," I told her from the netbooth in the lobby of the courthouse. "The whole time I was in there, he watched me. It was creepy."

Kara's face loomed large as she leaned close to the screen. "They're going to find him guilty, right?"

I told her about the evidence. Hair, saliva, and semen had been found at the crime scene: a perfect match. Although the bite marks had been inconclusive, the rest was damning enough. "I think I feel sick."

"*He's* sick," Kara said. "Did he say why he did it?"

"He denied killing anyone. Claimed he was innocent."

"Of course he would say that, but it doesn't make it true."

I sighed, leaning my head against the scratched, dirty glass of the booth, recalling Jules in the witness chair, insisting that he wasn't a murderer. And how, for a moment, I had almost believed him. Almost believed the perverse story he had spun about what, precisely, he had been doing at Grandmother's house right before she had been killed. "Kara, he fucked my grandmother. And my sister."

"And you," Kara added.

"He *ate* them."

"Consider yourself lucky that Richard showed up when he did, or you would have been dessert."

Alone in the storage comb, would anyone have heard me scream? And, then, once he'd finished slavering over me, had swallowed my flesh and sucked the marrow from my bones, would he have gone upstairs to where my little sister lay sleeping and done the same to her? And my mother, too? "I hope the fucker fries."

"You can't trust anyone."

You would think I'd learned that lesson from my sister, not to trust a stranger. From now on, I would be more careful. My mother, Violet, and Kara were the only people I could trust. And Richard, of course. I did consider myself lucky. Lucky because this time, at least, Richard Woodsman had arrived in time to save the girl from the Wolf.

* * * * *

256

When the trial was over and Richard proposed, I knew how Dorothy must have felt. It was as if a whirlwind had swept me up and set me down in some fucked-up fableland. My sister thought it was exciting and romantic. My mother thought I was too young to be engaged, but despite her warnings, there was an undercurrent of relief. It had been weeks since the verdict and the monster condemned, but these events lingered like soot that could not be scrubbed from our skins. So when Richard appeared with two tickets to Las Vegas, Mother just smiled and said she was sure that the distraction would do me some good, and that she and Violet could manage the shop for a few days without me.

Once we were in the taxi heading towards our hotel, there couldn't have been a girl who brooded more. I had the sinking feeling that I'd fucked up. Running off with Richard, agreeing to marry him – it had all been a mistake. A knee-jerk reaction. I'd mistaken gratitude for love, fear for need.

I had dinner alone while Richard was in the other room on the net with the Bureau. I had ordered a steak but couldn't eat. I just sat, trying not to think about what I'd done with the man who had murdered half my family – or how much I had *liked* it – as the blood steadily pooled against the rim of the plate.

Later in bed, scrunched up on one side of the mattress, I believed that Richard – always the perfect gentleman – wouldn't try a damn thing.

I was wrong. After turning off the lights he reached for me. I resisted his touch. He forced me to turn and tried to kiss me. Disgusted, I kept my lips tightly shut. Still he persisted. When he grabbed me again, I slapped his hand and jumped

257

from the bed. "Richard, *stop*."

"I can touch you if I want. We're engaged. Now. Come here."

"No. I don't want to. I don't even love you."

Fury distorted his features, twisting them into a grotesquerie of human flesh. "You little cunt," he hissed. "You horrid bitch. I know what your problem is. You're just like the rest of them. You can only get off with whores. That's the only way you can get off, by paying whores to fuck you."

"I... what...?"

Richard snarled. "You're nothing better than a whore yourself!"

He lunged.

I tried to run.

Claws dug into my shoulders and then a shove forced me down to the table. Silverware rattled as something cold spattered across my cheek – blood from my untouched dinner. His hands curled around my throat and I struggled for air as he started to throttle me.

I'd made another mistake.

Richard leered down at me, as saliva dripped from his lips. "I think I'm going to enjoy eating *you* the most."

My head spun. I needed air. With one hand I failed to pry his fingers from where they pressed into my throat. The fingers of my other hand crawled desperately across the table until they stumbled upon the knife.

I woke up in a small white room I didn't recognize. There was a dull throb of pain in my side and my hand. I had rows of tidy black stitches in both. My mind was boggled, heavy with fog, and I couldn't remember what happened or how I had gotten here. All I could remember was a dream in which I'd been walking through the Woods to bring a basket of goodies to my sick Grandmother's house, and Jules emerging from the shadows, taking my hand and warning me to not talk to strangers.

I heard voices from the hall, and then a face appeared at the tiny barred window of the door. "Feeling better?"

I held my tongue. I was huddled in a corner, feeling small. "What am I doing here?"

"That's what we're here to find out," said the face. "I'm Dr. Smith and I'm here to help you."

"What big eyes you have, doctor."

"Yes, Scarlet, all the better to see you with. Now, tell me, my dear, what's the last thing you remember?"

"What big ears you have, doctor."

"Yes, yes, I'm listening. Tell me. What do you remember?"

"Grandma's house," I said. "No, Las Vegas."

"What else do you remember, Scarlet?" he asked, flashing a toothy grin.

"What big teeth you have, doctor. And why do you keep calling me Scarlet? And Richard!" I jumped up, ignoring the throb of the stitches pulling at my skin. "What happened to Richard Woodsman?" I seized the bars, rattling them. Startled, the doctor skittered back from the window. "He's the Wolf! Richard Woodsman is the Wolf!"

The doctor called for some strongmen while I screamed and pleaded. A key rattled in the lock. The strongmen pinned me down, baring my arm for the doctor's shot. Instantly a velvet-coated hammer smashed down upon my head, knocking the fight right out of me. The doctor told me to rest now, that everything would be fine, and then they all went away. I lay there and started to cry for no reason. It took me a minute to even realize that I was crying.

And then I heard it, the noise at the door. Scratching and snuffling at the metal hinges, whining and worrying at the cracks. Even when I covered my ears with my hands, I couldn't block the noise. Nothing could stop it. Not even the velvet hammer could make it go away.

I'm not crazy, you know. The wolves are all still out there, howling at the door, trying to get in. And they are so... very... *hungry.*

Listen.

Fairy Tale

"Why he didn't spin more of it into gold for himself, no one can say, but the writers of fairy tales do seem to have rather perverse imaginations."

Peggy Landsman's work has been published in many online and print literary journals and anthologies. Her poetry chapbook, To-wit To-woo, is available from FootHills Publishing. Her romance novel, Passion's Professor, which she wrote under the pen name Samantha Rhodes, is available on her web site. She lives in South Florida where she swims in the warm Atlantic Ocean every chance she gets. You can find Peggy at peggylandsman.com and samantharhodes.com.

"All I can say is that 'Six Degrees of Rumpelstiltskin' started out as a poem that I was unable to complete. About twenty years after I abandoned it, I finally realized it was meant to be written in prose."

"Six Degrees" is a light, tongue-in-cheek story, which probably shouldn't be taken too seriously – unless you're Kevin Bacon.

Six Degrees of Rumpelstiltskin
Peggy Landsman

After the unfortunate affair with the miller's daughter-turned-queen left him literally beside himself – split in two – Rumpelstiltskin recited his mouthful of a name two hundred and seventy times backward and got himself together again. Good as new.

But, of course, he hadn't learned his lesson. (It's only the *readers* of fairy tales who learn anything, never the fairy tale characters themselves.)

Rumpelstiltskin was still lonely and too unattractive to find a mate, so the next time he came across a wretched young woman, he demanded the same price for helping her out of her predicament. And that time he was rewarded. "A deal's a deal," she said, and handed over her very first bundle of joy.

Rumpelstiltskin took the cherished bundle back to his place in the forest. "Today I bake, tomorrow I brew, but this baby needs teeth before she can chew."

Rumpelstiltskin had never seen a baby up close before and was indeed startled at her absolute lack of pearly whites. He had no idea how or what he was going to feed her. It never occurred to him that she'd drink milk. (He himself never touched the stuff, couldn't stand the thought of it.) And how she wailed! He couldn't believe his ears or his headache. Why had he ever thought he wanted a baby? No, it was painfully obvious, the life of a single dad was not the life for him.

To make a long story short, Rumpel, for short, wound up doing the only sensible thing he could do: he dumped his burden on the steps of an orphanage. He didn't just lay the little bit of flesh and bones naked on a cold stair. No, most assuredly not! First, he tucked her carefully into a basket filled with straw. (Straw was obviously a very plentiful commodity. Why he didn't spin more of it into gold for himself, no one can say, but the writers of fairy tales do seem to have rather perverse imaginations.)

After leaving the baby, who, by the way, was destined to become the girl Goldilocks, Rumpelstiltskin wandered off. He had many new and challenging experiences which transformed him into a much more reflective soul. He developed a greater understanding of his own past and, in more ways than you'd expect from a typical fairy tale character, he expanded his consciousness.

When he thought back to the nights he spent with the miller's daughter – all the straw he spun into gold to save her life, only to have her throw her life away on that bastard king – he wondered why she never offered him her friendship. That's all he ever wanted. But no, he had to come up with that "first-born" thing. What a way of saying "I want to be a part of your life. Invite me over for dinner now and then." (Okay, he had been *very* afraid of rejection.)

But, he's quick to remind himself, it did all work out for the best. He took some needed time off and traveled around the world. There was so much of it outside the forest! He met all sorts of people and other terrestrial creatures. Eventually he realized that what he wanted for a companion was something or someone more like a teddy bear – not a woman or a baby human – and one night, while Papa Bear was attempting to teach Mama Bear how to prepare a proper Japanese-style bath, Rumpelstiltskin, with great quantities of Maya Mountain honey, lured innocent Baby Bear out of his bedroom window. That's why Baby Bear doesn't figure more prominently in this story.

Goldilocks began her growing up in one of those institutions for little unclaimed humans. The good woman who first stumbled over the baby in the basket (she had been on her way down the stairs, whistling a happy tune at the time, and not paying attention to her feet) tried, but failed, to ascertain the identities of Goldilocks's biological parents. By the time Goldilocks could wash dishes and scrub floors and toilets, there was nothing else to do but rent her out, or, as they prefer to say, put her into foster care.

The Three Bears were a dysfunctional family, a bad choice on the part of the overburdened child welfare system. They never should have been entrusted with little Goldilocks. And when you think about it, Papa and Mama should have been charged with negligence after Baby disappeared. They had failed to provide a child-safe environment. It had been nothing but dumb luck that had prevented Baby from *falling* out of the window before being lured out of it, as he eventually was. Papa and Mama never even missed Baby. And, no, it wasn't because with him gone they had more porridge for themselves. They couldn't stand the stuff. They ate sushi. They simply resented the low ratio of reward to responsibility involved in caring for their young.

Goldilocks, however, never minded being a latchkey

kid. She didn't feel neglected at all. She didn't care where the Bears were when they were away. In fact, she wished they'd stay away forever. Papa and Mama skimped on all her needs, pocketed as much of the monthly allowance as possible and believed they deserved it for all their trouble. To make matters worse, they looked at her funny, as if she were missing a tail or something. But, don't worry, she didn't have to stuff her face with porridge for very long. The woodsman who killed the wolf and saved Little Red Riding Hood came along in no time. The fairy tale world *is* a small world after all.

Between you, me and the four walls – Papa and Mama Bear were still out – the real down and dirty is that after the woodsman rescued the girl in the hood, he was so pumped up that he carried her off to Papa Bear's Bed-But-No-Breakfast. He had a thing going on the side with Papa Bear, who rented out his beds by the hour at rates competitive with those of the smaller Japanese love hotels. That's why Papa, who'd begun this sideline long before Baby's disappearance, always made sure to get Mama and Baby out of the house under various pretenses at discrete intervals. They were never to know of his domestic enterprise or to share in its profits. He was saving up for a trip for himself to Hokkaido to see his relatives and maybe get to Tokyo for a bit of true geisha experience. He'd given up on Mama Bear's ability to satisfy his needs in that department.

Meanwhile, back in the bedroom, the horny woodsman was just about to get it on with Little Red Riding Hood in Papa Bear's bed when, lo and behold, he discovered another well-rounded tush, rosy and warm, under the blankets.

Goldilocks and Little Red Riding Hood made quite a

handful. They were both obviously under age, but the woodsman had been watching and rewatching that scene from *Blow-Up*. He couldn't resist. He just had to indulge his urge for a *ménage a trois*.

Hell, an opportunity like that doesn't come along every day!

Quite an orgy was underway when Papa and Mama Bear suddenly appeared in the doorway. And, yes, the porridge was gone! The woodsman, Little Red, and Goldi had probably done some smoke and gotten the munchies.

Mama Bear did not want to believe her eyes. For a moment, until she took in the absence of any stage director, she tried to convince herself that she'd walked in on a rehearsal for a theatrical reenactment of a scene from the life of Lucius Domitius Ahenobarbus.

"What kind of a house do you think I'm running?" she asked, narrowing her eyes suspiciously at her mate. She'd been getting pretty fed up with Papa Bear's shenanigans and she knew, she just *knew* that he had something to do with this. "And I'm not going to buy any of your nonsense about the local witch casting another one of her spells! So don't even start." Giving him a shoulder cold enough to trigger premature hibernation, she removed herself from the unbearable scene and returned downstairs.

All she wanted was to wrap herself in her favorite shawl, settle into her rocking chair with a cup of warm *sake*, and treat herself to the next chapter in *The Adventures of Babette, She-Bear of Paris*. But it was not to be.

At almost the precise moment that Mama Bear stepped off the bottom stair, the Ugly Duckling popped in. He explained to her that he'd heard from a friend of his, who'd heard it from a reliable source, that she – for a price which he was more than willing to pay – could perform various controversial procedures.

Calculating the profit she stood to make, Mama Bear listened attentively to this tiny, desperate creature heaving his downy breast before her. Yes, she was acquainted with the delicate species-change operation he had in mind. Yes, she'd be happy to help him out. Yes, of course, she understood. Young ducks can be so cruel!

The Horned Women

"She knew she had been tricked. These were the dreadful witches her grandmother had warned her about in the old cautionary tale she used to tell."

David Turnbull was born in Edinburgh and grew up in the Scottish borders. He now lives and works in London. His short fiction has appeared in numerous anthologies and small press magazines, most recently he has had short stories included in the Mertales *anthology published by* Wyvern Publications *and the* Terminal Earth *anthology in Poundlit Press. In 2011 he has stories due for publication in the Urban Horrors edition* Morpheus Tales *and in the* Rebel Wing *fairy story anthology of Rebel Press. Also, his children's fantasy novel* The Tale of Eua Redcap *is due for publication by the Pixiefoot Press imprint of Wyvern Publications in late 2011.*

David always believed that the Horned Women in the original Celtic folk tale would have stewed for a long time about having been cheated out of their "blood cakes" before planning their revenge.

Often in fairy tales (including the original "Horned Women") the heroine triumphs because she receives supernatural aid. In David's "The Blood Cakes," however, the protagonist must find a solution to her predicament using only her wits.

The Blood Cakes
David Turnbull

In their filthy hovel at Slievenamon the coven of the horned women congregated to gripe and grumble about the trick that had been played upon them and how they had been cheated out of their blood cakes.

"When I think about those cakes and the sweet blood of the little children that went into making them..." moaned the sister with four horns on her head.

"Don't!" cried the sister with seven. "The very mention of it makes my mouth water."

"Hoodwinked, we was," hissed the sister with nine.

"Swindled," agreed the sister with five.

"Those children will be all grown up now," said the one with eight.

"Blood sours with age," sighed her eleven-horned sister.

Three Horns looked through the steam from the cauldron. "Her children will have children of their own now."

"If only the spells that protect the house could be broken," said Twelve Horns. "Then we could enter and take what is rightfully ours."

"The beam will still be fixed in the jamb," said the sister with two horns. "And the feet water will still be on the porch."

"And the mantle we sewed with our own hands will still be hung in the window," agreed Ten.

"How do we know that's true?" asked a haggard voice

from deep in the gloom.

The oldest and most crooked of the sisters leaned forward from the shadows in which she'd been lurking. The crusty warts and weeping boils on her wizened face were illuminated by the flickering glow of the fire. The thirteen horns that afflicted her head were hoary and bleached white with age. She smacked her narrow lips over her pink, toothless gums and asked again.

"How do we know? How do we really know that spells that protect the house are still in place? Every night we sit here and lament the loss of our blood cakes when all this time we may have well been able to walk into the house as easy as pie."

"One of us ought to go and look," said Eight.

"One of us ought to go and check," agreed Five.

Old crooked Thirteen lifted her old crooked arm and pointed with her old crooked finger.

"One Horn will go," she said.

"Why is it always me who has to go and do chores like this?" demanded One Horn, sulkily.

"You're the youngest," replied old crooked Thirteen. "You're the swiftest."

"Besides," said Ten. "It's much easier for you to disguise your one measly horn than it is for us."

"Think what it would be like disguising eleven horns," said Eleven.

"Think what it would be like disguising twelve," said Twelve.

So One Horn went down from Slievenamon and made her way under the tiny quarter moon to the house of the infamous treachery. She prowled about the garden and lurked around the barn and she soon saw that all the accursed protective spells were still in place. The beam was still in the jamb. The feet water was still on the porch. The mantle that the horned women had sewn with their own hands still hung in the window.

She was about to turn back for Slievenamon to break the terrible news to her sisters when the sound of gentle singing came lilting from the meadow that bounded the far end of the garden. One Horn felt a twitching of her ears. She sniffed the air with her hooked nose and caught the unmistakable aroma of sweet young blood.

On investigation she found a red-headed girl of no more than sixteen, softly humming to herself in the middle of the meadow as she stared up at the midnight sky. The girl jumped when One Horn spoke and revealed herself.

"Who might this be out here in the meadow after the midnight hour?" she asked.

"I may well ask you the same question," replied the girl, eyeing One Horn with caution.

"Just a passing stranger," said One Horn.

"Well," said the girl. "My name is Erin and I am my grandmother's granddaughter. I have every right to be out here in the meadow that bounds her garden after the midnight hour."

"You grandmother owns that house?" asked One Horn, stroking her pointed chin.

"She does," replied Erin.

"And are you her only grandchild?" asked One Horn.

"Oh no," Erin said. "My grandmother has plenty of

grandchildren. But my brothers and sisters and all of my cousins are tucked up fast asleep in bed."

"I see," said One Horn.

"What's that on your head?" asked Erin, pointing at One Horn's horn.

"I bumped my head," lied One Horn. "On a tree."

"It's a funny looking bump," said Erin.

"It was a funny looking tree," replied One Horn.

"Tell me," said One Horn, "what exactly is it you're doing out here?"

"Looking at the stars," said Erin. "I find that they always twinkle far brighter when they only have a fingernail moon to compete with."

"You should see the stars at Slievenamon," said One Horn, quick as a flash. "There's not a star in all the wide universe that twinkles brighter than the stars in the sky above Slievenamon."

"Slievenamon?" said Erin. "It seems to me that I've heard my grandmother mention that name before..."

"Oh, everyone has heard of Slievenamon," cooed One Horn seductively. "Your grandmother no doubt told you what a wonderful place it is. I could take you there right now, to see the bright, twinkling stars."

"Would I be back home before my brothers and sisters and all my cousins woke up?" asked Erin.

"There and back before the cock crows," said One Horn.

Erin pondered, chewing her lip and twirling a lock of her red hair around her finger.

"The stars there are really that bright?" she asked.

One Horn nodded enthusiastically.

273

"There and back before the cock crows?"

One Horn nodded again.

"And you'll make sure that I don't go bumping into any funny looking trees?"

"I know the safe way there and the safe way back."

"Then I'll come," said Erin, unraveling her hair. "I'll come to Slievenamon to see the bright, twinkling stars."

It seemed to Erin that the journey to Slievenamon took no more than a blink of her eye. One moment she was in the middle of the meadow, in the cool night air, beneath the fingernail moon, the next she was in the most dank and dismal place she had seen in all her sixteen years.

There was not a star to be seen in the thick treacle of darkness that oozed above her head. Rancid smelling steam swirled all around her. Billows of acrid smoke stung her eyes. Things popped and cracked under her feet. When she looked down she saw that she was walking on a jagged carpet of discarded rodent bones.

Then she became aware of the coven of horned women emerging eerily all around her from out of the steam and smoke. She knew she had been tricked. These were the dreadful witches her grandmother had warned her about in the old cautionary tale she used to tell.

She tried desperately to escape. But whatever direction she turned, a horned woman was waiting, long-fingered hands curled into claws, ugly face contorted into a snarl. Finally when all seemed hopeless Erin slumped down amongst the rodent bones and began to cry. Through her tears she heard One Horn boasting about how she had enticed her back to Slievenamon and how she was the granddaughter of the woman who had cheated them out of their blood cakes. On hearing this, all of the horned sisters began to squabbled and squawk about what terrible thing they should best do with her.

"We should toss her in the cauldron straight away," said one. "Boil her good and proper, till the flesh falls from her bones."

"That's not the way," argued another. "We should cut her to quarters. So we can save some for later."

"Eighths!" insisted yet another.

"We should eat her alive bite by bite," said someone else. "Sweet young blood is all the sweeter when it runs hot and free."

Then a grizzled old voice spoke up in the darkness beyond the fire.

"We should get her to make our blood cakes."

Erin looked up to see crooked old Thirteen Horns leaning out of the gloom where she had been lurking. In her crooked old hand she held a long, sharp knife with a gleaming blade.

"Take this, girlie," said Thirteen Horns. "Use it to slit the throats of all the children asleep in your grandmother's house. Fill up a bucket with their sweet young blood and mix it with oatmeal so that we can at last have our blood cakes."

"I will not!" cried Erin, scrambling to her feet. "Those are my brothers and sisters and cousins. I'll do nothing to harm them. So you better just eat me up right now because the first chance I get I'm going to run from here as fast as I can."

"You will do as I bid you," insisted Thirteen Horns, drooling over her slack lips. "As soon as you entered this place you fell under my enchantment and I'll have you back here whenever I please."

"What are you talking about?" asked Erin.

"Home!" said Thirteen.

In the blink of an eye Erin found herself back in the meadow in the cool night air beneath the fingernail moon. She was about to run back to her grandmother's house when she heard the grizzled old voice of Thirteen speaking inside her head.

"Slievenamon!"

In another blink of an eye she found herself back in the hovel of the horned women.

"You see," boasted Thirteen. "I'll have you back here whenever I please."

The air filled with the cackling laughter of the horned women.

"Only if you do as I bid and bring us our blood cakes will I lift the enchantment," said Thirteen.

Erin was no fool. She was her grandmother's grand-daughter. She knew that she had to buy some time by making the horned women think that she was going to go through with the terrible deed.

"I've no choice then," she said. "I'll have to do as you bid."

"You'll take the sweet young blood of your brothers and sisters and cousins?" asked Thirteen, handing her the long, sharp knife with the gleaming blade.

"Yes," replied Erin.

"You'll mix it up with oatmeal?"

"Yes," replied Erin.

"You'll fetch us our blood cakes?"

"Yes," replied Erin.

"Tomorrow night, after the midnight hour?"

Erin gave a solemn nod of her head.

"Home then!" cried Thirteen, with a loud clap of her old, crooked hands.

The next morning when her brothers and sisters and cousins were seated at the breakfast table eating their porridge, Erin plucked courage to tell her grandmother what had happened.

Her grandmother was furious.

"What have I told you about wandering around out in the meadow after the midnight hour?"

She stomped around the kitchen, rattling pots and pans and clattering the breakfast dishes into the sink. When at last she calmed down, she sent all the brothers and sisters and cousins out to play in the yard and took Erin to one side.

"I got the better of those bothersome horned women once," she said. "And, by hook or by crook, I'll get the better of them again."

Erin though about the old well out in the yard that was long dried out and all filled in.

"Didn't the spirit of the well help you last time?" she asked her grandmother.

"He's long gone now," said her grandmother. "You and I will have to come up with a plan on our own."

Erin pondered, chewing her lip and twisting her red hair around her finger.

"I could fetch a chicken," she said after a while. "We

would use its blood for the blood cakes and then make a broth for supper."

"Wouldn't work," said her grandmother. "The horned women would know we'd tricked them straight off."

"How about a goat?" asked Erin. "We could bleed it and then make a stew for supper."

"Wouldn't work," her grandmother. "They'd taste the goat blood in the blood cakes."

"A pig then?" said Erin. "Pig's blood is closest to human blood. We could have roast pork for supper."

Her grandmother shook her head. "They won't be fooled that easily," she said.

Now it was Erin's grandmother who chewed her lip and twisted her grey hair around her finger. After a while she turned to Erin and said, "Do you think you could trick one of them into coming back here with you?"

"I suppose," said Erin, not entirely convinced that she could.

"Then here's what we'll do…"

That night after the midnight hour Erin climbed over her grandmother's garden fence and walked out to the middle of the meadow. No sooner had she got there than she heard Thirteen Horns' grizzled old voice in her head. "Slievenamon!"

Erin found herself back in the hovel amongst the horned sisters. In one hand she held the long sharp knife with the gleaming blade. The other hand she concealed behind her back so that the hags would not see the fresh bandage that was wrapped around it.

"Where's our blood cakes?" demanded Thirteen Horns

from deep in the shadows.

"Not made yet," replied Erin, exactly the way she and her grandmother had rehearsed it.

"Not made?" cried Thirteen Horns. "What trickery is this?"

"No trickery at all," said Erin. "I did exactly as you asked. I slit the throats of all my brothers and sisters and cousins and filled up a bucket with their blood."

She held up the gleaming knife and showed them the blood stains on the blade from where her grandmother had made a little cut into the palm of her hand.

"Looks like sweet young blood," said Five Horns, leaning in to examine the blood on the blade.

"Smells like sweet young blood," said Nine Horns, leaning in to sniff the blood on the blade.

"Tastes like sweet young blood," said Eleven Horns, leaning in to lick the blood on the blade.

"Then why have you not made our blood cakes?" demanded Thirteen Horns.

"The bucket of blood was too heavy for me to carry farther than the porch," replied Erin. "And the sack of oatmeal was too heavy for me to carry from the barn. I'm going to need one of you to help me..."

"I know what's coming," groaned One Horn.

"All in favor of One Horn going back to help the girlie, say aye," said Thirteen.

"Aye!" chorused the horned sisters.

"I knew it," grumbled One Horn.

With One Horn at her back Erin moved swiftly through

the meadow and across her grandmother's yard. When they reached the porch she turned to One Horn and said, "There's the bucket of blood. See if you can lift it so that we take it to the barn and mix it up with the oatmeal."

"Sweet young blood for blood cakes," said One Horn and smacked her lips.

But when she dashed across the porch and peered into the bucket she cried out in surprise. "There's not a drop of blood in this bucket!"

"There soon will be!" cried Erin.

Out of the shadows stepped her grandmother, brandishing the kindling axe. Before One Horn had any time to react she swung the axe and brought it down on her head. Straight through the middle of her horn went the blade and cleaved her skull in two.

"Quickly!" said Erin's grandmother as One Horn slumped onto the porch. "Lean forward her head so we can catch her blood in the bucket."

Half an hour later Erin returned to Slievenamon carrying a breakfast tray on which sat twelve perfectly rounded cakes made from a mixture of oatmeal and One Horn's blood.

"Blood cakes!" chorused the horned women, crowding greedily in on Erin. "A last our precious blood cakes!"

"Wait," said Thirteen Horns before they each could grab one. "Where is our sister? Where is One Horn?"

"Mixing the second batch," replied Erin.

"The second batch?"

"There was so much blood in the bucket from all my brothers and sisters and cousins," lied Erin, "that there is more than enough for a second batch."

"Two blood cakes each!" cried Four Horns.

"One for now and one for later," said Seven Horns.

"One for supper and one for breakfast," said Twelve.

"They're almost ready," said Erin.

"Go back home right now," said Thirteen. "And tell One Horn to get here as soon as she can. Tonight we feast on sweet young blood."

Erin laid the breakfast tray with the twelve blood cakes down by the horned women's fireside. "First you have to keep your side of the bargain," she said. "I did as you bade me. Now you must release me from the enchantment that allows you to call me back here whenever you wish."

"Very well," agreed Thirteen Horns. "Click your heels three times after I send you back to the meadow and then no matter how hard we try we will never again be able to call you back to Slievenamon."

Erin clicked her heels three time before sprinting across the meadow. She was climbing the fence into her grand-mother's yard when she heard the voice of Thirteen Horns inside her head.

"Slievenamon!" she cried over and over. "Slievenamon! Slievenamon! Slievenamon!"

But it was no use, the spell was already broken and Erin could not be called back. Now the horned sisters came hurtling down out of the dark night sky.

"You tricked us!" they howled.

"Not sweet young blood at all!"

"Sour blood!"

"Vile blood!"

"Foul blood!"

Furiously they each tried to make a grab for Erin. She had to duck and dodge and dive to keep out of their wicked clutches. With horned women hot on her heels she leapt across the feet water on the porch whereby her grandmother slammed the front door shut and fixed the beam in the jamb.

When the horned women came upon the cold corpse of their sister, still with the kindling axe embedded in its cleaved skull, they began to wail like banshees and spit out curses in the ancient tongue. But none of it worked. The spells that protected the house stayed their ground. The feet water could not be crossed. The beam remained firmly fixed in the jamb. The mantle went on hanging in the window.

When at last the sun rose over the hill and the horned sisters went skulking back to their hovel at Slievenamon, Erin turned to her grandmother.

"I'll never again venture out to meadow alone after the midnight hour," she vowed.

And to this day she never has!

$\mathcal{P}$eter $\mathcal{P}$an

"This was not going well. Either I didn't exist, or she hated me."

Josie Brown is a noted political nerd, fashion fiend and windmill-tilter from Worcester, Massachusetts. She splits her time into nanoseconds and dedicates them to a variety of activities, though the bulk of said nanoseconds go to her Political Theory Ph.D program at Boston University. She writes about fairies to retain her ability to communicate with people who don't talk about things like "idiographic-nomothetic synthesis" and other such wonkery.

Josie was previously published in the anthology Elf Love and blogs regularly at theoutlawjosie.blogspot.com.

Josie was contemplating this anthology's theme over an absinthe cocktail when it occurred to her that La Fée Verte had been sorely mistreated by the fairy tale community, with little in the way of back story or description of powers. After a few more drinks, she realized that all that green was just dying for a connection, and "Career Changes" was born.

Fashion, books, faeries and absinthe come together splendidly in this contemporary sequel to Peter Pan.

Career Changes
Josie Brown

I found the rare bookstore about a month after moving to Sarasota. It had taken me a while to learn the lay of the land, and the bookstore was the best of my discoveries. The shop's owner was everything my landlord wasn't – friendly without needing reports on my every movement, helpful without being nosy, and strange without giving me the sense that he might hide my body in the basement. He allowed me to rifle through the store looking for books for work and for fun, and I brought him the occasional lunch or bottle of wine. Over the weeks, we struck up a solid friendship. I loved being in a place so full of words and in the presence of someone dedicated to their care and keeping.

After a time, I noticed that someone kept making their own little section where the Hemingway belonged, and that several books had been pulled out and set on top of the others. Given the shopkeeper's meticulous organization of his shelves, this was quite startling, and even more so for its repeated occurrence. Shoved in beside the used copies of Hemingway were collections of Wilde's plays and Maupassant's short stories, as well as a beaten copy of Jarry's *Ubu Roi*. A short time later, an unusual collection of Baudelaire's writing appeared along with a shiny critical compendium of Van Gogh's works. It was a strange collection, but when the battered *Peter Pan* appeared in the mix, I couldn't resist asking the storekeeper what this bizarre assortment was all about. When I asked him, he laughed out loud – "Oh, those are the Fairy Queen's books." This didn't do much to explain the situation. I asked him what he meant, and all he would say was that I should come by on a weekend.

Visiting friends kept me from a weekend rendezvous for the next few weeks, but I was eventually able to come to the shop on a sunny Saturday, bearing coffee and croissants for my bookish friend. Rather than accepting the coffee, he dug around under the counter and produced a small, vaguely cloudy bottle of whiskey. "You'll get more out of the experience if you Irish up that coffee and share it with the local royalty," he said with a wink. I took my usual seat in front of the faux fireplace and cracked open a copy of *Essays Presented to Charles Williams* and began reading. An hour passed quickly as I turned pages and the shopkeeper packed the warm, worn books into their shelves.

The first I saw of her was a piece of stained blue and white cloth trailing around the corner. I heard books being shifted, and then a small, intense "*damn,*" at which the cloth whipped out of sight, only to be replaced by the most dizzying spectacle I'd ever seen.

Her skirt was a shout of color, like a butterfly war over the tulip fields of Amsterdam. An infinite selection of fabrics was tacked and twisted around her hips, sometimes pinned with glittering brooches and sometimes with clumsy stitches. There were cottons and tulles and silks and even a piece of burlap, pinned clumsily at her waist, and these fabrics whirled around to precede and follow her wherever she moved. Her impossibly tiny waist was encased in a spectacular green corset, looking like nothing so much as a waiting cocoon, sparkling all over with some kind of incredibly fine glitter and trailing a whorl of green gossamer down into the riotous skirt. A tiara of mangled wires was twisted through the hair piled dramatically atop her head, working to outshine the frenzy of costume jewelry and sea glass wrapped around her neck. The shop had gone completely silent as she made her way to the counter, and I realized that she moved this miracle of fashion from place to place in bare feet.

"Peter, my friend, wherrrrre is *The Sun Also Rises*?" The voice was like Eartha Kitt on helium. The shopkeeper told her that he had sold the book that morning, but would order a new copy. She looked dissatisfied, and one big toe began an irritated tapping. "But," Peter said, "I think I've found you a new friend. She has been coming here for a while and she wondered about your books." He gestured towards me, and I held up the spare coffee in what I hoped was a non-threatening and welcoming way. The Queen turned slightly towards me – or maybe just towards the door, or maybe to align herself with some kind of astrological ley line, who knows – and then turned back to the shopkeeper. "Did she take my book?" This was not going well. Either I didn't exist, or she hated me. "No, darling. She never touches your books." She did the half-turn again. "You know I don't like pants." As Peter tried to convince her that jeans were acceptable for women these days, I crossed my legs under my chair and tried to decide if it would be best to run or to hide amongst the stacks. "Just talk to her, she's curious," I heard him saying, and as I looked up, I saw her moving towards me in her swirl of skirts.

She took the seat next to me without looking at me,

speaking to me, or, as far as I could tell, thinking about me. She rustled around in her skirts for a cigarette and was just seating it in a long holder when Peter *tsk-tsk*ed at her. With no small amount of fuss, she relocated her smoking paraphernalia, then turned her eyes on me. "Well, what do *you* want?" I was completely unprepared for every last moment of this day. I told her that I'd seen her books, and that I thought whoever assembled the collection must be a fascinating person, because I couldn't figure out what tied their tastes together. Then I panicked and told her I loved her outfit.

As it turned out, fashion was the way to her heart, such as it was. She lit up at its mention, and visibly relaxed. She took the coffee I'd set on the pile of books between us, and snuck a silver flask out of her skirts to pour quick doses of clear brown liquid into both our cups. "I learned to sew when I had to manage those damn children," she said, sipping from her spiked cup and drawing circles on the floor with her toe, "but once I got free of them, I kept seeing fabrics I liked, so I began working on this dress." I asked her what children she was talking about, and had to ask her to repeat herself when she said "the Lost Boys." I looked closely at her face, wondering how that could be possible. She didn't look older than thirty – the age her mad behavior added was another matter entirely – but here she was telling me she'd played a starring role in a story written almost a century ago. "Are you...Wen..." I started, but was brought up short by the expression on her face. "*Wendy. Darling.* Would never have this skin tone. That old bat died years ago, with all the ugliness in her showing on the outside. She only encouraged those idiot children anyway." I figured it was time to go for broke before my curiosity killed me outright.

"I'm sorry if this is rude, but I'm dying to know your story. Peter called you 'The Fairy Queen'... are you... are there really... who *are* you?" She smiled and sat up in her chair. "I am, and there are. I've had so many names, but the first one was Mab. Before that bitch Titania came along and sucked everyone into her theatrics, my reign was unchallenged for centuries. What a mess that court is now," she huffed. "When I was there, we had the *best* parties and the most brilliant people. We urged on scientists and writers, and used our magic to make them question their place in the universe. Many of us got quite good at it... learning what tiny movements could shift thought, like an apple shaken loose from a tree at just the right moment. Now it's like those television plays people watch, the General Hospitals." "Soap operas," I corrected. "Yes, those. Everyone's been reduced to silly pranks and completely pathetic parties where everyone sits around talking about the minor inconveniences they've sprung on humans. A lot of the younger ones can't even *dance*.

"After Titania smothered all the life out of the court, I went looking for something else to do, and went off to the forests of Neverland, where at least no one would bother me. It used to be quite a popular resort, you know, but it had fallen completely out of favor by then. I was just planning to take some time off, and then find somewhere else to settle down. I'd only been there for a few weeks when those damn boys came blundering through, and I think they caught me at a weak moment. They were wearing big sheets of cloth tied with rope they'd made themselves, and had to stop every few steps to gather up their sheets. I told them I would make them new clothes, but they were so hapless that I didn't want to leave them alone. I never imagined that they would literally never grow up. Once that business with the Darling children went on, I'd had enough. I think it was time anyway... if you'd seen the way they latched on to that idiot girl you'd understand. They were ready for someone else."

She went quiet for a moment. I looked over at Peter, but he was paging through his catalog and humming to himself. "So anyway I wanted to get the hell away from children," she said suddenly, and I laughed and told her I sympathized. She continued, "I thought about places where children weren't allowed to go, and eventually I just wanted a drink, so I went off to Paris and found a bar in Montmartre. The people there seemed to have some of the spark the old courtiers had, and engaged in none of the inane drivel that those Lost Boys spewed constantly, so I took a job behind the bar and found myself a little apartment upstairs. At first, I missed the deference I'd had at the court – I *am* a damn Queen after all – but as time went on, I began to enjoy the camaraderie. Still, I wanted some of that old influence over humans, and particularly over these humans – they had so much brilliance and so much life, but they dedicated most of their time to drinking across the bar from me.

"Many of these people were hopelessly trendy and drank whatever the tastemakers told them was the newest thing. I began working on a drink that could open more doors for them, turning to wormwood and delicate herbs, knowing that minds were clearest when they brushed against death. When I was happy with my creation, I slipped it to the snobbiest of the trendy drinkers, telling them it was a secret concoction reserved for my *favorite* customers alone. Of course, they couldn't keep such a secret to themselves, and before the week was out, everyone was clamoring for my absinthe." She got up and walked over to her shelf, pulling out the books in her section. When she came back, I was still blinking in surprise. "So, 'the green fairy'... that wasn't just a random reference, it was you? Did they *know*?" She shook her head. "No, no. I've always worn green, like this," she said, waving at her gown, "and it just stuck. Or maybe they did know, deep in their hearts. I've never figured out when humans can tell we're fairies. Either way, Montmartre blossomed under my influence. Look at all these things we made!" She began handing me books, cracking them open to favorite passages and paintings. You couldn't question the brilliance; these were some of the most notable authors and artists of the period. I wondered why she'd ever left, and asked her.

She sat back, still holding the copy of *Ubu Roi*. "After a while, all my friends left or died," she said, stroking the cover with long fingernails. "I started thinking about where I would go when they were all gone. Everyone seemed to be talking about America, with its inventions and its wild thinking. It seemed to share the same spirit of Montmartre at its height. One day, I set my apartment back as I had found it, and left for America. I came to New York, but I'd heard people talking about the Fountain of Youth and wanted to see the area, so I started down the coast." I looked at her. "Oh it's not *real*, darling. No one who'd be able to use it needs a damn fountain to stay young. But I assumed that any area that would make people think it existed would be worth seeing, and it is, don't you think?" I agreed, saying Florida was certainly lovely. "So

you've been here all this time? That must be over fifty years."
She looked at Peter and smiled, "I found a courtier here, and
the forests of Neverland, with a decent bar or two if you're
willing to look for them. I go traveling on occasion, but I like
having a home here. It will do for now."

We parted long after the coffee had gone cold and the
sun began to set. When I returned a few days later, Peter told
me that I'd officially been inducted into the Queen's Court,
explaining that mostly meant sharing an occasional drink and
keeping her from smoking in inappropriate places. When a
Queen chooses you for her Court, there isn't much you can do.

The Six Swans

"With your very own hands – with these soft white hands – you must knit seven shirts from the stems of stinging nettles."

The second of Anne's contributions to this collection, it is a re-telling of a variant of the Grimms' tale. Generally, in the "Swan" tales, a princess must knit a number of shirts (out of an impossible material) in order to return her brothers – transformed into swans – to their human state, and thus achieve a happy ending.

All Anne says about "The Seven Swan Brothers" is that she was very depressed when she wrote it.

The Seven Swan Brothers
Anne Waldron Neumann

Once upon a time, a king with seven sons and a daughter lost his dear wife to sudden illness. The new queen proved treacherous and cruel. She had learned witchcraft from her nurse and hoped her own son would one day inherit her husband's kingdom. When the king was far from home on affairs of state, she transformed the seven princes into swans and ordered her huntsmen to drive them from the palace.

She had meant to change her stepdaughter, too. But the princess, returning unexpectedly from a visit, saw the evil queen's wickedness and fled into the forest to escape her brothers' fate.

For three days, the princess wandered forlorn, tearing gown and slippers on branches and stones, weeping bitterly, trying to quiet her terror with songs and her hunger with mushrooms. On the third morning, however, the princess was wakened from her wretched sleep by seven swans. These, the princess understood, were the brothers the stepmother had transformed. And indeed the swans caressed her with feathered wingtips, offered her ripe berries, and showed their love with tear-filled eyes.

When the princess had wept and embraced them all in turn and eaten the food they brought, the swan brothers, circling slowly overhead, led their sister deeper into the forest, to the cottage of an old woman who knew magic. "Help me change my brothers back to fine young noblemen and thereby prevent my cruel stepmother's wicked plan," the princess begged the old woman.

"With your very own hands – with these soft white hands – you must knit seven shirts from the stems of stinging nettles," the old woman told her. "When you throw the shirts over your swan-brothers' heads, they will change back to their proper shapes. Can you make this painful sacrifice?"

"Oh yes!" the princess cried. "I am sure I am capable of it. Dearest brothers, let us find a place where nettles are plentiful and where we can live together secretly and safely for however many days we must. With my own hands I will knit the shirts to undo your cruel transformation."

And so, guided once more by her brothers flying before her, the princess crossed the border of her father's domains, waded a swift and icy river, climbed a mountain range, descended its steep slopes, and picked her way through another tangled forest.

At the edge of this forest flowed a stream whose muddy banks grew thick with nettles. In a cliff near the stream was a cave. Here the princess and her brothers settled down to live while the princess gathered nettles and prepared to knit them into shirts.

Nettle shirts were more difficult to knit than the princess could ever have imagined, however. The rocky path from cave to river bank was painful for her now-slipperless feet. Gathering nettles was painful. Stripping leaves from stems was exquisitely painful. Even treading stripped stems into shreds that could be twisted into string and knitted was painful. As the first day drew toward late afternoon, the princess could no longer hide her agony from her brothers. They gathered round her with troubled eyes, gesturing with graceful necks and widespread wings for her to set her task aside. But she persisted till dark, though her slender white hands and feet were red and blistered.

At nightfall, she could hardly eat the food her swan brothers had gathered during the day. Only the tears they shed, when they gathered around her that night to comfort and pity their sister, seemed to bring her some relief from the burning pain.

Each day, the pain grew worse. But the first shirt was beginning to take shape. The princess told her brothers she would set aside each shirt in turn till all were completed and the brothers could return with her in triumph to their father's castle. But she was unsure whether their swan natures under-stand human speech, though they certainly understood human anguish.

It seemed that the brothers could speak together, however. On the day the first shirt was finished, the largest swan stepped forward and bowed its head, indicating that the princess should clothe him. The swan was transformed in-stantly into the oldest prince, dressed as he was on the day he was bewitched. The princess looked down at her stained gown and blistered hands in momentary shame. But her brother knelt before her, caught her hands in his, and kissed them tenderly.

"Dearest sister," he said, in a voice hoarse from emotion and disuse, "and I speak for all our brothers: know how much we honor and admire your painful service. We have resolved, now the first shirt is ready, that I should return immediately to our father's castle. There will I communicate our stepmother's treachery to his majesty. Look for me to return in seven days with the king our father and with horses and soldiers. An apothecary will prepare ointments to heal these poor hands, and servants will bring fine raiment befitting the most devoted of sisters. We have further agreed that our stepmother must be dragged here in chains and forced, in the king's presence, to undo her wicked spells. Therefore, dearest of all possible sisters, you need no more wound your poor hands with these cursed nettles."

At these kind words, the first she had heard for many weeks, the princess burst into tears. She was still weeping with gratitude and relief as she waved goodbye to her eldest brother.

Seven days passed without bringing the soldiers and horses, however, and then twice and thrice seven. Some dreadful fate had surely befallen the eldest brother. Had he been eaten by wolves? Left for dead by brigands? Or, more probably, waylaid by their ever-vigilant stepmother and her huntsmen? Wearily, the princess collected more nettles. And six tearful swans bowed their heads in shamed acquiescence.

When the second shirt was at last finished, the second brother stepped forward like the first. Transformed to his proper self by his sister's sacrifice, he was full of fiery resolve to avenge his oldest brother's all-too-probable fate and then replace him as their father's rightful heir. The princess called tearful goodbyes and warnings till her brother disappeared from view. But this time she waited only seven days before beginning the third shirt.

The third shirt grew more slowly than the first and second. The princess's fingers were swollen into sausages, and she found it harder than ever to twist shredded stems and knit them as before. Starved for human speech, she muttered while she worked: "Oh dear, oh dear, oh dear. My fingers are *so* swollen. My feet are *so* sore. These stems are *so* stiff. Whatever shall I do? Oh dear, oh dear, oh dear." She talked to herself when the five remaining brothers left to gather food and when she supposed they would not hear her. But they did hear. And they began to fear for their sister's fragile sanity.

Thus, after the third shirt was finished, and the third brother stepped forward and was transformed, he made an unexpected proposal. "This painful service is too hard for you to continue alone, dearest sister. Allow me to remain with you in human form while you prepare a shirt for our fourth brother. Though none but you can perform this painful task – so the wise old woman told us – you need not and shall not labor alone without human support and companionship."

The princess again burst into tears. "Dear brother," she sobbed, "how kind you are to me. How kind you *all* are. Surely, with such warnings as we have had of our stepmother's vigilance and treachery, you can contrive to send a message to the king and meet him *outside* the castle walls. There, in secrecy and safety, explain everything and devise a plan to save me and our four remaining brothers without such delay as you propose. I beg you to forget my foolish weakness. Save one, save all. Look, I will begin a fourth shirt immediately – not from any doubt of your success but to pass the time and, if I am diligent, to spare at least one other brother the shame of appearing before our father in his altered state."

But the princess did in fact doubt the third brother's success, and silent weeks confirmed her fears. Meanwhile, the fourth brother and his sister had reached an unspoken understanding. When the fourth nettle shirt was finished, he did not put it on but flew toward their father's castle still disguised as a swan, carrying the shirt in his beak. Perhaps, if he could somehow change into his real shape before his father's eyes, he would escape his stepmother's vigilance and *show* the king the queen's cruel fraud.

The fourth brother was soon invisible against the westering sun. He had flown too far for the princess to hear the twang and hiss as a watchful huntsman's arrow pierced his swan's heart. But, as the princess doggedly began the fifth shirt, she felt a dreadful pang in her own breast. Her cries of despair sank to inarticulate moans only with sleep.

As a fifth shirt took slow and painful shape, the fifth brother formed a private resolve. He had never expected to inherit anything – neither kingdom nor dukedom nor position at court, nor even so much as a small estate and hunting lodge. He had always suspected he and his younger brothers must live by their own wit and skill at arms. He would not risk death for something he had never hoped to gain and a court life he could scarcely remember. When the fifth shirt was completed, and the fifth brother was transformed, he thanked his sister with averted eyes and disappeared into forest shadows in the direction of his father's castle. Then, when night fell, he doubled back along the stream, planning to follow it and what-ever river it joined to seek his fortune in some foreign army.

After the fifth brother's departure, the princess no longer counted the days until his probable – his possible – nay, his *im*probable – return from their father's castle. And, as she began work on a sixth shirt, she seemed to have lost if not diligence then purpose – discarding not only nettle leaves but also stems she had just stripped and shredded, or unraveling an already knitted row in the slowly growing shirt.

The sixth brother, too, seemed to have forgotten who he was and who *they* were and what they were doing and why they were here. One October morning, when dawn mists parted to reveal trees reddening with cold, the sixth brother flew south with the wild swans. The princess, who had lost count not only of her knitting but also of her brothers, did not notice his disappearance.

More months pass. The seventh and final brother no longer invites his sister's tender gaze with his own tear-filled eyes. He still brings fish or cattail shoots or shriveled berries but bridles and hisses as he drops them at her feet. Sometimes he even fights his sister for the food, squawking and snapping and beating his wings.

The princess, in turn, has forgotten why she spends her days collecting and stripping nettles. Her hands and forearms are always swollen now, red and deeply blistered. They burn and bleed when new wounds open between old scars.

Each morning, the princess stumbles down the stony path to the river on feet as puffy as bread loaves. There she bathes her arms in mud and gathers the day's supply of nettles. The rest of the day she spends before her cave. Seated on a rock, she wags her head from side to side as she strips nettle leaves from their stems. "Eeh, eeh, eeh," she keens. Sometimes she rises and spins in circles, stamping nettle stems with cracked and callused heels. "Eeh, eeh, eeh." As she dances, she twists outstretched hands through hanks of knotted hair that hang below her knees, holding her tresses out in some dim memory, perhaps, of opulently skirted ball gowns. Or is she simply resting weary arms in the cradles of her hair? Or perhaps she longs to lift herself from earth, still spinning, and float into the clouds to join the brothers she no longer remembers.

The Frog Prince

"'Just one thing I want to make clear,' she said. 'Absolutely no tongues, all right? I know what you've been catching with it.'"

Born in 1980, Stuart Sharp is a freelance/ghost writer living in East Yorkshire. He has a PhD in Medieval History, but somehow never seems to be able to write historical fiction.

*As a ghost-writer, he can't really brag in detail about the eight YA novels he was responsible for last year, but he has published two urban fantasy novels (*Searching *and* Witch Hunt, *both by Double Dragon Publishing) under his own name, as well as producing a steady stream of slightly whimsical fantasy short stories.*

"I went through a bit of a turning characters into frogs phase last year, and towards the end of it, it occurred to me that I should probably at least try to play with the traditional tale. That happened to coincide with a few job interviews, and the effects are clear to see."

Find him at www.stu-stusplace.blogspot.com.

Testing the Water
Stuart Sharp

Princess Aurelia had become something of an expert, when it came to ponds. You did, after a while. There were limpid ones and stagnant ones, deep ones and ones that barely came past the ankles of the royal wetsuit. This one came up to her knees, murky and smelling faintly of mould.

It was at least reasonably free from rubbish. Aurelia hated it when she had to wade through mountains of shopping trolleys on her way across. After all, it wasn't as if any of the five kingdoms even had supermarkets. She could only assume that they appeared spontaneously, like mushrooms, or servants.

Finally, she found what she was looking for over in the far corner, sitting on a lily pad and watching her with something akin to hope. Aurelia strode over to the frog as purposefully as it was possible to while knee deep in water, scooping it up in one well-manicured hand before heading back to the bank.

The frog didn't squirm, which was generally a good sign. It was always embarrassing, kissing a frog that turned out to be just a frog. It probably wasn't very kind to the poor little things, either, even if Princess Aurelia *had* been judged "fairest princess" three years running by *Magic Mirrors Monthly*.

Her Aunt Matilda was waiting with a towel and a flask

of hot tea. The older woman wore black with the confidence of someone who could use glamour spells to look as she wanted, which was, in this case, rather more stunning than Aurelia did. The princess knew she only did it to annoy her. Aurelia handed her the frog, discretely wiping her hands on the towel.

"Why does it always have to be me who fetches the frogs?"

"Because this is for your benefit, dear," Matilda said. "Besides, you *know* I don't really react well to water. I melt."

"You do *not*. Your glamour just washes off, and then people can see that you're going grey."

"Well, isn't that bad enough? I think it's important to maintain appearances. Shall we get on with this?"

Aurelia sighed. "Oh, very well. Hold it up."

Aunt Matilda presented the frog and Aurelia prepared to pucker up. "Just one thing I want to make clear," she said. "Absolutely no tongues, all right? I know what you've been catching with it."

Closing her eyes, she planted a single chaste kiss on the frog. There was a familiar tinkle of bells.

Aurelia opened one eye, and then the other. The man in front of her was about her age, and certainly handsome, being dark-haired, square-jawed, and pleasantly muscular. She could see the latter because frogs didn't tend to turn back with very many of their clothes intact. She could see rather more than that when she risked a glance downwards. Good, up to spec in all obvious departments.

"Um... I couldn't borrow your towel, could I?" the man said. His voice was, predictably, aristocratic and dreamy.

Aurelia handed it over. "I'm Aurelia."

"And I am Prince Greenrick," the man replied. "Um... that would that be *Princess* Aurelia, wouldn't it? It's supposed to be a beautiful princess who does the turning back, you see, so that we can live together happily ever after."

"She's a princess, all right," Aunt Matilda put in. "I wouldn't be quite so quick on the happily ever after front, though. We've got some questions first."

The prince looked rather confused at that. It was, Aurelia decided, not a good look for him. Square-jawed heroism, yes. She could see that working. Confusion, on the other hand, made him look rather like a stunned duckling. A slight black mark there, perhaps.

"Um," Prince Greenrick said, "what sort of questions? Only, no one told me that there might be questions, and you don't exactly get much chance to revise, when you're a frog. Unless you want to know about ponds. I know quite a lot about ponds."

"Not as much as we do, sunshine," Matilda said. She started filing her nails. "We must have traipsed round half the ponds in the five kingdoms by now."

"Oh. Okay. Um... what do you want to know?"

Says "um" a lot, Aurelia thought, putting it on her mental checklist. Now, should that go down as an annoyance or an endearing quirk?

"Well," she said, "first of all, you're definitely a proper prince? Father a king, mother the queen, and so on?"

"Um... yes. Or they were, last time I checked, anyway. Why do you ask?"

"It's just that *some* people think that it's all right getting these little certificates off the crystal ball channels that just say they are, and it gets so *annoying*."

"Yes, I suppose it would. Um... can I just ask what all this−"

"And you're the heir to a proper kingdom, aren't you? Somewhere that brings in a proper income? Call me old fashioned, but I like a man who can pay his own way."

"Um... no, I don't think there are any problems there. I mean, we had a royal treasurer and everything, so presumably there must have been some treasure lying around somewhere."

The um...ing was getting a little annoying now. Still, there was no harm in going through a few more questions. He might grow on her.

"Right," Aurelia said, "something a bit more practical, now. Say I'm being held captive by an evil dragon that wants to eat me. What do you do?"

"Why, I ride in on the old warhorse and kebab the blighter with my lance, of course! Can't have damn great newts abducting beautiful young women." As Aurelia blushed at the compliment, the prince appeared to think about it. "Horrid things anyway, newts. Always stealing the best bits of the pond when you aren't looking. Is that the right answer?"

"Oh, definitely," Aurelia said. "Well, except for the thing about the newts, and I suppose we can give you that, under the circumstances. You'd be surprised at how many of the princes I've tried didn't get it, though. One went on about dragons being an endangered species, while another started going on about risk assessments and the proper use of fire extinguishers. What sort of handsome prince does that?"

Silence fell. The sort of silence where one half of a conversation has just worked out that something is rather wrong, while the other half is busy stuffing her fist in her mouth over what she has just said.

"So you've, um... done this before?" Prince Greenrick asked.

"Once or twice," Aurelia admitted. "The first time was... well, an accident, but after that..."

From the side, Aunt Matilda cackled. She'd always been good at cackling. "Once or twice? Try twenty-three times! Weeks we've spent, knee-deep in ponds, looking for a suitable candidate!"

"Suitable candidate?" The confused look was back. Aurelia was sure she didn't like it now. "You mean that all these questions are so you can *choose* whether... whether..."

"Whether to order the big white dress or throw you back," Aunt Matilda said. "Exactly."

Prince Greenrick drew himself up to his full height. "Now see here! That is *not* how this works! The beautiful princess kisses the frog, he turns into a prince, and they live happily ever after. It isn't a precursor to some sort of *interview*!"

Aurelia frowned prettily. She knew she did it prettily. People had told her. "Well, that doesn't seem very sensible. I mean, just leaping into an ever after with the first frog you meet? That's no way to guarantee happiness."

"And you think this is?" Prince Greenrick stormed.

"Please don't shout," Aurelia said. "I *hate* it when princes shout at me."

"I will damn well shout as much as I like! Why, I have a good mind to drag the pair of you before my father the king!"

"You and what army?" Aunt Matilda said. She took a

stick out from somewhere in the folds of her dress.

"I'll have you know, madam, that I have a perfectly serviceable army just over… ribbet."

Aunt Matilda blew smoke from the tip of her wand while Aurelia stared down at the frog, or at least at the frog-shaped lump in the towel. She sighed. "You know, aunty, I really thought that he might be one to keep."

Her aunt put an arm around her. "I'll grant that he seemed all right until he started yelling, but think about it, dear. If he's shouting now, what will he be like in twenty years? Besides, I never think it's a good start to a relationship when you're threatening the prospective in-laws with an army."

Aurelia nodded rather sadly. Her aunt was probably right. At a croak from beneath the towel, she lifted it up to reveal the frog. It glared at her and croaked again.

"Oh, please don't be like that," Aurelia said. "I know it isn't exactly what you wanted, but isn't it better being a frog than winding up with someone you'll only annoy with all the 'ums'?"

The frog croaked again, and hopped for the pond.

"It's not you," Aurelia called after it, "it's me." She thought about that. "All right, so it mostly *is* you, but I'm sure that another princess will be along soon. Probably. And if you play your cards right and don't say 'um' too much, you might still get your happily ever after."

She turned to her aunt, and sighed. "You know, I really thought that dating would be easier than this."

Aunt Matilda shrugged. "Well, there's always the other traditional option."

"Hang around in a tower waiting for someone to come

along? No chance. I mean, yes, you get to catch up on your beauty sleep, but pruning all those rose bushes must be hell afterwards."

Aunt Matilda, whose own love life was as varied and complicated as she could make it, thanks to the glamour, nodded. "You could just try getting out to a few clubs, you know, letting your hair down a bit."

"Aunty, I'm a princess. People would only try to climb up it. No. It has to be this way. We'll just have to try more frogs. Where's the next pond?"

The other woman waved vaguely over to the left. There was probably one there somewhere. There seemed to be one everywhere else.

"I'll just bring the van round."

Princess Aurelia nodded, and her aunt headed off. She took another look at the frog. Maybe she could live with the ums? After all, this was starting to get rather trying. No. What was the point of being a princess if you couldn't be at least a little picky? Now, she should probably get on. Happily ever afters didn't make themselves.

The Wedding of
Sir Gawain and Dame Ragnelle

"When you looked like a geriatric toad and smelled like the midden — not to mention being imprisoned by your mad brother — invitations to court were rarely forthcoming."

Michelle Markey Butler holds a doctorate in English Literature, which is all Thomas Malory's fault. When not writing, she tries to stop her preschoolers eating gum off the floor, save a Queen Anne from the ravages of 1970s remuddling, and plot her return to academia. She blogs about parenting at www.heirraising.wordpress.com and is pleased to report that despite their best efforts none of the children have escaped. Recently.

Michelle's story "Little Hands" won an Honorable Mention in the Second Quarter 2010 Writers of the Future Contest, while her book-in-progress, Lord Garland's Daughter, was named an Honorable Mention in Textnovel's 2010 contest. Her story "Farewell the Dove" appeared in the January issue of Digital Dragon Magazine. More about Michelle can be found at: michellemarkeybutler.com.

"The fifteenth-century 'The Wedding of Sir Gawain and Dame Ragnell' has long been my favorite Arthurian story, so I was pleased at the opportunity to speculate about what their lives together might have held. Once started, I couldn't resist dovetailing my sequel with Marie de France's 'Lanval,' another favorite."

Part mystery, part romance, and part court drama, "Sovereynte" is the only story in the collection based on an Arthurian legend, and also an entertaining read.

Sovereynte
Michelle Markey Butler

Ragnell knew he was looking at her, wondering if she were awake. But she didn't roll over. She lay still — probably too still. Gawain would realize she was avoiding him. Whatever. She wasn't up to dealing with him.

Finally she felt the bed shift as he got up and headed into the dressing room. The king was leaving later that day, taking the queen to visit her father for a week. Gawain was among the knights accompanying them. She was relieved. How wrong was it that after just four months of marriage, she was grateful to get away from him? She waited until she heard the outer door close before getting up, feeling cowardly for dodging him. The relief, however, remained.

Who did he think he was, ordering her to a feast? God's wounds, she hated court functions. They were boring, she always offended someone, court ladies snubbed her, and everyone — *everyone* — stared at her. He asked. She refused. He insisted. When she still refused, his face reddened and he *commanded*, as her husband. So much for the *sovereynte* he'd promised. He agreed on their wedding day she was her own master, and that broke her brother's enchantment. It was the answer to the riddle: what do women want? *Sovereynte*, to direct their own lives. Now he was issuing proclamations. She went — but she hadn't spoken to him since.

She threw back the covers, sliding through the canopy

into the chilly October air. With no fireplace, the other room was even colder. She dressed quickly, but not so fast that she didn't pause, as always, to admire her feet. Pale, normal feet. The magic had made her a mass of lumps, warts, moles, ill-placed hair, and wrinkles. Why had it bothered her most that her feet were hideous?

A knock sounded on the outer door.

"Queen Guinevere." She bowed, doubting she hid her surprise.

The queen looked no less astonished. "Do you not have a lady in waiting? You are the wife of Gawain. You should not answer doors. Think of his reputation."

"I haven't found one who doesn't stare at me when she thinks I'm not looking." It wouldn't be wise to ask about Guinevere's lack of accompaniment. If Ragnell shouldn't open doors, the queen definitely shouldn't knock on them.

Her eyebrows shot up, her face taut with offended pride. Ragnell's mind searched frantically, wondering what she'd done to give offense, and so soon. She'd barely exchanged a dozen words with her... without addressing her properly. "My lady," she added hastily. God's dripping head! She'd never get used to court customs. She'd never had to before. When you looked like a geriatric toad and smelled like the midden — not to mention being imprisoned by your mad brother — invitations to court were rarely forthcoming.

The regal eyebrows descended minutely, as if on alert for other infractions. "You have a great deal to learn, Dame Ragnell."

"No doubt, my lady." She *had* already learned Guinevere's reputation for holding grudges, so she swallowed her annoyance. Was that reference to Gawain a threat? Most likely. The queen excelled at those too. "How may I serve my lady?" She hoped she concealed a wince as she forced the words out. Guinevere obviously wanted her to do something. Probably something she wouldn't like. Royalty sneaking around was invariably sketchy.

Guinevere's nose unwrinkled enough that she looked like she'd bit a sour cherry rather than that she'd just realized one of the dogs had farted under the table. At least the knights always blamed the dogs. "You have a reputation for solving puzzles."

"I've been some small use to the ladies of the court, my lady." Though wary, they'd apparently decided a magician's sister might know a trick or two. They began trickling in for her help — often lost items, but sometimes bigger concerns. Was a lover faithful? A servant loyal? Ragnell had no magic, but she was clever and she had a skill for knowing truth when she heard it. She solved their problems.

"My brooch is missing."

Ragnell drew a deep breath. She might escape yet. "My lady, I've helped others recover things. But wouldn't your attendants do better? They know where you go, and so where to look."

The queen waited a heartbeat. "I do not believe it is lost."

Ragnell waited, but she didn't continue. "Yes, my lady?"

Again Guinevere hesitated. "I am certain it has not merely fallen off. The clasp is strong."

"You think it's misplaced in your chambers? Or..." she paused, wondering whether to go on. But the queen's sharp gaze demanded she do. "One of your attendants stole it?"

Guinevere looked surprised. "Of course not. My ladies are of the highest rank, from the best families. They would never betray me."

Ragnell looked down at her court slippers. No shoes had fit her transformed feet. "Betrayal happens, even in the best families."

"What do you mean?" The queen's voice was sharp. Ragnell realized — again too late — she'd given offense. Guinevere assumed she alluded to the rumors surrounding Arthur: his father'd tricked his way into his mother's bed, or worse, Arthur had been tricked into his sister's.

"My brother." She gestured along the length of her body. "I'm only lately restored, my lady. It pains me to think of it." But not as much as Arthur's refusal to give her ten minutes alone with the bastard after his enchantments broke.

Guinevere looked abashed, as she'd meant her to. But queens do not apologize. After an awkward moment, Ragnell spoke again. "What do you think happened?"

"It was... misplaced."

"Misplaced?"

The queen's gaze shifted downward as if embarrassed. "I have an admirer."

"You have an *admirer*?" She blurted before she thought. "You have a *husband!*" She inhaled as if she could suck the words back in, waiting for the explosion.

It didn't come. "What does that matter?" the queen said coolly. "Arthur does not restrict his entertainments. I have no intention of doing so."

Ragnell clamped her lips. She must not say what she

316

was thinking. The morals of royalty were roughly those of feral cats? Not her place to comment.

Her distaste must not have been evident, at least not so strongly Guinevere felt she had to deal with it. "He was seated beside me at the feast last week." She gave a soft sigh. "The one for the Breton knight."

She remembered. It was the feast Gawain demanded she attend with him.

"He may have taken it then. A token." She tucked a strand of golden hair behind one ear. "Sweet. But I need it back. It was a gift from Arthur. If I do not wear it next week at the feast welcoming that Cornish knight, he will notice."

She combed her memory. Who sat beside the queen? She closed her eyes, picturing the scene. "Lanval or Bedivere? My lady?"

"Not Bedivere." She gave a derision-charged sniff. "Lanval." Her voice shifted, all sunshine and honey. "Yes. Lanval." Her gaze sharpened again. "We leave in an hour. I want that brooch when I return."

Ragnell waited until the door closed before growling her annoyance. God's ankles! First Gawain. Now Guinevere. This was court etiquette? Maybe she'd been better off as a hag.

She let her breath out slowly, picturing her irritation leaving like a mist. Succumbing to anger didn't help — how many times had she learned that during her captivity? — it just felt good. She needed her wits instead.

She had no doubt she could find the brooch. Arthur's court was a small community. She'd be able to track it down, particularly if Lanval had palmed it. But Guinevere's deadline was irksome. She could do it, but in a week? That wasn't much

317

time.

And — something about the queen's story itched. Maybe the talent *was* magic and her soul crept away from naming it, but untruth galled her like wearing someone else's boots. What part was false? Arthur's philandering? She'd heard no whispers that the king sought pleasures beyond his marriage bed. Guinevere's claim could be rationalization of her own outside interests. Lanval wasn't the first to pursue the queen. Guinevere's beauty was like the moon on a smooth lake — and any other romantic clichés one cared to think of. Men found her irresistible. Last year she'd been kidnapped by a besotted neighboring king. Ragnell had heard about it from Gawain, who'd been a member of the rescue party.

Not hearing rumors about Arthur's pursuits didn't mean it wasn't true. She hadn't heard anything about Lanval's interest in Guinevere either, but he'd been there at the feast, chatting her up and probably pocketing a keepsake. She wasn't part of the court gossip's beaten path.

Something about the queen's story had been untrue. She sat, trying to puzzle out when the familiar discomfort began. Finally she shrugged. She sensed all lies, important or not. It made talking to anyone tricky. Most people lied in small ways every day. "No thank you, I'm not hungry," someone would say while visiting a friend, when in reality she knew that the other woman's cook wiped her nose on her hand. Guinevere's falsehood could be meaningless — perhaps she only worried Arthur would notice if she didn't wear the brooch, not that she knew he would. Most likely, irrelevant. What *was* relevant was the queen expected to see that brooch in her hand in one week. God's muddy feet. One week.

318

* * * * *

A decade as a hag does not tend to develop subtlety. Ragnell waited two hours — she'd been at court long enough to know that outings involving the queen never happened on schedule — then went to Lanval's room. Straightforward is not the same as foolhardy; she made sure he was away from court and that no one saw her. It wasn't difficult. Most of the knights were gone, either with Arthur, on quest, or visiting their own holdings; Guinevere's ladies were with her; and the household servants had vanished. Those not gone with the king and queen were probably somewhere with their feet up, enjoying a well-deserved rest.

One glance showed that Lanval was a lower-ranked knight than Gawain. He had one small room, less than half the size of their dressing room, and no fireplace. But he was a tidy soul. His bed was made, the canopy properly pulled back. The chest at the bed's foot was closed. His court robe hung on its hook. There were no dirty small clothes or hose on the floor. She shuddered. How disgusting would that have been? She wasn't even used to seeing Gawain's yet.

Where would a Guinevere-struck knight hide a purloined love token?

There was a belt-pouch hanging behind the court robe, but it was empty. She stepped to the end of the bed and examined the wooden clothes box. Gawain said sometimes knights left their chests rigged; theft was not as unknown at court as Guinevere liked to believe. She found no contrivance, and raised the top an inch, waiting to see if anything sprang loose before lifting it further. Lanval was apparently not as concerned as some of his brothers-in-arms.

Or he simply had less to steal. The chest was almost empty. An extra pair of hose. A ratty tunic — what was that about? He wouldn't dare to be seen anywhere near court in that. A cracked wooden spoon. Maybe he just didn't throw things out? A pair of soft court slippers...

Hang on... the right slipper was heavier than it should've been.

She exhaled in anticipated relief that the task had proven so easy, and reached into the slipper.

Not so fast. As soon as her fingers grazed the object, she knew it wasn't what she sought. It was a ring. A ring worth three or four of Guinevere's missing brooch. The queen hadn't said anything about a lost ring, and Ragnell knew it wasn't hers. It wasn't anyone's in Arthur's court, or at least it hadn't been made by or for them. The silver sat ice-cold on her palm, too cold for even the unheated room to explain, and seemed to be growing frostier, as if it knew it did not belong in her hand. She'd seen those designs before. How had Lanval come by an elvish ring?

Shrugging, she slid the ring back into the slipper, replaced his belongings, and closed the chest. Not her problem. If it wasn't supposed to be there, the elves were more than capable of reclaiming their property.

There was one place left to look. She glanced away even as she stepped towards it. She was newly married; beyond a canopy was a mystery, a mingled blush and wonder. She thought of Gawain, and the red deepened in her cheeks.

God's bony butt, was this what marriage had done to her? She gave a deliberately uncouth snort, remembering the hag who'd scratched and spit at Arthur's table, and pushed through the bed curtains. She felt under the pillow and ran her hands along the smooth bedclothes. Standing again, she bent to examine the ropes supporting the mattress. Nothing.

If Guinevere was wrong, how was she going to find the brooch before her return? It would be just like that thoughtless idiot to drop an impossible task in her lap, skedaddle for a week, and expect her to have it fixed before she got back.

Maybe she'd missed it. She should check again, just to be certain. But the belt-pouch was still empty, the chest held no further surprises, and there was nothing but bed-clothes — albeit fresher ones than you might expect from a bachelor knight — on the mattress. She shook the bed curtains, setting the hanging rings jingling but no brooch clattered helpfully out.

She stood, her words about Guinevere, Lanval, and the court in general now so foul she spoke them only in her head. The upside was that Gawain looked good by comparison. Maybe she'd overreacted. Was it that unreasonable to want his wife to attend court feasts with him? He couldn't know how much she hated the stares. The goggle-eyed, open-mouthed stares, remembering what she'd been and wondering when her time would run out. But she wasn't going back. She glanced down at her feet. She *wasn't* —

Dust...

She paused in her silent rant, staring at the floor. Lanval was a tidy man, but the servant who cleaned his room wasn't. Dust coated the floor. Which was not as intriguing as the two small tracks in it. Lanval's bed had been moved recently; it used to stand a hand's breadth further from the wall. Now it was almost against it. She frowned. Why would anyone do that? The bed curtains could touch the wall and leech cold and damp from it. Since their purpose was to keep the sleeper's warmth within the bed, it seemed counter-productive bordering on stupid.

She crawled back onto Lanval's mattress, examining the far side more closely. She shook the bed curtains again, focusing on the section beside the wall. *Here* it hung free, although just a hair from the plastered stone wall. *Here*, too, it swung easily. *Here...* she smiled, slipping her hand between the mattress and wall... it bunched, creating a little velvet pouch, just enough to hold... a brooch. Guinevere had been right after all.

Ragnell liked solitude, which was good, because hags were generally left alone. But after three days of neither seeing nor speaking to anyone — her meals appeared in her room as if brought by ghosts — even she was ready for reassurance that other mortals still walked the earth.

She went to the kitchen. She'd made friends with Arthur's cook, although she wasn't able to see her often. Yet another of the court's prohibitions was socializing with ser-vants. She didn't care, but it was inconsiderate to Gawain to flout customs too often. No matter how dumb they were.

"Dame Ragnell." If it was possible for a voice to sound floury, Hafren's did.

She toed a three-legged stool closer to where the cook stood dusted to the elbows, kneading bread dough. "Nice to see you."

"I thought I might before now," Hafren's voice held a hint of reproach, "with most of the court gone."

Ragnell looked down. "I'm sorry." She was, too; she should have realized it was the perfect opportunity. And it was warmer in the kitchen. "The queen left me a job."

"Ah." Hafren clucked sympathetically. "Got it done?"

"Yes."

She set loaves aside to rise. "Something difficult or just unpleasant?"

Ragnell snorted. The cook had Guinevere pegged. "Unpleasant." She pondered how annoyed the queen would be if she found out she'd discussed it, then decided she didn't care. Something still rubbed wrong. Maybe talking it out would help. "Finding a brooch."

"She lost it?" Hafren set the bowl aside for one of her underlings to wash later. Only then did Ragnell look around the kitchen, noticing its emptiness, so different from the usual bustle. She really *was* distracted.

"I put my staff on half-days during the king and queen's absences," the cook said. "I can handle breakfast for the half-dozen people who want it. My folks've earned some time off."

Ragnell wondered when Hafren got a break but decided against asking. The cook was speaking again. "Strange she asked you. Her ladies'd have a much better idea where to look."

"That's what I said. The queen insisted it wasn't lost. Just 'misplaced.'"

"Uh-oh," the cook said. "That sounds like royalty for 'it's complicated.'"

"You got it. She claimed a knight swiped it for a love token."

Hafren added flour to a fresh bowl. "Lanval?"

"What makes you say that? I haven't heard any

rumors."

"Pfft. Spend more time with us. We hear 'em all. You found it?"

She patted her belt pouch. "In his room."

The cook tsked. "I wouldn't've believed it."

"You just said you'd heard stories."

She sprinkled salt into the bowl and stirred. "I hear 'em. Doesn't mean I believe 'em."

"Why?"

She began to cut lard into the flour mixture. "Lanval's not the type."

Ragnell kicked the leg of her stool. "I didn't think so either."

"It's the flashy foreign knights that catch the queen's eye. Lanval grew up not ten miles from here. I know his grandmother. She'd be disappointed, let me tell you. In his taste."

She snickered. No wonder she liked Hafren. She was the only person at court brazen enough to speak her mind. She suspected the cook was careful to whom she said such things, but it wouldn't matter. Guinevere knew better than to force Arthur to choose between his cook and his queen. Hafren's pies were marveled about as far away as Normandy, and he adored pie.

"But now that I think about it," her hand hovered over the bowl, adding water, "he has been acting odd lately. Like he's in love." She shook her head. "I just wouldn't have guessed him for the queen's new toy. I'd heard those rumors, but only from her ladies. Where'd you find it?"

"In his bed."

Hafren's eyebrows shot up. "More than flirtation, then."

"You think...?"

"Don't you?"

She hadn't. She'd assumed Lanval had moved his bed, creating an ideal hiding spot for his pilfered token in the bunched-up bed curtains. Was Hafren suggesting that the brooch had been dropped during... an encounter... an encounter vigorous enough to scoot the bed? She felt her cheeks go crimson.

"This why you've been hiding upstairs? Guinevere's unsavory recovery mission? She should be more careful than to drop jewelry in her lover's bed."

Hiding? Ragnell opened her mouth to object. But Hafren was right. She had been hiding. Not from the queen's task. That was finished, although her mind continued to turn it over, perplexed by the rough edges that snagged her thought. Gawain. It was Gawain she was hiding from, even though he wasn't there. Not wanting to think about their quarrel, she'd "forgotten" to visit the kitchen, knowing Hafren would sense it as soon as she spoke his name.

Or if she didn't.

"What's wrong?"

"Nothing."

"Uh-huh. Now, what's wrong?"

She kicked the stool again. "It's just... well... it's Gawain."

Hafren gave a wry smile. "I already knew that."

She looked away but she could feel the unrelenting stare. Finally she blew out her breath and began talking.

"Uh-huh," the cook said again when she'd finished. "Does he know why you don't like feasts?"

"The stares?" Ragnell shook her head. "It's foolish. I can't tell him."

Hafren began patting out the dough. "Then how will he know?"

"It shouldn't matter. I said I didn't want to. He should keep his promise."

"It doesn't work like that. He agreed you'd be your own master. Not his."

"If he did know, it wouldn't matter. He wanted me there."

"Maybe. But he knew his reason — to show off his wife, I'd guess. He didn't know yours. He probably thought he had the better claim this time."

Ragnell sniffed. "What if he always thinks he has the better claim?"

"That doesn't sound like Gawain. Though it reminds me of certain queens I won't mention."

"You are a wicked woman. Guinevere must hate you."

Hafren reached for a bowl of apples. "Let her. If *I'd* been kidnapped, it wouldn't have taken months to get me back. The king eats apple pie at least once a week."

Guinevere must have come directly to her rooms when the traveling party arrived. Ragnell opened the door to find the queen still in her riding clothes. Dust swirled from her as she stepped into the room. "Well?"

"How nice to see you again, my lady. Was your journey pleasant?"

The queen gestured impatiently. "Either give me my brooch or admit your failure."

Ragnell drew it from her belt-pouch.

Guinevere stroked the piece's largest jewel. "Where did you find it?"

"In Lanval's chamber. In his bed. But you already knew that."

The queen blushed prettily. "It was a possibility."

"No," Ragnell said. "You *knew*."

The queen paused, her hand on the door.

"You put it there yourself."

"Take care, Dame Ragnell." Her voice was like the low growl of a bobcat.

"You want Lanval. But he's not interested. So you set a trap." She took a step closer. "You had your ladies spread rumors he fancied you. Then you planted your brooch in his bed. Once it was found, and with the stories already whirling, who'd believe his protests?" Ragnell struggled to keep her voice cool, to check her welling fury, the same rage that had enflamed her soul the day before. Fingering Guinevere's brooch and wondering about the oddness of men, she'd thought about what Hafren had said. Mulling it over, she'd realized what Guinevere had done, and what she meant to do. With Ragnell as her tool. "After all, the brooch was found by me, who the court ladies've been coming to for months with their little problems, and known to be outside court intrigue. An impeccable witness. Lanval might as well acquiesce. Or if he keeps refusing, you can denounce him to Arthur. Either way, you win." She was pleased to hear her outrage manifest as contempt, undergirding her words like steel.

The queen turned. She was at least a hand taller than Ragnell, and pulled herself up to her full height. "I would never. I do not have to. You are lying."

"I'm not. But you are. Now. And before, when you said Lanval was an admirer. Didn't your ladies tell you I can sense lies?" She paused. God's privy members. Maybe the talent *was* magic. It certainly wouldn't hurt to let Guinevere think so. "One can't be held in the thrall of sorcery as long as I was and not be touched in some way. A poor recompense for ten years of stinking ugliness."

The queen paled. Not in fear but cold white fury. "You will wish yourself back there if you speak of this to anyone. I *will* have Lanval!"

"Love can't be forced."

"Who are you to talk? Gawain did not choose you."

Ragnell inhaled. "Our marriage was arranged — in an unusual manner. But noble marriages are often arranged."

"You forced him to promise you *sovereynte*. That's all I want. *Sovereynte*."

"*Sovereynte* isn't getting everything you want. It's having a say."

"I know people better than you do." Her voice was a low hiss. "You take what you want. No one is going to give it to you. I want Lanval. He *will* be mine!"

The door opened. Gawain stared as the queen brushed past him.

He stepped inside, his face tight.

She took a deep breath. "They stare."

Confusion clouded his features.

"At the feasts. They stare."

He blinked. "Let them! They sneered at you before. Now they see you, beautiful and clever as you are, and remember that of all the knights, you picked me."

"Who else?" Her voice softened. "Who had the courage to face the Green Knight? Who had the courage to face *me*?" She sighed. "But they're not jealous. They're waiting for me to change back. Not just the knights. Everyone. The court ladies. The servants."

"Is that how it seems to you? Look closer. They're green as a holly leaf with envy. Come with me again, and see."

She felt a corner of her mouth turning down. "I don't know."

"I'll watch, too. Maybe I'm wrong. If they are looking to see what you turn into next, we won't go to any feasts but the ones Arthur directly orders."

She wavered. It was a start. Did her eyes hold the depth of misery his did? Guinevere was right. He hadn't chosen her. She'd demanded him, her reward for saving Arthur's life. But he had later, and he did now.

He opened his arms slowly, as if afraid she might not come to him. She flung herself forward, her head going to his shoulder, his nose into her hair.

Rapunzel

"You're done giving me things. You locked me up, and then they locked you up. The difference was that you deserved it."

Once upon a time, Mat MacKenzie expected he would be a novelist when he grew up, going so far as to major in writing, but not so far as to grow up. He found himself making computer games instead, out of a hope that they could blossom into a new narrative medium – but has found that, for storytelling, the old ways are still the best ways.

Mat's main avocation is his toddler, whose presence in his life inspires daily wonder, lifelong responsibilities, and certain fears.

"Dreams of the Tower" is a twenty-first century sequel to the story of Rapunzel that explores the realms of dreams and magic in the context of family life.

Dreams of the Tower
Mat MacKenzie

The lady behind the counter glances at the MasterCard, and raises her eyes guardedly. "I'm sorry if it's a bad question, miss, but aren't you the Rapunzel girl?" That's how they said it on TV, *the Rapunzel girl*, even before they leaked my identity on FOX.

"I was. My name's Rachel now. It's on the card."

She fussily gathers my things into the CVS bag. "I'm sorry, miss. That was out of line. Here's your card, and the bag has the receipt." She perks up through a visible effort. "And you've got two real angels there. Everything works out in the end." Gregory and Lisa pile up behind my leg and peer out. Even at five they're tired of this routine.

"Yeah, I guess it does." When I was sixteen and pregnant, the story was still current, and I could barely stand to go outside. But no matter what happens, I've seen worse: Mrs. Gothel had me in that tower for four years. Four years. They can remember that pitiable waif on TV, but I'm a grown woman with a husband and two happy kids.

We've barely started down the sidewalk when my phone plays "Purple Rain," the special ringtone for Erik. The twins look up eagerly and I put him on speaker. "Hi, Daddy," I say, "we're headed home now."

"Rache, I can see a robin! All the way across the yard –

and on the first day of Spring!"

"You're sure? They said it would take a month—"

"Honey, it's the first time they've put implants in someone who grew up sighted. I saw it, the orange on the breast. It's mostly a blur but I'm already getting there. My God, by next week I'll be able to see Greggy's face. It's incredible. Hi, Lisa, I'm going to see you!"

We rush the three blocks back to the house and the kids sprint across the kitchen to Erik. "Is the robin still there?" "How many fingers am I holding up?" "Show me the robin!"

He spreads his arms and finds his children by touch, but plainly he's trying to use his vision too as he hoists them side-by-side onto the bench under the window. "It's straight across the yard, on the fence."

I set down the bags and come to peer over his shoulder. "Honey, there's red there but it's the birdfeeder. It's, like, two feet tall." The kids pull away from the window. I blew that one.

Erik squints where his eyes used to be, those soft hazel eyes. "Oh, hey, you just missed it. I guess it flew away." You can barely see the scarred flesh behind the special glasses. I'm used to him wearing dark glasses. The wires running around back, and under the bandages, those still creep me out.

"Oh, Daddy," says Lisa, hopping back down. Gregory sits and watches his legs dangle.

I give Erik's arm a conciliatory squeeze and go back to sort out the groceries. "Yesterday you could barely tell where the window was. This is good."

He smiles gamely. Then he looks across the kitchen and says, "Can I help you?"

"Thanks, but I've got it."

"Hello. Can we help you with something?" He's looking past me.

The kitchen has a door to the back yard. Erik advances a step, placing himself between Lisa and the entrance.

"There's nobody there, honey," I say.

He stops abruptly, unclips his telescoping cane from his trouser pocket, fingers the strap. "I was so sure that time." He sits. "Maybe it was the shade from outside."

I'm in the downstairs part of the tower, a windowless round room with old posters taped along the wall, each one a ghostly moonrise framed by trees or mountains, with mystical runes added by hand. Mrs. Gothel and I are in the two splintery lawn chairs. It's winter in Maine, and the tower stands unheated and drafty. Even the shiny brass lamp on the table has a bluish LED, illuminating without warmth.

She dresses in layers of flowing, hand-painted robes. Tonight's ensemble is purple, topped with a shawl, with the thin leather belt traced with a silver dragon motif. My whole life she's been old and creased and imposingly tall, with narrow shoulders and a thin, angular nose. Her eyes are huge and penetrating and I never did figure out what color they were.

I am dressed just like her, with the robes hiked up and tucked in to accommodate my smaller frame. My long, silken hair is combed out meticulously, and I'm wearing midnight blue eye shadow and coral lipstick, identical to hers.

She leans forward in her chair, brandishing *The Wicca Pogroms*, a world history text self-published by a member of her circle who's in, I think, Detroit. We spent half of my thirteenth year analyzing it paragraph by paragraph.

Erik's voice whispers in the periphery of my hearing: "Once you know you are dreaming, the dreamland is yours. Command it, firmly." He's quoting from *Own Your Dreamland*, a book he picked up for me last summer, part of my recovery. Every bedtime he recites its mantras using his best hypnotist voice.

"Mother, that book was bullshit. When I read about real history I felt like I'd been brought up in North Korea." That was good: after a hundred dreams like this, I took the initiative. But I called her *Mother*. "Mrs. Gothel, I mean."

She shifts somehow, like she's snapping into focus for the first time. With a bemused glance at the book she lays it aside. "Oh, my sweet, how I've longed to see you again. Still such a beauty, if no longer the maiden. And you've been studying dreams – how enterprising!"

"I have a few issues to talk about. Let's start with locking up children and never telling them their fairy tales."

"Little Rapunzel, all children are their parents' captives, and carry their parents within them." She studies me for a moment, appraisingly. "But I have come to tell you your future, not your past. You remember, I am sure, that the magic follows the blood?"

—*and the blood may be inborn or may issue forth*. I always took that as some indefinite threat. "I remember everything," I tell her, "but I got over believing it. Perhaps I should say that you told me the wrong fairy tales."

"Do not court my temper, my child. I am your mother, and your grandmother, and twenty generations before them, and it is time for a new generation to receive us. You are heir to an immortal gift."

"You're done giving me things. You locked me up, and then they locked you up. The difference was that you deserved it."

"Oh, no, my child. I am here because I am no longer confined in Windham. I have the magic."

"I don't want your magic and I was never your child."

She rises imperiously, her robes sheer and solid like a column, and her shadow seems to engulf the walls. "You will do as you are instructed. You are my child, but not of my blood: therefore blood must issue forth."

"I command you to sit down, Morrigan Gothel."

"You shall not address your mother by her given name." She flicks her left hand into a severe gesture, her long fingers down and straight like a cage, a ghostly lunar glow dancing between the dagger-like nails.

"This is too much. I'm making you go away, and the tower, the whole thing. You've infested my dreams long enough." The stones and posters scatter like leaves in a typhoon, revealing a honey-lit field of spring poppies, and warm sunlight floods across us.

She glances around and the tower slams back into place. "You refuse, then, to so much as listen. Perhaps you will reconsider, for the sake of your children. But first, you must relearn respect for your elders."

Her hand rises, colossal, surrounding me, and begins to squeeze.

The pain pierces me and my hands are clamped to my temples and blackness crushes in and I'm falling back twisting and my spine freezes and my legs are trapped my hand bangs on something in the dark my eyes are shattered there is water rising cold to my throat and I hear a ragged scream and I'm gasping I'm choking I'm awake, sweaty sheets adhering to my back, my legs tangled up, shivering. Erik rolls over, groggily, and holds me in the dark. At night the glasses come off, and I feel his stubbly face nuzzling my forehead. I realize I'm crying. "You're OK," he says. "You're OK. I've got you." He rocks me, warm skin on skin, and slides his fingers along the base of my skull, where I get my tension headaches, the wrong spot but the right thing to do. I cry harder, letting it out, letting it out.

One more convulsion and I start to regain myself. As if by some signal, we both pause, and lie there vigilant, like so many nights before. After a moment, he whispers, "I don't hear them." The kids' room is next to ours and some of my night-mares have been harder on them than on me. I start to breathe again.

"I tried to get rid of her. She won't go away. Erik, make her go away."

"Another tower dream, am I right?"

"Downstairs, a lesson. But I knew it was a dream – that's the hard part, right? Then I can have control?"

"Rache, I change my dreamland all the time now. I actually command it out loud. Just do it like that."

"You don't understand. It hurts, it's like a migraine, up along here. The book said dreams can't do that."

"Yeah, like with falling dreams, where you never hit the ground. That sucks all to hell, getting the headache too. But it's over now." His arms give another squeeze.

It's not an answer, but it's what he's got – and me, I've got a headache from Hell and a chronic fear of sleep. We chat gently until I'm not shaking any more, and then I let him slip off into his dreams while I hold mine rigidly at bay, staring at the unchanging ceiling, remembering the tower.

The window in the upper room looked across to Mrs. Gothel's rustic cottage, where I spent my early, comparatively happy years. We never did the "Rapunzel, Rapunzel, let down your hair" routine, but she would call up, "Rapunzel, my sweet, drop the ladder down. I've come to give you a lesson." The ladder was this fire emergency thing, chains and narrow steel rungs. If I talked back instead, she would say, "The choice, my child, is yours," and press something in her hand, and instantly I'd get a pulsing migraine aura and would double over – and that would be the lesson for the day.

It seemed a great act of kindness, the next day, when she came up after all, and gave me some extra, warm food and a vial of peach schnapps.

Now and then I tried to sneak down. Within a few rungs my head would start to swim, and the wild bushes below seemed to writhe and lash their thorns at me, driving me back. I never reached the ground.

I wake after dawn, hollowed out like a Jack-O-Lantern, the pain almost faded.

Monday. Erik stayed home for the morning, then went into Boston to busk on the Orange Line with his vintage Suzuki keyboard and drum machine. We mostly manage on his inheritance but he brings in grocery money with poppish covers of Metallica and Ozzy.

Lisa and Gregory and I are deep into building a Lego museum, exhibiting *Found Objects: Living Room*, when the phone rings. I don't know the number on the ID, but it's local, and this is a good time for adult contact. "Hello?"

"Hi, I, um, figured I would get the machine. This is Uncle Clyde."

"You're not my uncle." Mrs. Gothel's half-brother was never bad to me; but I've always suspected he knew what was going on, and didn't tell.

"I'm going to keep this short. I thought you should know she's gone."

"She fucking *escaped*?" The twins look up, eyes wide. They only know bits of the story but they know I'm jumpy sometimes. I'm pacing with the phone, trying not to go berserk.

"No, no, it's... suicide. Yesterday, at the prison in Windham. She talked them into giving her her old clothes and stuff. You know how she talks people into things. How she talked. She had this little dagger, hidden somehow. I thought you should know first."

I halt mid-step, almost trip over myself, feel my chest take in air, like I've been relieved of a forty-pound overcoat I'd forgotten I was wearing. "Thank you. Thank you, Clyde."

"Maybe she couldn't live with it anymore. This, what, angiosarcoma, all the pills. You knew she was sick, right?"

"No."

"It had spread to the heart, the left ventricle, very rare. They gave her a week, two, tops. Anyhow, she left a note, not addressed to anyone, but maybe it will mean something to you. It's kind of weird."

"Of course it is." I take a seat, putting on a good display of calm for the twins, who come over to touch. "Go ahead." Paper crinkles on the other end.

The Maiden came I, silver and sky, shoots of spring to rise,
  the rowan and crocus to bear.
The Mother became, golden aflame, grown erect and wise,
  to nurture the whelp in my care.
The Crone today, iron and clay, my power shall prevail
  by the spell of the Samhain drum.
The Eye shall I find, eternal of mind, to pierce the icy veil
  the Mother once more to become.

It's her usual symbols, seasons mixed with the stages of the Goddess, Greek elements, yadda-yadda – not even real Neopaganism. And Samhain is Halloween, half a year away.

I push my right sleeve up to the elbow. She's naming my old tattoos, which still shimmer like the windows of a cathedral, using God-knows-what for ink. If Clyde knew anything I'd ask him about the eye, the one I haven't got. And why go from the Crone straight to the Mother? What happened to the Maiden?

Once I've convinced him I can't translate this stuff for him the conversation wraps up. Our goodbyes are cordial. I explain to the kids, as little as I can get away with, and then call Erik, my finger trembling over the buttons. He's elated, and not only on my behalf: the woman's weird, thorny bushes cost him both his eyes. We talk dreamily of sirloin and wine, and then I call around and rummage up a babysitter.

The next morning, Erik announces that he can see well enough to fry some eggs, while I have "doctor's orders to stay in bed." Soon I can smell bacon, and when I'm summoned down the stairs, the eggs are mangled from some attempt to

340

flip them, but they're soft how I like them, seeping into the toast. The twins are rooting for him, awed, as he sets down the plates without feeling first for the table.

"You know what you never get?" he asks me as we dig in. "A day off. And me, I never get to look around. So. I've been thinking about the attic, all the crap up there, how I haven't ever done much cleaning. And then all that stuff I haven't seen in years, stuff I never got to share with these guys."

"A day off sounds wonderful. But not everything up there is, totally... good, you know."

"Yeah, I'll take care of it. How about if you have today to yourself while the three of us do some housecleaning? It can be our little adventure."

The twins chatter excitedly. Normally the attic is off-limits.

In minutes I'm in sweatshirt and jeans. Out on the porch I take him aside. "I've got my phone if you need me." He nods, taps a finger to the glasses. "And keep them out of my old chest? They shouldn't see that stuff, not yet." After they convicted Mrs. Gothel, we snuck into the tower, using Erik's backwoods route, machete and all, and took some of my things. It was a crappy childhood, but it was mine.

And off I go.

The art in the Isabella Stewart Gardner Museum is that much nicer when you can stop and look instead of wrangling two kids. I resolve to get Erik to come next time.

Then I'm wandering the open spaces downtown, never checking the time, letting the last few days soak in, the miracles of the daytime and the horrors of the night. As dusk draws me home at last, I notice I'm humming, and the song is

Ding Dong, the Witch is Dead. I sing it softly, and then with abandon, on the subway and up the hill. I do the helium munchkin voices. "Which old witch? The wicked witch!"

I smell the smoke and see the open windows before I reach the door. Then I smell the barbeque sauce and the chicken. Erik greets me sheepishly – he salvaged enough for dinner, and microwaved some pot stickers for a side dish.

Dinner is show-and-tell. Lisa holds up a small silvery key. "I never knew Daddy had a motorcycle. That is so cool."

"That was a long time ago," Erik says. "I still owe Mommy a ride, I think."

"I liked the pictures on the walls," says Gregory. "The kitty was my favorite. You could see it moving."

Erik rubs his chin. "Did you find a picture of Metalli-cat? I can't see too well in the dark."

"The lamp was nice and bright," Lisa points out.

I shoot him a sharp glance.

"It's OK," says Erik, measuring his words. "I took it out before they came up." So they saw the old brass lamp – but not the robes, the one faded poster, the witchy stuff. I silently forgive him and move on.

The kids probe eagerly about the artifacts spread around the house: the machete, on the top shelf in the living room, out of their reach; the pavement-scraped leather jacket with the anarchy symbol in red acrylic; the lead pipe which was supposed to be a bomb but had the wrong mix of chemicals. It takes a genuine miscreant to scale the tower and rescue the damsel, but still, I feel for his parents. After dinner I offer to wash the dishes if he'll take the bags of attic refuse to the curb.

Later, I notice the lamp glowing coldly in a corner. As I

switch it off my arm aches beneath the tattoos, like there is sand in my veins. Later I switch it off again. Damn thing.

The kids are tucked in and we're settling into bed. We touch lightly in the dark.

"You know, I used to think Mrs. Gothel couldn't die. I mean, literally. She was going on about it again in last night's dream."

"She really got you when you were impressionable."

"She did, yeah – she got me. But I saw things, even when I was old enough to know the difference. One time, I was nine or ten, and she turned my big dressing mirror into a window, and we watched a house, somewhere far away, burning. She closed it when I tried to put my hand in – I never told you that one because you wouldn't believe." He grunts noncommittally. "I think that was my birth parents' place. Anyhow, tomorrow we need to take my old trunk down to the dump. Everything from the Gothel place."

"If you're still sure in the morning, we'll rent a car. Settled?"

"Settled." The talk wanders, to his two dead parents and my three, and on to more comfortable places. During the *Own Your Dreamland* recitation I start to stroke him on the thigh, and he sidles closer and I can hear his smile. "I'm going to turn on the light," he says. "I want to see you this time."

It isn't how we've ever done it, with the glasses and the light on; but it's good. He tells me that I'm still beautiful. We let it build slowly, taking it long into the night.

The morning is overcast and I wake lazily and late. Erik

343

is sprawled like a lanky puppy, snoring lightly, and I notice he managed to get his glasses onto the charging stand. The kids must have been up for hours and I'm surprised and grateful that they didn't bang on the door. Maybe they've gorged themselves on Fruit Loops.

I throw on my bathrobe and groggily make my way down the stairs. I hear giggles, and see light flashing from the living room. "Lisa, Gregory, good morning," I call out, in that same voice every mother uses. "You haven't been watching too much TV, have you?" It's a real question and a standing joke.

Lisa bounds into view, a pixie in her lime pajamas. "No TV, mommy. We're playing the painting game." She's got something black smudged on her face, and on her arms and hands. It looks like tempera, which at least washes off.

"What game was it? Can I play too?"

"The game with the kitty, the game in the lamp. You can join next turn!"

She leads me into the living room. The brass lamp stands in the middle of the floor, dazzling as a lighthouse, and the light it throws has transformed the room with projected shadow shapes. Twisted runes and long sinuous lines cover the walls and stretch across the blond pinewood like a dark bed of vipers.

Gregory is crouched with a paintbrush and a tempera jar, carefully filling in a shadowy line. A cat made of shadow watches by his feet, flat on the floor like a paper cutout, with eyes like little moons. He says, "Now it's my turn to catch the kitty!" Gleefully he stabs with his brush, almost tagging the cat. It bounds away to another shape and flicks its tail coyly. Gregory advances.

Nausea rolls through me, and I rock back on my heels like I've been shoved; but I say, flatly, "Lisa, Gregory, come over here right now. The game is over and I need you to go upstairs."

They look to me searchingly. The cat turns its head my way, and paws its next rune impatiently. Gregory studies his dripping brush.

"Lisa, go upstairs and wake up Daddy." She shuffles her feet, I squeeze her hand as she passes, and she starts on up. Gregory lingers as I force myself to approach the lamp, holding up one hand against the painful brightness, half-familiar runes splashed against my legs. If the off switch doesn't work I'll destroy it with a hammer. In fact, I'll do that anyway.

I'm nearly to the lamp when I smack into something.

I put out my hands: it's all around me, an invisible wall, and it feels like frozen air, colder than a nightmare and sheer as steel. Mrs. Gothel did this once, when I worked myself up into an adolescent rage and started screaming at her. She made me stand in this design on the floor, a circle made of ropey lines, and I was caught there until I pleaded for forgiveness. Our floor has the same pattern, repeated over and over, some shadows and a few painted in.

"Mommy! Mommy, help." Gregory's imprisoned a few feet behind me. I try to reach over but the wall is in the way.

"We'll be OK, Greg. I'll get you out." How suddenly I'm desperate. Is this some leftover magic, meant to keep me in the tower? Erik doesn't know a thing about witchcraft, but he can pour water on the tempera. The runes will stop working if we smudge them. Or he can break the lamp, or something.

Gregory bashes against his invisible wall with his forearm, too hard, and winces. I try again to reach for him but my wall is impenetrable. He holds hands flat against the air like a street mime. "Mommy, I'm sorry about the game. I didn't know it was wrong. I'm sorry about the floor."

I hear creaking on the stairs. "You didn't do anything wrong, Gregory honey. Daddy's coming down now. We'll be all right. We'll be all right."

Erik appears at the bottom of the stairs and instantly the lamp goes dark, leaving a floating pink afterimage etched with runes and a cat. He surveys the room with his glasses, slowly, and a broad grin builds across his face. "I've been waiting for this one for a long time," he says.

A mad fantasy flashes through my mind where he's scheming with Mrs. Gothel, like in a straight-to-video movie. But I know him. "Honey, this sounds weird, but I'm trapped here, and Gregory too. We need you to do some things."

Gregory's sobbing, trying to reach his brush, which rolled outside the invisible wall when he dropped it.

Erik cranes his head way back, looking far up past the ceiling, and cups his hands and calls up. "I know you're trapped, honey. I'm coming right up. Get the ladder – or, what the hell, let down your hair!"

"I'm right here, Erik. Can't you see me? We're right in front of you."

Suddenly he backpedals and thrashes his leg to get something off, cursing. And then he shakes his head light-heartedly and chuckles, and holds out his hand, like a king requiring his scepter. "This is my dreamland. I command my machete into my hand." He waits a second, hand out expectantly, and lowers his arm. Then he spots the machete and fetches it from the shelf.

"Erik, Erik, I'm right here. You're in the living room."

He holds the machete with both hands, like a slugger before the pitch, right in front of his son. "Rache, I know you're not here to see this," he says, "but when we wake up you're going to love hearing happened to your mom's rose bushes."

I press myself against the floor, face-down, and order Gregory, "down on the floor, *now*. Get down like this." He does it just as Erik takes a wild, slashing swipe, straight through the invisible wall, and the machete misses by inches. Gregory lies frozen, peeking up at his father in disbelief. From here I see one spot in my circle that isn't filled in. I stretch an arm through but I can't reach him. His circle is complete.

Erik slashes again, grinning wildly, and deftly switches around his grip to strike straight down. Gregory tries to squeeze to the side but there's no room and the machete slams into his thigh and there's a crack of steel on bone and the blood sprays out over Gregory and on my face and my arm and he howls, a desperate wolf howl, a cornered wolf cub crying for *Mommy, Mommy*, and I can't reach him. Across the room Lisa faints and collapses, bumping down the stairs and spilling into the room like a dead thing.

Erik's smile vanishes and lets go of the machete, which stands with its tip in the floor, the lower part buried in flesh. Gregory's scream blurs my senses and the only thing in the universe is him, huddled, needing me. With a blinding surge I force my head through that gap, scraping my nose, ripping my hair, and I press my lungs flat, sliding sideways, clawing the polished floor for purchase. I'm curled around the edge of the icy wall, emerging with my back to Gregory, my back to the machete.

Erik is pleading with his dream. "My son is hurt. I need to wake up." He slaps himself across the face, hard. He tries it again.

I get out all the way, and totter to my feet, and the rush recedes a little. Gregory's blood feels obscene on my arm. As I watch, the tattoos draw it into themselves, hungrily, growing flush upon it. Finally I understand that this wasn't any leftover magic. Mrs. Gothel was alive in the lamp. She was alive in my dream and she's alive in Erik's glasses. *The magic follows the blood. Time for a new generation to receive us.* At this crowning moment of insanity I know why I was in the tower.

Pressing my hands against the frozen air around Gregory, I crouch and tell him, "I'm going to get you out." He looks up, eyes pleading and wet, pajamas spattered red, and quiets, starting to succumb to the cold and shock. But I can't help him and stay beside him too. I get the lead pipe that was supposed to be a bomb, and smash the lamp, and smash it again, scattering shards of plastic and glass. That's one less place she can go.

Gregory's huddled motionless now, curled face down like a fetus, pinned like a moth on a board.

"Erik," I say. "Can you see me? I'm standing in front of you now."

"Rachel, are you out there? I'm in a dream, at the tower, but something's wrong. I can't get out, it's like your dreams, it's not working. Gregory's hurt somewhere. I think I heard him for real. If you can hear me you've got to help him."

He reaches straight for me, uncertainly, and I dodge. The phantoms around him must have shifted again.

348

But she's still not letting him see me. I pounce with both hands and snatch the glasses, and they won't come and I yank harder and he grimaces and grabs the back of his head. Shit, there's some kind of catch you're supposed to release, he's clutching the wires. The catch pops and I back away. Later, we can talk later. Now that I'm holding the glasses, she has me where she wants me.

And I feel her, pushing up through my wrist like an invading pulse. With a sharp prickle, a new tattoo surfaces next to the others, a midnight blue line, and I realize my fingers can't let go of the glasses. The line blinks open into an eye, the iris every color, no color, like a spider web. It wells up out of my skin, an eye with lids and dark lashes, and she swivels it to look straight at me. Her presence is expanding up my forearm, following the blood to my heart, and my elbow flexes, experimentally, without my command.

Wrapping my other hand around the wrist I jam my thumbnail into her iris, forcing it in, and the eye tries to squeeze shut. My blood, Gregory's blood, her eye jelly pool up and I push in harder, and maybe it hurts her like it hurts me. At the same time I'm marching myself toward the hall to the bathroom. The glasses are electronic.

I use my knee to bang the toilet seat upright. "You won't take me again," I tell her, realizing as I say it that she has no ears, not yet.

She's spreading upward into my chest. My breathing is off-kilter, the right side out of synch with the left. I plunge both hands into the cool toilet water, and a wash of pink spreads from the wound. Nothing happens. The glasses are waterproof. I bang them around, fighting against my possessed arm, and finally there's a snap, and searing heat, and my arms jolt up and I force them back down, the red water frothing, searing my fingers, scalding my face.

The toilet bowl cracks and I slip and topple sideways onto the slick floor and the glasses bounce away. The clash of wills within me melts away. The room shifts somehow, like it's snapping into focus for the first time. I can move both my hands. The eye is still there, but it's only a tattoo on skin, flat and blind with a gouge weeping red right between the tendons.

Erik appears, feeling his way. "Rache, quick, Greggy's hurt, there's blood, and he's unconscious. I called 9-1-1 but I don't have the glasses. Are you all right? I need you."

"I am unhurt. Help me up." He locates me and helps me to me feet, debris filtering off my robe, and we dash back to the living room.

The invisible walls are gone. "Gregory's leg is broken," I report, "but he's alive. Lisa is over by the stairs." She shivers at my touch, already awake but playing dead. She collapses into my lap, and I rock her, feeling her warm breath on my hands. The next generation will be easier.

Erik kneels solemnly and strokes Gregory's head, careful not to move him. The siren of the ambulance is approaching.

"They're going to think I did this to him. I'm don't know, maybe I did. I was sleepwalking, or something, and I couldn't control the dream. But I could hear when he was hurt. Hang on, Greggy, they're almost here. Hang on."

"You're not responsible. Mother came back, using her magic. She needed blood from my bloodline." And so little of it benefited the ceremony, so much was lost. It was all ad hoc, only fortune providing even the blade.

The ambulance stops out front, and cuts the siren, and there are voices and bustle.

"Magic, was it? I'm trying to believe you. I don't have an answer. You're sure she's not coming back?"

"She taught me more than you know, my sweet. I have the magic."

Fairy Tale

"'Why would he do this?' The Wolf softly touched a row of stitches up his abdomen. 'All I did was eat Little Red Riding Hood. And do you have any idea how hurtful being called 'Big Bad' is?'"

Joe Mogel is a resident of Worcester, Massachusetts, where he attends college and works part time as a math tutor. He is a published fiction and non-fiction writer. His articles "The Remarkable Mr Golub" and his work for the Quinsigamond College newspaper Open Door, are both available online. Joe's fiction can also be found online, such as the story "Outlaw's End" at Rope and Wire. He is currently working on two novels, a play and several short stories. His website is JoeMogelAuthor.YolaSite.com.

"The inspiration for this story came from the fairy tales themselves. How could anyone go through any one of those stories without needing therapy? Then came a great deal of research, both in the stories and psychology. The issues I gave each of the characters seemed to me to be the best fit. Once I had the characters and the setting hashed out, I built each section as a compression of several months of therapy. Add a dash of real history and my own takes on some of the personalities of the fairy tales and voilà! we now know what makes them tick."

What Makes Them Tick
Joe Mogel

With a loping stride, the short, briefcase-wielding man mounted the stairs to the Fairytale Kingdom Mental Health Clinic. The large, castle-like, brick building sat in the middle of a sprawling health center, surrounded by enchanted woods, which made his morning commute stressful. The small man, clad in fedora and trench coat, assailed the revolving door.

Tromping through the foyer, he breezed past the marble slab desk. Bustling behind was an Arabian princess secretary. She flipped her long, black, braided hair as she flopped a stack of file folders onto the desk. The tinkling bells on her bedlah outfit caught his attention.

"Dr. Norton, your cases for today," she cooed, batting long lashes on her big, hazel eyes.

"Yasmin," Dr. Norton hummed, "how have you and your father been getting along lately?"

She gave a broad lipped, little pout. "Fine."

Dr. Norton raised a spare, questioning eyebrow. He snatched the folders with his free hand and tucked them under his arm.

"Elektra complex," he muttered as he strode to the bank of elevators in the back of the lobby.

The fourth floor had peach-toned walls and drab, tan Berber carpeting. White, paneled doors with large frosted windows lined both sides of the unending hallway. Brass numbered plaques listed the offices and occupants. There was a potted ficus punctuating the space between each office. An electric buzz issued from the florescent lights.

Dr. Norton tromped down to suite 13, fiddling with the lock for a moment before he stepped into his office's waiting room. Lights were flicked on, jacket and hat tossed onto hooks, and magazines organized on the coffee table. He grumbled into his back office, almost tripping over his white noise machine.

He flopped the folder down on his desk and sank into his swivel chair. A second coffee table, sofa and a rocking chair were set opposite his desk and under a cape style bay window. A monolithic filing cabinet, draped in leaves from an unkempt potted plant, stood guard in the corner. He stretched out for a moment, then glanced at the wall clock.

Crap, she'll be here in about ten minutes, almost no time for a snack.

The outer door creaked open then slammed closed.

Damn. She's here early.

The leggy redhead strutted into the office. The buzz of the white noise machine muffled the clop of her high heels. She pouted her surgically-enchanted lips as she sat on the rocking chair. She wore a skimpy peasant's skirt and blouse; a bright red riding cloak was draped over her shoulders.

"Good morning, doctor," she cooed.

"Good morning, Little Red Riding Hood," Dr. Norton replied cordially.

Her eyes softened as she smiled. "Please call me Lil' Red, all the men do."

"I'm sorry, I always forget that, Lil' Red." Dr. Norton shook his head as he plucked Lil' Red's folder from the pile.

"You're taking your medication regularly?"

"Yes!" she snapped, sitting bolt upright, her eyes going wild. "Why would you think I'm not?"

Dr. Norton set the folder in his lap, leaned his head back and interlaced his fingers.

"Ok, ok." She sank into her seat. "Maybe I haven't been as regular in taking my meds as I should. There, I said it, ok?"

Dr. Norton relaxed, leaning a little forward in his seat.

"That manic response will be more common if you don't take your medication as prescribed."

She weakly nodded, giving sad, puppy dog eyes.

"Bipolar is a manageable condition if you stay on top of your meds and work at those techniques we discussed last time."

"You're right." Lil' Red sighed. A slight smile curved her lips.

Dr. Norton furrowed his eyebrows. "That doesn't mean you can fall back to your old habits."

Lil' Red dropped her chin to her chest and folded her hands in her lap. She let out a little sniffle.

"Sex addiction isn't an effective way of managing your manic episodes."

She rolled her eyes and groaned.

"Remember what happened after you were eaten by the Big Bad Wolf?"

"I had sex with the woodsman as a thank you."

"And?"

"I had sex with the wolf as an 'I'm sorry you were cut

open.'"

"Mmmm... Hmmm..."

"And I had sex with grand..."

"That's enough."

"I still can't sleep, I feel deep dread about the people who are trying to kill me."

Dr. Norton rubbed his eyes and pinched the bridge of his nose.

The tall, fair-haired man in the gold trimmed cape paced the room. His gold buttoned blue shirt wrinkled as he wrung his hands.

"I just, I just know they want me out of the way. I can't stop thinking about them, it's driving me nuts!"

"Prince," Dr. Norton hummed, "perhaps you should sit down. We've already established that your pacing is a physical manifestation of your anxiety. So if you sit down, you'll be exercising control over the chaotic elements in your Id."

The Prince sat down and drummed on his knees. The gold piping on his white trousers jumped with every rap of his fingers.

"I just know that they want me gone," gulped the Prince.

"Who are they?"

"I don't know, but they want me gone."

"Why do they want you gone?"

"Because they suspect that I'm something else. They think I'm not a real prince."

Dr. Norton audibly exhaled.

"What is it they suspect?"

"That I might be..." The Prince paused, looking about the room. He slowly leaned in and whispered, "I might be gay."

Dr. Norton arched an eyebrow and looked the quivering, caped noble up and down.

"You don't say."

"Yeah, I know, it's crazy." His cape ruffled as he straightened his back. "I mean I've had Rapunzel, Snow White, Sleeping Beauty, that girl who kissed me when I was a frog..."

"You were a frog?"

"Yeah, I was a frog and this peasant girl kissed me and *voilà!* Here I am!" His arms twanged out and back to his sides.

"Now why do you think people think you're gay?"

The Prince jumped in his seat. "Who said I'm gay?"

"You said you thought people wanted you dead because these unnamed folks thought you were gay. Is that right?"

"Oh, yeah. I did say that, didn't I?"

Dr. Norton rubbed his eyes again.

"I think," the Doctor said, leaning back in his seat, "that you're projecting onto others. I think you're the one who thinks you're gay."

"How could I be gay? I'm Prince Charming!" exclaimed the Prince.

Dr. Norton grimaced and hunched his shoulders forward.

"I think the frog is a metaphor. The fact that that animal is not a body breeder is symbolic of your detachment from your inner feelings."

"Ok, I guess so." The Prince twitched.

"Your feeling that this amorphous 'they' wants you dead is really you, wanting your self doubt to go away. But most of all I think this comes down to a repressed desire on your behalf."

The Prince knotted his eyebrows and thrust his lower lip forward.

"Do you know what I'm getting at, Prince?"

"Yeah, I think I do."

Dr. Norton relaxed into his swivel chair. A calm smile slipped across his face. Quick words were scribbled into Prince Charming's file.

"This is all because..." the Prince began.

"Go on."

"...secretly, deep down..."

"Go on."

"...I've been repressing..."

"Yes."

"...the fact that..."

"Yes."

"...I want to be a frog again."

"Yes, wait, what? No!" Dr. Norton abruptly sprang almost out of his seat.

"It all makes sense now, Doc." An uneasy smile fractured the stress on his royal features. "I've been running around saving all these damsels in distress, kissing them, living happily ever after until the next damsel come along. Why? Because I'm trying to convince myself that what I want is human girls, when what I really want is to live in a swamp on a lily pad."

Dr. Norton slapped himself on the forehead and ran his hand down his face, flicking his lower lip with the tips of his fingers.

"Yeah, it's all coming together now. This must be why I want to snap at flies with my tongue."

"Wrong type of fly," Dr. Norton muttered. "On the bright side," the Doctor slapped his thighs, "our session is over for this week. Be certain to arrange our next meeting with Yasmin on your way out."

"Do you think the Wicked Witch could turn me back into a frog?"

"If she does, please be aware that I don't provide amphibian food for my clients."

The oversized wolf sat gingerly across from Dr. Norton. A half empty box of tissues in his furry lap, full rubbish bin by his side.

"Why would he do this?" The Wolf softly touched a row of stitches up his abdomen. "All I did was eat Little Red Riding Hood. And do you have any idea how hurtful being called 'Big Bad' is?"

A loud bang shook the office door. Two laughing voices cackled from the waiting room. Dr. Norton groaned as he stood up. The Wolf sniffed again and dabbed the corners of his eyes.

"Excuse me for a second, it seems my 3:15 appointment is already here making trouble."

The Wolf's puppy eyes were as big as frying pans. "Ok, just don't leave me alone too long."

They kicked the underside of the coffee table, causing a heap of magazines to cascade off the sides. The blond, blue-eyed young man and woman snickered and smirked at Dr. Norton's pained expression. The young man wore an embroidered, button front shirt and green lederhosen. The young woman wore a tan dirndl dress and a puffy sleeved, peasant's blouse.

A grating sound emanated from Dr. Norton's clenched jaw.

"While I understand that you two may be required by law to be here as part of the Judge's decision, I'm not going to put up with your misbehavior, especially when I'm dealing with another client. Clear?" Dr. Norton growled.

"Sure, Doc," Hansel grunted.

"Whatever, pops," Gretel snorted.

As Dr. Norton turned to go back into his office the kicking and laughing started again. He clenched his fists and spun back.

"Stop that!" the therapist snapped.

"Or what? You'll sic the Big Bad Wolf on us?" Gretel sneered.

The Wolf popped his head out of the office, behind Dr. Norton.

"See? I told you!" he yelped. Hansel and Gretel stared, jaws open and eyes bulging. The Wolf sniffled. "They have no idea how hurtful this is. I have to put with this kind of stereotyping daily. It just isn't fair."

Dr. Norton turned back to his lupine patient.

"Please sit back down, I'll be back with you in a moment."

The Wolf slipped back into the office, muttering how unjust the world was. Dr. Norton turned back to the Germanic vandals, a slicing grin on his face.

"Can you behave yourselves until the end of my current session?"

"Yes," they replied in unison.

"Good," Dr. Norton grumbled as he moved back into the office. He closed the door with a loud sigh. He flopped back down into his seat.

"Did you hear what they were saying?" The Wolf moaned. "Why does everyone have to pick on me?"

"They aren't necessarily picking on you. Have you looked at this thing from the alternative perspective? Consider the woodsman." Dr. Norton stroked his temple. "His girlfriend was in your belly."

"That's no excuse." The Wolf sniffled, and then blew his nose. "You do know that unwanted, impromptu surgical procedures by unlicensed surgeons is a crime, right?"

"Of course I know that." The Doctor inclined forward, pressing his palms together. "But you have to realize that eating people is wrong. What we need to do now is find the source of your drive to eat people."

"I guess it goes back to my childhood." The Wolf slumped back into the rocking chair; he looked up at the ceiling. "My Mom stopped breast feeding me early. She said she just had to take care of these crying brats, Romulus and Remus."

"Fascinating." Dr. Norton jotted in his file. "Seems you're the half brother of the Roman Empire, in an odd sort of way."

"I'm sure the Celts and Dacians will be thrilled to hear that."

"Historic connections aside..." Dr. Norton hummed. "Didn't Little Red Riding Hood sleep with you as an apology?"

"It's hard to enjoy sex when your spleen and intestines

362

are hanging out."

"Excellent point." Dr. Norton nodded. "Anyway... This fixation of yours makes sense now. Two humans steal your mother from you during the oral stage of Freudian development. To both get your mother's attention and take revenge, you're consuming the species that took her from you in the first place."

The Wolf sniffed and blew his nose again.

"Is there any way for me to get better?"

"Naturally there is." Dr. Norton bent forward and patted the Wolf on the knee. "With my help and your own efforts, you'll be on the fast track to recovery in no time."

"Would you, could you give me a hug? I really need one right now," sniffled the Wolf.

"As long as you don't eat me."

Dr. Norton sighed and flipped open the youths' file.

"It seems," the Doctor started, "that the old woman you two shoved into the oven suffered third degree burns on ninety percent of her body."

"Bitch wanted to cook me!" Hansel snapped.

"You pushed an eighty-year-old woman into a four hundred degree oven and shut the door."

"Ho had it coming, trying to eat my twin brother," squawked Gretel.

Dr. Norton exhaled. "Had it coming?"

Hansel and Gretel snickered and looked at each other, fox-like expressions on their faces.

Dr. Norton looked the twins over. He ran his tongue across his teeth, then another quick study of the file.

"Did you enjoy burning that old woman?"

"Hell yeah, the screaming and crackling?" Hansel sneered.

"It was a blast!" Gretel's eyes lit up.

Dr. Norton's face flattened, his mouth pursed and shoulders drooped. Fast notes were scratched into the file.

Extreme sadistic tendencies, possible masochism.

"What did you do after?"

"We had sex," Hansel said.

Dr. Norton froze. He slowly looked up from the folder. Gretel slung her leg across Hansel's lap.

"You are in an incestuous relationship?"

Hansel and Gretel looked at each other, then at the flabbergast therapist.

"Gee, what could have given you that idea?" Gretel hissed.

"You do know that incest is against the law, right?"

"So? We're both legal adults, we can decide who we do and don't want to screw," Gretel clucked. Hansel stroked her leg.

Dr. Norton cocked his head to the side and rotated back and forth in his swivel chair.

"Sadistic and incestuous? Hmmm..."

Gretel and Hansel bent forward, studying the mental health expert.

"What 'hmmm'?" Gretel asked.

Dr. Norton smiled as he stopped rotating.

"Describe your relationship with your father."

"Our Dad? Why do you want to know about our Dad?" Hansel balked.

The Doctor smiled again. "Humor me."

"Well, Dad is... not around much these days," Gretel started.

"And when he is around, it's like having a mannequin for a parent," Hansel added.

"He's distant."

"And disconnected."

"Uninterested."

"That's it!" Dr. Norton exclaimed. "It's all about your father. The sadism and incest are just cries for help and attention from him. Once we unravel all the misconceptions in your subconsciouses, the sadism and incest will just melt away."

The twins gave sad, large-eyed looks.

"Does this mean we won't set squirrels on fire then..." Hansel began.

"Have hardcore bondage se..."

"Yes, it means you'll stop those very disturbing behaviors," Dr. Norton interrupted loudly. "Now stop petting your sister's leg."

"Of course I was, like, trying to kill him." The blond girl blew a bubble and continued chewing, twirling her hair and kicking her leg. "The gay bastard, like, left me for, like, Snow White. Like, apparently he likes sloppy eights."

Dr. Norton dropped the file folder into his lap. He studied the pink-chemise-wearing, twenty-something woman. She open-mouth chewed a wad of gum.

"You can justify wanting a man dead for rejecting you?"

"Duh. I mean, like, he rejected me, ME! Like, who the fuck does he think he is, rejecting me?" She cranked her head back and curled her lips, showing teeth. "I'm motherfucking Sleeping Beauty! Beauty, do you, like, get that? My Dad is, like, a fucking King."

"But Prince Charming's father is also a King."

"Like, really? His Dad isn't a King like my Dad is a King." Sleeping Beauty chewed away.

"It was your father who sent you to me, right?" Dr. Norton picked the folder back up and cleared his throat.

"Yeah, like, he said I needed to be more regal and shit. Like, that I'm not good enough to be Princess, fuck!" She kicked her leg and loudly blew another bubble.

"Don't you feel shame for wanting to harm another person though? And what about Snow White? You seem very hostile towards her."

Sleeping Beauty threw her hands into her lap, groaning.

"Like, why should I feel bad? That queer frog-obsessed pansy pissed me off. I, like, have the right to get even with him." She lip-smacked the gum. "And Snow White is white 'cause her face is covered in dirty midget..."

"That's enough." Dr. Norton interjected. "Don't have to finish that sentence." He rolled back a few inches. "You also seem to harbor negative feelings toward homosexuals and Little People."

"I don't hate gay people. Like, my stylist is gay and I don't, like, hate him. You think, like, a straight guy could make my hair look this good?" She pointed to her shellacked bouffant. Dr. Norton rolled his eyes. "But those midgets are, like, so grody."

"They prefer to be called diminutive mining technicians."

"Whatever." She looked away, sticking her hand out. "Like, talk to the hand, 'cause, like, the face don't care."

"Why did we ever stop using electroshock and lobotomies?" the Doctor grumbled to himself.

"What did you say? Like, I didn't hear you."

"Oh, nothing."

"I just don't feel like myself. Even sending the flying monkeys after people just leaves me feeling empty." The green woman with the pointy black hat sighed, shoulders slumping. "It doesn't help being called 'Wicked' all the time, either." She slid her long, bony, clawed fingers along the arm of the rocking chair.

"Let's talk about the strategies you're using to deal with your depression," Dr. Norton chimed.

"You know I'm not big on medications. At least those not eye-of-newt based."

The doctor exhaled. "While I'm fully aware of that, it doesn't change facts; you need your anti-depressants."

"I know, I know." The witch moaned and put her head in her hands. "I'm just so out of it, I forget sometimes."

"What about exercise?" Dr. Norton asked, making a note in his file. "Are you getting enough?"

"Well, I go out broom riding at least twice a week." The witch sighed. "It just isn't the same without my big and little sisters there."

"You would go out riding with your sisters?"

"Yeah, but they were killed a while ago."

"My condolences." Dr. Norton bit the erasure of his

pencil. "If you don't mind answering, how did it happen? Witch hunters? A mob of villagers?"

"Nah, falling house and a bucket of water."

"Oh, I see."

"Yeah."

"You never mentioned you were grieving. Any particular reason?"

"I thought it went without saying." She sat up and slapped her legs. "I mean, when have you ever heard of things working out for a witch?"

Dr. Norton gaped and shrugged.

The witch pursed her lips and crossed her arms. "That's what I thought.

"You know that my mother was recently burned by those Teutonic twerps, Hansel and Gretel. My big sister was smooshed by a mud-farmer's ranch and my little sister dissolved by a bucket of water.

"But did you know that my aunt was banished from her home? For trying to rid us all of that slut Snow White and that asshole Sleeping Beauty. Not to mention my three cousins, including my favorite relative, Winifred, were hanged in Salem. Oh sure, they came back, only to be turned to dust by sunlight, like some cheap vampires."

"Well, I'll have you know that the Count is one of my other clients."

"Really? What's his deal?"

"Wasn't breast fed as a baby."

"Makes sense." She thrust out her jaw and examined the wall, in concentration. "Anyway, my cousins were hanged and my Uncle Jafar, from Saudi Arabia, has completely disappeared. His obnoxious pet parrot is still hanging around, but my Uncle has vanished.

"Last, but certainly not least, my grandmother, Morgana, was dropped by her HMO. Seems they don't cover people over five hundred years of age. Bastards.

"As you can probably tell I don't have a lot to be happy about. There just isn't any reason to get out of bed in the morning."

Dr. Norton rubbed his chin, staring at the ceiling. He rocked back and forth.

"It's too easy for you to dwell on the bad. Besides the meds and exercise you need excitement." He leaned over the file in his lap, the tips of his fingers pressed together in an arch. "A change of scenery, a vacation. You need to mix things up, rekindle the spark in your life."

"Well," she perked up a bit, "there are these villagers I've wanted to turn into toads for a while, maybe I could try that. I might even try turning Prince Charming back into a frog, or maybe some beast-like creature. Possibly turn his servants into pieces of living furniture."

"That's the spirit," Dr. Norton said cheerfully, then turned serious. "But you do know that you would be liable for any magical damages to your therapist, right?"

The sun was setting as Dr. Norton filed down the hall, folders tucked under his arm. The elevator buzzed and the door chunked as it opened. He scurried as fast as he could to the desk, throwing down the folders.

"Dr. Norton..." the Arabian Princess sang out.

He froze mid-stride, slowly turning to the desk.

"Here's your list of patients for tomorrow and there's a package here for the Wicked Witch." She held up an oil lamp-shaped parcel. "The label says it's her uncle. What should I do with it?"

Dr. Norton took a slow, deep breath.

"Leave it and the list for me to check tomorrow. Ok?"

"Of course, Dr. Norton." She tilted her head, smiling dopily.

The Doctor spun and strode for the door. As he exited for the parking lot, he muttered under his breath. "Time to hit the Scotch."

Come, Come Blackbird

"This is not a fairy tale, Fionn."

Heather Fowler received her M.A. in English and Creative Writing from Hollins University. She has taught composition, literature, and writing-related courses at UCSD, California State University at Stanislaus, and Modesto Junior College. Her fabulist fiction has been published online and in print in the US, England, Australia, and India, as well as recently nominated for both the storySouth Million Writers Award and Sundress Publications Best of the Net. She was Guest Editor for Zoetrope All-Story Extra *in March and April of 2000. Fowler's story, "Slut," won third prize at the 2000 California Writer's Conference in Monterey. Her poetry has been nominated for the Pushcart Prize, was recently featured in* The Nervous Breakdown, poeticdiversity, *and* The Medulla Review, *and has been selected for a joint first place in the 2007 Faringdon Online Poetry Competition. Her debut magical realism collection* Suspended Heart *has just been released by Aqueous Books (partial author's proceeds will be donated to the San Diego Family Justice Center, a center to help displaced families and battered women and children). Her website is www.heatherfowlerwrites.com.*

"'Come, Come Blackbird' was inspired by a mixture of fairy tale tropes and language and a modern sort of fabulism. A woman trapped with small magic in a marriage that diminishes her seeks a happy ending in the view outside her window. Her imagination flourishes again, as soon as she can see the potential for flight."

Although "Come, Come Blackbird" is neither sequel to – nor retelling of – an existing tale, the editors felt that it was too beautiful to pass by, and that it makes a fitting conclusion to the anthology.

Come, Come Blackbird
Heather Fowler

It is ten minutes to midnight in South Bend, but this is no fairy tale. There's no coach, and there's no prince for miles. It's late, a night with a deceptively light sky, and Fionn tends her hearth in a dark home where only a small fire burns. Her heart is angry and her man is mean. Though this would qualify as understatement, it is no exception.

A baby cries in the distance, this distance more mental than physical, Fionn's sweet girl wailing straight down the cobblestone hall Fionn strides with bare feet. The mommy, Fionn, begins humming even before she even reaches the child's door, soothing then lifting her small girl into her arms and nuzzling the infant's doughy face.

"Now you pretend you didn't hear daddy yelling, all right, angel?" she asks, though the child is so young it is more about her motherly cooed tone than any meaning to the words. Fionn keeps her voice low. "No yelling between us," she mutters. "Promise? Don't forget to swear. Fucksake."

The soothed babe smiles. Fionn puts her down in the crib for a second, spins, and her dress has altered to the cloth of a princess. No need to wait till midnight, child. It's a blue dress now, blue as the Aegean sea. Long and covered with seed pearls in the shapes of roses and pears.

"If he knew I still did this here, now, all the time," she tells the child, "and if he could, he would take my ability away

373

too, like he takes everything I love. Shoves it into boxes or throws it in the yard bin for the dogs – like the trash, like the bones! But he's gone now, baby. Want to see another dress? Look what your mama can do!"

She spins and wears red velvet embellished with gold rope, low cut, the stuffed head of a lion sewn into the sweep.

The baby laughs.

"Don't worry," she tells the baby. "I didn't really kill a lion for this."

In this day with strange magic, Fionn loves her skill of self-wardrobing. It's a weak magic, as magics go – better to be able to make televisions or gold watches out of thin air – and her dresses each disappear at midnight, but no magic should be discarded. "I should have known I would never keep a love hot as coals, baby," she says then, watching her child watching her back. "Mama started as a whore for her own father, then touch slut for the relatives at family parties who watched as she remained unprotected – but you won't be done that way! Don't tell anyone that old story either. This is our secret! Not that grandmama's love was ever given me – a boy's name she offered! And what did my twin get – Fiona? So I was never the favorite and my twin rips me up, has what I need and what I want – but you, you will be the favorite, Crystal! That's why I called you Crystal, so no-one could speak ill of you." She picks the baby up again, cooing, "You're so shiny. And it's quiet here in the house now that our man's gone. Sometimes I wish every man would just stay gone. This is why I hold you so much," but the child tucks her head into Fionn's neck and sleeps. Fionn still humming intermittently, says, "You'll sleep all night now; not to worry – all night, Crystal, and no one will bother you.

374

Mommy can never sleep."

Her mean man returns. She can almost taste the hair of his beard. The force of his kiss. "Fionn? Fionn? I left my keys here. Came to get them, but I'm leaving again." The sound of his voice chills her, his shoes and heavy footfalls.

She steps out of the infant's room. "I'm here," she says, confirming his unasked question.

They stare in the hall. She does not worry that he will hit her because he isn't violent, but she wonders where the kindness in his eyes has gone and where he left it. "You going to try and do something useful while I'm gone?" he asks, staring her up and down, speaking with his deep, measured tone.

"I'm watching the baby," she says. "That's useful. You like my dress?"

"Mind tricks!" he says. "I hate your skills. The dress will be gone in a minute and then what? Rags again, Fionn. You'll be wearing rags."

"That's cruel," she says.

"I'm not trying to hurt you," he says. "But you are always wearing rags. Just because people can look at you all day long in a fancy dress doesn't mean it doesn't disappear at midnight. This is why you should go back with the gypsies if you no longer want my protection, because only traveling sales people can make millions overnight with your fancy gowns, but your product is so good that when it disappeared they would hunt you down if you stayed – all those angry people cheated to find only air in exchange for your dresses after midnight. Thief, they'd call you. Deceiver. And I've tried to think of a way we can sell your magic –"

"Kind. Kind of you," Fionn interrupts.

"But it's not coming to me, so you're a useless wife. All you ever want is to walk around the fields, stand in tall grass in the rain, touch yourself here with the door locked, or sit smothering yourself in the bath."

"You never touch me anymore," she argues. "Unless you're angry. I am alive. What am I supposed to do? If you didn't lock me in so much..."

"I protect you," he replies.

"You defeat me."

"Yes, and you leave me cold," he says. "Why would I touch you? I didn't hold your past against you, but now I can hardly look at you."

She touches the hem of her dress, creates the faces of moles all along its trim. She turns to the window. "You used to touch me."

"You hadn't sold me out then," he replies. "You hadn't permitted what you later permitted."

"So, what did I do?" she asks. "Can you be specific? How did I lose you? In and out of this house, you work all the time. I'm not permitted to take lovers, but you won't even give me the slightest comfort?"

The clock tolls twelve.

"This is not a fairy tale, Fionn."

"And what is your fairy tale magic, Jonathan? Your magic used to be your patience and your kindness. That you could make people smile. I think it's a gone magic. I think you lost it somewhere."

"I think we should stop talking," he says. "We'll say yet more we didn't mean."

"Go dream your fantasy, Fionn, you say – but don't endanger us? Well I am tired of dreaming in this cold house. Give me something, darling. Anything."

"I gave you a child," he replies.

"Reluctantly, but thank you. Who will I talk to when she grows old enough that she understands my words?"

"You can make friends; you always have."

"Out here in the nowhere?"

"Anywhere, my dear."

"Cold, cold," she says. "I'm about to freeze."

Jonathan turns on his heel. "Your dress has just turned to rags, to tatters," he says. "Look at you now. So. Well. Make another dress. Oh, except you can't do that until the sun comes up, right? Poor Fionn."

Fionn stands before him and says, "Cold. Cold. Cold. Cold." She drops the rags like garments from her body. Luminous pale in moonlight, in starlight, her white full shape and dark hair create a vision by the window. She stands up nude and proud, nipples outthrust, glaring at him. "You can't tell me you don't want me," she says as she watches his desire rise. It's always there when she's nude, simmering. "Should we make another baby, Jonathan? Right now? Here on the floor? Among the rushes and the thyme?"

He's drawn, she knows, but resists. "No," he says, pulling her in hard to kiss her in a way that punishes. "No." And walks out.

She checks back on the baby. Still sleeping. Whispers: "This is what happens, baby, when you don't know what you get before you let a man lock you down. It's terrible."

Still naked, she shivers. "Friends, Jonathan?" she says

to his absence. "Who will come get me? We live so far away." She shakes her head. "Here is an abomination. You are all I have baby, Crystal!" she whispers fervently. And she walks to the hearth to tend the fire, naked, regardless of sparks. She could put on her rags again, but they make no sense and no difference. A blackbird arrives at her windowsill. The baby sleeps. The blackbird whistles.

She sees a spot of red on his shoulder. "Oh, look at you, redwing," she says. "Look how beautiful! Did you get lost among the cattails and then find your way here?"

He tilts his head, though she doesn't expect a response. She opens the window. He lands on her outstretched fingers, making one bleed. She strokes the blood red patch on his wing. "I wish Crystal could see you," she says.

"Crystal can see me, Fionn," he replies.

While she is still gaping, he turns into a man, similarly naked, but with more muted human shades of flesh and hair. "It's my magic," he says. "I can be a bird. I can be a man. Though no one can touch me when I'm human. This part is the illusion. Like your dresses are mist after midnight."

"Oh," Fionn says.

He settles in. They talk. It turns out that he has been watching her for days. It turns out he has heard each thing she's said. It turns out he has one more magic skill to offer. "Want to fly?" he asks. "I can take one forlorn girl up in the sky with me, but only for a brief while."

"Yes," she says. "Yes. Me."

The window is open. He touches her wrist with his beak and she becomes a streaky brown female blackbird. When he speaks to her now, it is in blackbird, but because she is a black-

378

bird, she can still understand.

"Learning to fly is hard," he trebles. "Careful now. Watch my wings! Good. Follow the air. Feel it! Let the current ride beneath you. Yes! Very good! But we can only be out briefly, as making myself a human and then a human into a bird exhausts me, but I'll be back, Fionn. Soon. We'll talk again. Let's aim for the window."

They fly. She and he fly out above the telephone wires and into the moonlight. He sings a tumbling song. She loves his song. She sings and tumbles.

Soon enough, they return. It's long after midnight now, at least an hour. "I have to stay with my man," she tells the blackbird. "With my baby, too. But thank you for the flight. It was a beautiful thing, flight. You're a beautiful bird."

"You were always capable of flying, Fionn," the blackbird replies. "And me, I'm just a blackbird."

"My heart is so angry and my man is so mean," she confesses. "I love him, but he doesn't seem to love me anymore. He hates my magic and has none of his own."

"Does he envy you your magic?" blackbird asks. "I only have two magics. But they are good, aren't they? I live in that tree right there, lady. You see it? Where the red and green leaves alternate. You can see it from your window. Look for me one day. I will come to see you dressing. And then we can – we can wait and see."

It's like the blackbird might say more, but he does not. He flies out the window and is gone. For a good hour, she says nothing. She checks on Crystal. She licks the rusty blood from her finger and remembers the wind beneath her wings, even when her mean man comes home. Her arms feel like wings.

379

She stands in rags at two in the morning, stretching her arms to either side, and thinks about how tomorrow she will think up gorgeous dresses that have birds embroidered all over them.

No more moles. No more lions. She will wear a dress of flaming herons first, to get blackbird's attention. She will blow a kiss out the window at her little pet and invite him to sit upon her shoulder. She will dance with his bird man, in the air or on the ground. Lots of fun things will happen.

But this is no fairy tale.

At three in the morning, her mean man comes home. He gets into bed beside her, making sure to avoid touching any plane of her. He rolls away, says nothing. He does not need to speak to hurt her. Speech is an old trick; he trades now in silences. Passive aggression post-wooing.

But she closes her eyes then, lying down beside him for just an instant before deciding instead to stand. She keeps standing until the purring rumble of his snores is full enough to believe – running her nails up and down her flesh as if to score herself with talons – thinking clearly now, thinking heartfully, carefully remembering his black feathers and the body of her flight.

Illustration Credits

CIARAN GAFFNEY *crash-landed on this planet in 1989. The initial panic was soon replaced by immense adoration for furry little whiskered things most people refer to as 'cats,' and quickly made sure he acquired many of these for his very own. He lives in Vermont with his family and partner, surrounded by winter.*

CAITLYN LAMBERT *is currently a student at Quinsigamond Community College, where she studies Applied Arts. She has lived and studied in Worcester, MA, her whole life. Her favorite hobbies are playing with cats, teasing her boyfriend, and doing art on sunny days in her dark, depressing room.*

Keeper of one too many cats, JADE LIEBES *is a comic artist and illustrator who may or may not run entirely on chai tea and cupcakes. She is not a huge fan of digital art, though she's known to throw color around in Photoshop, but she prefers drawing entirely by hand with pencil and ink. She has one self-published comic called* Maps.

ROSE MAMBERT *is a writer and occasional painter, photographer, print-maker, and illustrator with a background in graphic arts and printing. Her work has appeared on T-shirts and CDs, collective art shows, and most frequently in the form of band flyers tacked onto telephone poles.*

Information about DUNCAN EAGLESON *can be found in the introduction to "Snovhit" on p.194.*

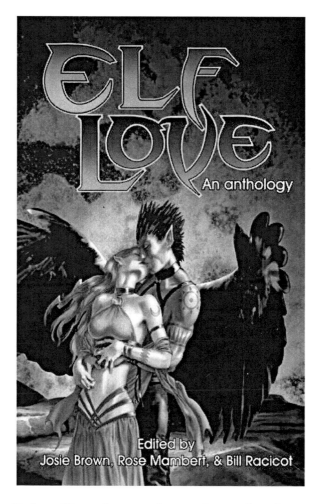

CPSIA information can be obtained at www.ICGtesting.com
Printed in the USA
LVOW011604251111

256475LV00008B/38/P

9 780982 991312